CAPTIVATED BY HER ITALIAN BOSS

ROSANNA BATTIGELLI

THE BACHELOR'S BABY SURPRISE

TERI WILSON

MILLS & BOON

First Published in Great Britain 2018
by Mills & Boon, an imprint of HarperCollinsPublishers,
1 London Bridge Street, London, SE1 9GF

Captivated by Her Italian Boss © 2018 Rosanna Battigelli
The Bachelor's Baby Surprise © 2018 Teri Wilson

ISBN: 978-0-263-26519-4

0818

MIX
Paper from
responsible sources
FSC™ C007454

This book is produced from independently certified FSC™
paper to ensure responsible forest management.

For more information visit: www.harpercollins.co.uk/green

Printed and bound in Spain
by CPI, Barcelona

CAPTIVATED
BY HER
ITALIAN BOSS

ROSANNA BATTIGELLI

To Calabria, a land of resilience and enchantment
that continues to captivate me.

And to all my Calabrese relatives and friends
worldwide, starting with those in Camini,
where my heart first began to beat.

CHAPTER ONE

WHEN NEVE SPOTTED the ad in the Vancouver newspaper in the second to last week of June, she felt a shiver of excitement run through her. It was an ad requesting applications from Canadian nannies for a position for the summer. In Italy. And Southern Italy, at that. A place she had visited with her mother when she was eighteen. Her parents had traveled through Calabria and Sicily on their honeymoon, and her mother's nostalgia had drawn her back for what would have been their nineteenth anniversary.

Neve had loved the leisurely five-week tour through the seaside towns and mountain hamlets, culminating with the last week in Valdoro—Valley of Gold—on the southeast coast of Calabria. It was the town where Neve had been conceived. Neve could still envision the shimmering, color-changing waves of the Ionian Sea. And the dazzling sun that rose at dawn, its face an orange-gold orb that soon took dominion of the cerulean sky. By 8:00 a.m., the temperature would register over thirty degrees Celsius, and Neve couldn't wait to head to the beach.

Her imagination had gone wild as they explored the ancient places she had read about in the works of British authors who had traveled to the area over a century earlier. Because of Greek colonization a thousand or so years ago, the area had become known as Magna Grecia, or Great

Greece. Neve had read the books her parents had discovered about the South, including George Gissing's *By The Ionian Sea* and Norman Douglas's *Old Calabria*. She had particularly enjoyed Edward Lear's *Voyages in Southern Italy*. Lear had traveled to the South with another artist to paint landscapes. As he traveled from hamlet to hamlet, he had written about his experiences in a journal. His accounts of peculiar townsfolk and the places they had stayed had put Neve in stitches, like the story of a pig running out from under a table as they were feasting on a dinner of macaroni. As an adolescent, Neve had dreamed of returning to Italy one day to rediscover the places that had so enchanted her.

Reading the details in the ad, Neve's jaw dropped. What were the chances of coming across a job opportunity in Valdoro for the summer? And one that she could easily apply for, since her job as a kindergarten teacher meant she had summers free. The ad read:

Canadian Nanny wanted to prepare child for Kindergarten.
Summer Position.
Only highly experienced applicants will be considered.
Skills in Behavioral Management and Modification a must.
Child has experienced trauma and requires a special caregiver.
Three nannies have been recently dismissed; please do not apply if you believe this will be a vacation.
Position is full-time, with one day off per week.
Send a letter including your CV to my assistant, Mrs. Lucia Michele, email address below.
Do not inquire as to the status of your application.

You will be contacted within one week for an interview if I am interested.

Neve read the ad over several times. The prospective employer obviously wanted to make it quite clear to the applicant that this job was not going to be an easy one. She wondered at the trauma of the poor child. A death? Divorce? Abuse? Her stomach twisted. She had a special place in her heart for children; she always had, even as a teenager. She had babysat regularly in her neighborhood, and she had decided early on that teaching would be the career for her. She had been teaching now for three years, and maybe that didn't make her *highly experienced*, but she *had* dealt with a few difficult and sensitive situations, and as a result, had taken specialized courses to help children who had experienced trauma of some kind.

She herself had experienced the loss of her father as a child. He had succumbed to a sudden stroke when she was eight, and it still made her heart twinge when she remembered the day she had come home from school and had found her house filled with relatives and family friends, some gathered around her mother. Bewildered, she had run toward her mother, who had sobbed the news to her before collapsing. Sadly, over the years, her mother had been more preoccupied with *her* loss and less over Neve's trauma of losing her father.

Neve's eyes prickled. She squeezed them shut, then focused on the ad.

Who was the sender? The most logical answer was that it was a parent who couldn't stay at home and needed someone to help the child deal with the trauma and help prepare him or her for the challenge of another transition: school.

A tall order. Especially since progress so far had been

limited. At least that was what she had inferred from the terse statement: *three nannies have recently been dismissed.* She felt a twinge in her heart at what the child must be going through and the poor, desperate parent. A thousand thoughts swarmed her mind about the sad possibilities, and then one thought pushed the others away: *I'm going to apply.*

And why not? She had the sensitivity required for such a position, given her own personal history. And she had dealt with behavioral and trauma issues in her three years of teaching, everything from stubbornness and aggression to grief over the loss of a parent or pet.

Yes, she would have loved to return to a *vacation* in Valdoro, but just being there and knowing she would be helping a child in distress—or attempting to help—was enough to motivate her. She would be content with reacquainting herself with the area on her day off. Of course, that was *if* she was hired for the position.

Neve had been ready to go to bed when she had picked up the newspaper, but now she was too excited to sleep. She reached for her laptop and typed up a letter. She read it over twice, added a section, read it over again and then attached her most recent CV. Taking a deep breath, she typed in the email address and pressed Send before she could change her mind.

With a shiver of anticipation, Neve ran a bath, her imagination sparked. As she stepped into its bubbly warmth, her floral-scented body wash reminded her of the jasmine and other flowers blooming in the pots on the balconies at Villa Morgana, where she had stayed with her mother in Valdoro. She inhaled deeply and closed her eyes, her memories reactivated.

Visions of the villa came rushing back: the spacious, elegant rooms with their sparkling marble floors; the colorful glazed pots on the balcony, bursting with blooms of every color; and the scent of the nearby bakery wafting up to her when she stepped out on her balcony—

Neve's eyes flew open. She blinked. There was something wrong with this picture. *Well, not wrong, exactly.* It was just missing one thing. *One person. The guy walking down the road. The guy whose intense gaze had seemed to blaze across the street to connect with hers.*

She had been drying her hair outside after a cool shower, enjoying the balmy heat of the midday Calabrian sun. Her mother and their friends, the owners of the villa, had been taking their usual siesta after the sumptuous lunch they had all feasted on. The merchants had shut down their businesses for the afternoon, and would reopen in a few hours. Nobody strolled about in the scorching afternoon heat, which is why Neve had been taken aback to see him walking by. His stride seemed to have slowed down when he was directly across the road from her balcony. And although other boys in Valdoro had openly demonstrated curiosity about her with sly nudges and winks when she walked in and out of the ice cream shop or bakery down the street, they hadn't turned her knees to jelly, like this guy had just done.

He must have been working on a farm. His dark hair had been tousled and sweat-dampened, and his white T-shirt and jeans had been streaked with earth. He had been carrying a large burlap bag on his back, filled with greens and vegetables. But it had been his eyes that had galvanized her. Ebony eyes that had sent a shiver coursing through her veins. Eyes like river stones gleaming in the sun. And even with a coating of dust on his face, Neve had been able to make out his chiseled features, straight nose and sensual curve of his lips.

Suddenly flustered, Neve had shifted her gaze and in

mere seconds, had taken in his tanned arms—his biceps bulging from holding the burlap bag—and his well-fitting, straight-leg jeans. *He is not a boy*, she remembered thinking. She had guessed him to be in his early twenties. And she had been eighteen… For a few moments she had felt a strange weakness overcome her and had wondered if she was about to pass out.

And then he had stopped. She had felt him staring at her and had looked up. *Is he going to say something?* she had wondered. Their eyes had locked. And then he had given a slight nod and, readjusting his bag, had kept walking. The following day Neve had watched him from behind the wooden shutters, too shy to suddenly appear on the balcony. But when he had slowed down and looked up toward her balcony, her heart had fluttered. *He had been hoping to see her.*

Neve realized she was holding her breath and let it out in a rush. And then other memories of that summer eight years ago came tumbling out. The way he had started going by the villa several times a day, not just to and from his farm job, but also later in the evening. He had made evening trips to and from the bakery, the Pasticceria Michelina. Sometimes he had walked; other times he had rumbled by on a motor scooter. Neve had felt herself falling under the spell of the Southern ways, the age-old custom of locking gazes, communicating with eyes only, a slow dance of intuition and anticipation. Her heart had thrummed all evening and night after that first encounter, and over the next few days she had found she could concentrate on little else.

Her mother, Lois, had caught the exchange once. He had been walking by after his work on the farm, and Lois had come into Neve's room and walked toward the balcony at the same moment that he had paused to look up and smile at Neve, who had taken to sitting out on the balcony with a book every afternoon. Neve had returned the smile, and then had become aware of her mother's presence.

"What are you doing?" her mother had asked. "You don't pay attention to farmhands, Neve. That could get you into real trouble."

Neve had flushed, embarrassed to have been discovered flirting and even more embarrassed to think that *he* had heard or understood. But when she had looked back toward him, he had walked on and was almost out of sight. She had glanced at her mother, whose frown had deepened.

"I've read stories about how some men in the South used to kidnap young ladies, take them up to a mountain cave and compromise their honor so their family would have no choice but to let them get married."

"Mom! Really? Are we talking about the same century?" Neve couldn't believe what she had just heard. "I wasn't doing anything other than smiling back. And I didn't get the feeling he wanted to marry me," she had added flippantly. "I don't think you have to worry about him carrying me off."

Her mother's cheeks had reddened. "Neve, you are not to give him or anyone like him any attention. You're in Italy, remember. Men are more…*passionate* here. You came here a virgin. I don't want you to fall for the first Romeo that pays attention to you and let him—"

"Mom! Oh, my God!" Neve had jumped up, *her* face flaming. "Just *stop*! Give me some credit, would you?"

She had barricaded herself in her private bathroom, ignoring her mother's calls and halfhearted attempts to apologize. She had come out after her mother had gone, and wiping her tear-streaked eyes, she had walked to the balcony…

* * *

For the next few days Neve had been too busy with her school obligations to think much about the ad. When an email from a Mrs. Lucia Michele arrived, informing her that she was one of the applicants who could proceed to be interviewed, Neve's heart had done a leap. She had thought it was a long shot, as there must have been hundreds of applicants, if not more, and her pulse had quickened at the thought that she might actually stand a chance of being hired.

Mrs. Michele's email had informed Neve of the interview details. It would be conducted by *her*. The employer would be watching the interview privately. Due to the sensitive nature regarding the child, she had been instructed to keep the employer's identity confidential until the chosen applicant actually arrived in person in Southern Italy.

And now here Neve was, communicating with Signora Lucia Michele, who was asking her in halting English about her philosophy of discipline. Neve felt a little self-conscious doing a Skype interview while her prospective employer watched from his computer.

Neve paused for a moment, wondering what stance "the boss" expected her to take. She looked beyond the woman, almost expecting that he—why she thought it would be a *he*, she didn't know—would appear, and took a deep breath. She could only answer truthfully.

"I believe that consistency is essential in discipline," she replied, her voice steady. "The child must know what you expect, and as a kindergarten teacher, I tell my children right at the beginning that I expect to be treated kindly, with respect, and that I will be treating them in the same manner. I make sure they know right away that A, their parents have trusted them to my care because I will keep them safe and take good care of them, and B, they will learn and have fun with me."

She couldn't help smiling, thinking of her school kids as they looked at her with wide eyes on the first day of school. "Those are the two main things they need to know. And then, day by day, they will learn how to interact, how to solve problems, how to be a good leader." She looked straight at the camera. "And they will learn about consequences when they do something inappropriate. I believe in positive discipline and fairness, and flexibility when it is required...without laying a hand on the child."

Signora Michele gave a curt nod. "And I see you have... ah...some *esperienza* with children who have suffered— how do you say?—oh, yes—loss?"

Neve tried to control her eyes from misting. Yes, she had experience, she replied, and bit her lip. She told the *signora* about the courses she had taken to help understand what children who had lost a parent through death or separation or divorce were going through. "You can't assume that every child who enters your classroom has had a happy, cheerful childhood," she said wistfully. "If only..." She blinked and thought of a frail-looking girl called Tessa, who had lost her mother to cancer a month before starting kindergarten.

Don't cry, she told herself. *Hold it together.*

And then Signora Michele turned slightly and touched her ear. Neve spotted the hearing device that was obviously the means of communication between her and the employer.

She nodded and turned back to Neve, her face expressionless. "Thank you for your time, Signorina Wilder. You will be contacted with an answer within a day or two. There are still a few other applicants to consider... *Grazie*."

Neve nodded and gave her a small smile before the

woman left. She looked again right into the camera at the top of her screen, knowing the employer would be watching until the last moment. Neve stared briefly, then nodded, her eyes never faltering.

"Grazie," she addressed the unseen employer before shutting down her laptop.

Davide Cortese's pulse leaped. If he had entertained the smallest doubt when she had first appeared on his laptop screen in his study, after mere seconds he could no longer deny it. The interview had lasted twenty minutes or so between his assistant and the applicant, but it had taken him only a few stunned moments to realize the latter's identity.

Neve Wilder. He hadn't seen her name and the others in the file Lucia had prepared; he had wanted to see all the Skype interviews first. Neve was the thirteenth applicant to be interviewed by Lucia, and Davide had almost lost hope that a suitable nanny could be found for his five-year-old niece, Bianca.

His expression softened at the thought of his niece. She looked like the mirror image of her mother, his sister, Violetta. Her face still had the cherubic roundness of babyhood, but she had grown taller, even since the accident. *The accident.* Just those two words caused his body to freeze, just like the first time he was told by Violetta's friend Alba that Violetta and her husband, Tristan, had skidded on an icy mountain road after their skiing weekend in Banff and had died instantly when their vehicle hit a tree.

Alba, who had been babysitting Bianca, had delivered the news tearfully by phone, and all at once Davide had felt numb, devastated, angry, sad and desperate. His only sibling, *gone.* She was six years his senior, and he had always looked to her for guidance growing up, especially after both their parents had died. Their father had passed first when Davide was ten, and their mother, heartbroken, had succumbed to cancer a year later.

Life had been hard enough without his gentle father around, but losing his mother so soon after was a blow that had siphoned what remained of Davide's childhood spirit. Davide had lost his joy, his appetite, his interest in school. He had become frail, withdrawn and had often missed school.

He and Violetta had been looked after by their uncle, Zio Francesco, a priest in their town of Valdoro. Zio Francesco had told Davide when he was older about how he had begun to despair of reviving Davide's spirit and physical health. He had wondered if bringing him out to the farm and letting Davide occupy himself with planting jobs and the tending of the animals might restore him in some way.

His uncle had wept while reciting his rosary after noticing how several days on the land had brought a change in Davide's behavior and outlook. After a few weeks Davide had willingly returned to school, but had continued to work on the farm after school and on weekends, as well as throughout high school and in the summer when back from university.

Davide's heart tightened. He would never forget what Zio Francesco had done for him.

Davide's sister, Violetta, had been shaken but more stoic than he was after the deaths of their parents. She had overseen the household responsibilities that their mother had managed while still at school, but when Violetta was eighteen, she fell in love with a tourist from Canada and she married him at twenty and moved to his home in Steveston, about a half an hour from Vancouver. Tristan had worked as a tour guide at a whale-watching company, while Violetta had worked to develop a small home business with her sewing talents. She had been so happy that she could work from home once they had had their baby, which was five years ago. She had studied English and learned it quickly, and when Bianca was born, she had made sure to speak to her in both languages.

Davide's English was also fairly good. Violetta had encouraged him to study it with the possibility of moving to Vancouver one day, and he had, but destiny had had other plans for him and he had remained in Valdoro.

Valdoro was where he had first spotted Neve. *Neve*, pronounced *Neh-veh*, meaning *snow* in Italian. She had been standing on one of the balconies of Villa Morgana, owned by one of the wealthiest families in town, a family that derived their wealth from the bounty of the bergamot groves on their outlying properties. Their coral-colored villa was on the main street heading into Valdoro, with ornate wrought iron balconies and ceramic planters bursting with flowers. The entire roof of the villa was a terrace with bougainvillea spilling over the railing. Chairs with bright yellow and blue upholstery were scattered around a table protected by an *ombrellone*, a huge umbrella tilted to one side.

Davide had been returning from his uncle's small farm, which he tended to from before sunrise till late morning, as the scorching sun was too prohibitive past noon. He had been later than usual that day, having had to chase after a goat that had found an opening in the enclosure and had wandered off. Afterward, Davide had gathered some of the garden vegetables in a huge burlap bag, and as he had passed the Villa Morgana, he had spotted a girl on the balcony. He hadn't seen her in Valdoro before. Her hair was wet and she was air-drying it.

Davide's T-shirt had been sweat-soaked, his jeans earth-stained, and he could feel his face prickling with perspiration. As he had passed in front of the villa from the opposite side of the road, the girl had tossed her hair back and caught sight of him. She had cocked her head and Davide could feel his steps slowing. He had wanted to stop completely and just feast on the vision before him.

He had been mesmerized by her light skin, her strawberry-blond hair catching the rays of the sun and shimmering like spun gold, the white halter dress with big red polka dots, her lean legs. His heart had thumped erratically at her gaze, which couldn't have lasted more than a few seconds before she had started to blink, and he had noticed her eyes traveling past his eyes and down his body.

Davide remembered the embarrassment he had felt at his dusty and sweaty appearance, although she hadn't give him any sign of arrogance, and he had nodded slightly in the respectful way he had been taught when encountering girls or women, and had forced his cement-like shoes to keep walking.

Showering at the house he had shared with his zio, Francesco, his insides had quivered at the thought of the girl. She had looked to be around seventeen or eighteen. He had been twenty-two, home for the summer from university, and although some of the mothers in Valdoro had discreetly made it known that he was welcome to court their daughters, he had been more intent on his studies. He hadn't said so much to his uncle, but he was hoping to join his sister in Vancouver after university. His parents had left him and his sister with very little; what money they had was tied up in their small farm property, so his uncle had encouraged him to keep working the land, and he would support him with a modest salary.

That had been the plan.

Until Neve Wilder's arrival in Valdoro.

* * *

Now, looking at her face on the screen, and knowing she couldn't see him or ever imagine his identity, Davide felt his gut tighten. He wasn't a love-struck young man anymore, and how and why fate had thrown Neve Wilder back into his life after eight years was a bizarre mystery to him. When he had tried to meet her back then, her message to him had been very clear. She had wanted nothing to do with him. He was below her and should remember his place.

She had crushed him then and Davide had spent the next few years trying to forget her and vowing to never be *below* anyone again. He would finish his university education and make something of himself. He didn't need *her* or anyone like her.

He had discovered that her family was visiting from Vancouver, where he had planned to go after his graduate studies. Overcome with bitterness, he had changed his mind immediately. He wouldn't move anywhere where there was even the *remotest* chance of bumping into her. No, he never wanted to see her face again.

This was a cruel twist of fate, watching an interview with the same girl who, eight years later, was applying for a job as a nanny for his niece. Only she wasn't a girl anymore. Her pretty looks as a teenager had blossomed into what he had to admit could only be called stunning.

Her fair skin was luminescent, with a faint smattering of freckles over her nose and peach-tinted cheeks, and that mane of hair, although restrained in a loose chignon, seemed even more burnished. Her eyes, never close enough for him to determine their exact color, were a dark bluish-green that reminded him of the sea in winter. *And that mouth.* Her lipstick was a luscious magenta pink, the same color as the delicious inner fruit of the cactus pear.

She could be a sea witch, he thought, a modern *Scylla*, the whirlpool in the waters off the coast that was personified in Greek mythology as a female monster impeding the way of the hero Odysseus…

Davide watched as Neve's eyes shifted to the camera. She leaned forward and her face filled the screen. He swallowed, his pulse drumming wildly as a corner of her mouth lifted and she nodded. And then said *"Grazie,"* her witch eyes never blinking once.

Twelve interviews, and none of the applicants had impressed him. *Until the thirteenth.* Thirteen was a lucky number for Italians. But the last thing he felt now was lucky. If it had been anybody but Neve, he'd have hired her on the spot. Her qualifications were spot-on; her answers had been genuine. She had seemed so humble, so *caring and devoted.* How could this be the same Neve who had arrogantly put him down and rejected him?

Bianca needed a competent nanny. She would be starting school in a couple of months, and the trauma of losing her parents had shattered her world. None of her previous nannies had worked out. The first hadn't been sensitive enough, the second had been caught snooping through his desk papers and the third had shown more interest in wanting to help *him* through his grief, using her physical allure…

Bianca's occasional tantrums and crying outbursts had increased. Davide's gut was telling him to offer Neve the job.

His bruised heart was pounding No!

Davide watched as Neve shut down her laptop. He stared blindly at the screen and let the voices in his head battle it out. The memories of Neve in Valdoro eight years ago clashed with his fresh memories of the interview. Wearily, he finally stood up from his desk and drummed his fingers along the edge before buzzing for Lucia in the smaller office next to him.

"What did you think of the last applicant?" he said curtly in Italian.

"She was the best, Signor Cortese."

Davide trusted Lucia's opinion; she was his valued research assistant and friend, and genuinely cared for Bianca. When she addressed him in such a formal manner, he knew she was very serious.

"Yes…she *was*," he murmured, his fingers beginning to tap again.

He cleared his throat. This wasn't about *him*, he tried to convince himself. He had to do this for Bianca. What were the chances of finding someone as perfect as Neve Wilder for the position of nanny?

"Send her an email offering her the position. Sign it with your name, not mine. And tell her her flight and all travel costs will be covered. Rail, hotel, food, everything. I understand she's finished with her school year toward the end of June. I want her here for the first or second of July. Please and thank you."

"*Prego*, Davide. Let's hope for the best." She gave his hand a reassuring pat and left the room.

Davide sat back down at his massive sixteenth-century carved walnut desk. He opened a drawer, and then reached farther into a hidden back drawer and retrieved a folded note. His heart thudding, he gently opened it and read the message inside:

I will *not* meet you.
    Your bold request is inappropriate and offensive.
You would do well to remember your place.
Neve

Davide felt the heat rise from his chest to his neck and face. The silly note still got to him. His jaw clenched. Eight summers ago, Neve Wilder had succeeded in humiliating him and putting him in his place with her arrogant reply.

And now she'd be working for *him*. How could he not help feeling even the tiniest temptation to put *her* in her place?

CHAPTER TWO

THIS NANNY JOB, if she got it, would be like winning the lottery, Neve thought wistfully. She wanted to get away. No, she needed to get away. Her mother, who was controlling at the best of times, had become especially clingy and obtrusive lately.

Neve sighed. She wished that some of the attention her mother was directing toward her nowadays had been given when her father had died and afterward. Neve could still remember feeling heartbroken and confused in her youth. Devastated that her dear father would no longer accompany her to any of her school events or swimming lessons, or read her any fairy tales at bedtime, and bewildered by her mother's emotional distance. While her mother had eased her grief with a drink while staring out a window, Neve had often cried herself to sleep hugging the plush dragon her father had bought her for her seventh birthday. Her eyes prickled at the memory of her dear father, always encouraging, never judgmental of her or others.

Unlike her mother.

It hadn't taken Neve long in her youth to recognize certain traits in her mother that made her feel uncomfortable, especially in public. Lois Wilder, who had enjoyed a wealthy lifestyle since she was young, expected and often demanded service from others. Saw herself as above certain people. Neve had become embarrassed more than once by her mother's arrogant demeanor, even with some of her school friends. Whenever she had brought a friend over, Lois had always asked them about their parents' jobs, scrutinized their clothing and ultimately tried to manipulate whom Neve should socialize with.

She had even tried to dissuade Neve from pursuing such a common profession as teaching. "Why don't you accept a position in your father's company?" She owned the company now and had pressed Neve constantly to get on board. "You could have it made, sweetheart, instead of trying to educate rug rats. And in kindergarten, how much teaching will you actually be doing? They're still babies. You'll be spending most of the time on your knees, cleaning up after their accidents, wiping snotty noses, dealing with tantrums. And you'll be making peanuts compared to what you'd be earning working in your dad's computer business."

"Mom, I have no interest in the world of computers. I want to make a difference with kids. Help them to love learning."

"Well, at least get your masters and doctorate, and then you'll be able to teach at the university level. *That* would give you some status."

"I'm not interested in status, Mom." *Like you...*

Neve had had to control herself from being rude, although sometimes she had come very close. By the time she had graduated with her teaching degree, she had been more than ready to leave home. Lois had tried to bribe her with a luxury car and promises of travel if she stayed put.

Neve was having none of it.

Her mother had been hinting about a new manager in one of the departments that she thought might be a good match for Neve. The last thing Neve wanted was a man her mother approved of. A man who had similar qualities as her mother. Rich and snooty. Controlling and manipulative.

No, Neve had started her search and had found herself a bachelor apartment in a section of a house owned by Italian immigrants, and her teacher's salary had covered her rent and expenses. The "allowance" her mother insisted on sending her, Neve had put in her savings and travel accounts. Lois had insisted that she wanted Neve to have her inheritance—or at least some of it—before she passed away. "That way I can see you enjoying the finer things in life, darling."

Neve was immersed in watching a recent YouTube video of Valdoro when her cell phone chimed. She glanced down on the counter where she had left it and felt a swirl of butterflies in her stomach at the sender and the subject.

Lucia Michele. Re: Your Application

She hadn't expected to hear back the same day, let alone after half an hour. It had to be a form letter, fired off that quickly. Her heart sank. What had she expected, anyway? There had obviously been other applicants with much more experience than she had…

Neve sat down at the kitchen island and opened up the message on her phone. Her heartbeat quickened at the first sentence.

Dear Miss Wilder,
You have been accepted for the position of nanny. I will be sending you another email with information about the child's situation as well as other pertinent details you should know. The child's name is Bianca. She is five years old and living with her uncle.

I trust that you will be satisfied with the proposed salary and conditions of employment. After you have read the email, please download the attached contract, sign it and either scan and resend, or take a photograph and email it to this address.

Once this is done I will book your flights and send you an email with itinerary details. On July second you will be met at Lamezia Airport and a driver will bring you to your employer's residence.

Cordially,

Lucia Michele

Neve blinked, stunned. *She had the job!* She read the email again. She couldn't exactly call it a *warm* letter; it was very matter-of-fact and to the point. There was no commentary on her qualifications, the interview itself or anything else. The employer had obviously been satisfied with her detailed CV and with how she had responded in the interview.

Neve thought about everything she needed to do in the next two weeks. *Less than two weeks*, actually. Finalize report cards. File. Clean up her classroom. Pack. No, shop first. She needed some light dresses and new shorts. And definitely a couple of new swimsuits. Her favorite one, a fuchsia one-piece, had faded from the chlorine at the local swimming pool. And not that she'd have much time to herself, but the ad did say there would be one day off. Well, she would most certainly be frequenting the nearest beach on that day.

Neve thought about the little girl she would soon meet. *Bianca.* Such a lovely name. What had occurred in Bianca's young life to cause her such distress? Why was she living with her uncle? Dozens of questions swarmed in Neve's mind... She would get the answers soon enough.

She opted for an early night after a quick shower. The school was having their end-of-year play the following day, and she needed to store up her energy for the scheduled activities that included her class of twenty-four kindergarten students. There would be fun and laughter, but Neve was prepared for the possible tears and other behaviors that some of her five-year-olds might display after a few hours in the sun.

Yawning, she changed into a light blue baby doll and snuggled under her covers. She thought about Bianca's uncle. It was hard to get any kind of impression of him from his assistant's email. Did he have a wife, and if so, she must be working, or else wouldn't she be taking care of Bianca? *Stop*, she told herself. She'd know more when she got Mrs. Michele's next email.

Neve felt her eyelids getting heavier. *What if Bianca's uncle is single?* And the sudden thought: *What if that guy from across the street is still in Valdoro?* He may very well have moved to work in a bigger city up north, like Rome or Milan, as many of the Southerners tended to do. But if he *was* still in Valdoro, would she recognize him? He'd be maybe twenty-eight or so, and he'd probably be married with a couple of kids… *Or maybe not…* The picture of him she had kept in her mind had faded and blurred a little, but even so, she felt her pulse quicken.

And the image of his intense black eyes was the last thing she saw before she drifted into sleep.

Davide shut down his laptop. He left his study and strode to his bedroom. He opened the shutters and stood for a while, gazing at the twinkling lights dotting the countryside, and the indigo streak beyond—the Ionian Sea. It had been another scorching day; the locals had said it was the hottest summer in history. A smile curved his lips. For as long as he could remember, Valdoro's residents had said the same thing every summer. And the people in neighboring hamlets and towns were no different.

He almost felt like driving down the mountain to have a swim in the refreshing depths of the sea. But Bianca was sleeping and Lucia had gone home. They had decided to carry out the interview in early afternoon Vancouver time, which was nine hours behind Italian time.

Davide peeled off his shirt and pants and tossed them over a chair. There was hardly a breeze, and the night air had dropped a dozen degrees, but it was still too warm. He didn't have to worry about his neighbors seeing him, though. Last year he had purchased this house on a steep mountain on the outskirts of Valdoro, a few kilometers away. There were no neighbors to look across from their windows or balconies to his.

He smiled wryly. It wasn't actually a *house*; it was an eighteenth-century castle that had been built by the Baron of Valdoro. Fortified castles had been built inland on impossibly high mountains throughout Calabria, and their lords or barons had employed the locals to work the land of their vast properties, or *latifundi*, as they had been known. The last descendant of the Baron of Valdoro had died childless a hundred or so years earlier, and the land around his castle had long been abandoned. Although the castle was within the boundaries of Valdoro, it had not been maintained; the town simply hadn't had the financial means to restore it.

Three years ago, when Davide's first novel had been awarded Italy's prestigious literary award—the *Premio Strega*—followed by international sales and a film and miniseries option that made him a multimillionaire in months, he had spent the first year swirling from interview to interview, in between countless literary readings and festivals all over Italy. His face had been on the cover of practically every newspaper and magazine.

He had been one of the youngest recipients of the *Strega*. His hometown had attracted tourists, which had boosted the economy and profile of Valdoro, pleasing both the town officials and the residents alike. Davide was given the ceremonial key to Valdoro, and he had celebrated with his uncle and neighbors in a day of festivities culminating in a spectacular show of fireworks.

He still couldn't believe that the words he had penned about a family during the unification of Italy in 1861 had garnered such fanfare. It had been compared in scope to *Il Gattopardo*, the famous novel written by Giuseppe Tomasi di Lampedusa. Davide had studied *The Leopard* in high school, had been riveted by its rich complexity, propelling him to pursue further studies in history and literature.

He had made a promise to himself the summer Neve Wilder had visited Valdoro with her mother. And that was to let Neve's harsh words on the note she sent him burn into his soul until he had accomplished one goal, and that was to elevate himself to the point where she, or anybody else, could not look down on him.

That meant continuing to further his education and to *make something of himself.* His uncle had lived very humbly as a priest, and had stretched himself to the limit to provide for him. Davide had been very appreciative, but he had realized that he had to push himself to go beyond his or his uncle's normal expectations.

In between his studies and work on the farm, Davide had taken to writing. Late at night and before dawn, he had let his knowledge of history, his culture and his imagination combine and transform into the fictional story of the daughter of a Bourbon lord, who had become captivated with the ideals of General Giuseppe Garibaldi in his quest to oust the Spanish Bourbon regime and unify the South with the rest of Italy. The girl had fallen in love with one of Garibaldi's soldiers during the revolution and successful ousting of the Bourbons, and had abandoned her family and relinquished her status to elope with him in the mysterious Aspromonte mountain range in Calabria.

Writing this story had been bittersweet, and his hand had sometimes trembled with emotion as he created the scenes between the two lovers. His protagonist, Serena, had turned out to be an Italian version of Neve, dark-haired but with the same fair skin and blue-green eyes that were not often seen in the South.

Davide had made Serena everything he had fantasized about Neve before she had crushed his illusions…and Vittorio was the name he had called the man who had captured her heart.

Davide gave a harsh laugh. What a fool he had been eight years ago. A romantic fool.

After first catching sight of Neve on that balcony, he had used every excuse possible to walk by. He had had asked his friend Agostino, whose mother had been working as a housekeeper at the Villa Morgana, to keep him informed of any excursions Neve's family was planning, and Davide would innocently show up around that time. *Just to catch sight of Neve.*

When he had had the good fortune of first spotting her on the balcony, he had dared to hold his gaze for longer than a casual glance. And to his delight, after gazing away shyly, she had returned it. But then, with each subsequent walk-by, she had attempted a quirky smile, her face flushing like a ripe peach.

After a couple of days Davide had made the bold move of crossing the road to walk on the same side of the villa on his way home from working on the farm. And then later, once he had showered and changed, he had returned. The local bakery was just down the street from the villa, and this had become his excuse to walk by every day.

Zio Francesco had commented about Davide's sudden sweet tooth, for Davide was bringing home a bag of brioche filled with custard one day, or a few marzipan fruit cookies or hazelnut biscotti the next day. Davide couldn't very well reveal the real reason for his purchases to his uncle; he had shared his feelings only with Agostino, who had revealed the girl's name to him.

When Agostino had told him one evening that Neve's mother was planning an outing to the sea, Davide's stomach had churned with anticipation. *He would go, too!* He had convinced Agostino to join him, for it would have looked odd for him to show up alone on the beach used by the Valdoro locals. They had set out on Agostino's Vespa and had spent the morning alternately sunning and swimming, with Davide trying to keep his observations of Neve as unnoticeable as possible.

He and Agostino had laid out their beach towels a short distance from Neve and her mother, who had rented an umbrella and had brought a picnic basket. Davide's heart had started to pound when Neve, still unaware of his presence, had removed her beach wrap and started to apply sunscreen to her slender arms and legs. She was wearing a blue two-piece swimsuit with pink polka dots. He had smiled; she had had a thing for polka dots, obviously, and they had suited her something crazy.

He had felt the sun and the inner heat suddenly get to him, and slapping Agostino on the arm, he had challenged him to a race out to the third marker in the water, indicating one hundred meters.

"Race you there and back," he had urged. "I'm burning up."

They had splashed their way back to shore, with Davide winning by three meters. Laughing, they had dried off and collapsed on their beach towels. That was when Davide had looked across and realized Neve was watching him. Her mother had been busy laying out the picnic food. *Had Neve seen the whole race?* Self-consciously, he had given her a nod and after checking to make sure her mother was still occupied, he had waved.

She had waved back and seemed self-conscious herself, looking around as if to see if anyone had noticed her wave to Davide. Tossing her hair back, she had tiptoed quickly on the hot beach sand and had ventured a little way into the water before immersing herself completely in a graceful dive.

It had all happened in slow motion. The sights and sounds around Davide had blurred, and all he had been conscious of was Neve, her lithe body ascending from her dive with the sun reflected in every glistening drop on her skin. And when she had shaken her head and sent a rainbow spray around her, his breath had caught in his throat, and he had known in the deepest reaches of his soul that he had fallen in love with this bewitching sea nymph. *An impossible love that could never be returned.*

The realization had overwhelmed him. How was he going to deal with this? Agostino had told him earlier that Neve's visit to Valdoro would end in a couple of days, and then she and her mother would be returning to Canada. He had felt a series of unbearable twinges in his heart from wanting Neve but knowing his desire could not be reciprocated. Fate wouldn't allow it. Davide had immediately felt deflated, already anticipating the impending loss... Neve would be gone tomorrow, and he would be left with this torturous flame in his chest.

He had to meet her.

The thought had made his breath falter and his heart thump erratically. If he couldn't have anything else with Neve, at the very least he had wanted a few moments with her. A moment, even. To tell her how he felt, and to hear her response. His gut had told him that she had felt something, too… He had seen it in her eyes.

It had been too much to hope that Neve had fallen in love with him, as well, but Davide had been prepared to accept that. *Or at least, he thought he had been.* Some primeval instinct had been telling him that he just had to let her know, even if it was the last time he saw her lovely face.

He had stolen a last glance in Neve's direction. She had had her back to him as she and her mother enjoyed their picnic lunch. Unable to bear staying at the beach any longer, he had given Agostino a nudge and they had shaken off their beach towels and headed back to Valdoro. While cooling off with a gelato at a bar near the town square, Davide had devised a plan to meet with Neve. He would write Neve a note, and Agostino would make an excuse to show up at the villa with the pretense of talking to his mother and figure out a way to deliver it personally to Neve.

With any luck, Neve would agree to meet him at the bakery down the street, where they could sit down and he could treat her to a cappuccino and a pastry while divulging his feelings to her. It would be a perfectly respectable meeting place that would look like a casual encounter to anyone who might be frequenting the shop.

Staring across to the twinkling indigo sky, Davide felt a sharp twinge as he recalled how stupidly love-struck he had been, waxing poetic in a note that now seemed ridiculous with his naive and laughable choice of words.

Signorina Neve,

Only our eyes have met, and forgive me for being bold, but you have pierced my heart with your beauty. I feel that it is in our destiny to meet. With all my respect, I wish to see you before you depart for Canada. I only ask for a few moments of your time so I can express what is in my soul. My intentions are honorable...

If you can grant me this gift, I will be forever indebted. I will be at Michelina's Bakery after it reopens later this afternoon.

D.

Davide felt a tingle along his nerve endings as he thought about his imminent reunion with the girl who had so thoroughly put him in his "place" with her harsh reply. How would he react? How would *she*? His jaw clenched. Maybe he shouldn't have hired Neve Wilder so quickly. Maybe she had every right to know who her boss was before agreeing to the job.

But she wouldn't have agreed to the job if she had known it was you...

Davide felt a jolt. His inner voice was right. But somewhere deep inside the pain that was still trapped in his heart, was the pulsing desire to see Neve again. And keeping his identity from her—at least until she arrived—was the *only* way he could make that happen.

CHAPTER THREE

"MY GOODNESS, NEVE, you could have told me about this job opportunity sooner." Lois Wilder's voice was half-scolding, half-offended. "Hearing this a day before your flight hardly gives me a chance to process all this." She waved her hands helplessly, indicating Neve's open suitcase.

Or interfere in some way, Neve couldn't help thinking. "There's nothing to process, Mom. And I was busy finishing up my school year. You know I have no time to chat when I'm in the middle of report cards and end-of-school activities."

Lois expelled a sigh of frustration. "But, darling, had I known, I could have booked a flight, as well. Not that I would have expected to be put up at the same place as you," she added quickly. "I still have my friends at Villa Morgana. I'm sure they would be thrilled to have me visit."

"This is not a vacation, Mom. It's a job. Six days a week." Neve tried to keep her voice steady. "And I'm sure that on the seventh day I'll be too exhausted to do anything but rest." Neve was inwardly horrified at the thought of her mother coming to Valdoro. Knowing her, she'd find a way to insinuate herself in Neve's work and leisure time. No, she had to make it clear to her mom—without being mean—that she should stay home.

"Mom, I can't discuss the details, but this assignment

is highly sensitive. I will not be able to spend *any* time with you at all. And besides—" Neve had a brain wave "—you're hosting that big event in a week—the annual technology symposium—at the company, remember?"

Lois frowned. "Yes, of course. I suppose I can't miss that, seeing as how your dad started it all..." Her eyes began to mist. "Although the thought of returning to the special place where your dad and I..." She sniffed and pulled out a tissue from her designer purse. "May he rest in peace."

"Mom, I really have to finish packing. It's going to be a long couple of flights, and I need to get to bed early. It's only been two days since school ended, and I haven't even had a chance to unwind." Neve continued folding light cotton tops, Capri pants and dresses into her medium-size suitcase. She hoped her mother would take the hint.

Lois peered into the suitcase. "Don't forget your sun protection, Neve. You know how quickly you freckle." She took a step forward to scan Neve's face. "And you might start thinking about using some wrinkle cream. I have a new tube in my purse..."

"Thanks, but no thanks, Mom. I like the natural look." Neve realized that her tone was more clipped than she intended, but she had to stop her mother before she offered another dozen suggestions or reminders. "I'm twenty-six, Mom. I can handle this."

Lois raised her professionally shaped eyebrows. "I forgot to ask. Who is your employer? Can you give me his number? And make sure he has mine, in case of an emergency. Oh, and how much is he paying you for this job? Is the flight included?"

"Mother, you need to go, or it'll be midnight before I'm done here." Neve put an arm around her mother's shoulder and gently ushered her to the door of her apartment.

"I'll text you the information. Don't worry, it's all good." She gave her a hug. "See you at the end of the summer."

"Let me know as soon as your flight lands, Neve. I'll be waiting anxiously."

"I will, Mom," Neve replied wearily. "Good night."

"Buon viaggio," Lois called out before Neve closed the door. "And watch out for those Southern Italian men!"

Neve gave a sigh. She always felt somewhat energy-depleted after spending time with her mother. She often wondered at her mom's clinginess; she certainly hadn't been like that while Neve was growing up. Could it be that Lois had realized that some of her maternal skills had been lacking back then—especially after her husband's death—and was feeling guilty and trying to make up for it?

Neve had a hard time with it. At this point in her life, she didn't need her mother hovering over her. Lois's controlling and opinionated ways were grating, and Neve often felt her patience dwindling around her.

It wasn't that she didn't love her mother; she just wanted her to loosen the apron strings. No—she wanted Lois to untie them completely, and to fold the apron and put it away. It had gotten to the point where Neve had actually contemplated moving out of town. And then she had gotten her current job as a kindergarten teacher, which had prevented any further plans of relocating.

Neve checked the time and quickly finished packing, pushing away any more thoughts about her mother. All that was left to do now was to have a soothing bath and go to bed. And tomorrow, after a leisurely breakfast, she'd head to the airport. She thought of the plush orca she had purchased for Bianca—the perfect West Coast gift for a child—and smiled. Difficult and troubled though Bianca might be, Neve was confident that she could help her.

Lucia Michele had provided more details about Bianca's

situation, her daily routines and Neve's trip arrangements in a subsequent email, including the fact that Bianca's uncle would be covering all her travel and food expenses. *How very generous, and obviously very wealthy*, Neve had thought, and had wondered what he did for a living.

Feeling her eyelids start to droop, Neve pulled the stopper and stepped out of the tub, shivering despite the warmth of the room. She wrapped her terry-cloth robe around her and dried herself briskly before changing into a knee-length nightshirt. Under the covers, she let out a deep sigh. *She was really doing this.* Her travel clothes were laid out, and she was ready to fly to Italy and be a nanny! She hugged her pillow and let the memories of sun-drenched days, delicious Southern cuisine and the magical Ionian Sea lull her to sleep.

Davide drummed his fingers on his desk. He checked the time on his cell phone. Neve's plane should be landing in minutes at the Lamezia International Airport. Tomaso, his occasional driver, would be waiting for her, holding a card up with her name on it. Hopefully, there wouldn't be a delay in claiming her luggage. If complications arose, Tomaso would take care of them.

Davide wondered if Neve still spoke some Italian. The second time he saw her on her balcony, he had smiled and said, *"Ciao, signorina."* She had hesitated, given a quirk of a smile, and replied, *"Ciao."* It came out sounding more like the English "chow," and, embarrassed, she quickly repeated it with less of an aspiration at the start of the word. He had nodded in approval, and as he continued walking, he couldn't resist looking back and saying, *"Ciao, bella."* But she had already gone in.

Davide had tried to push recurring thoughts of her away after she had left Valdoro and returned to Vancouver. But if he had managed to accomplish that even temporarily during the day, he had been plagued by dreams of her at night.

His zio, Francesco, had noticed his malaise and had encouraged Davide to confide in him. *Is it about a girl?* He had eyed Davide with furrowed brows. Davide had been too embarrassed to talk about his feelings. *Especially to his uncle the priest. How could he have possibly discussed his unquenchable desire for Neve, and his feelings of bitterness and humiliation?*

"The best thing is to concentrate on your studies—and perhaps frequent Sunday mass a little more often," his uncle had solemnly suggested.

Davide smirked. He had taken his uncle's advice about his studies, but not so much on the second suggestion. Davide had had an issue with God and the whole destiny thing, and at twenty-two, forgiveness was not a strong male virtue. Davide had still gone to mass on special occasions, like the main holidays and an occasional funeral mass for a family friend, but other than that, he had stayed away. Besides, he had had goals he needed to accomplish.

And he had. He gave a bitter laugh as his gaze fell on the copy of his award-winning novel on his desk. Maybe he should thank Neve personally for *her* part in his literary success. Maybe he should have included a few words about her in his acceptance speech. After all, it was *her written words* that had ignited the chain of events leading up to the writing of his book.

Let it go, an inner voice whispered. Davide took a deep breath. *Indeed.* Why should he continue to be bitter about the words and actions of a teenage girl? He was a man now. His young ego may have been bruised then, but surely he was mature enough to have moved on?

Davide thought he had dealt with all those immature emotions, but he couldn't deny the sharp twinge in the core of his heart when Neve's face had appeared on the screen. She was still beautiful. *Bellissima.* He had watched the interview a few times after Lucia had gone home. Studied Neve's face as she spoke. Paused to go over her every feature. He had drunk in the sight of her like a man coming across a source of water after days of walking in a scorching-hot desert.

Could he handle her living in the castle with him, interacting with him daily, watching her deal with his beloved niece? *Only time would tell...*

His phone indicated a text. He checked the message, written in Italian.

Signorina Wilder has arrived. We are on our way.

Va bene, Davide replied swiftly.

He set down his phone, strode over to the credenza and poured himself a shot of brandy.

CHAPTER FOUR

As soon as Neve stepped out of the plane, the dry July heat enveloped her like a swaddling blanket. She was glad she had packed light. Her carry-on contained her laptop and a few emergency items in case her luggage was lost. And in her one piece of luggage, which she would shortly claim, there were just enough items to last her three weeks. She would alternate clothes over her two-month stay, and if she really got tired of wearing the same thing, she'd go to any one of the outdoor markets and buy something new. After all, she wasn't there to be in a fashion parade; she was there for work.

Neve took a moment to text her mother that she had arrived, and joined a slow-moving throng to get clearance from the uniformed officials. She then proceeded to the baggage claim area. She looked eagerly for a middle-aged man holding a sign with her name on it, as Lucia Michele had indicated in her email, and when she had spotted him, she waved and walked briskly toward him. He welcomed Neve in Italian and introduced himself as Tomaso Rocco. She smiled back at him and thanked him in Italian for having come to the airport to pick her up and drive her back to her employer's house.

Neve noticed that his eyebrows had lifted at the word *casa*. Maybe he was surprised that she could speak Italian. She had studied it since her trip to Italy as a teenager, and made it a point to use it with her Italian landlady and landlord, so she felt fairly comfortable communicating right away with Tomaso. Strangely enough, he switched to a faltering English after she had spoken.

"Would you care for a refresh before we proceed?" Tomaso pointed to a nearby kiosk. "Or a *panino*?"

Neve smiled. "*Grazie*, Signor Tomaso, but I had a nice meal on the plane. I wouldn't mind finding a ladies' room, though."

He nodded and once she returned, she positioned herself near one of the conveyors to scan the moving luggage. A few minutes later she spotted the suitcase with two extra-large stickers of the Canadian flag and the Italian flag placed side by side. Tomaso deftly grabbed it and a few moments later they were driving south along the coast. Neve was glad that Tomaso was not a man of many words, as the view around her had her total attention. She caught her breath at the shimmering expanse of the Gulf of St. Euphemia in the Tyrrhenian Sea, and the pastel-colored facades of villas and apartments. The familiar sight of oleander trees, with their profusion of white, pink and fuchsia blooms, growing not only around homes but also along endless stretches of railroad tracks, made Neve think of an impressionist painting, with its mesmerizing combination of multicolored strokes.

Despite the stifling heat of the afternoon, Tomaso had opted to roll the windows down instead of putting on the air-conditioning, and Neve actually didn't mind as she breathed in the sweet scent of the oleander blossoms perfuming the air.

Before long Tomaso had changed direction and was heading inland. The view changed from seascape to hills and valleys, with miles and miles of olive groves.

Neve loved the look of the olive trees, with their gnarled branches and silver-green foliage. She started as the vehicle jerked to a sudden stop, and Neve, turning her head, discovered the cause: a herd of goats crossing the road. The goatherd ambled by, waving at Tomaso, and he gave a resigned wave back. "People not like to hurry here," he said to Neve in his broken English. He drummed his fingers on the steering wheel. "You understand? Sometimes is like a thousand years ago."

"I understand." Neve stifled the urge to chuckle. "It's like time standing still."

Tomaso gave her a baffled look and then exclaimed as some of the goats started to backtrack. He gave a quick blast of the horn and the goats finally crossed over. Neve settled back to enjoy the magnificent views as the road snaked its way through what she discovered as she checked her map, was the Aspromonte mountain range. *The Bitter Mountains.*

She couldn't help a slight shiver as she recalled reading about some of the nefarious happenings within the dark recesses of the heavily wooded slopes. Stories of bandits, or *briganti*. Some had been the Italian counterpart to Robin Hood, but others were immortalized in folk songs for their notorious deeds.

Neve marveled at some of the hamlets perched on top of a hill. Some had been abandoned for years, and the houses were crumbling in areas. But even these ghost towns, with their borders of cactus pear plants and hillsides of golden broom, had a mysterious and romantic air about them, conjuring all kinds of stories in her imagination.

Totally absorbed in the mountain landscape, with its dark gullies and sheer cliff sides with often no guardrails, Neve found herself holding her breath. It was like seeing everything with new eyes. Perhaps at eighteen she had had other things—or people—that had grabbed her attention, but now the mountains, trees and the scintillating waters were even more majestic and striking than she remembered.

Tomaso started whistling an old folk tune; she had heard it at a festival during her last trip to Italy. She knew the title, *Calabrisella Mia*, and if her memory served her right, it was about a young man who spotted a young lady washing clothes at the public fountains and was captivated by her. Well, maybe nobody went to do laundry at the fountains or by the river anymore, but Valdoro still celebrated the chivalry of the "old days" at their annual summer festival, the *Festa della Calabrisella*, where couples dressed up in traditional vintage clothing and danced the *tarantella*.

The hamlet came alive for the festivities, with its numbers swelling from visitors near and far. Merchants sold their artisanal goods in an outdoor market in Valdoro's *piazza* during the day, and everything from stuffed eggplants to fried calamari and cuttlefish were sold in the town banquet hall in the evening before the outdoor activities resumed, with musicians performing back in the square until midnight.

Neve's mouth watered at the memory of the food fair, and in particular, the sizzling stuffed zucchini flowers that she loved, their golden orange blossoms filled with a chunk of *fontina* cheese, and then floured and quickly deep-fried. Neve hoped she would be able to attend with Bianca, or during her day off.

"*Ecco!* We are approaching Valdoro," Tomaso suddenly exclaimed, and Neve realized she had been lost in her thoughts and had missed the road signs. She sat up straighter and wondered at how much of what she saw seemed completely new. And then she saw the fork in the road that led right into Valdoro.

"The Pasticceria Michelina!" She recognized the peach-colored facade of the bakery on the same street as the Villa Morgana. "They had the best marzipan cookies and cannoli! Could we stop?" She would love to buy some treats for Bianca.

"I'm sure you will have time to go back soon enough," Tomaso said with a tone of regret. "But your employer is waiting and expects us very shortly."

Was her employer that inflexible? She wouldn't have taken more than five minutes to get what she wanted... Neve started as Tomaso suddenly swerved to follow the left fork, which took them away from the main road.

"Wh-where are you going?" Neve said, confused. "I thought we were going to Valdoro."

"We are still in Valdoro, *signorina.* Your boss lives on the—how do you say?—outside skirts."

Neve smiled, but didn't correct him. As Tomaso drove farther along, fewer and fewer homes appeared, and then suddenly, there was nothing but stretches of olive groves, uncultivated land bordered with endless cactus pear bushes and what looked like giant aloe vera plants, and massive clay hills. Tomaso veered into a side road, and Neve realized he was starting to ascend a path that wove its way around a mountainside, giving her flashes of the Ionian Sea through the dizzying blur of trees.

Neve's stomach gave a flip at the change in elevation. *Who would build way up here? Was there a cluster of homes at the summit?* She had seen photos of mountaintop villages or monasteries all over Italy, and they had always made her catch her breath, trying to imagine the toil of the men and mules employed to carry out such a task centuries ago.

Neve closed her eyes at one point. There were no guardrails at all, and the thought of the vehicle skidding down the mountain made the butterflies in her stomach crash wildly into each other.

"Siamo arrivati," Tomaso announced after what seemed like an eternity.

Neve felt the car come to a stop. She opened her eyes and allowed her stomach to settle for a moment. Tomaso came around to open her door, and she stepped out hesitantly, thanking him. He nodded and as he went to retrieve her luggage, Neve's gaze shifted eagerly to her employer's house. She froze and then felt a slow tremble along her nerve endings.

This was no house. Neve's gaze traveled from one side of the centuries-old castle to the other. *A castle! Was she dreaming?* She pinched her hand. No, no dream. And no wonder that Tomaso had had that funny expression when she thanked him for picking her up to take her to her employer's "house." Parked outside were three other vehicles, one an electric blue that dazzled in the sun. As they approached, the golden bull brand confirmed her guess: a Lamborghini. The second one was a red Alfa Romeo, and the third, a Fiat Cinquecento.

Neve followed Tomaso numbly toward the massive rounded portico. The low heels of her sandals clicked on the granite slabs of the walkway, and she felt as if she was walking into a fairy tale. The few scattered clouds seemed to be within reach, and the air was fresh at this elevation. Neve breathed in the scent of the nearby pine trees. They seemed to be twinkling with the sun's rays poking through spaces in their thick boughs. The sun gleamed off the casement windows, and Neve wondered if her employer was watching from behind one of them. She swallowed. *What was she in for?* She felt an inner shiver and had a feeling that there were a lot more unexpected things to come.

Tomaso ignored the heavy iron knocker and pressed a

buzzer on a panel below. Okay, so there was one modern touch, but what if her employer was an eccentric?

She knew next to nothing about him. Who was this enig-matic boss who lived at the top of a mountain and who hadn't wanted his identity revealed? And how could he be raising his niece here, so isolated from other people? From kids?

A hundred questions swarmed her mind, but they dis-sipated when the doorknob turned. She bit her lip.

The door opened with a slight creak, and Neve was almost expecting to see a disheveled, wild-haired scien-tist or inventor type, dressed in a lab coat and smelling of formaldehyde and carrying a beaker with some swirling concoction. *What appeared was anything but.*

She looked up to meet the unsmiling and spectacled gaze of a thirty-something man who was hardly the Fran-kenstein she had envisioned. The fresh citrus scent of his cologne tingled her nostrils. He hadn't shaved, but that didn't detract from his attractiveness. *No*, his well-groomed scruff was absolutely charming. *If only he would remove his sunglasses.* Somehow, Neve felt at a disadvantage...

His dark brown hair was cut short but revealed curls on the top, and he had a firm, straight nose and strong jaw. And perfect lips. Although she didn't want to stare, Neve couldn't help taking in his physique in a two-second glance that wandered from his face to his body, noting the broad shoulders and snug-fitting sleeves; the crisp black shirt open at the neck, with buttons tapering to a flat stomach; and the tailored cream trousers and polished black shoes. *Italian leather, of course.*

Neve's heart did a flip at the way he was staring at her when her gaze returned to his face. He smiled, revealing a dimple that was the icing on the cake as far as she was concerned, and she began to reciprocate but realized with a gulp that he was directing it to Tomaso, who stood behind her with her suitcase in hand. He opened the door wider and directed Tomaso in Italian to carry her suitcase to her room. When Tomaso disappeared, he looked appraisingly at her, and the half smile that still lingered on her face began to waver.

But then he held out his hand and flashed her a smile. "*Benvenuta*, Signorina Wilder."

Neve would have truly felt his welcome was genuine, had the coolness of his tone not indicated otherwise.

From his study window, Davide had watched Neve come out of his Fiat van. His pulse had quickened with her every step toward the castle. The way the sun had caught in her hair and made it shimmer had taken his breath away. Her calf-length, pale lavender dress, with its filmy skirt layers and uneven hem, made her look like a mystical fairy. All she needed to do was to kick off her shoes and dance around the castle grounds...

Stop! What are you doing? This fairy wanted to have nothing to do with you, remember? She made it quite clear that you were below her. And she's not here for any reason other than to take care of Bianca.

Davide realized he was clenching his jaw and relaxed it. The fact was, Neve Wilder had had the best credentials for the job, and he had to forget what she had been like at eighteen. What had devastated him at the time—*and afterward*—had probably not affected her one bit. She had most likely forgotten the whole incident. *And maybe him, as well...* In any case, he had no intention of bringing it up...unless *she* did.

Making his way down the gleaming oak staircase to the main floor, Davide had thought of how opportune it was to have arranged for Bianca to be away for a few days. Thank goodness Bianca enjoyed spending time with Lucia, his trusted research assistant and friend. Davide didn't know how he would have gotten through these past few months without Lucia's help. She had been there to pick up the pieces after he had dismissed the last three nannies, and for that he would be eternally grateful. Lucia was married with no children of her own but had grown up in a large family, and had a wonderful way with children.

Davide was grateful that Lucia had gained Bianca's trust, but Lucia wasn't there to be a nanny. After the disappointments of the past, he intended to discover whether Neve Wilder was truly the right choice. He'd decided not to introduce Bianca to her new nanny right away, and risk upsetting her if he had to fire Neve.

Davide was sure that he would be able to determine if Neve's character was genuine, or if she had just put on a good act during the interview. And if his judgment *had* been faulty, he'd waste no time in sending her back to Vancouver.

David had stipulated that Neve would have a "trial period" in the contract, but he had omitted to mention that Bianca wouldn't be there at that time. He shrugged, his mouth twisting.

His prerogative. He was the boss.

When Davide had opened the thick wooden door, he had felt a surge of electricity zip through his veins. His gaze had flown first to Neve, then he had smiled at Tomaso to bring up Neve's luggage to her room. "The one in the turret," he had directed, and then had focused his attention to Neve. Nothing in her gaze had indicated that she had recognized him. *Good. Maybe that was for the best...* But her smile had suddenly faltered...and then he had realized that his expression had hardly been welcoming.

No matter what he thought of her, he had reminded himself that he had to be civil, for Bianca's sake.

Davide had forced himself to smile, and despite the hard, twisted knot in his gut that he had lived with for the past eight years, faking his welcome had made him feel like a cad.

Now he swore inwardly as he saw something shut down in her blue-green eyes. She had perceptively picked up on his less than genuine gesture.

Neve had not even been in his presence for a minute, and he was feeling emotional turmoil. Realizing now that he was staring at her, he cleared his throat and tried softening his tone. "I apologize, Signorina Wilder. I've had little sleep these past few months. It has been a very difficult time, as you can imagine." He offered her his hand.

Her aquamarine eyes widened. "Yes, of course, *signor*." She gave his hand a gentle squeeze. "I'm very sorry for your loss…and Bianca's."

The touch of her hand in his, albeit brief, ignited his nerve endings.

He nodded and focused on what she was saying. *Were her eyes actually misting?* "Thank you. May I take your carry-on?" He wanted to veer away from any further mention of his sister and brother-in-law. The last thing he wanted was to be emotional in front of her.

Fortunately, Tomaso's reappearance distracted them both. Davide thanked him and offered him a cool refreshment, but Tomaso respectfully declined. "My wife texted me to say her eggplant parmigiana would be ready when I get home," he chuckled. "And believe me, she makes the best *melanzana alla parmigiana*."

"I don't blame you for hurrying back." Davide nodded. "It's not every man who can go home to a good meal—and a good woman," he added drily. He shook Tomaso's hand,

and as Tomaso headed toward his Fiat Cinquecento, Davide motioned for Neve to enter the castle. He could see that Neve was impressed by what she saw. He gave her a few moments as she took in the rich oak staircase curving sensuously to the second level, the vaulted ceiling and pale mint walls, the luxurious peach marble tiles and the gleaming walnut and oak inlaid furniture pieces, including the round central table, enhanced by a large crystal vase filled with fresh flowers of every color. Davide had them delivered and arranged once a week. He enjoyed the look and scent of them in the foyer—the mix of peony and oleander, jasmine and rose, and any other combination of flowers native to Calabria.

"I imagine you're tired after your trip, Signorina Wilder. I'll show you to your room." He gestured toward the staircase.

Neve hesitated for a moment before nodding, and as she proceeded gracefully up the stairs, Davide couldn't stop his gaze from sweeping over her. Her dress molded to the curves of her body, and its flared and layered skirt swayed with her hip movements. Davide swallowed as his eyes swept farther downward along the length of her calves and to her low-heeled sandals. She suddenly stopped on the landing, and he looked up too late to stop his body from bumping into hers. She faltered, and his arms instinctively dropped her carry-on bag and reached out to steady her.

For a moment his body went into shock. The feel of her trim waist almost completely encircled by his hands made his nerve endings sizzle. His mouth was inches away from her neck, and, oh, how he had often dreamt of—

He felt her stiffen. And he remembered that his fantasies of holding her in his arms, of brushing a path of kisses against her neck before moving upward to taste her coral lips, had died with his hopes long before, splintering like the waves that dashed against the boulders on the shore.

"Mi scusi," he apologized curtly, moving away to pick up her bag. He preceded her down the hall, walking past a half-dozen doors until he stopped at a curved section, one of the four turrets in the castle. Davide wanted her in the spare room next to Bianca, and both were across the hall from his bedroom and his study.

Not that he had any ungentlemanly intentions toward Neve. No, despite his undeniable attraction to Neve *still*, his pride would not allow him to even venture in *that* direction. She was here to do the job he had hired her for. Nothing more, nothing less. He opened the thick, rounded door. "I hope you will be pleased with this room, Signorina Wilder."

She glanced past him and her mouth opened in wonder. Turning, she gave him a dazzling smile. *"Pleased?* This is every girl's dream come true," she breathed. "A castle and a room fit for a princess—I feel like I'm in a fairy tale…" She went straight to the casement window to check out the view. The breeze rippled through her hair, and Davide felt a twist in his gut at the reality that she was actually here in person.

"I'm glad you like it." He gave her a piercing look as he set down her bag. "Just keep in mind, though, that your experience here may not be like the fairy tales you're familiar with. And hopefully, you'll last longer than the previous three princesses…"

CHAPTER FIVE

NEVE STARED AT the door that had just closed behind him. She felt foolish now for having gushed about the place; he must have thought her materialistic, or at the very least, fanciful. And she had a strong feeling that fanciful was not what he wanted in a nanny.

Neve looked around. She wondered what kind of a job her boss had to allow him to renovate an ancient castle in such a lavish manner. There had been nothing in sight to enlighten her in any way about this. Perhaps he had inherited money and didn't have to work...

She had grown up accustomed to a wealthy lifestyle, but *this*, this place was over-the-top. The floor was a stunning pale rose marble with veins of gold. The bed stood in the center of a rich Renaissance-style rug. The duvet and pillow shams had the dreamy colors of an impressionist painting, with assorted custom pillows in turquoise and gold. The massive armoire matched the gleaming wood of the bed and the night tables, and on the top of each end table stood an antique lamp with carnelian tassels hanging from the rim of each shade. A luxurious burgundy recliner was positioned by the window.

This was obviously decorated for a woman's use, Neve thought, eyeing the ornate dressing table against one wall. *Had her boss designed it for his lady? Or wife?* She hadn't seen a ring on his finger, which didn't necessarily mean he wasn't married. Neve felt her stomach tighten at the thought of how his hands had felt around her waist. With his gorgeous looks, how could she even think he wasn't attached in one way or another? Those hands of his were probably in high demand…

Neve forced herself to stop that train of thought. *What was the matter with her?* She was here not even an hour, and already she was thinking about her boss in a way that an employee should not be.

She strode to the mahogany four-poster bed, with its matching step-up stool. After removing her sandals, she climbed up to sit on the bed. Much as she wanted to lie down and have a nap, Neve's mind was too preoccupied to let herself sleep. On the plane trip, her thoughts had kept returning to the little girl that she would soon meet. *Would Bianca be upset or hostile to yet another nanny showing up?* Not that there had been any mention of her being hostile, but Neve couldn't help wondering at the cause of the dismissal of three previous nannies.

They had obviously displeased Neve's uncle. Could one of them have been negligent in her care of Bianca? Had one been too harsh with her? Or had one of the nannies been more attentive to their boss than to his niece? Neve turned over every possibility that she could think of, and had finally convinced herself to stop. Just because three nannies had disappointed their employer, it didn't mean that *she* would. In any case, all she could do was try her best. Use all the skills and compassion she had to try to reach this little girl.

Neve felt a twinge in her heart, thinking of Bianca's tragic loss. *Not one parent, but two.* A double trauma. And then to be whisked away to a new country where she had nobody but her uncle as family. Neve took a deep breath. *No, this was not going to be a vacation.*

She frowned. And how strange was it that she still didn't know her employer's name? He hadn't introduced himself, and taken by surprise at his appearance, Neve hadn't even thought of asking...

A couple of taps at the door made her start. "*Scusi*, Signorina Neve. I thought you might like some refreshments."

Neve slid off the bed and put on her sandals before hurrying to open the door. He was holding a silver tray with a bottle of water and one of orange juice, a small platter of grapes and golden plums and a variety of cheeses and crackers. He was still wearing his glasses, which Neve found rather unnerving.

"That's very thoughtful. Thank you, Mr...?"

He looked at her intently. "Cortese," he said curtly. "You're welcome." He strode to the dressing table and set the tray down. He walked back to the door and then looked over his shoulder at her. "After you have rested and when you are ready, please come to my study across the hall and we'll go over my expectations..."

Neve's eyebrows arched. *Hadn't Lucia Michele informed her of all his expectations?* She felt her stomach muscles contract. There was something in the way he was looking at her that made her stomach quiver with apprehension. And when exactly was he planning to introduce her to Bianca? He hadn't said anything about her whereabouts. She was most likely having an afternoon siesta, and Neve would meet her afterward...

"I'm not feeling that tired right now, Signor Cortese. But I wouldn't mind having some water and fruit." Neve gave him a tentative smile. "I'll be over in a few minutes, and by then, I'm hoping that Bianca—"

"Bianca's not here," he said swiftly. He swiveled to face her. "She's away for a few days. My assistant—Signora Michele—has a niece visiting, and I arranged for Bianca to spend a few days with them. I thought that we could use the time to review a few things..."

Neve had to stop from gaping as she stared back at him. She felt a shiver run through her. She was alone in a castle miles away from anyone, with a man who had wanted his identity protected. Could she trust him? What if—?

"You have nothing to worry about, Signorina Wilder," he said coolly. "I'm not planning to compromise your virtue." His ebony eyes swept over her body deliberately before locking with hers. "I had you brought here for my niece, not for me." He turned to leave. "And I have no interest in taking up in *that* way with *straniere*."

Neve's stomach tensed at the way his voice had chilled at the word *foreigners*, specifically foreign women. Speechless, she stood watching him, and even after he had shut the door firmly, she stood immobilized for another minute. Finally, she walked over to the dressing table, had a long drink of water and sat down on the stool, her heart racing as if she had just completed a marathon.

She had no choice but to meet Signor Cortese in his study. But first she needed to cool herself off. After finishing the bottle of water, Neve stood up and taking a deep breath, headed for the door.

Davide had left the door of his study open. He heard Neve's door open and shut and her footsteps as she crossed the hall. He remained at his desk, looking out to the view of the countryside and to the strip of azure sea beyond. "Come in," he said curtly when her footsteps ceased at his doorway.

He had been thinking about the startled fawn look on Neve's face when he had told her that Bianca wasn't there.

I'm not planning to compromise your virtue, he had stated, and almost blurted afterward, *if your virtue is still intact...*

Davide swiveled to face her, but remained sitting. He gestured to the maroon leather chair in front of her. "Please...have a seat."

He reached beyond his laptop for a file on the left-hand corner of his desk, and slid it toward him. He saw that Neve was gazing at the small pile of books on the other side of his desk.

"So now you know what I do for a living..."

Her eyes widened. *"You're an author?"*

Davide nodded. "I suppose you must have wondered what I did to enable me to buy this place and renovate it." He saw a flush spread over her cheeks.

"Well, it *had* crossed my mind," she admitted, shrugging defensively. "But most writers don't live... I mean... can't live—"

"Like *this*?" Davide smirked. "You're right, Signorina Wilder. I was one of the lucky ones whose first novel—and the only one published so far—was not only awarded the *Strega*, Italy's highest literary award, but was also optioned immediately by a major film company. And a television series is also in the works. If I wanted to, I could retire right now and live happily-ever-after..." The muscles in his jaw flicked. "But I have no intention of retiring. And *happily-ever-after* is not an option right now." He tapped his closed laptop. "Eventually I'll get back to working on my second novel...when Bianca is more settled..."

"I'm sure luck was not the only factor in your success, Signor Cortese."

Neve's soft voice was like a hammer against his heart. No, it hadn't been all about luck. It had been about her rejection, about heartbreak, about losing himself in a fictional world to escape his own reality...

"Perhaps I can read your book while I'm here..."

No! Letting her read the story of Serena and Vittorio would be allowing her a glimpse—no, an entire window—into his soul, and he wasn't ready for that... He had revealed a vulnerable part of his soul once to her, only to have it scorched by her harsh words.

"Perhaps," he forced himself to reply nonchalantly. "But I'm sure you'll be too busy tending to Bianca..." He straightened in his chair. "But we're not here to talk about me or my book," he said curtly. "Let's get down to business and not my personal life."

"I'm sorry," Neve replied quickly. "I didn't mean to—"

"Apology accepted."

"I—I hope I haven't offended you."

Davide surveyed her for a moment. The flush on her face had deepened, and her discomfort was palpable. "I'm not offended in the least," he replied crisply. *At least not about the present. The past was a different story...* He leaned forward, out of the direct sunlight. "Now, let's go over Bianca's routines..." He removed his sunglasses, his eyes boring into Neve's.

CHAPTER SIX

NEVE'S LIPS PARTED with a sudden uptake of breath. His black eyes were so intense…like smoldering volcanic shards. She couldn't pull her gaze away. She felt something stir in her memory… Black eyes that glistened like raven's wings…

Neve felt her heart begin to beat a warning drum against her chest.

Could it be? The Italian who had made it a point to walk past her balcony every day while she had stayed at the Villa Morgana? Who had shown up at the beach with his friend when she was there with her mother?

She scanned his face, trying to imagine him eight years younger, without the groomed shadow or styled hair.

Yes. Sparks shot through her veins. It was *him.*

Neve stared at him speechlessly. Eight years ago he had had longer hair and no groomed shadow, and he had been more lanky. Now he exuded maturity, worldliness and wealth. With his expensive clothes and styled hair that was short on the sides and back and curling on top, he looked as polished and sophisticated as a model in a magazine. His face had lost its adolescent leanness, and was strong, chiseled—*and heart-stopping.*

What were the chances of *him* being Bianca's uncle and her employer for the summer?

And then her mind stilled. *He had known who she was when he had hired her*. He had watched the interview conducted by his assistant.

Neve didn't think she had changed that much in eight years; she had no doubt that he would have recognized her right away. That is, if he had remembered walking past her balcony at Villa Morgana and gazing at her with such intensity...

She had been young, but not so young that she hadn't been instantly aware of the meaning of his look. It had riveted her, caused the first stirrings of sensuality, made her wonder what it could lead to...and after three days of this, she had felt a molten heat begin to spread throughout her veins even at the anticipation of seeing him return from his work in the countryside.

And then one day he had shown up at the beach. When she had seen him and his friend Agostino, whom she recognized as the son of the housekeeper at Villa Morgana, she had tried to be discreet about watching him. She had directed fleeting glances at his tanned, muscled body, always when her mother was distracted with preparing the picnic lunch or sunning on the beach chair. Neve had brought a book along, and she had held it up in front of her, pretending to read, but all the while, gazing at *him*. She hadn't known his name, and she'd never seemed to have the opportunity to ask Agostino...

And two days before she had to leave Italy, Davide had stopped coming by. The first day Neve had left the balcony with a heavy feeling in her chest. She had pleaded a headache and stayed in her room instead of joining her mother and hosts for dinner. Her appetite had left her. Her mother had checked in on her, but Neve had pretended to be sleeping.

On the evening before their departure, Neve had had

no choice but to join the group, despite the fact that she was feeling even worse.

The next morning she had left Valdoro with a desperate scan of the streets from the backseat of the vehicle that had sped toward the airport. The flight back home had been just as dismal, and for the next few months Neve had felt listless and down. Her mother had claimed it to be a hormone imbalance, and had supplied her with over-the-counter remedies. Neve had pretended to take them, but all the while had flushed them down the toilet.

Her gut had told her that it wasn't pills she needed; it was time. Time to get over the crazy feeling that she had lost someone she had just begun to fall in love with…

Neve's gaze dropped to the name on the book. *Davide Cortese…* How often had she wondered about his name? Carlo, Luciano, Marco, Roberto, Vincenzo… She had gone over every Italian name in the alphabet, trying to guess at his. For a long time he had appeared in her adolescent dreams, and during the day she had found it hard to concentrate on her classes.

When her marks had started to slip, her mother had threatened to send her to a private school and Neve had forced herself to slip out of her malaise and get back to reality. She was in Canada and *he* was in Southern Italy. They were from different worlds, and there was no chance of those worlds colliding…

Yet here she was, eight years later. *In a castle that she'd be living in for two months with him…and his niece.* She shook her head and wanted to pinch herself, but knew it was futile.

This was not a dream…

Davide had noticed the changes in Neve's expression. The slight furrowing of her eyebrows suddenly smoothing out, her blue-green eyes widening and her lips parting. And her chest rising with a quick intake of breath. She had recognized him.

So now what?

She would have figured out that he had recognized her from the interview. How would she react? Perhaps she was wondering what his real motive was in hiring her. Or feeling threatened that someone she had spurned eight years earlier had masterminded her return to Valdoro? Maybe she wondered if he was some kind of psychopath who was bent on revenge... He searched her face for any sign of fear, but all he saw was surprise. And confusion. He saw her glance down at his books and back at him. Her cheeks had darkened to a deep shade of pink, the same pink as some of the roses and oleander flowers on his property.

Her eyebrows had lifted in an unspoken question, but Davide wasn't ready to comply with a response. And it didn't look like she wanted to be the first one to bring up the now very obvious elephant in the room...

"*Va bene*, let's discuss your goals concerning Bianca before I reinforce my expectations." His eyes narrowed. "And please respond with specifics about how you intend to achieve those goals."

Davide checked the time on his phone. He had grilled Neve long enough, and to his surprise, she had answered his questions unwaveringly, providing a detailed knowledge of behavioral strategies and demonstrating a genuine empathy toward children. But the color that had suffused her face earlier had dissipated. In fact, she was looking a little pale...

He stood up abruptly. "I think we've discussed enough for now. Once you have rested, please feel free to go down to any of the rooms on the main level or out in the courtyard or gardens." He watched as Neve nodded and turned, the uneven hem of her violet dress swirling to reveal a flash of her thighs. His pulse jumped erratically. Despite the efforts he had made to recover emotionally from Neve, his body was obviously not on board.

Stifling a growl of frustration, he waited until he heard her bedroom door click shut behind her and then busied himself with email, responding to several communications from his publisher, who had been checking on him regularly since Davide had brought Bianca back from Vancouver. Afterward, he went downstairs to make himself an espresso. Sitting with it in the courtyard beyond the kitchen, he couldn't help thinking about Neve.

He forced himself to face a hard fact. *He was not immune to her physical charms.* The eight years of trying to quench his desire for her had been futile. Watching her on his computer screen had activated his pulse, but having her in his presence, within his touch, was a sweet torture that took every ounce of his energy to conceal.

Maybe hiring Neve Wilder, despite her stellar CV and qualifications, had been a mistake. How could he not have imagined the effect that her presence would have on him? Eight years ago he would have given anything to have met her, held her hand, revealed his feelings. But she had denied him even the chance to meet. Then she had left the country, leaving him with a gnawing regret and a crushed spirit.

If he had thought that he could be neutral having Neve as a nanny to Bianca without his emotions being affected, he had been delusional. The feel of her hand in his...just that momentary touch had sent a spiral of heat through him, and his heart had hammered against his rib cage, drowning out some of her words... And then she had told him how sorry she was for his and Bianca's loss, and those azure eyes had started to mist.

How could he endure two months of having Neve so close? What on earth had he hoped to accomplish, other than to find a nanny who could help Bianca and prepare her for school?

Davide recalled the flash of recognition on Neve's face.

What was she thinking now? Would she stay, now that she knew who he was?

He clenched his jaw. *She had to stay.* Whether she liked it or not. Even if she was uncomfortable with him. She had signed a contract. And ultimately, she was here for Bianca, not for *him.* He would stay out of her way as much as possible.

Davide felt the familiar stabs of sadness and concern over Bianca's trauma. Since the accident, she had awoken occasionally during the night with a bad dream. He had made sure to have the room across his set up for her when he brought her back here, and he had always kept his door open to listen for any signs of distress from her.

It had been a trauma for him, too; he had loved Violetta and had been crushed at the news of her and Tristan's deaths. He still shuddered every time he thought about the phone call that night. How his body had gone numb, and then trembled in icy shock. There had been no sleep for the rest of the night. He had paced through the castle like a man possessed, feeling a desolation that was as dark and deep as the Ionian Sea nearby. And a helplessness that he could do nothing for little Bianca while they were oceans apart.

He had known that Violetta's friend Alba would take good care of Bianca until he arrived, and Davide had made her promise that she would let *him* tell Bianca. Like a zombie, he had thrown together a few clothes in a medium suitcase, and had driven straight to Lamezia Airport. He had flown to Rome and then had made two more connections to his final stop in Vancouver.

And he had crashed for a few hours in a hotel before hiring a driver to bring him to Alba's condo.

That had been five months ago. Before that he had still felt young and relatively carefree. Any sense of happiness over his literary success and his progress with his second novel had dissipated like the morning fog at the news of Violetta and Tristan. And the hardest thing that he had ever had to do was to look at Bianca's sweet little face, all lit up over his arrival, and tell her about the accident.

The shadow that had crossed her face, and the cries of *"Mummy! Daddy! I want them to come home!"* while he held her in his arms, had almost done him in, but he had forced himself to stay calm and strong for her sake, and had stayed with her until she had cried herself to sleep. Alba had prepared a spare room for him, but he opted for a spare cot to be brought to Bianca's room, in case she woke up in the night, scared or in shock.

Davide had thanked God countless times that he had been able to fly to Vancouver regularly since Bianca's birth. Violetta had bestowed him with the honor of being Bianca's godfather, and he had been determined to have a special relationship with his niece. He had not wanted Bianca to ever feel that he was a stranger.

Davide had been so grateful that the success of his first novel had provided him with the means to take regular trips and stay connected with Violetta's family.

Since he had brought Bianca home with him, Davide had put his writing on hold. Helping Bianca had been his priority. And still was. But now that Neve was here, he might be able return to his novel in progress. *If she lasted...*

CHAPTER SEVEN

NEVE OPENED HER EYES, blinking at the unfamiliar light fixture, a chandelier that featured dozens of colorful Murano glass flowers in various states of bloom. And then she remembered where she was. She had returned to her room and emotionally drained, had taken off her sandals and had lain down on the bed. Despite the turbulence of her thoughts, she had felt herself drifting.

Now, checking the time, she realized that she had been napping for almost two hours. Still feeling somewhat groggy, she slid off the bed and ambled to the washroom. After a refreshing shower, she towel-dried her hair, combed it out and slipped on a headband. She opened her suitcase and chose an aqua cotton top and a pair of white Capri pants.

There was no avoiding the situation. She couldn't stay in her room indefinitely. Taking a deep breath, Neve headed downstairs.

She found her way past the elegant dining area to the most spectacular kitchen she had ever seen. From the gleaming granite countertops to the oversize appliances, the room shouted luxury. The new complemented the old, which Neve could see was the original stone hearth and an antique harvest table. In the center of the table was a large terra-cotta jug filled with flowers that Neve did not recognize, but she breathed in their delicate scent and loved the way they made the room homey despite its size.

She started as her boss suddenly spoke behind her.

"Would you like a cool drink or perhaps a cappuccino?"

"Thank you. I'd love a cool drink—*un'aranciata*?"

"Yes, certainly." He opened the restaurant-size refrigerator and grabbed a bottle of orange soda and a beer. "Let's go out into the courtyard…" He strode over to open a large rounded door. "After you."

Neve caught her breath. Was there no end to the wonder of this place? It was a garden of Eden; there was no other way to describe it. Lemon and fig trees. Bay laurel and medlar. Wild rosebushes and a huge grape pergola. And a large trellis, draped with an enchanting canopy of wisteria in full bloom. Glazed pots of every size and color, filled with rosemary, oregano, parsley, sage and thyme. And beyond, a vegetable garden and a profusion of cactus pear bushes.

Davide set down the drinks on an ornate glass table and pulled out a chair for Neve.

She thanked him and sat down. As Neve sipped her orange soda, she gazed at the more rugged terrain across the mountain, and then beyond that, to the cobalt strip of the Ionian Sea. *It was unreal, being here. Never in her wildest imagination had she thought she'd be working in a place like this.* She glanced again at the cultivated areas of the property and imagined all the work that had gone into it.

Neve turned to see Davide sit next to her, a beer in his hand.

"You must have a gardener," Neve said, unable to keep the awe out of her voice.

"You're looking at him," Davide replied curtly.

Neve was taken aback at his tone. *Had she said something that had offended him?* "Oh… I just thought…"

"That someone with my money would have hired help?" He gave a biting laugh. "No, when I bought this place, I decided that I needed to restore it to its previous glory and functionality. Inside and out. And I wanted to do the work outside myself, as I had done on my uncle's farm years ago." His eyes speared hers. "Let's just say that I needed to get over something…and hard, physical labor under our summer Calabrian sun will make you forget just about anything…or *anybody*."

Neve's heart did a half flip at the intensity of his gaze. Why did she have the gnawing feeling that Davide was inferring something that she would understand? Davide's mouth opened as if he was going to add something, but he promptly shut it, and the look he gave her was almost… *reprimanding*.

Perhaps she was misinterpreting things. *Why would he be reprimanding her?*

Neve glanced away, her cheeks already feeling the effects of the late-afternoon sun. *Or was it more than the sun?*

Davide excused himself as he stood up. "My housekeeper/cook is away for a week," he said. "So you're going to have to put up with some of my cooking." While Neve sauntered into the garden, Davide went inside to prepare a tomato salad and lemon rosemary chicken scallopini.

He set down the plates on the kitchen island, and he brought out a slightly chilled white Greco wine.

Davide had pulled out a chair for Neve at the kitchen island. *"Buon appetito,"* he said, gesturing for her to start.

"If the rest of your cooking is this good, I won't mind that your housekeeper's away," Neve murmured after her first taste. She glanced across at him shyly. "I can make basic meals, but I must say I was glad that cooking wasn't part of the requirements of this job…"

Davide arched an eyebrow. "I'm surprised…"

Neve's fork paused in midair. "That I'm a mediocre cook?"

"That you'd be so candid about your perceived culinary shortcoming."

Neve shrugged. "I see no need to lie about myself, or pretend I'm something I'm not."

"That's a good virtue for a nanny to have." Davide swirled the wine in his glass without averting his gaze.

They ate in silence for a few moments, and Davide wondered if it was the right time to venture into the past and confront Neve about the letter. *About how less than virtuous she had been in the way she had treated him…*

No; now was not the time. Neve had just arrived today. It wasn't fair to bombard her with something that had happened eight years ago, and that had probably bothered *him* a lot more than her. He would have to be patient and wait for the right opportunity…

Lucia would be bringing Bianca back after two days, leaving him tomorrow and the day after to evaluate Neve's character and suitability to take care of Bianca. Tomorrow he planned to take Neve to the market. He wanted to observe and interact with her in a variety of settings, with a variety of people. If any red flags went up in his mind, he could address them with her and then decisions would be made.

Davide offered Neve coffee, but she declined, thanking him for the lovely meal before excusing herself to return to her room. He watched her leave, and after setting the dishes in the dishwasher and turning it on, he decided to turn in, as well.

Lying in his king-size bed with his sheets pulled back,

Davide listened to the night sounds outside his windows, unable to sleep. He heard an owl, and a few minutes later, a kestrel. He shivered involuntarily, despite the warmth of the night.

Neve had been in his castle only one day, and already she had begun to affect him. From what he could determine today, she would be good for Bianca.

But would she be good for *him*?

CHAPTER EIGHT

NEVE'S PHONE ALARM woke her up and she rolled over to silence it on her night table, her eyes still closed. Her first thought was what to wear for school, and then her eyes flew open. School was over. She stared up at the ceiling, looked down at the unfamiliar quilt and gazed around her without lifting her head off the pillow. Her mind cleared. She was in Davide Cortese's castle, and she had been hired for the summer as nanny to his niece, Bianca.

But it would be a couple of days more before Bianca returned. *A couple of days more for Davide to ascertain whether she would be right for the job.*

Neve stretched and rolled off the bed, almost losing her balance when she missed the stepping stool. She wondered what Davide had planned for today…and her nerve endings began to tingle… She didn't blame Davide for wanting to ensure that she would work out; what unnerved her was knowing that she'd be alone with him…

Stop. Now. Focus on what you're here for…

Neve headed to the bathroom, opting for a shower. She marveled again at the spaciousness and luxury around her. The wooden shutters on the two casement windows were open, and the sun splashed into the room, which was bigger than the kitchen in her apartment back in Vancouver. Everything gleamed, from the marble floor to the granite countertop and silver fixtures. The crystal chandelier, casting its prismatic colors on the opposite wall, was intertwined with a sculpted garland of leaves and roses in various states of bloom. Neve couldn't believe how lifelike they looked.

Eyeing the enormous claw-foot tub, she imagined it would be better suited for two, and she couldn't stop the thought that perhaps Davide had made use of it in the past...

Lathering herself in the shower, question after question filled her mind: *Why had Davide stopped walking past Villa Morgana? Had he been sorry to see her go? Had he married? What had made him choose such a remote location in which to live? And besides wanting a qualified nanny for Bianca, had he hired her for another reason?*

She'd have to be patient for the answers. *If he ever chose to enlighten her.*

After changing into a striped coral T-shirt and mint Capri pants, Neve made her way down to the kitchen. Davide was having an espresso but put his demitasse down and stood up, greeting her with a *"Buon giorno,* Signorina Neve. *Espresso o cappuccino?"*

Neve returned the greeting. *"Cappuccino, grazie."*

Moments later Davide returned with Neve's cappuccino and a tray of biscotti and assorted pastries. A platter of fruit was already on the table, along with little tubs of yogurt.

Neve thanked him again and took a sip of her cappuccino. She eyed the assorted pastries. *Were they from the Pasticceria Michelina?* She chose an almond brioche with custard filling and after taking her first eager bite, she couldn't help sighing with pleasure.

A smile flashed across Davide's face, showing perfectly straight white teeth. A warm feeling spread inside her at how *absolutely gorgeous* he looked when the outside edges of his eyes crinkled… "I'm going to enjoy these while I can," she said, tilting her head in feigned defiance. "*When in Rome*, as they say…" She took another bite.

"You have custard on your nose, *signorina*," he informed her drily.

"Oh!" Neve gave an embarrassed laugh. "It's a good thing you told me before I ended up swimming in custard."

Davide gave a wry laugh. He leaned across the table to wipe the custard off Neve's nose with a napkin. She blinked and then reached for a marzipan pastry and popped it into her mouth, her gaze locking with his as he brought his cup to his lips.

God in heaven, he was having some unholy thoughts. And memories of Neve swimming while he and Agostino watched… Davide set down his demitasse. The image of Neve swimming now—

"I—I wasn't expecting you to be working here as an author…"

"You mean to be doing your job with me around?" His eyes pierced hers. "I suppose that wasn't mentioned in any of the correspondence. Well, now you know." He watched Neve's blue-green eyes blinking a little more rapidly than before. "Don't worry, *signorina*, I won't be following you like a lost puppy." He gave a curt laugh but this time, his raven eyes were devoid of humor. "You do understand that the three of us will be spending certain times of the day together?" He leaned toward her, murmuring, "I am hoping that we will be able to establish a workable routine… for the sake of my niece."

"Of course, Signor Cortese," she replied, this time a little stiffly. "I am here to do my job, and nothing else."

And nothing else… Was she referring to their mutual

flirting eight years ago, signaling that she had no intention of venturing in that direction? *And why should she?* She had made it quite clear in her note that she considered him below her. He nodded and abruptly stood up.

"Since Bianca is not here and it's a beautiful day, I thought you might want to consider going for a ride in the countryside to the market in Reggio."

"I…well, yes, okay. That would be…nice."

His gaze swept over her face and bare arms. "Did you bring a sun hat? The temperature was thirty-two degrees Celsius an hour ago. The sun will bake your fair skin."

"Yes, I have one in my room." Neve stood up and started to gather the cups and dishes, but Davide put up his hand. "Please leave those. You are not here as a housekeeper. That is not your *place*."

"But your housekeeper's not here…"

"I'll take care of them." His voice brooked no argument. "I'll be waiting for you in the foyer."

Davide held the door of his Alfa Romeo open for Neve, his eyes sweeping over the curves of her slim body and the soft lines of her profile. He rolled up his sleeves and took his place behind the wheel. He caught a whiff of Neve's perfume, a delicate floral scent that reminded him of an awakening spring garden. A glance her way confirmed she had fastened her seat belt, and he repressed his desire to linger on the curves of her body so tantalizingly close to him. He was glad she was looking out her window, though, reluctant for her to see the desire in his eyes.

He couldn't deny it. He still desired her, despite her past rejection of him. Despite the eight years that he had tried to extinguish that desire. But what good would it do to let her know how he felt? Or to show her? *And risk being rejected once again?* He reached for his sunglasses and concentrated on driving. *No, he needed her now for one purpose only.* And that was to do the job she had been hired to do.

As he maneuvered his way carefully down the mountainside, he noted how rapt Neve was with the view. She was leaning forward in her seat, taking in the stretches of woodland, the dizzying drops of ravines and the dazzling blue of the Ionian Sea. Several times she swayed toward him when he rounded a corner, and once her bare arm skimmed his forearm. The unexpectedness of her soft skin against his made him swerve slightly, and he cursed inwardly for his reaction. *Stay in control, man*, he berated himself.

When he reached the turnoff at the bottom of the mountain leading to the main coastal highway, he inserted a CD of classic Italian hits from the yearly Sanremo Music Festival, and for the next forty minutes, drove along the coast. The market he was heading to was in the capital city of Reggio di Calabria, and not sure if he had mentioned this to Neve, he turned down the music and told her.

Neve's eyes lit up. "Oh, wonderful! We had come to Reggio to take the ferry across to Sicily, and we did have time to go to the museum to see the famous Bronzi di Riace, but we missed the market."

"And what did you think of the bronze sculptures?" He was interested about her impression of the eight-foot-high statues discovered in the sea near the boundary of the Marinas of Riace and Camini. They were thought to be representations of Greek warriors created during the era of Greek colonization of Southern Italy.

Neve flashed him a curious look. "They were…amazing, just like the other items in the museum. I loved ancient history when I was a teenager—and I still do—and I remember thinking it would be great to become an archaeologist and go on digs and discover something fabulous."

She laughed, a sweet, gurgling sound that reminded him of the brook on the outskirts of Valdoro.

"So what made you decide on teaching?"

She laughed again. "I realized I liked kids more than digging."

He couldn't help chuckling. He stole a glance at her and felt his pulse jump. *She looked so...fresh and wholesome.* And now that he was physically closer to her than he had ever been in Italy, he could see the sprinkling of freckles over her nose and part of her cheeks. *Charming.*

"I babysat a lot in my final years of high school and through university." Neve paused, smiling, as if she was remembering some of those moments. "We lived in an upscale neighborhood with lots of CEOs, both male and female. Lots of late evenings, social events, staff parties, last-minute business trips. And kids of all ages. Bouncy babies all the way up to testy teens." She gave another tinkling laugh. "I never had to work at another job. I spent many evenings and most weekends looking after all these kids. And plenty of overnights, too."

"It sounds like you enjoyed it, that it wasn't a—what is the word?—chore? Most teenagers would rather be out socializing...and on dates." He kept his eyes on the road, but when she didn't respond right away, he glanced quickly at her. *Had her cheeks become more flushed?*

"I wasn't much of a socializer," Neve murmured. "I was kind of shy..."

Davide didn't know how to respond. This picture of Neve was so different from the one he had drawn up after she sent him that note. A picture that had grown more and more dark, at least when it came to Neve's personality.

She was confusing him. *Making him doubt his previous perceptions.* Maybe he had misinterpreted her note based on his insecurities at the time. He *had* felt somewhat inferior. Not inferior in character, but in wealth and status. His ancestors had been landless laborers and his parents, although they had managed to acquire a piece of land to farm, had enough food to provide for their family, but barely enough for extras.

Davide and Violetta had worked alongside their parents after school and on weekends to carry out all the seasonal rituals: drying tomatoes in the summer sun, picking mushrooms in the fall, harvesting vegetables and fruits, picking olives, getting them pressed into oil, growing and picking the winter greens and seeding in the spring. The only socializing they had done was at communal activities, such as the chestnut roast in early winter, or during the religious processions for their town's patron saint, San Nicola. And it had been even more work-intensive after their parents had died.

No wonder Violetta had jumped at the opportunity for a new life in another country. After she had married Tristan, Davide had been left to carry out most of the work on the farm, since their uncle had obligations not only in Valdoro but also in the next community. It was after Neve's message that Davide had felt the stirrings of dissatisfaction in what he had been doing. He had wanted *more*. And fortunately, when he had expressed his desire to pursue his masters degree, Zio Francesco had sold the farm, actually relieved to not have to worry about its upkeep. He had divided the money three ways, and had provided Davide with the means to continue his studies, Violetta with a cash endowment and a nest egg for himself. Sadly, his uncle had died during Davide's last year at university.

A series of honking and bleating made Davide slow down and then come to a full stop. A herd of goats was haphazardly crossing the road, and traffic had stalled on either side to let the animals pass. The goatherd ambled along as if he had all the time in the world, oblivious to some of the impatient calls from the vehicles. His dog was scrambling about, doing its job, its sharp barks adding to the cacophony.

Neve had leaned forward, clearly delighted with the whole scene. Their windows were rolled down, and Davide couldn't help laughing at some of the more colorful remarks aimed at the goatherd, who grinned good-naturedly and ambled on.

"The market's not far now," Davide said. "A couple of minutes…" He maneuvered his way through several congested streets, looking for a place to park, and then finally pulled into a spot two blocks away. "Wait here a moment," he told Neve, and climbed out of the vehicle to go around to her side. He opened the door and held out his hand. "*Prego.* Please allow me…"

Her turquoise eyes widened and she hesitated briefly before taking his hand. As she stepped out, she used her left hand to put on her sun hat and as she took a step forward, she stumbled over one of his feet. Davide immediately encircled her with his other arm and helped her regain her balance. "I'm beginning to think you're deliberately trying to trip me, Signorina Neve," he said wryly. "Three strokes and you're out." He smiled, attempting a joke.

"It's three *strikes*," she blurted.

Davide watched Neve's face flush before his eyes.

"Yes, of course," Davide replied gruffly when the different meanings had registered. "My English is not always… exact." He let go of her. "My apologies." *Now, how was he supposed to get that suggestive image out of his mind?*

A few people walked past, smiling at them.

"*Che bella coppia.*" He heard a lady say. "*Avranno dei belli bambini in famiglia.*"

What a beautiful couple. They'll have beautiful babies in their family.

Neve must have heard it also, and for a second their gazes locked and the sounds around them seemed to meld into a distant hum.

It took every ounce of Davide's energy to keep the stab of pain in his heart from showing on his face.

CHAPTER NINE

NEVE COULDN'T BE SURE, but she thought she saw something flicker in Davide's expression.

A momentary crease in his forehead, as if a headache had started. Had the lady's comment hit a nerve? Had Davide been struck by a surge of grief at the mention of family? After all, his family had been shattered with the loss of his sister and brother-in-law. And how could he *not* feel the loss that Bianca was experiencing?

Neve felt a rush of empathy toward Davide. *Poor man.* What an enormous responsibility he had on his shoulders. She didn't doubt that he loved his niece, but from her experience with single parents of children in her class, he would need a lot more to sustain him in the difficult months, and maybe years, ahead.

She wondered if Davide had been able to express his grief to anyone. This made her think of the loss of her father, and how she had wished she had been able to share her grief with her mother... Feeling a prickle behind her eyes, she averted her gaze. She was relieved when they finally reached the market grounds.

The sights, smells and sounds made an instant impression on Neve, and for a moment she just stood there, gazing around at the colors and bustling crowds. Her nose crinkled at the strong smell of fish and seafood. A nearby vendor had a swordfish on display, its two halves glistening on a heavy plank, its eyes glassy. "*Pesce spade, pesce spada, signore e signori.* Swordfish, ladies and gentlemen. Fresher than a gentleman from the south of Italy!"

The nearby crowd erupted in laughter, and Neve couldn't help joining in. She saw that Davide had a smirk on his face.

Neve was looking forward to going through the vendor stalls and finding something unique to the area for herself. Suddenly, she felt as if everything was right in her world. This is where she was supposed to be, in a market in Southern Italy, among the bustling crowds, surrounded by bursts of color and the sounds of parents cajoling or scolding, their children laughing or crying, and couples bartering with animated gestures to vendors who were just as animated.

Neve had studied the standard Italian, but she was able to pick up some of the Calabrese dialect she heard and couldn't help smiling at the singsong nature of the voices of two women perusing the products displayed on the table at the next stall.

When they reached the stall, the ladies had moved on, and Neve was able to clearly view the delicate lingerie items displayed on the lacy tablecloth below.

Neve felt her cheeks tingle with heat and she didn't dare look at Davide. There were samples of silky bras and panties, sold separately or in sets, in colors ranging from delicate pastels to dusky purple, red and black. There were also exquisite nighties with Venetian lace accents in elegant boxes. Her gaze lingered on a filmy coral nightgown with intricate rose lace edging. *If she had been here on her own, she might have been tempted to buy it...*

The vendor was an attractive man in his late thirties or early forties, and the way he was sizing up her size and shape made Neve want to squirm, especially with Davide looking on. To add to her mortification, the vendor winked at Davide and suggested he treat "his lady" with a *regalino da ricordare*, a gift to remember. And then a second wink.

Neve felt as if she were melting under a bright spotlight. She gave a self-conscious laugh. *"No, grazie,"* she told the vendor and turned away. "I was thinking of a different kind of souvenir," she murmured to Davide in English. "Like something for the kitchen."

"But you can use any of these items in the kitchen," the vendor replied with a laugh.

Neve's cheeks burned. She hurried past to the next stall, which featured handbags and shoes. A few stalls farther down, they came to one selling pottery. Although the stalls provided some shade with their awnings or large beach-style umbrellas, Neve felt the Calabrian heat affecting her. Her hat helped, but even with her T-shirt and Capri pants, she felt overdressed and overheated.

She closed her eyes for an instant and felt herself swaying slightly. And then she felt Davide's arms bracing her, the citrus scent of his cologne tingling her nostrils. "You need water," he said huskily, his touch and words jolting her. She blinked at him wordlessly. "You stay here. I'll go buy some."

Davide called to the vendor, who quickly ushered Neve toward a chair behind his main display table. She sat gratefully, but was annoyed with herself for her momentary weakness. Davide came back with two bottles of water. He opened one and handed it to Neve.

The water wasn't refrigerated, but it refreshed her all the same. She drank half the bottle without stopping. Davide finished his bottle and then offered to hold Neve's while she looked around. "You're sure to find something you like for your kitchen here," he said, a gleam in his eyes.

Neve handed him the bottle and nodded, her pulse re-activating. She quickly turned to the collection of pottery. Davide chatted with the vendor while Neve looked over the items, but as she tried to decide on the glazed or un-glazed ones, she sensed his gaze on her...

Neve's head was bent, her strawberry-blond hair falling in front of her. The sun reflected in the strands, made them look like gilded waterfalls. He caught his breath.

What were the chances of a nanny called Neve taking care of his niece, Bianca? Snow and white. *Snow White.* He felt a corner of his mouth lifting. As the vendor moved away to attend to a customer, Davide couldn't help think-ing about fate again. Fate and fairy tales.

Fairy tales had their dark elements, both physical and psychological, and his and Bianca's lives had certainly had their share of those. And they also usually involved a physical and inner journey—with periods of isolation, daunting challenges and malevolent forces—finally lead-ing toward a happy ending.

Well, he had often felt moments of isolation. Some lon-ger than others. Even during all the social and public events celebrating the success of his first novel. Davide had had no shortage of female company, with beautiful women seeking his attention—and he had sometimes taken what was offered—but despite the satisfaction of his physical needs, his emotional needs had remained unfulfilled. He hadn't known what exactly he was looking for—and he still wasn't sure—but none of his dates had tempted him to make a serious commitment.

As for challenges, the one of raising Bianca had to be the most difficult of any he had faced. He had had no other choice, given the loss of her parents. But it was a challenge he had embraced. He had loved Bianca from the moment he had seen her, and taking care of her was now at the top of his list of priorities, challenges and all. Davide felt a twinge in his chest. Hadn't his uncle done the same for him and Violetta after both their parents had died?

Noticing that Neve was paying for some items, Davide strolled toward her. Neve had chosen a set of three unglazed terra-cotta jugs, the small one about the size of a lemon and the largest about the size of a small teapot.

She handed them to the vendor, who proceeded to arrange them in a sturdy bag with bubble wrap. "I love things that are made from the earth," she told him in Italian. "And not mass-produced. These are lovely. I have the perfect spot for them in my kitchen."

The vendor beamed and told Neve that his family had been making them for several generations, and now he was teaching the trade to his grandchildren.

Neve thanked him with a smile and was about to take the bag, but Davide reached for it first. "I'll carry it," he said. "You can keep looking. You have about forty minutes before the market closes."

Neve shrugged, smiling, and continued going in and out of the market stalls, trying on bracelets and bangles, sunglasses and sandals. Davide suddenly realized that he felt a lightness that he couldn't remember feeling for a very long time. *Or was it contentedness?*

On the way back to the castle, Davide put on some quiet music and, glancing in Neve's direction a few times, he noticed that her eyelids were drooping.

When he finally brought the vehicle to a stop, Neve shifted a little but didn't wake up.

Her chest was rising and falling gently with her every breath. Davide's gaze settled on her mouth and he felt desire sizzle through him. Right or wrong, he wanted to reach over and taste those lips, feel their curves, savor them oh…so…slowly.

He closed his eyes for a second. *What was he doing?* He couldn't risk losing Neve as a nanny because of his unwanted advances. *Don't ruin a good thing.* Davide's eyes fluttered and he realized with a start that he had actually started to lean toward Neve. He was about to move back, but a flicker made him look across at Neve. *Too late*.

Neve was wide awake. Her eyes were so close to his that Davide felt like he could dive right in and swim in their blue-green depths.

He gave her a crooked smile. "I was just about to wake you, *Snow White*. We're home…"

CHAPTER TEN

AFTER WAKING UP in the car last night to Davide's intense gaze only inches away—and feeling his breath gently fanning her face—it had taken every bit of Neve's self-control not to close the gap and kiss him. To finally feel the lips of the one who had ignited her desire eight years earlier. After a few seconds of holding her breath, she exhaled in relief when Davide moved away.

Kissing her boss before she officially began her job would not have been a good choice. Nor a very professional one. Walking briskly toward the castle, carrying her bag of pottery souvenirs, Neve reminded herself that although they had been attracted to each other from afar in Valdoro eight years ago, and there was obviously a magnetic force that still existed, encouraging any involvement with Davide Cortese under the current circumstances would be not only unwise, but also foolhardy.

In the foyer, Davide asked if she'd like to join him for a drink or a cup of tea in the kitchen. She thanked him but declined, her cautious inner voice sounding off warning signals.

Besides, she was feeling the jet lag…

Davide gazed at her speculatively. "All right, then, before you turn in, I want to ask you…"

She paused and waited, her curiosity piqued.

"I'm flying to Milan tomorrow for a meeting with my publisher at one. Bianca won't be back until the day after. Why don't you join me? At least you'd get to see another part of Italy." He raised his eyebrows. "While I'm at the meeting, you can visit the Duomo and the Galleria if you like. Are you familiar with these places?"

Neve's eyes widened. "Only from what I've seen in books or videos."

The stunning Gothic cathedral that had taken nearly six centuries to build was a place she had always wanted to visit, and who wouldn't want to peruse the shops of the famous gallery next to it? A spiral of excitement wound its way through her, and she gave him a tentative smile. "I'd love to go. Will we be taking a train? I suppose we'll have an early start, then?"

Davide's mouth curled in amusement. "Not too early. I've chartered a private plane. Once my meeting is over, we can meet in the Galleria, and then later, fly back. We'll have dinner on the plane." He nodded. "All right, then. *Buona notte*, Signorina Neve. *Sogni d'oro*."

Neve watched him head toward the kitchen. *Yes, she would certainly have sweet dreams tonight...*

Davide concealed a smile as he watched Neve's childlike delight as the private plane picked up speed on the runway at the airport in Valdoro and soon nosed its way upward. The sky was a brilliant blue with no clouds, perfect conditions to enjoy the view. Neve kept track of the flight progress, exclaiming when they flew over the wooded and mysterious landscapes of Sicily and farther north toward Naples, where the dark, looming mass that was Vesuvius made her visibly shiver.

Their conversation was limited to discussion about the

places they passed, with Neve asking questions and Davide answering them.

When the male flight attendant brought them lunch, Neve's eyes widened at the sight of the steaming risotto with porcini mushrooms, served on white china with gold edging and accompanied by gold-plated cutlery and white wine that Davide had selected. The second dish consisted of a platter with calamari, cuttlefish and other seafood delights lightly fried to perfection. Strong coffee and a tiramisu mousse ended the meal.

At Milan's Linate Airport, a black limousine was waiting for them. It wound its way through the busy streets and made its first stop near the Duomo and Galleria. Davide walked with Neve to the massive sculpted doors of the cathedral. "I know you'll enjoy the tour," he said, "and afterward, you can begin your shopping adventure. I'll text you when my meeting is over, and you can meet me at the front doors of the Galleria." He gave her a pleasant smile and waited until she had disappeared into the cathedral before striding toward the limo.

The two-hour meeting to discuss his second novel went as well as could be expected, given that he hadn't made any progress with it since his sister and brother-in-law's deaths. His publisher asked him how he and Bianca were doing, and after a shared espresso, had him go over the story line. As Davide recounted what he had written so far and what he still had to accomplish, he felt the desire to write re-igniting within him. Shaking his publisher's hand and bolstered by his encouragement, Davide left with the resolution to return to his novel…

Neve was waiting for him at the entrance of the Galleria. She had a couple of shopping bags, one of them from the Duomo and one from a bookstore. He raised an eyebrow.

"I bought a reproduction of a painting in the cathedral,"

she told him, her eyes sparkling, "and in the Galleria, I found a book about brigandage in Calabria. And a pictorial history of Milan that has a lovely section on the history and architecture of the Duomo, which I absolutely loved!"

During the flight back to Valdoro, Davide opened up his laptop and started to review the chapters he had written so far. Neve divided her attention between her books and the view. At one point he watched her unnoticed, rapt in her book. He shut down his laptop. The click made her look up and glance at him across the aisle.

"So other than babysitting and becoming a teacher, what else is there to know about Neve Wilder?" He gazed at her quizzically. "You read, you enjoy traveling, you appreciate good food. What am I missing?"

Neve closed her book. "Um, I'm not sure what you're asking…"

"Do you ski, have a particular hobby, go out dancing on Friday night—"

Neve burst out laughing. "I'm too exhausted from teaching all week to go out dancing on Friday night. Usually I just curl up with a good book or movie and veg."

"Veg?"

"Relax." She smiled. "And yes, I ski. And swim and hike. I like to be outdoors as much as I can…"

He glanced at her ring hand. Neve caught his gaze and blushed.

"And no, I don't have a boyfriend…at the moment," she said a little defensively. And then she cocked an eyebrow at him. "And you?"

"I'm too exhausted from parenting Bianca to go out dancing on Friday nights," he said, his mouth quirking. "And I don't ski—didn't have time to learn while working on the farm and doing my graduate studies—but I do swim and hike. And enjoy gardening, as you already know."

Neve was looking at him intently, waiting for him to go on, and a curious sensation washed over him. *She wanted to know if he had a love interest...*

"I'm happily unattached," he added bluntly, and turned to the approaching flight attendant, who announced that their dinner was ready.

They lowered their trays, their conversation over, and were served a plate of ricotta cheese and spinach cannelloni in a roasted tomato sauce followed by a mixed salad and pork tenderloin medallions. Dessert was a variety of fresh fruit.

Relaxing with his espresso, Davide thought that the day with Neve had worked out pretty well.

And he had to admit that Signorina Neve had some redeemable qualities after all...

At the castle Neve thanked Davide for allowing her to join him on his trip to Milan. She would make it an early night, she said, stifling a yawn, and was looking forward to meeting Bianca in the morning.

Davide went upstairs to his study and placed his laptop on his desk before heading to his room. In bed, he stared at the opposite wall for a long time, watching the shaft of moonlight change with the movement of the clouds. He thought about the woman in the room across his, and how today he had not seen any indication of snobbery or arrogance. He closed his eyes, not sure if the contentedness he was feeling stemmed mostly from his time with his publisher or with Neve Wilder.

CHAPTER ELEVEN

NEVE WOKE UP before her phone alarm went off. She had heard voices a little earlier and footsteps leading to the room next to hers. Bianca was back. As Neve finished dressing, she felt a flutter of anxiety at her imminent meeting with the child. Generally, she had plenty of confidence when dealing with kids. But with Davide Cortese watching her…

As she put on her sandals, she heard a cry and then another.

Was Bianca rebelling at the thought of meeting *her*? Neve inhaled deeply. *Coraggio*, she told herself. *You can do this.* Before she could change her mind, she opened the door and stepped into the hallway.

Davide rushed into Bianca's room after her first cry. Lucia had dropped her off a half hour earlier, and she had been playing quietly with her toys while he had gone to his study to return a phone call to his publisher. Now she was sitting on her bed, her face puckered in a frown. Her braids had come undone and she was holding the ribbons within two tight little fists.

Davide sat next to her and put his arm around her. "*Che c'è*, Bianca? What's the matter, sweetheart?"

"My hair's wrecked and I want to go to the market!"

Her voice ended in a wail, and Davide's jaw tightened as he wondered what strategy he could use to prevent Bianca's distress from escalating into a tantrum.

"Come, Bianca, let me fix your hair in pigtails. And then you can have breakfast and you'll feel better."

"I don't want pigtails!" Bianca's voice rose. She slid off the bed. "And I'm not hungry! I want to go to the market today!" She ran out of the room, crying, "I want Mommy and Daddy!"

Davide strode quickly after her. He stopped short in the hall. Neve and Bianca were sprawled on the floor, and Bianca was staring at Neve, looking dazed. Neve's shapely legs were exposed and realizing that her dress had hiked up, Neve quickly readjusted it, her cheeks flushed as she met his gaze.

Davide rushed to help them both up. Bianca stood there wide-eyed while he helped Neve.

After making sure that neither of them had bumped their head, Davide said wryly, "I see you've both hit it off with a bang. Bianca, this is Signorina Neve, your new nanny. *Signorina*—my niece."

Neve shifted her gaze to the little girl in the white shirt and red jumper who had instinctively reached for her uncle's hand. Bianca had delicate features, with eyes the color of caramel, and the longest lashes Neve had ever seen on a child. Her hair was golden brown and had tumbled down, showing the pleats from her previously tight braids. Her eyes held a gleam of curiosity and at the same time, suspicion.

"*Ciao*, Bianca." Neve smiled warmly. "I'm so glad you and I didn't crack like Humpty Dumpty when we fell." She made her eyes widen deliberately. "Can you imagine? Your poor uncle would have had to pick up all the pieces and put us back together," she laughed. "And what if he got the pieces wrong and I ended up with your hair? And you with mine?"

Bianca's mouth twitched. And then she giggled. "You're silly!"

Neve smiled, relieved. Appealing to a child's sense of nonsense was one of the strategies that often helped defuse a situation in her classroom.

"Please join me and Bianca for breakfast," Davide said, his gaze shifting to her.

"Only if Bianca doesn't mind having a silly nanny around." Neve winked at Bianca.

"I don't mind," Bianca said brightly, tugging her uncle's hand. "Come on, Zio Davide, I'm hungry."

Neve caught a flash of surprise in Davide's eyes. *And was that a flicker of approval in his gaze?* A warm rush swirled throughout Neve's body as she recalled how his gaze had swept over her when she had lain on the tiled floor… Blinking, she returned to the present. "I'd like you to come into my room a minute, Bianca. I have a little something for you…"

"That wasn't necessary," Davide said curtly. At Bianca's crestfallen expression, he added, "but it was kind of you."

He stood in Neve's doorway as Bianca pulled the blue tissue out of the gift bag excitedly and then reached inside. He could only see Bianca's profile from where he stood, and the lips that were starting to quiver as she stared at the plush creature in her hand. *An orca.* Davide groaned inwardly. It was probably the worst gift Neve could have brought for Bianca.

Bianca burst into tears, threw down the orca and ran out the door. Davide didn't stop her.

She headed to her room, and he would go there very

shortly. But first, he had to explain Bianca's reaction to Neve, who looked as if she had just received an unexpected slap on the cheek.

"I—I…" She looked at him with her mouth open. "I don't know why…"

"I'll tell you why." He rubbed his jaw tiredly. "Bianca's father worked as a tour guide at a whale-watching company in Steveston." He picked up the plush toy. "This just reminded her that her daddy is dead."

"I'm so sorry." Neve's voice broke. "I didn't know—"

"No, you didn't," Davide said, and the words sounded even more abrupt and bitter than he had intended as he left Neve's room.

Today was Neve's first official day of work as Bianca's nanny. *How long would she last?*

CHAPTER TWELVE

NEVE SAT DOWN on the edge of her bed. Only minutes with Bianca and she had already screwed up. But how was she to have known? She had bought the orca from a vendor at the Granville Island Public Market in Vancouver, thinking it would be the perfect West Coast gift. Neve bit her lip. She could see now that working here would be full of ups and downs. She had imagined that it might be, but the positive start between her and Bianca had given her false hope.

Of course there would be outbursts and episodes such as this one. Bianca was sensitive, and how much more sensitive could a situation be than one where both your parents were suddenly gone from your life? *Forever. She* had lost one parent, and *that* had devastated her...

No; it was not going to be an easy job. And having Davide around much of the time would be even harder. Watching her with those gleaming black eyes...

They were not the eyes that had made her adolescent hormones do a wild dance, though. *Eyes that had hinted of passion and promise...*

Neve hadn't seen that look in the guys she had dated. And not that there had been many... After her trip to Italy, none of the guys at university had appealed to her. Somehow, their appearance and manner always seemed so...so young and immature. And none of them had looked at her with the same intense gaze as Davide had…

She had dated a couple of guys, three years apart, but there had been no sparks. Both had been more interested in trying to get to know her physically than in making an emotional connection. She hadn't welcomed the pressure; she had wanted to *feel* something before making *that* kind of commitment.

Neve started at the sudden knock at her door.

"May I come in?" Davide's voice was calm.

Neve's pulse began to thrum. "Yes." She took a deep breath as he entered. "How's Bianca?"

Davide took a few steps toward her then stopped. "She has calmed down," he said, his gaze steady. "I told her that you wanted to give her a special gift. Then I suggested that every time she felt sad about her daddy, she could give the whale a hug. And her daddy would be happy, because he would feel the hug, too."

Neve felt her heart swelling. "Thank you. That was very insightful… You've given Bianca something concrete to do to deal with her feelings of loss." She stood up and gazed at him, smiling with relief. "Is it okay if I go and see her now?"

Davide's mouth curved briefly. "Yes, of course."

He made a half turn then glanced back at her appraisingly. His gaze flew to the unmade bed, lingered there for several seconds, and returned to her. "I hope you're finding this room comfortable and meeting your standards," he said, his dark eyebrows lifting.

Neve had felt a current sizzle its way through her veins at the way Davide's gaze had swept over the bed, taking in her nightie tossed among the sheets. Feeling the warmth in her cheeks, she nodded quickly. "It's very comfortable, thank you."

Davide nodded abruptly, opened his mouth to reply, but at that moment his phone rang.

"*Buon giorno*, Lucia," he said warmly, and with a quick nod at Neve, strode out the door, his voice carrying down the hall. Neve felt a twinge as he gave a deep laugh.

Neve bit her lip. Would Davide ever laugh like that with *her*? Or speak about the past? Enlighten her as to why he had suddenly stopped going by the Villa Morgana? There were so many things she wished she had the nerve to ask him... But now was not the time. She closed the door behind her and hurried to Bianca's room.

Davide was putting his phone away and telling Bianca that he would take her for a gelato in town and that they would go to the market another day.

Bianca gave a happy squeal and ran to him. "Is Signorina Neve coming, too?"

Neve liked the way Bianca addressed her name the Italian way, just like *he did*. She smiled at Davide expectantly.

Davide felt his jaw tighten. "No. Signorina Neve is not coming." He saw Neve's smile disappear. "She can come next time." Although he had been speaking to Bianca, he had kept his gaze on Neve. Davide saw her open her mouth as if to disagree with him and then shut it, a deflated look in her eyes. She was disappointed. And maybe a little hurt.

Had he wanted to hurt her? Give her a taste of what rejection felt like? He pushed aside those thoughts impatiently. No, it was not his intention to strike back at Neve this way; he simply wanted to go over a few things with Bianca before Neve began her duties as nanny.

The puzzled expression in Neve's eyes at his abrupt "no" puzzled *him*. And that fawn-like innocence in her expression wasn't helping to ease his conscience. As he strode away, the satisfaction that he had thought he'd feel turned out to be more like a twinge of remorse. He stopped and turned around. She deserved an explanation, at least.

"Bianca and I may visit friends in town for a while," he said, "or we might not. In any case, I'd like to go over a few things with her before you take over as nanny..." He paused to see if she would respond, but she just nodded. "If you're hungry, feel free to go down to the kitchen and help yourself to anything in the refrigerator," he added gruffly. *"Ciao."*

Davide closed the side door of his Fiat van and then settled Bianca into her car seat in the back. Driving, he occasionally glanced in the rearview mirror at Bianca. She was hugging her whale, and Davide felt his heart constrict. He marveled at a child's capacity for forgiveness and wondered cynically about his own propensity for it.

Tesoro mio. Bianca *was* a treasure—and his now, to cherish, love and raise. He swallowed hard. He couldn't bring back her parents, but he would do everything in his power to make her happy. And making sure she had the right nanny was at the top of his list.

As Davide drove down the mountainside, an image of Neve flashed in his mind, and the momentary furrowing of her brows when he said she was not joining him and Bianca. A split-second action, but long enough to indicate that she felt hurt, confused that he would exclude her so soon after meeting Bianca.

Could it be possible that Neve had totally forgotten how she had treated him in the past, how she had insulted him by telling him to "remember his place"? Maybe to someone else, those words might not have been a big deal, but they had delivered a sizeable blow to his ego. *And heart.*

The words on the note might have been civil in and of themselves, but he had had no trouble reading between the lines: *You're not good enough to be with me. You're inferior. Poor. You have no business trying to associate with someone in a class above you...*

Davide enjoyed his second espresso at the Pasticceria Michelina while Bianca worked happily away at her hazelnut gelato. For a long time he had avoided coming to this bakery that had evoked so many painful memories and dashed hopes...

Davide checked the time on his phone. He didn't want to head back to the castle just yet. And he hadn't really intended to visit friends in Valdoro; he had just needed some space. *Time to think.* Time to process the reality of having Neve Wilder living under the same roof with him and Bianca...and most important, to make sure Bianca was ready to be with her new nanny...

When they arrived at the castle, there was no sign of Neve. Davide's pulse relaxed. He helped Bianca prepare for an early bedtime, and after reading her a story in Italian from the collection he had bought her, he gave her a gentle kiss on the forehead. *"Buona notte, tesoro,"* he murmured. He set the book down on the night table and went to sit in the rocking chair in the corner as he always did until he was sure Bianca had fallen asleep.

Davide had never imagined how a parent must feel until he had assumed the care of Bianca. Yes, he had visited her in Vancouver, but he had never had to provide for her in a material or emotional way. It had been the latter that had changed him. And it had made him aware of how Bianca had felt, bewildered and shaken...the same way *he* had felt, losing his father and his mother soon after.

Sometimes, the ache of growing up without either of his parents had made him withdraw from situations where he'd have to witness his friends interacting with their families in their homes or at community events. It wasn't that he had begrudged them their happiness; it was just that it made his own sense of loss that much more acute. He had felt more comfortable being by himself, either working on the farm or in his room, losing himself in books and later, writing…

Before the accident, he had had only himself to take care of. Now he had a child. Not his biologically, but as close as it could possibly get. He no longer had the freedom he had enjoyed as a bachelor and celebrated author, but he didn't care. Although the deaths of Violetta and Tristan had catapulted him into a whirlpool of grief and loss, they had also given him a new awareness of the fragility of life and his responsibility of raising Bianca.

He had embraced that responsibility without any hesitation. Bianca belonged with him. He would protect her, care for her and provide every opportunity for her. He had loved her from the moment he had seen her, a week after she was born.

Davide felt a twinge at the memory of Violetta holding Bianca up to him, her dark eyes shining with pride and love. She had swaddled Bianca in a soft pink blanket, and her tiny face, perfectly round and with open eyes, had melted his heart.

Noting Bianca's rhythmic breathing, Davide turned off the lamp and switched on her night-light. The two espressos he had had would keep *him* up for a while. Maybe now was a good time to go to his study and review the research notes that he had abandoned months ago…

As he left Bianca's room, he glanced across to the rounded door of Neve's bedroom. *Would she be in bed? Or by her window, looking out to the sea?* There was no light emerging from the crack at the bottom of the door, and no sounds of movement. He imagined Neve in her filmy nightie, her hair reflecting the shaft of silvery light from the moon…

Davide strode down the hall to his study and turned on his desk lamp. For a moment he tapped his fingers on the polished walnut desk. *Who was he kidding?* He was too restless to concentrate on his research notes. Sighing, he turned off the lamp and went to his room, hoping sleep would come quickly.

CHAPTER THIRTEEN

AFTER DAVIDE AND BIANCA had left, Neve had gone downstairs and out into the courtyard with a book, but she hadn't been able to concentrate. Why would Davide rush Bianca off so quickly after they had just met? She wondered at the real reason why Davide had been so adamant about her staying behind. Had she simply imagined that his gaze had hardened for a moment, as if she had done something to displease him?

Whatever it was, she was determined to find out what the problem was.

And then maybe he'd look at her again like he had eight years ago...

The tread of shoes in the hall outside her room had briefly registered in her light slumber, but Neve hadn't fully awakened until she heard a series of shrieks sometime later. She jolted upright, disoriented, and then consciousness hit her like a wave.

Bianca. Was she having one of her nightmares?

She grabbed the matching robe and hurriedly put it on, tying the straps before bolting out the door.

Bianca's door was partially open, and Neve didn't hesitate. In seconds she was at Bianca's side. Bianca was sitting up, her face puckered and streaked with tears.

"You're safe, Bianca," Neve murmured, putting an arm around her. "You must have been dreaming. I'm here."

"And *I'm* here."

Davide's voice made them both direct their gazes to the doorway. In several strides he had reached the bed, and had crouched down to kneel on the mat. Taking Bianca's hands, he gave them a kiss and then met Neve's gaze. "You can go back to bed," he said curtly. "I'll take care of this."

Neve felt a stab of hurt. She had been hoping to comfort Bianca with a little rhyme she had shared with her kindergarten students after reading them a story about having bad dreams. "I just—"

"I want her to stay," Bianca cried, tugging at her uncle's hands.

Neve saw Davide's jaw tighten, the muscles flicking as he gazed from Bianca to Neve.

"If you wish, and if Signorina Neve doesn't mind," he said gruffly.

"I don't mind at all," Neve said. She glanced at the bookshelf nearby. "Maybe I can read Bianca a story…"

Bianca's face brightened. She clambered out of the bed and ran to grab a book. Neve felt her heart melting at the sight of Bianca in her nightshirt, her golden-brown hair streaming down her back, her slender legs bronzed from the summer sun.

Although she kept her eyes on Bianca, Neve was very conscious of Davide's proximity. *And gaze.* He was still on his knees and inches away from her own. An image of his head cradled in her lap flashed in her mind, and her hand caressing his hair, and she felt a series of sparks shoot through her. She was sure her cheeks were flaming and she was glad when Bianca jumped back on the bed between them.

"This is my favorite," she said, turning the book to reveal the cover: *Bianca Neve.* "I'm in it!" She looked up at Neve, her eyes fluttering as if she just realized something. "And so are *you*! Can you read it to me?"

"I don't think Signorina Neve can read Italian," Davide said brusquely. "I'll read it."

"I can read it," Neve said quickly. "I studied Italian in high school and at university."

"Va bene." Davide nodded, crossing his arms.

Neve's heart flipped. *She had expected him to leave the room.* Bianca thrust the book toward her. Neve felt as if she was on a stage with the spotlight gleaming down on her. Lifting the cover that displayed Snow White in the arms of the prince, she turned to the first page, took a deep breath and started reading...

"C'era una volta..."

Davide felt something tighten in his chest at the sight of Neve reading in Italian to Bianca. As if someone was squeezing his heart. He tried not to wince. Was he resentful of Neve? Jealous? No... The pain came from the thought that his sister, Violetta, should be the one tucking Bianca in at night, comforting her after a bad dream, reading her a story. Not a stranger. He swallowed and felt himself clenching his teeth.

He was angry.

Angry that God had taken away his only sister. Angry that at least one of Bianca's parents couldn't have survived. *Furious* with God that Bianca had to suffer this loss at so young an age. And frustrated that he didn't have all the answers to making things better for Bianca. *And himself.*

He stroked Bianca's hair absentmindedly. *Poor child.* He felt a protective surge run through him. He squeezed his eyes tightly to stop the tingling at the backs of his lids.

When they reopened, they settled on Neve. He watched

the flitting of expressions on her face as she became each character on the page. Heard the lilting cadence of her voice in an Italian that was charming, with only a few syllabic mistakes. Saw how totally absorbed she was, looking up regularly to meet Bianca's enthralled gaze. *She must be a wonderful kindergarten teacher.*

This thought collided with the impression he had held about her for the past eight years. *She was spoiled, entitled, arrogant, a tease.* She had teased him with her gaze every day on that balcony, hadn't she? She had appeared around the time he was returning from the farm. Had sat there with a book, or a cool drink, or had stood watering the flowers. Except for the first time their gazes locked, she hadn't averted her gaze, which, even from several paces away, reflected a mutual attraction. And a hundred thoughts had flitted through his mind, a hundred ways that he could try to meet her and get beyond the stage of just devouring her with his eyes...

And then she had shattered any hopes he might have had by expressing her true feelings in that note... She had probably gotten a real kick out of imagining his reaction upon reading it...

"E vissero felici e contenti..."

And they lived happily-ever-after...

He started at Bianca's sudden clapping. All signs of distress from her dream had gone. Neve's face was flushed, her mouth curved in a smile as she gazed at Bianca.

He felt the initial tightness in his chest suddenly dissolve. No matter what Neve had done in the past, she had done something just now that he couldn't fault. For the second time today she had made Bianca smile and laugh.

He had worried that Bianca would never display the lightheartedness that was part of her character before the accident, the lightheartedness inherent in most children.

He had done everything possible to lift her spirits these past few months, even when his own spirit had felt dead. After what seemed like an unbearably long stretch, she had finally rewarded him with a smile, then two, and he had cheered inwardly, knowing that she had started to move along the lengthy road toward healing.

But she was still a long ways off. *And so was he.*

He stood up. "Well, Bianca, now you can have a good sleep. Say good-night and thank-you to Signorina Neve." He riveted his gaze to Neve, who stood up promptly.

Bianca complied and gave Neve a shy smile before putting her arms around her uncle's neck and kissing him on the cheek. She settled under the covers and Davide tucked her in.

"*Buona notte*, Bianca," Neve said softly.

Davide flicked off the light switch, leaving only a night-light on. When he and Neve were in the hall, he gazed down at her. Despite the shadows under her eyes, she was still a beautiful woman. And in minutes, she would be taking that robe off and going to bed herself...

His pulse quickened. *Don't go there*, his inner voice reminded him. *You've tormented yourself enough over the years, imagining her...*

"*Buona notte*, Signorina Neve," he said huskily, "*e grazie.*"

"*Buona notte,*" she said with a quick nod. "And you're welcome." She turned toward her room in the turret.

He watched until the last thing he saw was the swirl of her robe and the door clicking shut.

CHAPTER FOURTEEN

NEVE WOKE UP with a dream that she was lost in a dark cleft of the Aspromonte mountains, and that she was calling for help, but the only response she got was from the howl of an Apennine wolf. She sat up in a sweat, her breathing accelerated, and despite the earliness of the hour, knew she couldn't get back to sleep.

After a quick shower Neve wrapped a turquoise towel around her head and put on the white robe that was hanging on the back of the door. She'd take a minute to check on Bianca.

Neve glanced across the hall. Davide's door was partially open. She felt a quiver run through her, wondering if he was still sleeping...

She hurried into Bianca's room and smiled at the sleeping figure. *Poor baby*, she needed the rest. Back in her room, Neve retrieved a paperback from her handbag and plopped down into the burgundy recliner by the window.

When she heard movements in Bianca's room, Neve put down her book and checked the time. She was shocked that two hours had gone by. She hurried over and saw that Bianca had changed into a T-shirt and shorts. Neve greeted her warmly and told her to wait while she changed, and then they could go down to the kitchen together.

Neve decided on a red skort and a white peasant-style top with short, gathered sleeves. As she slipped on white sandals, her phone signaled an incoming text. She glanced at the series of long messages and felt herself tensing. *Had her mother forgotten that she would be busy with her job?* Before she left the room she quickly replied.

Working; will text later.

Bianca was not at her window seat. Neve hurried to check the washroom, and wondered if Bianca had decided to go to the kitchen on her own. She'd have to make it clear to Bianca to follow her instructions and not take off anywhere without her.

Neve flew down the stairs and by the time she reached the kitchen she was breathless. Davide was at the stove, but he was alone. She looked past the doors leading to the courtyard. No sign of Bianca. She met Davide's narrowed gaze. "Bianca promised to stay in her room while I got dressed," she blurted. "I couldn't have been more than five minutes."

Davide shut off the gas element and the look he gave Neve made her stomach twist. "Bianca cannot be left unsupervised. Not even for five minutes. There are too many dangerous spots around the castle for a child. She could go wandering off and topple over a ledge or bluff." He strode quickly out of the kitchen, adding harshly, "I've lost my sister. I can't risk losing Bianca, too."

She followed him out and watched as he took the steps three at a time. "I'm going to see if she's in one of the unused rooms of the castle." He paused to glance at her. "You check the main rooms."

Neve nodded, shuddering at the thought of Bianca in

one of the scenarios Davide had mentioned. She wouldn't be able to live with herself if Bianca got hurt, or worse…

No, that's not going to happen, she tried to convince herself. *Bianca will show up.*

"Bianca!" Davide's booming voice echoed in the halls. Neve's heart pounded as she checked Bianca's room again, her own room, and then hesitated a moment when she came to Davide's bedroom. She couldn't *not* check it…

The room was breathtaking. *Masculine.* And elegant, with a double-sided marble fireplace dividing his room and en-suite bathroom. The floor was a huge expanse of gleaming hardwood, the walls a sage green, the bed coverings a pewter gray. The sight of them pulled back and rumpled from Davide's sleep made her pulse kick up. Could Bianca be under the bed? Neve called out for her and was about to look under it when she heard Davide's loud voice in the hall. And then Bianca's faint, "I'm here, Zio Davide."

Neve rushed out and saw Davide disappear into his study. She strode over and paused at the door. Bianca was crawling out from under Davide's desk, a sheepish look on her face, and Davide was standing by, his eyebrows furrowed and his jaw muscles tensed.

"Why did you not stay in your room and wait for Signorina Neve as she asked?" Davide's voice was calm but firm. "You can't just run off, Bianca."

Bianca's lip started to tremble. "But I wanted to play hide-and-seek."

"You were told to stay put. You *have* to follow instructions, Bianca. From me or from your nanny."

Bianca burst into tears and ran out of the room, barely glancing at Neve. Davide started to follow but stopped at the doorway and gave Neve a piercing look. "I think you need to address this with Bianca, as well. *Now.*" He strode out of the room.

Neve took a deep breath. As she followed Davide into Bianca's room, she knew she had a double challenge: to get her message across to Bianca and to show Davide that she was as competent as she had made out to be in her application and interview.

Bianca had thrown herself facedown on her bed, her crying reduced to quiet sniffling. Neve spotted the plush orca on Bianca's night table and picked it up. She sat down gently at the side of the bed. "You know, Bianca, I love to play hide-and-seek." She saw Davide raise an eyebrow, probably wondering where she was going with this. "And we can play after lunch. But first, we need to go over the rules, so nobody is in danger."

Bianca turned over to one side and wiped her eyes. "What danger?"

Neve made her eyes widen. "Well, I've never been in a real castle before, and I'm afraid I might get lost on my own. And end up in the dragon's den," she added, making her voice tremble.

"We don't have a dragon," Bianca sniffed. "That's just in fairy tales."

"Are you sure?" Neve looked around fearfully. "I thought every castle had a dragon."

Bianca scrambled to sit cross-legged next to Neve. "Silly Miss Neve!" She took Neve's hand. "I'll stay beside you, I promise. And don't be scared. If there was a real dragon, Zio Davide would protect you!"

I would? Davide's eyes narrowed and glinted like shards of obsidian. And then he smiled and Neve caught the twinkle in them. "Of course I would." He sat next to Bianca and put an arm around her, giving Neve a thumbs-up sign at the same time.

Neve felt a warm glow spread throughout her body. She

hadn't been sure that her strategy would work with Bianca, but it had and Davide had approved.

Davide was the first to rise. "I'll get back to making lunch." He ruffled Bianca's hair. "Maybe Signorina Neve can tame your hair first." He gazed at Neve. *"A presto."*

Neve nodded, her words sticking in her throat. *Yes, I'll see you soon. Gladly.*

She watched him leave, then stood up and smiling, held out a hand to Bianca.

Davide found himself humming as he stirred the sliced cherry tomatoes in the pan where he had first sautéed onions and garlic in extra-virgin olive oil. He had already put the spaghetti into the boiling salted water. All the ingredients were from his garden, the oil from his olive groves and the pasta was locally made and sold. He rinsed a generous sprig of basil that he had snipped off one of the plants in the courtyard and added it to the pan.

As Davide set three place mats on the harvest table, with his at one end, and Neve's and Bianca's on either side of him, he replayed the scene between Neve and Bianca in his mind. Neve had known exactly what strategy to use to get Bianca to come around. She hadn't been stern or raised her voice. She had relied on her own understanding and experience with children to get her message across. And she had done it by tapping into Bianca's imagination and by communicating with her at her level. *Brilliant.*

Who was this Neve Wilder?

Yes, she was the beauty who had made his heart flip almost a decade ago. His Juliet on the balcony of Villa Morgana. The girl whose eyes had branded his every time he had walked past... And not one day had gone by since they had exchanged the first gaze that Davide hadn't thought about her, dreamt about being with her. But she had turned him down, hadn't even wanted to meet him. Every silent message that he had intercepted from her eyes had turned out to be wrong.

And now she was *here*. Sometimes he thought he must be dreaming and that he'd surely wake up and Neve wouldn't be in his castle. Nor would Bianca. But then reality would pinch him. *Hard. Really hard.* Bianca was an orphan and Neve was here as a result...

How could sadness and happiness be so intertwined?

Davide stopped at the sudden jolt of awareness. Yes, he was sad, terribly sad about the loss of his sister and brother-in-law. And even sadder for Bianca's loss. But he could not deny that happiness had somehow found a way to take root in the hardened core of his heart. He had felt twinges of happiness, contentedness and hope...all in the short time since Neve had arrived.

And it...felt...good. It made him almost want to forget the past. *Almost.* Maybe he and Neve would have the opportunity to delve into it while she was here. And then maybe not. But at the moment Davide didn't care. He had lunch to serve.

The aroma of freshly made tomato sauce with basil filled the air. Davide set the cutlery down and returned to the stove to check the pasta. *Perfect.* Davide drained the spaghetti, transferred it into a large colorful bowl that had been his mother's and mixed in some sauce. At the sound of approaching footsteps, Davide felt a surge of anticipation. He set the bowl on the table, and glancing up, he saw Neve and Bianca walking hand in hand toward him, the look on both their faces melting his heart.

CHAPTER FIFTEEN

NEVE HADN'T REALIZED how hungry she was until the scent of tomato sauce reached her before she even entered the kitchen. When she and Bianca walked into the room, Davide flashed them a grin.

"After *you*, ladies," he said, pulling out Neve's chair on his right and Bianca's on his left.

"*I'm* not a lady, Zio Davide!" Bianca giggled.

"Okay, little girl, but try to eat like one, *va bene*?"

"Okay." Bianca took her fork and twirled the spaghetti expertly and plopped it into her mouth.

Neve felt a little self-conscious. She hadn't really thought about all the time that she would be spending with Bianca and her uncle. She twirled her spaghetti mindfully, careful not to end up with a massive amount on her fork, and had her first taste. *Wow.* She had eaten Italian food numerous times in restaurant chains, but she couldn't remember any of them imparting this kind of instant impression on her.

She had a second forkful. "This is delicious," she murmured, glancing at Davide. *"Grazie."*

"Where are my manners?" Davide suddenly rose and went to a side cabinet that revealed itself to be a wine cooler. He pulled out a bottle, opened it and poured it into two wineglasses before returning to set them on the table.

"Here's to dragons and damsels who can handle them," he said, leaning forward to offer Neve a glass. Then he clinked glasses, his black eyes piercing into hers.

Neve felt her nerve endings pulsate. She averted her gaze to breathe in the wine's aroma, then brought the glass to her lips. *Exquisite. And strong.* Perfect choice with the tomato sauce.

Neve sat back, her body relaxed from the combination of delicious food and drink.

"Can we go play hide-and-seek now, Zio Davide?"

Davide nodded. "A quick game."

Neve was relieved at Bianca's query. She offered to help with the dishes, but Davide waved them on. "I'll join you in a minute," he said. "Bianca can start showing you around the garden."

The sultry heat of the midafternoon sun was palpable as soon as Neve stepped outside into the courtyard with Bianca. Neve was awed by the organized rows of flowering plants and pots bursting with herbs. One planter contained the largest rosemary bush she had ever seen. She couldn't resist snipping a sprig and pressing it together and inhaling its sharp aromatic scent.

Neve followed Bianca, who was skipping along the rows of plants, bushes and trees. Lemon trees with lemons almost the size of grapefruit. A trellis with cascading wisteria and rows of oleanders, with blooms of white, pink and fuchsia. *This place was magical.*

Neve recognized the large, flapping leaves of a fig tree and paused gratefully in its shade. Even with her sun hat on, the heat was stronger than she remembered.

"Perhaps we should wait for later in the evening to indulge Bianca with a game of hide-and-seek. It won't be so hot then."

Davide had come up right behind her. Neve turned,

startled, and her shoulder brushed against him. She sprang back as if she had touched a live wire and was instantly embarrassed at her reaction. Davide didn't move. His eyes narrowed slightly, though, and he gazed at her intently. "Thank you for the way you handled the issue with Bianca earlier," he said quietly. "I didn't expect that kind of approach."

Neve felt a coil of pleasure at his words. "Sometimes you have to turn into a child to get your message across to another child," she replied a little breathlessly. "What I mean is, you have to put yourself in their shoes, try to reach them at their own level."

"And you did," he said, nodding. "You have a way with children," he added huskily. "You must be a wonderful teacher."

Neve didn't know what to say. The unexpected series of compliments from Davide had made her tingle all over. And he had taken a step closer to her. Was he intending to—?

"Zio Davide! Signorina Neve! Are you coming?" Bianca had stopped skipping and had turned around, her hands on her hips, looking stern even from where they stood.

Davide chuckled. "We've been told. Shall we? I haven't played this game since I was a kid."

Davide gestured for Neve to walk ahead of him. He had to get a handle on his emotions. He had almost embraced her. Thank goodness that Bianca had called out.

Once they reached Bianca, Davide went over the rules. No climbing trees, no going past the border of cactus pear bushes. Neve could be "it." Home base would be under the fig tree, and Neve would count slowly to twenty while Davide and Bianca went to find a hiding spot.

"Remember, no peeking!" Bianca cried.

"No peeking," Neve promised, crossing her heart.

"Is everybody ready?" Davide looked from Bianca to Neve. Bianca clapped excitedly. Neve nodded, her cheeks flushed. "Okay, Signorina Neve, take your spot." He waited till she reached the fig tree. He winked at Bianca. They watched as Neve turned toward the trunk of the tree, covered her eyes and started counting. Davide waited to see where Bianca was heading and then took the opposite direction.

He couldn't believe he was doing this. *Playing a children's game with the girl he had fallen for eight years ago.* How could he have ever predicted this would happen? That he'd be raising his orphaned niece and hiring that very girl—*woman*—as her nanny? Davide shook his head and chose a grassy spot between a row of bushy magnolia trees and a cactus pear grove. He heard Neve call out, "Ready or not, here I come!"

Why was his heart thumping? He heard Neve's footsteps padding away, and then Bianca's little gasp and more running, and then suddenly footsteps moving in his direction. Davide waited silently, and when he caught a glimpse of her through a space in the oleanders, he considered making a dash for "home." He'd wait another few seconds… and maybe she'd turn right around. Turn she did, before suddenly pivoting and charging right around the corner. *And into him.*

Davide had just managed to stop them both from landing in the cactus pear grove, which would have been much more painful than the body slam Neve had just given him. His arms had automatically shot out and wrapped themselves around her like a vise while his legs stood firm as he took the blow. Fortunately for them both, her head had hit his chest and not his nose or mouth. They could have easily ended up with either a broken nose or teeth knocked out.

For a moment Neve's head lay flat against his chest and

if his heart had been thumping before, now it was clanging. *She was in his arms.* He could feel her chest heaving against his, and the knowledge that only two thin layers of material lay between them made his abdomen muscles tighten with a longing that almost hurt.

And then, as if she had just come to, Neve lifted her head to gaze up at him. Her eyes were wide and startling this close. An ocean of turquoise with teal depths. And dark pupils that seemed to drill right into him. Her lips parted as if she wanted to say something, and that was when something inside Davide broke loose. He lowered his head and covered her lips with his, savored their fullness, top and bottom. He expected her to push him away, tell him he was out of line, but when she didn't, he pressed her even closer to him, cupping the back of her head, and deepened his kiss. Wave after wave of desire washed over him, and if he didn't have Bianca around, he'd—

Bianca! He broke away from Neve so suddenly that he almost felt light-headed.

"You tagged me good," he rasped. "Now you better see if you can find Bianca."

Neve blinked and bolted away from him.

CHAPTER SIXTEEN

NEVE DIDN'T KNOW how she had managed to continue playing after Davide had kissed her. She had found Bianca hiding behind a giant ceramic planter and had proceeded to chase after the squealing child who managed to get "home" without being tagged. Davide had had his turn being "it" and Neve's heart had done an anxious dance, wondering if he would attempt to kiss her again.

What had felt like ages in his arms with that first kiss had actually been only about half a minute. Just enough time to send her spinning into another universe.

She had seen stars when she had slammed into him. Or rather, *felt* them. They weren't like the stars in cartoons when two people collided, but a shower of dazzling little orbs that made all her nerve endings tingle. And when his lips had touched hers…she had felt something bursting inside her, and she had realized that the awakening she had felt at eighteen had suddenly been reactivated in a rush of adult desire and passion.

They had to talk. Clear the air. And she had to find out, once and for all, the reason for Davide's disappearing act eight years ago.

The game had tuckered Bianca out. Neve had accompanied her to her room, and after washing up, Bianca had willingly gone for a nap, holding her orca tight against her. Neve had closed her shutters and then gone to her own room to shower.

Now, as she lathered herself with the mandarin-scented body wash, Neve couldn't help shivering at the memory of Davide's arms around her. And his lips taking possession of hers…

She rinsed and dried herself and instead of getting dressed right away, slipped on a teddy. She might even try to have a nap herself. Since they had had a later lunch, Davide had said that they would have dinner at about eight or eight-thirty. She wouldn't mind a little rest and some time to collect her thoughts before going down to talk with him.

Just as Neve lay down on her bed, her damp hair wrapped up in a towel, her phone rang. She reached for it and moaned. *Her mother.* What now?

"Hi, Mom," she said, trying not to sound testy. "I guess you didn't read my last text."

"Now, Neve, I'm just trying to make sure you're all right. And I called deliberately in the afternoon Italy time, when most people are having a siesta."

"Mom, I know you mean well, but you don't have to worry about me. I'm not a teenager anymore."

"Well, you *are* in a foreign place. And much as I love Italy, you still have to be careful. You'll be there for two months, and you don't have experience—"

"I certainly do. That's why I applied for this job, remember?"

"I didn't mean in teaching, darling. I meant in the world of men—"

"I'm not here to be with men, Mother," Neve retorted. *"Really?"*

"Well, just make sure you don't take up with any of the locals." Her tone sounded as if she was wrinkling her nose. "People in those small towns talk, and your name will be sullied."

"Mom, it's the twenty-first century, for God's sake. Things *have* changed in the last hundred years." Neve felt her jaw muscles tighten.

"And by the way, you barely gave me any details about this nanny job you've taken on. Who are the parents?"

"There are no parents. The little girl's an orphan."

"Oh. Poor girl. Well, who hired you, then?"

"The girl's uncle. He's her godfather and guardian."

"Is he married?"

Neve heard the sharp edge in her mother's voice. *Where was she going with this?*

"No, Mom. And I don't have time for this interrogation. I have to get back to work."

"But—"

"Sorry, gotta go. Bye, Mom."

Neve was too agitated to try to have a rest. If only her mother would respect her wishes and give her some space. Maybe next time she would just not answer the phone…

She changed into a tangerine halter dress and sandals, then unwrapped the towel and went to sit by a window to comb and dry her hair. She returned to the washroom to check her appearance and decided to add a touch of eyeliner and a hint of green eyeshadow, finishing with a dab of orange-red lipstick. Now she was ready to face Davide. And talk.

She took a deep breath and left her room. Davide's bedroom door was shut but the door of his study was half-open. She strode quickly to it before she could change her mind. Her pulse spiked at the sight of him, his broad back to her, his laptop open.

Davide had taken a shower, too; his hair was still damp, the tendrils curling at the top of his head. He was wearing a white T-shirt that outlined his shoulder muscles and black jeans that fitted his body perfectly. He was looking at the screen intently, scrolling through it with one hand while cupping his chin with the other.

Was he doing research for his novel? Neve felt a surge of pride, thinking of how hard he had worked to accomplish his goals over the years...

An image flashed in her mind of the first time she had seen him, returning midday from a farm or somebody's property, his hands and face earth-stained, his clothes dampened with sweat. Standing on her balcony at Villa Morgana, what had captivated her instantly had been his eyes. Black and intense, looking up at her as if he had been struck by a vision. They had set off a series of sparks inside her that she had never felt with anyone else, before or since.

Neve swallowed and knocked gently. Davide immediately shut his laptop and swiveled in his chair to face her, his brows furrowed. She saw his eyes narrow and quickly scan over her before returning to meet her gaze. He lifted his eyebrows but remained silent.

"I—I think we need to clear up a few matters, Signor Cortese."

"And I think you can call me Davide now that we've gotten to know each other a little more," he returned smoothly "Come in, Neve." He gestured to one of the recliners.

Neve walked over and sat down, a strange drumming in her chest. He always pronounced her name the Italian way—and she liked it—but this time, something in the deep resonance of his voice made her nerve endings tingle.

He rolled his chair over the hardwood floor and stopped a few feet away from her.

They sat looking at each other for a few moments, and unable to hold it in any longer, she blurted, "You had stopped passing by the Villa Morgana a couple of days before I left for Canada. You made me think that—"

"That I wanted you?" he said huskily, leaning forward. "Or should I put it more delicately…that I wanted to meet you?"

Neve bit her lip. She was no longer a somewhat naive eighteen-year-old. Still a little shy, maybe, but there was no reason why she couldn't be frank. "Yes."

He cocked his head as if she was a puzzle to him. *"And…?"*

She frowned. "And I wanted to know why…"

Davide looked at her as if she had two heads. "You know perfectly well why, Neve. Have you lost your memory?"

Neve felt the heat in her chest rising to her neck and face. "I don't understand what you're saying. I was there for two days after, waiting for you, but you just stopped showing up."

Davide let out a laugh, but there was no humor in it. "You made it quite clear in your note that you wanted nothing to do with me."

Neve's jaw dropped. *Was she in another dimension?* "Wh-what? What note?"

Davide stared at her intensely for a moment, then rose to return to his desk. Neve watched him open the drawer and then reach into it farther. He returned to sit across her and held out a folded note in his hand.

Davide wasn't sure if her memory was defective, or if she was pretending not to remember—for whatever reason— but she couldn't deny the contents and meaning of the note she was now reading intently.

He had it memorized, imprinted in his mind like a hot branding iron:

I will *not* meet you. Your bold request is inappropriate and not appreciated. You would do well to remember your place.

Davide watched her read the note again, before turning it over and discovering *his* message. She looked up at him, blinking as if in shock.

"I did not write that note." Her voice cracked. "But I know who did." She handed it back to him, her hand trembling.

Davide's heart had jolted at her words. And at the emotions flashing in her eyes in mere seconds. Shock. Awareness. Defeat. *And pain.* In an instant he knew she was telling the truth.

The realization pierced him to the core. "Who?" he ground out.

She bit her lip again and he saw that her eyes were misting. "My mother."

She dropped her head in her hands, pressing them against her eyes. "I can't believe it."

Davide felt his stomach begin to churn. "Are you sure, Neve?"

Neve nodded, still holding her head. "That's her handwriting."

"Why?" He couldn't control the edge of anger in his voice.

Neve let her hands drop limply in her lap. She looked across at him and said nothing. Her eyes had darkened like an angry winter sea. But there was a sadness in them that made Davide want to take her in his arms and hold her.

He took a long, deep breath and reached for her hands, caressing them softly with his own.

And that was when she burst into tears. He rose and gently but firmly pulled her up to cradle her in his arms.

He let her sob against his chest, soaking his T-shirt, while he stroked her head and back. The warmth of her tears against his neck ignited his primeval instinct to protect his woman, and he embraced Neve even tighter.

He lowered his head to brush her forehead with light kisses, and when her sobs began to subside, he tilted her chin up to his and kissed her as thoroughly as he had done in the garden. *In the way that he had dreamed about thousands of times in the past eight years.* He tasted salt from her tears and after gently wiping them away, he kissed her over and over, wanting every kiss to make up for the pain her mother had caused her. *And him.*

He still wanted to know why Neve's mother had done this. But he wasn't going to push Neve into answering. He could wait, now that the main mystery had been solved. "Bianca will be waking up soon," he murmured in Neve's ear. "We can talk later." He brushed a kiss on her temple. "Why don't you go and check on her, and then we can all go for a ride into town." He looked deeply into her eyes. "How do you feel about a gelato or some cannoli at the Pasticceria Michelina?"

The look in Neve's eyes made his heart and stomach flip.

Her lips slowly stretched into a smile. And then she stood on tiptoe to answer him with a kiss.

A kiss that made him forget that eight lonely and bitter years had ever gone by...

CHAPTER SEVENTEEN

NEVE SPLASHED COOL water over her face in her bathroom. Her stomach was still churning, thinking about her mother. How could she? She had had no right to manipulate Neve's life in the way that she had. Neve's first impulse had been to call her mother immediately, ream her out, but then had changed her mind. She had to think this one through.

Her mother had gone too far, interfering with Neve's business, her *private* business. She had been eighteen that summer. Old enough to accept a young man's invitation to meet, for God's sake. But no, Lois Wilder had to stick her controlling finger into Neve's life, poking it where it didn't belong. *Again.* Intercepting and responding to a note that had been meant for *her.*

Davide had asked why but Neve had been reluctant to explain just then. She had needed time to process what this all meant, how she would handle things with her mother and how she and Davide would deal with this new knowledge.

Neve knew exactly why Lois had done it.

Because she was a snob.

Neve had never liked this character trait of her mother's. Lois had always liked to flaunt her money, display her status through the clothes and jewelry she wore, or by the different cars she drove. And she had wanted Neve to do the same. "The way you look is *everything*, darling," she had said to Neve on numerous occasions. In fact, she had drummed it into Neve's head since kindergarten.

And she hadn't appreciated Neve's reluctance to comply.

Over the years Lois had cajoled, flattered or even scolded Neve in order to get her to be more like *her*. Subtly and not so subtly criticized Neve's choice of clothes as being too *common* and had tried to discourage Neve from associating with some of her friends whose families she had deemed to be in a lower financial or social status than theirs. Lois's eagle eyes had often judged people based on the way they looked.

So no wonder that Davide hadn't passed inspection. Her mother would have instantly been horrified, having noted Davide's dusty and dressed-down appearance. Neve remembered all too clearly how her mother had yanked her back into her room when she had caught her smiling at him across the street. And she obviously hadn't liked the way Davide had been staring and smiling back.

But how had she managed to intercept Davide's note and send it back? Neve felt another surge of anger toward her mother, but she took a few deep breaths, counted to ten and then headed to Bianca's room. They were going to be driving to the special place where Davide had wanted to meet, and the last person Neve wanted there was her mother, even if it was only in her thoughts.

The bakery's facade hadn't changed, but the interior had been modernized to appear retro, Davide told her with a smile. The owners had purchased the adjacent building so they could add a pizzeria and a bigger seating area.

Neve liked the look of the place. The round tables had pastel-colored surfaces with chrome edging and legs. Their colors of coral, robin's egg blue and buttercup yellow made the place cheery.

Neve noticed that people had turned to look at them

with unconcealed curiosity. Some greeted Davide and he smiled or waved back, but he did not introduce her to any of them. "If I do, I'll never have a moment with you alone," he murmured as he led her and Bianca to a table near the front window. "I hope you don't mind."

"Not at all." She smiled, relieved. "I'm not really in the mood for socializing." *I'd rather keep you to myself.*

Davide pulled out a chair for Neve and Bianca, placing Bianca between them.

"Zio Davide, can we order pizza? I'm starving." Bianca rubbed her tummy for emphasis.

Davide chuckled as he checked the time on his phone. "No wonder. You haven't eaten in at least five hours." He glanced at Neve. "Is pizza okay with you? We can have something sweet afterward." His gaze lingered on her lips before returning to lock with hers.

I already had something sweet...your kisses. "You pick. I'm sure I'll enjoy whatever you choose."

Davide ordered a *pizza alla melanzana*. "Something I'm almost sure you've never had—pizza with roasted eggplant," he said, flashing her a smile. "You might as well try new things while you're here…"

The way that Davide was looking at her was making her heart do jumping jacks in her chest. She lost herself in their depths for a few moments, imagining what would have happened if she had met Davide here eight years ago… Would she have let him charm her and take her to a more private place? Would he have kissed her? Made her melt like she had after his searing kiss in the garden?

The waiter came over with three glasses of water and Davide immediately stood up and greeted him with a hug before introducing him as Agostino.

"Piacere." Neve smiled. "Pleased to meet you." She

wondered why he seemed a little flustered all of a sudden, looking from Davide to her, and then back to Davide.

Agostino greeted Bianca and placed a paper place mat in front of her with a box of crayons before returning to the kitchen with their order.

"My childhood friend," Davide explained. "His mother worked at the Villa Morgana eight years ago. You might have seen him around... And he's the one I asked to deliver the note to your room."

Neve frowned. "Now that you mention it, he *does* look a little familiar."

"Well, from the looks of it, some of the locals here are probably thinking the same about *you*."

Neve glanced casually over her shoulder and met several smiles. She smiled back shyly and turning back to Davide, murmured, "They're *staring* at me."

"Why wouldn't they be staring? *Sei bellissima*..."

Neve flushed at his compliment.

"Besides, this isn't a big town. Word gets around. People know I've hired a nanny for Bianca, and they're curious." His mouth twitched. "It's in their nature."

Agostino returned with their pizza, its aroma making Neve's mouth water. The cheese on top was golden brown, with thin rounds of roasted eggplant spread all over. Neve had her first bite and nodded her approval at Davide. "My new favorite pizza," she said. "It's heavenly."

"I was drawing heaven," Bianca piped up, holding up her drawing. "See? There's Mommy and Daddy."

Neve swallowed. Bianca's drawing had a spiky sun in one corner and some clouds over mountains, with two stick figures standing on one cloud. They looked like they were holding hands. All around them, Bianca had drawn hearts. Neve glanced at Davide, and the look in his eyes made her heart hurt.

* * *

Davide had lost his appetite. Seeing Bianca's creation had given his heart such a jolt that for a moment, he wished that he were alone with the pain. And yet, seeing the empathy and compassion in Neve's eyes made him want to be alone with her, so she could comfort him as he poured out his grief and mourned his losses.

Months ago he had tried to be stoic at Violetta and Tristan's funeral, but there had been moments that had simply been too much. Seeing his little niece standing next to the coffin had been one of those moments, and he had not been able to hold back the tears. He had picked her up and they had both cried, Bianca clinging to him with big, sorrowful eyes that had haunted him ever since.

Her drawing was simple but so profound. Davide was shaken by the symbols that immediately flashed in his mind as he scanned the page, symbols that had come naturally to Bianca. The sun shining brightly and the mountains to represent her parents' ski trip. The stick figures on the clouds to show her parents up high, where heaven was. And finally, the detail that pierced his heart: the stick figures with hands joined.

Whereas *he* had questioned his faith and beliefs after the accident, here was a five-year-old who had suffered a trauma no child should ever have to suffer, yet her beliefs were clearly evident in her drawing. Beliefs that had obviously originated from her upbringing by two loving parents. And the hearts all over the page showed the reciprocation of that love.

There was no car in the drawing, or anything resembling a sign of the accident. Davide let out a long breath. "That's a beautiful and very special drawing, Bianca," he murmured, putting his arm around her shoulders. "We will have to frame it." He bent down to give her a kiss on the head. "Your *mamma* and *papà* would be very proud of you, as I am."

Bianca nodded as she bit into her second piece of pizza, seemingly unperturbed at the moment.

But Davide could tell that Neve was not going to eat much more. He called Agostino over and requested a box so they could take the unfinished pizza home.

Davide ordered an espresso for himself and Neve, and a spumoni gelato for Bianca. He held his hand up when Neve offered to contribute to the cost. "You are not paying for meals, remember?" He looked at her sternly. "That's part of your working conditions."

"Thank you, Signor Davide," Neve said, blushing as she added a touch of sugar to her espresso.

"And I told you to drop the *signor*, remember?" Davide gazed at her with raised eyebrows. "Since we're now on more...*familiar* terms?" He watched her light flush deepen and her eyelashes flutter briefly, causing a wave of desire to pulsate through his body.

Seeing that Bianca had finished her gelato, Davide paid the bill and said goodbye to Agostino, adding quietly that he'd be in touch soon. He held the door open for Neve and Bianca and ushered them into his van. He made sure Bianca's seat belt was fastened properly and climbed into the driver's seat. He glanced over at Neve. She was holding Bianca's drawing, a wistful look on her face. And then she looked over and caught his gaze. He had almost expected her to look away, but she held his gaze for five seconds...then ten...

"Zio Davide, I'm tired. Are we going home?"

Davide gave a start and looked back at Bianca. "Right now, *tesoro*. Close your eyes and rest. We'll be home in no time."

In minutes Bianca was asleep. As Davide maneuvered

his way out of town, he could feel the tension that had settled on his neck and shoulders. He would relax in his whirlpool bath when he got home. It had been an emotionally draining day, and he needed to digest what had happened—*and what was happening*—between him and Neve.

There were still plenty of questions that he wanted to ask her about her mother. And he was sure that Neve had questions of her own. It had sounded like Neve and her mother had issues that had originated in Neve's adolescent years. Or maybe earlier. At the very least, Lois Wilder was controlling and manipulative. *Had she been jealous of Neve?* Most mothers *wanted* their daughters to find a nice guy. But she had found a way to stop her daughter from meeting with him. Had she done the same with other guys?

Davide felt a chill as he remembered the words on the note. *You would do well to remember your place.* Maybe the issue hadn't been with Neve, but with *him*. Of course! He hadn't fit Lois's image of *a nice guy*. He had been grimy and dusty from his work on the farm... She must have cringed at the thought of her upper-class daughter stooping to meet *a farmer*.

Anger and disgust swirled in his gut. He couldn't abide snobbery. And he felt a stab of remorse for all the years that he had thought that it was Neve who had been the snob. *Eight wasted years.* Years of bitterness, regret and humiliation.

But maybe they hadn't been wasted. Those words that Lois had written—dripping with disdain—had actually pushed Davide to elevate his goals. This had eventually led to the writing of his novel, which had catapulted him to a level of success that he had only ever dreamed of. So in that sense, those eight years hadn't been wasted, but on the other hand, almost a decade of his and Neve's lives had been controlled by a force neither of them had been aware of. The force that was Lois Wilder.

Davide didn't know how things would be proceeding with Neve from this point on, but he knew one thing for sure: the feeling that had settled in his heart when he had first seen Neve had never disappeared. It may have flickered, like a match's flame on a windy day, but now, with the truth finally out in the open, the flicker was becoming stronger and stronger. All the judgments he had made about Neve after reading that note had dissipated when he had seen that stricken look in her eyes. The raw pain that she had been deceived by her own mother, by some one she had thought she could trust. And that look had pained him also, knowing that Neve had been hurt.

As Davide wound his way up the mountain, he suddenly thought of the novel that he had put on hold since the accident. Taking care of his sister's and brother-in-law's affairs after their accident had taken all his time and emotional energy. And once Bianca had returned to Southern Italy with him, he had spent time with her during the day and evening, trying to adapt to a new life that included a child.

He had hired a nanny right from the beginning, and then another, and a third, but each one had fallen short of his expectations. The first had exaggerated her qualifications, the second had crossed the line by snooping and the third had wanted to get to him through Bianca. All had violated his trust.

During all of this Davide hadn't felt the desire to return to his writing. So he had done the next best thing— continued his research. He had set this novel in the late nineteen-fifties, during the last great wave of Italian immigration to other parts of the world. Reading and compiling facts and significant details of that era had kept him moving forward, even if the creative part of it was on hold.

Fortunately, the resounding success of his first novel afforded him whatever time he needed to move through his grief and mourning without the worry about a paycheck not arriving. And even though his publisher and editor had been anxiously awaiting his next literary offering, Davide had refused to put pressure on himself. He knew that the desire to write would return, sooner or later.

And it *had*, especially after seeing that *look* in Neve's eyes. The utter defeat, mixed with shards of pain. A look that he could envision on his heroine's face after her discovery of her husband's infidelity in their newly adopted country—a scene that he had been about to write the night that he had gotten the call from Bianca's babysitter in Vancouver…

As Davide drove the final stretch onto his property, the lights he had had installed casting an amber glow on different sections of the castle, Davide felt a ripple of excitement run through him. *He would return to his writing tonight.*

CHAPTER EIGHTEEN

BIANCA WAS TOO tired for a bath and a story before bed. And earlier, too tired to walk into the castle. Davide had carried her from the van into the castle and up the winding staircase. Neve had followed, a warmth spreading throughout her body at Davide's tenderness toward his niece. And at the sight of his strong back and arm muscles...

The sudden image of him carrying *her* up the stairs made her pulse quicken and she was glad he wasn't able to see her face at that moment, probably close to the same color as her hair.

Davide kissed Bianca good-night and excused himself. Neve helped Bianca change and get into bed, and when Neve tiptoed out of her room, Davide reappeared from his study. He offered Neve a chamomile tea or a cool drink, and she hesitated for a moment, trying to read his expression in the dimmed hall lighting.

Would this lead to further discussion about the past and her mother's part in it? Or encourage something more intimate? A wave of exhaustion washed over her then, and although she was very tempted, she made herself decline his offer. "Thanks, but I... I think the best thing is for me to get to bed. Today has been somewhat overwhelming..."

He closed the distance between them and took her hands in his. The way his thumbs were circling gently over her palms was triggering a series of red-hot currents through her. And when she thought that she was close to letting out a soft moan, he brought her hands to his lips, planted a firm kiss on both of them and brought them gently down. "*Anche per me*, Neve. Also for me."

Davide looked deep into her eyes—activating another delicious swirl in the pit of her stomach—and murmured, "I have some work to do, but we will see each other in the morning. *Va bene?*"

"*Va bene,*" she managed to reply a little breathlessly. Of course it was okay with her. Neve watched him retreat into his study, leaving the door half-open, and she entered her room, almost regretting that she hadn't accepted his offer.

As soon as she stepped into the large, claw-foot tub in her en-suite bathroom, enveloped by the sweet, soothing fragrance of the floral bubble bath, she knew she had made the right choice. *At least for tonight.*

The muscles in her body were more tense than she had realized. Neve closed her eyes, glad she had dimmed the lights, and focused on doing some deep breathing exercises. After twenty or so minutes, she stepped out of the perfumed water, feeling much more mellow and relaxed. Wrapping herself in an oversize towel, she padded to her bed. She had put on a shower cap to expedite her bath routine, so she didn't have to worry about drying her hair. She switched on the night-light near the door to the en suite and turned off the Murano chandelier in her room.

Neve lay on top of the bed for a few minutes, enjoying the warm breeze from the open shutters. She felt like a pampered princess in her luxurious turret room. Before her eyelids became too droopy, she shifted to turn back the covers, and then flung her towel on the edge of the bed. The thought *did* occur to her to walk over to the armoire where she had hung up her nightie, but her limbs refused to cooperate.

The cool satin sheet against Neve's bare skin made her snap out of her lethargy. She felt a slow, sensual tingle along her nerve endings with every brush of her body against the satin, and the thought of Davide so close by in his study ramped up the sensations even more. With a sudden shiver, she pulled the top satin sheet over her and squeezed her eyes shut. She had to stop imagining Davide walking through that door and coming to her...

He was her boss! No matter that there had been sparks between them eight years ago, sparks that hadn't needed much to flare up since she had arrived. She could not encourage any kind of involvement with Davide while she was employed by him. Yes, it would be sweet torture, living under his roof and erecting an emotional barrier to prevent him from getting closer. But there was no other option, unless she quit her job and went home.

And she didn't have the heart to do that to Bianca. The child had had enough traumatic changes in her life, and Neve wasn't about to become the fourth nanny who hadn't worked out. The poor child needed some stability, and Neve had every intention of fulfilling her part of the contract and ensuring that Bianca was ready for kindergarten. She could see—and she knew Davide could, too—that Bianca was already warming up to her.

Neve inhaled deeply. She could only take it one day at a time. And even *that* might prove to be more difficult than she could imagine...

Exhausted, Neve closed her eyes and curled to one side, tucking the sheet under her chin, and willed herself to sleep.

Davide stared at the paragraph he had just finished typing up on the laptop. He frowned, his fingers drumming the keys softly without actually typing. Then he changed a few words, read it over again and smiled. He was back on track!

He rubbed his eyes and then checked the time on his cell phone. After 3:00 a.m. Well, he had accomplished what he had meant to do. The scene was done, and he felt emotionally spent but exhilarated at the same time.

Davide sat back in his leather office chair and let his shoulders relax. He dipped his head, moved it to one side and then the other, stretching his neck and then his shoulders. The sound of footsteps in the hall made him swivel. His first thought was that it was Bianca, but a couple of seconds later Neve appeared at the half-open door, her cotton robe tied loosely at her waist.

Her hair was tousled, framing her face in feathery strands, and her eyes were blinking, as if surprised to see him there.

"I—I woke up and thought I heard something," she said, her voice husky. "I opened my door and saw your light. I thought maybe you had forgotten to turn it off… so I was going to."

Davide couldn't help smiling. "Thank you for being concerned about my light bill, Neve."

Her mouth quirked on one side and her gaze flew to his computer. "Well, I guess I'll let you get back to whatever you were doing…"

Davide waited till her gaze returned to his. "No, don't go just yet… Come in."

He saw her hesitate and then pull the strap of her robe tighter around her. She walked tentatively toward him, stopping several feet from his desk. His laptop was still open, with the last page of his chapter on the screen. Davide saw her gaze fly to it quickly and then back to him.

He closed the laptop and stood up to face her.

"I have something I'd like to give you. A little gift to

express my gratitude for doing such a great job with Bianca." He held out a copy of *La Figlia Dei Borboni*. "The English translation is in the works."

Davide felt a swirl of pleasure as Neve's eyes widened, along with her smile. She took the book gingerly as if it was a priceless treasure. She scanned the cover and then turned it over to read the blurb. And then she flipped the first couple of pages to where he had inscribed it.

Per Neve,
Con ammirazione e gratitudine.

For Neve, with admiration and gratitude.
She looked up at him, her eyes a misty azure.

"*Grazie,* Davide," she said, blinking but unable to stop the teardrops from slipping out onto her cheeks.

He groaned softly and took the book out of her hands and dropped it on the desk. He pulled her close against him, wrapping one arm around her back and raising his other hand to press her head gently against his chest. He breathed in the fresh scent of her hair and held her for timeless moments, letting all his senses experience the intimacy he had dreamed of for years.

And then his need for her made him tilt her face toward him and hungrily seek her lips. When they opened almost immediately for him, an exquisite current ran through him as he tasted the fruit that had been denied him for almost a decade. *Madonna mia*, he thought, his breath ragged. He pulled away to trace a path of kisses down her silky neck, and with impatient hands, he tugged at the ties of her robe until it fell away.

Her sudden gasp at the touch of his hands over the thin nightie beneath her robe sent his heart catapulting against his rib cage. His lips sought hers again while one hand slid under her nightie. And then another gasp. With a muffled groan, Davide swept her up in his arms and carried her to his bedroom.

"I've been waiting a lifetime to make you mine, Neve," he breathed against her ear before setting her down on his king-size bed. He had so much he wanted to say to her…

But he let his passion say the rest…

CHAPTER NINETEEN

WHEN NEVE WOKE UP, she was alone in her own bed. A series of images flashed through her mind and made her pulse do hurdles. Had she been dreaming? There was no way that she and Davide had…

They *had.*

And her body was still thrumming from his touch.

The way he had begun his tender exploration, so slowly and gently, as if she were a delicate flower.

And the feel of his lips and touch becoming more passionate…and thorough…

He had sent her to the stars and back. There had been few words…his eyes had relayed everything she had needed to know. And afterward she had nestled against him, cocooned by his strong arms, his breath warm against her neck. *This is how she had always imagined lovemaking would be…*

Neve had wished she could have stayed there until morning, but they both knew that Bianca could wake up at any time.

Davide had helped her with her nightie and dressing gown, and had carried her back to her room. After a final passionate kiss, he had left, and Neve had eventually succumbed to a deep, contented sleep.

The unexpected ring of her cell phone gave Neve an

unpleasant jolt, and she reached for it on her night table, irritated at the interruption of her thoughts. Blinking, she read the text message.

Neve, I can't believe you didn't tell me you were living in a castle! And that your boss is the celebrated author Davide Cortese! Not that I knew about him before, lol, but my sources in Valdoro texted me to tell me that the two of you had been seen in Michelina's Bakery, of all places! So, 'fess up, darling. Is something going on that I should know about? Did you meet him online through a dating service? Is that why he hired you as nanny to his niece?

Neve paused, her stomach in knots. She could not believe that even this far away from home, her mother was still sticking her nose in her private business. And of course her mother's "sources" were her friends at the Villa Morgana. An employee at the villa had either been at the bakery when she and Davide had been there with Bianca, or else someone at the bakery had told a friend who had then told another friend…

And how was she supposed to respond to her mother's query? What had happened between her and Davide was too fresh, too private. And the last person she wanted to know about it was the person who had contrived—and succeeded—in preventing them from ever meeting. Neve still had to confront her mother about *that*.

But maybe her mother didn't know that Davide was the fellow she had responded to so disdainfully years ago… In any case, Neve needed to downplay the situation and convince her mother that there hadn't been any involvement between her and Davide.

No, Mom, we didn't meet through an internet dating site. I was hired because of my credentials and experience with children. And I had no idea he was an author when I accepted the position.

Her mom was quick to reply.

Well, I hope he's paying you well. If he's living in a castle he must be loaded. And I hear his book has been optioned for a film!

Neve's jaw clenched as she wrote back.

You don't have to worry about what he's paying me, Mom. And I have to go now. Bye!

She was about to turn off her phone, but her mother quickly texted again.

Well, I'll see you soon, darling, because I've booked a flight for Italy! I'll be in Valdoro before you know it! My flight leaves tonight. But don't worry. I don't expect to be put up in the castle of your prince—oops—boss, lol! I'll be with my friends at the Villa Morgana, of course! Arrivederci, bella! Can't wait to see you and meet him!

A moment later Lois texted Neve her flight number.

Neve stared openmouthed at her cell phone. And then she turned it off, not bothering to reply.

How could she stop her mother from coming? Stop her from interfering with her life?

Neve bit her lip, her nerves jangled. Her mother could not be stopped when she put something in her head. And her impulsive decision to return to Valdoro must have something to do with her discovery of Davide's status.

For as long as Neve could remember, her mother had

taken every opportunity to associate with people of distinction. So why would things be different now? Neve frowned at the thought of her mother's imminent arrival. Lois would be sure to find a way to show up at the castle and try to ingratiate herself with Davide.

And how would Davide feel when he found out about her mother's plans? Lois had humiliated him, and Neve wouldn't blame him if Davide wanted nothing to do with her. Surely he would see right through Lois...

Neve's attraction to Davide had nothing to do with his money or status. Yes, she was thrilled for his success, but the spark that connected them had been created in the past. It hadn't mattered to her then that he had come from humble beginnings, and it didn't matter to her now. If Davide had remained a farmer, she would still be attracted to him. What mattered to her was his devotion to his niece, and how he had put aside his work to make Bianca his priority and help her adjust to life without her parents.

Neve had to give Davide a lot of credit for accepting and carrying out his role as godfather. And her heart bled for the grieving he must have felt at the tragic news—and still must be feeling...

A rush of tenderness swept through her as she thought of ways to comfort Davide. Not just by taking care of Bianca, but by taking care of *him*. Neve felt a sudden longing that she had never felt with any other man, and it made her catch her breath.

She wanted Davide.

Not just in the physical sense, but in every way imaginable. She wanted to nurture that spark from eight years ago into red-hot flames that would burn for a lifetime. She had disappeared from his life once, but fate had brought them back together. She couldn't ignore or throw away the second chance offered to them, even if Davide *was* her boss.

But what if Davide doesn't feel the same? What if he's just needing something—somebody—to help him get through his grief? What makes you think he would want you permanently in his life?

Neve faltered at her inner voice. Maybe Davide *had* needed a physical release after the grief and pain of the past few months. She felt her cheeks burn at the memory of his passion, and how he had managed to make her reciprocate, even though it had been her first time...

Neve bit her lip as her thoughts took a dark turn. Perhaps one of the three "princesses," as Davide had called Bianca's nannies, had had a physical relationship with him before he tired of her and dismissed her. Neve frowned. Did she *really* know what Davide's true character was like? Maybe what she had seen on the outside was just a mask...

A gorgeous mask that she had fallen for. *Hard.*

No, she couldn't believe—*didn't want to believe*—that Davide had made love to her for the sole purpose of physical gratification. She couldn't possibly have misread the tenderness in his eyes, and that look of wonder...

Neve checked the time on her phone. Davide had told her to sleep in; he would see to Bianca's breakfast and *hers*, when she came down to the kitchen. Neve smiled. She'd have a quick shower first, and maybe she'd be in time to watch Davide make the frittata he had promised her...

In the stillness of dawn, Davide watched the sun rise up like a gleaming orange persimmon on the horizon, and the pale blue sky brightening with streaks of pink and gold. He had already been up for an hour, gone to make himself an espresso and returned to his room to enjoy it.

For the first time since Bianca had come to live with him, Davide had woken up without feeling like the proverbial weight of the world was on his shoulders. Without the responsibility of parenting seeming so *serious*.

Not that it wasn't serious, but since Neve had taken over as nanny, Davide had experienced some of the lighter moments of raising a child, and he had enjoyed them. Like the game of hide-and-seek. Bianca had laughed and he had, too, watching her squeal when Neve had gotten close enough to tag her.

Davide felt his nerve endings tingle at the thought of Neve. Not in a game of tag, but in his arms last night, *in his bed*. He hadn't planned it and he would have stopped the second she had shown any sign that she wanted him to stop… *But she hadn't.*

Discovering that *he had been the first* had taken Davide straight to heaven with the wonder of it. He had felt humbled, exhilarated and emotional all at once, and he had been careful to rein in his passion…until she was ready.

Bianca's call and knock on the door forced him to suppress any further thoughts of Neve.

He called out for Bianca to enter and she joined him on his leather chair, her orca with her, which, she told him matter-of-factly, she had named "Berry." Sitting on his lap, she watched the sun's ascent with him and told him about the whales she had seen with her father, called "Granny" and "Onyx." Davide listened quietly, inwardly rejoicing that Bianca was starting to talk about her parents without bursting into tears.

And then she proclaimed that she was hungry. Chuckling, he headed downstairs with her, and after preparing her cereal and milk, went out to the garden to get snippets of parsley and green onions for the frittata. He whistled a tune that had been a hit a decade earlier, performed at the Sanremo Music Festival. Whenever it had played on the radio, his heart had felt a twinge. It had haunted him then with its romantic melody, but no more.

Davide took out a bowl and as he beat the eggs with a mixture of milk, chopped parsley and pecorino romano, the cheese he preferred with its sharp bite, Neve walked into the kitchen. Davide stopped whistling, and his hand stopped beating. He took in Neve's sleeveless coral dress with its big retro buckle that emphasized her slender waist, and its skirt that flared and reached just above her knees. A matching headband made her look like a fifties glamour girl.

"*Buon giorno*, Neve." If Bianca wasn't with them, he'd have called Neve *cara* or *bella* or *tesoro mio*. But he couldn't very well call her *dear* or *beautiful* or *my treasure* in front of his niece. At least…not yet. He motioned for her to join Bianca at the table. "I'm keeping my promise to cook for you," he murmured as she walked by him. "Are you hungry?"

She paused and fixed him with a wide-eyed glance. Lashes fluttering open and closed like exotic fans. Eyes with an intensity that sent coils of electricity spiraling throughout his body.

"Very," she said, and then noticing that Bianca was watching her, made a fierce expression, adding, "I'm as hungry as the wolf in *The Three Little Pigs*."

Bianca let out a little squeal. "You can't have my cereal!" she laughed.

Davide resumed beating the eggs. Neve had such a remarkable way with kids. She made Bianca smile and laugh, and after the sadness and tears since the accident, hearing that little tinkling sound come out of Bianca's mouth, and seeing her brown eyes literally sparkle at Neve's silliness, Davide couldn't help but smile and laugh himself.

It felt strange to feel lighthearted. The past few months had been anything but. He had wondered sometimes if he and Bianca would ever laugh again. Her previous nannies had not elicited anywhere near the kind of reaction Bianca had demonstrated with Neve. All three had left him disillusioned with their less-than-honorable motives. He had been determined to find the right nanny for Bianca, one who was genuinely interested in helping her, and not using her as a means to get to *him*.

Aware of Neve's eyes occasionally shifting from Bianca to him, Davide heated the pan with extra-virgin olive oil and sautéed the chopped onions before adding the egg mixture. When the edges started curling in, he flipped the frittata over by sliding it first on the bottom of the pan lid and then quickly flipping it over into the hot pan. When both sides were golden brown, he transferred it to a large plate, cut it into wedges and brought it to the table, along with a plate of tomato slices and a crusty roll.

"I'll let you serve while I get the coffee," he said, and returned moments later with an espresso for himself and a cappuccino for Neve.

Bianca finished her wedge of frittata quickly and went out into the courtyard.

When she had gone, Davide looked closely at Neve. "Don't you like it?" He looked pointedly at her half-finished plate.

"No... I mean, yes, it's very tasty. It's just that..." She met Davide's gaze directly and then looked down, her shoulders slumping. When she looked back at him, her brows were furrowed and her lips were pursed.

"I don't know how to tell you this," she finally ventured.

Davide's stomach twisted. *Was she going to tell him that she regretted last night? That she now wanted to leave?* He leaned forward, elbows on the table, and hands clasped together in front of his mouth. The euphoria he had felt in his chest from just being with Neve started to seep out of him. Bracing himself, he said brusquely, "Just tell me."

Neve took a deep breath. "My mother is coming to Valdoro. She wants to meet you."

CHAPTER TWENTY

THERE—IT WAS OUT. Neve watched Davide closely, wanting to see what his first gut reaction would be.

It wasn't what she had expected.

The frown on Davide's face had relaxed, and unclasping his hands, his mouth had become visible, showing a crooked smile. "Why?"

"*Why?* Because she's curious, impulsive. Her friends at the Villa Morgana told her that we had been seen at the bakery." At Davide's puzzled look, she felt herself flush in embarrassment. "They told her about *you*. Your success, your castle, your…"

"Wealth," he finished, nodding. "And she wants to come and see for herself what high society circles her daughter has gotten herself into…" His black eyes gleamed. "Does she know who I am?"

Neve gazed at him for a moment, her heart contracting. *No, her mother had no idea who Davide was as a person. She was interested in Davide Cortese as a celebrated author who lived in a castle and was "loaded."* But Neve knew that Davide was referring to the past…

"No…she wouldn't know that you were the one she wrote the note to…" Neve sighed.

"The last thing I wanted was my mother around," she said, her voice breaking. "I'm sorry."

Davide leaned forward and grasped her hands. "You don't need to be," he said huskily, his thumbs caressing her palms. "Is she expecting to stay here?"

"No, thank God." Neve felt her shoulders relax. "She'll be staying with her friends at the Villa Morgana."

Davide released one hand to cup her chin. "That's just a peach," he chuckled.

Neve couldn't help breaking into a smile. *"Peachy,"* she corrected.

"Yes, just peachy." He gave a deep laugh. "Or we could have prepared a room for her in the castle dungeon."

Neve laughed. "Is there really a dungeon?"

Davide's eyes twinkled. "It's a cellar, and it actually has a secret tunnel that leads to a cave in the mountainside… Apparently, it was a hiding place for brigands in the eighteen-sixties."

"Brigands?" Neve stared at him incredulously. *"Really?"* She couldn't help shivering. "And the owner of the castle knew about it?"

"Probably. He may have been sympathetic to the brigands' cause. They were rebelling against the ousting of the Bourbon regime during Italy's Unification, mostly because of the hardships suffered by the peasants after the formation of the new government. The owner—a baron whose family had enjoyed the privileges of the old order for generations—probably used the brigands to covertly rebel against the government himself."

"Oh, my," Neve murmured. "Sounds like a very dangerous time."

Davide nodded. "It's a period known as *il decennio di fuoco*—the decade of fire. The government went after the brigands and employed the National Guard to find and capture them. *And* their women, the *brigantesse*."

Neve stared. "Their women went into hiding with them?"

"Some, but if they were captured, the law was generally more lenient with them, sentencing them to life imprisonment in a workhouse."

"That was more *lenient*?"

"More lenient than having them hanged or shot. Sadly, some ended up in the latter category."

Neve gave another shudder. She looked across at him with a sudden curiosity. "Do you know if…if any of your ancestors might have been *briganti*?"

Davide's eyes narrowed, glinting amusement. "Possibly. When I was researching the municipal archives, I came across the names of some distant relatives who had disappeared around that time…"

Neve's mouth dropped. She imagined the castle engulfed in fog over a century and a half earlier, and a brigand with Davide's features furtively making his way through the castle tunnel with his *brigantessa*, and hiding out in the dark mountain cave. The brigand would have wrapped his cloak over his woman and she would have snuggled against him, trying not to think about the bats clustered in masses on the walls and ceiling…

Davide's laughter shattered her thoughts. "Wh-what?" She blinked at him.

"You looked horrified for a moment. Did the thought of my possible brigand heritage shock you?"

Neve looked at him sheepishly. "No… I was just thinking about the bats in the cave."

Davide's burst of laughter made Bianca run over to them.

"Zio, can we go to the beach this morning?" She turned excitedly toward Neve. "Did you bring a swimsuit?"

Neve glanced at Davide. "Don't feel you need to… I'm sure you have some work you might like to do…some writing?"

"I can do that later. I have a better imagination at

night…" Davide's gaze locked with hers for so long that Neve began to feel a flush spread to the most vulnerable zones of her body.

He glanced at the time on his cell phone. "We can leave in twenty minutes or so. I have a quick call to make to my publisher." Davide grinned at them. "You ladies get what you need—sunscreen, hats, a good book… Have you read the latest Strega Prize–winning novel?" he said teasingly. He gave Neve a wink. "*Ciao.* I'll meet you in the foyer."

Davide watched Neve and Bianca walk toward the staircase, with Bianca reaching for Neve's hand. He felt a rush of warmth at his niece's gesture. She trusted Neve.

And so did he.

With a lightness he thought he'd never feel again, Davide called his publisher in Milan to tell him that he had returned to the writing of his novel. They discussed a few details and timelines, and then Davide scheduled another meeting with him for the middle of the week. *And he could take Neve with him again…*

Whistling, Davide returned to the kitchen. His publisher had been thrilled, and he was just as thrilled. But right now he had other things to think about, like packing up a few items for the beach. They would be there till around noon, and Bianca would be sure to get hungry.

He found a large insulated bag in the pantry and set it down on the table. He decided to keep it simple: panini and some cheese, olives and tomatoes. He gathered up a few more items from the fridge and a bottle opener. And finally, he added a bottle of red wine and two crystal glasses, wrapped up in several tea towels.

Davide thought about Neve's initial words, *I don't know how to tell you this*, and how he had braced himself for Neve's declaration that she regretted what had happened between them and that she would be resigning, no longer able to work for him under the circumstances… The tension had put his stomach in knots.

But those knots had instantly relaxed with Neve's announcement that her mother would be coming to Valdoro. Not that he was exactly delighted with the news, but it was something that wouldn't cause his heart to break, like Neve's leaving would do.

Davide froze with a sudden realization. *He didn't want Neve to leave.*

Not now…*or ever.*

CHAPTER TWENTY-ONE

Neve accompanied Bianca to her room first and helped her
with her swimsuit and clothes to wear over it. Bianca insisted on bringing Berry the orca with her. While Bianca
waited in Neve's room, Neve changed into a red one-piece
swimsuit in her en-suite bathroom, and then slipped on
a pair of white shorts and a green eyelet peasant blouse.

As she brushed her hair in front of the dressing table
in her room, Bianca came over and watched. "Can I brush
your hair?" she said suddenly. "My mommy used to let me
brush hers...and then she would brush mine. She would
call me *principessa* when she did my hair."

Neve's heart ached at the sad note in Bianca's voice.
She handed Bianca the brush. "Yes, of course you can, Bianca." She leaned forward so she was eye to eye with the
child. "I know you miss your dear mommy, Bianca. And
your daddy. Just remember that they love you, and they
want you to be happy."

"But why did they have to die and leave me all alone?"
Bianca's lips started to quiver.

"Sweetheart, you're not alone," Neve said softly. "You
have your Zio Davide. He loves you, and your mommy and
daddy chose him to take good care of you. That's why they
made him your godfather when you were born."

Bianca's face puckered into a frown. "Did they *know* they were going to die?"

"No, love. Just try to remember that when you're missing them, think of something beautiful, like an angel, or a twinkling star, or a rainbow, and think of them being right beside it. *Imagine it.*" She smiled brightly. "Your mommy and daddy will always be in your heart and mind and memories, Bianca. And in your imagination."

"But that's *make-believe*," Bianca said, her chocolate-brown eyes widening. "I want it to be *real*."

"When you *believe*, it feels real," Neve said, trying to keep her voice steady. "Now how about I pick a special name for you? Your mommy called you 'princess,' and since you're taking such good care of your little whale, I'd like to call you—" she pretended to think "—Queen of the Orcas! How does that sound to you, *Your Majesty*?"

"I like it, Miss Neve!" She grinned and proceeded to brush Neve's hair.

"And how about you just call me Neve?"

"Okay, but can I sometimes call you Snow White?"

A gentle cough made them both look toward the doorway. Davide was leaning casually against the door frame. *How long had he been there? Had he heard Bianca's words about her parents?*

Neve caught a glimpse of sadness on Davide's face. Or was it just her imagination?

"My telephone conversation didn't take as long as I thought it would," he said. "I came up to tell you we could leave as soon as you were ready." His jaw muscles flickered. "So let's go, Snow White and Queen of the Orcas! Your carriage awaits!"

"I should call you Miss Italy with the colors you're wearing, Neve," Davide murmured, his gaze sweeping over her again. That green peasant top that she had positioned just slightly off her shoulders, those white shorts that hugged her curves and the red peeking through the eyelets of her cotton blouse... *Bellissima*.

She didn't reply, and as she walked past him with Bianca, she just gave him a twitch of a smile, her blue-green eyes startling in their clarity.

During the drive down the mountain to the beach, Davide put on a CD of Bianca's favorite tunes, and she hummed along while alternately throwing her orca up in the air and catching it, or making it dance to the rhythm of the song.

Davide had deliberately planned the musical distraction. He had caught much of the conversation earlier between Neve and Bianca. When he had arrived at Neve's bedroom door, she was telling Bianca that she knew that she missed her mommy...

Neither of them had seen him, and there hadn't been the opportunity to announce his presence, so he had waited in the doorway. And the words Neve had communicated to Bianca had made something shift inside him, creating room for his heart to expand. The feeling had been so exquisite that he had almost cried out. It took everything he had to act casual, to hide the revelation that his body—and soul—had just revealed to him.

He loved Neve. He loved her gentle spirit with Bianca, her compassion, her understanding of how to help a grieving child. She had come up with a way to empower Bianca to hold on to her parents through her memories and her imagination. He had felt a prickling behind his eyes at her words. They had sparked something in him, as well—the realization that he could handle his grief in the same way.

Moreover, he had felt a wave of regret about the opinion he had harbored about Neve for nearly a decade. He had been so wrong. So…very…wrong. Well, he would do whatever it took to make it right. He no longer wanted her just as a nanny for Bianca. He wanted her for himself, too, if she would have him.

Yes, he wanted her to spend a lifetime with him. As his wife. As his fairy-tale princess. As his lover. As the guardian of his little Queen of the Orcas.

Davide wanted the three of them to be a *family*, to share everything a family shared.

He stole a glance at Neve. She was swaying gently to the music and singing the words to the nursery rhymes. Davide felt like his heart would burst. He needed to tell her how he felt, but he would be patient and wait for a time when they could be alone.

His assistant Lucia had texted him earlier to say that she was babysitting her niece Rosalia again, and could she pick up Bianca later in the afternoon and bring her back the following day? Davide had agreed. Bianca needed to be with kids her own age and he was grateful to Lucia for arranging regular visits.

He couldn't help smiling. Tomorrow would be the day, then. After Bianca left, he would take Neve for a special drive through the countryside to one of his favorite seaside spots. They would share a wonderful dinner, and afterward he would reveal what was in his heart.

And with any luck, she would accept his proposal.

The road from the castle veered off to a private road at the base of the mountain that was available to him exclusively, and after a few final twists in the road, they arrived at the beach.

Davide parked the van at the end of the path, and they had walked several hundred feet to the beach.

The pale, silky length of it seemed endless, stretching as far as the eye could see in either direction. Davide watched Neve taking it all in, and he felt a spiral of plea-sure that he could share this place—*his place*—with her.

She darted an awe-filled glance at him, and her blue-green eyes were as dazzling to him as the sun-speckled waters of the Ionian Sea.

Bianca immediately plunked herself down on the sand and while she played with her sandcastle toys, Davide set up the beach umbrella and the lounging chairs that he and Neve had carried from the van. He proceeded to take off his T-shirt and jeans, leaving only his swim shorts.

He'd wait a while before plunging into the sea.

Out of the corner of his eye, he could see Neve doing the same. At the sudden flash of red, he turned, and the combination of the curves emphasized by the silky red swimsuit and her shapely legs made his heart flip wildly against his rib cage. She must have known he was watch-ing her, because a soft flush had crept into her cheeks. She immediately sat down and pulled a book out of her bag. *La Figlia Dei Borboni.*

He was so tempted to tell her that he didn't want her to go back to Vancouver, that he wanted her to stay… There was no doubt in his mind that she was physically attracted to him, as he was to her. The passion they had shared had rocked his world. But was that enough for Neve to uproot her entire life and move to Italy?

He had to find a way of convincing her to stay…and never disappear out of his life again.

He lay back on the reclining beach chair. "I'm going to let myself heat up a little more before I dive in," he told her huskily. "I'll leave you to your reading. Oh, by the way, my assistant Lucia will be coming by later this afternoon to pick up Bianca. She's babysitting her niece again, and she asked if Bianca could go over and stay the night. Lucia will bring Bianca back tomorrow."

Neve nodded and lay back herself, but only a couple of minutes had passed before Bianca called out for her to help build a sandcastle. Neve put away Davide's book and sauntered over to Bianca, who handed her a yellow pail. "Can you get some water, Neve?"

"Yes, at once, oh Queen of the Orcas." Neve curtsied and with a smile, went to do Bianca's bidding.

Davide watched them together between half-closed lids. He felt drowsy and...*content*. The world—or at least *his world*—suddenly felt right. *Maybe this is what starting to heal feels like*, he thought in wonder. Shards of pain replaced by rays of hope.

It was just too bad that Lois Wilder would be arriving soon, like a meteor about to crash into his world.

CHAPTER TWENTY-TWO

IT TOOK NEVE'S every effort not to constantly glance at Davide's body. He was lying back on his chaise longue, his sunglasses on. His leanness a decade ago had become solid muscle, and as her gaze swept over his chest and sculpted muscles of his abdomen and legs, she quivered inside, remembering how that body had felt against her...

And although she had nodded nonchalantly at the news that Bianca would be having a sleepover, her nerve endings were tingling at the thought of spending a night alone with him in the castle...

When he suddenly sat up, she started, and spilled the bucket of water she had been carrying, splashing herself and Bianca.

"I think it's time for a real splash," he chuckled. "Come on, Bianca."

Bianca dropped her beach toys and ran to clasp Davide's hand. "Come on, Neve," she called.

Neve followed and moments later they were all immersed in the gentle ebb and flow of the surf. Davide's hands firmly held Bianca's as she bobbed and kicked her legs. Not long after the first exhilarating dip, Neve's body acclimatized to the temperature of the water, and with the sun beaming down, it actually started to feel balmy. The taste of the salt water, the turquoise waves glittering with millions of specks of light and the glistening body of Davide…it was all making her feel quite heady…

Afterward, Davide spread out the picnic lunch he had prepared: panini and a variety of luncheon meats, cheeses and condiments. He met Neve's gaze and tilted his head to direct her attention to Bianca. Bianca's little cheeks were full, and while she happily munched away, she broke off little bits of cheese from her plate and pretended to feed it to her orca.

Neve smiled and when her glance returned to Davide, he was grinning back at her. Seeing his eyes crinkle at the edges, his delight and love for Bianca reflected in their depths, Neve felt both joy and sadness. Joy for having witnessed the depth of Davide's feelings for his niece, and sadness, knowing that she herself was only a temporary addition in their lives.

Yes, Davide and Bianca were a family…and maybe one day Davide would meet someone he wanted as his wife and godmother to his niece…and then their little family would grow… Feeling a sudden prickle behind her eyelids, Neve turned away, pretending to watch the surf.

"When did you say your mother was arriving?" Davide asked moments later.

Neve groaned. "I hadn't. But if she made all her connections, she should be getting in around three at the Villa Morgana. And she'll probably want to make her way here sometime after that. I'm sure she'll text right away."

"Shall we return to the castle and get ready for her arrival, then?" He smiled at her. "Pull out the red carpet?"

"Please, Davide, you don't have to do anything special, especially after the way she treated you."

His smile widened. "I…was…teasing, Neve. I don't have a red carpet." He looked over at Bianca. "I see our queen is feeling drowsy. She'll have a good nap when we get back." He gazed back at Neve, lifting an eyebrow. "Shall we pack up?"

Neve checked her phone anxiously. Her mother had settled into Villa Morgana and had texted Neve to say that she was ready to be picked up. Could her boss send a driver out to the villa?

Neve had relayed her request to Davide, apologizing for her mother's assumption that "her boss" would take care of her travel arrangements. "I'm sure she could have hired someone through her friends at the villa," she said, her cheeks heating up in frustration.

Davide's lips quirked. "She's obviously expecting the royal treatment. Shall I pick up Her Highness in my Lamborghini or Alfa?"

Neve stared at him. *"Really?"* She shook her head. "Is there not a taxi she can take?"

Davide's eyebrows lifted. "Well…there *is* a taxi driver I know who hasn't been getting much work. His name is Santo. Why don't I call him?"

"Perfect." Neve sighed, relieved.

"And I'll call the Pasticceria Michelina and order a box of pastries. Santo can pick them up on his way here. The least I can do is to offer her a *caffè* and biscotti," he said, winking at Neve.

Bianca was still napping when Neve heard the taxi arrive. She was waiting in the foyer, sitting in one of the two wingback chairs with a magazine. Davide had gone to work in his study and must have seen the taxicab from his window. He joined her, wearing black trousers and a crisp white shirt, unbuttoned at his neck. He flashed Neve a smile that sent her pulse skittering. "Are we ready for this?"

Neve sighed. "Do we have a choice? I should apologize in advance for anything she might say or—"

"You don't have to apologize for anything," Davide said firmly. "And don't worry on my account. I can take care of myself." He reached for her hand and gave it a squeeze. "And you can, too. Take care of yourself, I mean." He opened the thick door and motioned for Neve to precede him. *"Coraggio,"* he murmured close to her ear as they walked out.

"Neve!"

Neve watched her mother scramble out of the taxicab and begin striding toward her. She was wearing a light blue pantsuit and nude pumps. Even from this distance, Neve could see that she was frowning. The cab driver followed more leisurely, holding the box from the bakery. Lois slowed down as she caught sight of Davide's cars, and her frown seemed to deepen. As if she suddenly realized where she was, she stopped and gazed up at the castle and the view around it.

Neve and Davide closed the gap between them. Neve gave her mother a dutiful hug and then stepped back to introduce Davide.

Neve saw Lois's gaze sweep over him. *Recording every bit of data her senses took in.*

The fresh, citrus scent of his cologne, his styled hair, his gold chain, his expensive shirt and pants, his gleaming leather shoes...

Davide courteously held out his hand and Lois took it with a smile, also scanning his fingers for gold.

When Davide excused himself to go and retrieve the package from the cab driver, Lois turned so that only Neve could see her face.

"Neve, I can't believe that your boss is living like a king here—" she gestured toward the luxury vehicles "—and the best he could do was to send a cab! The driver reeked of cigarettes and garlic, and his air-conditioning was not working." She brushed off her pants as if germs were still clinging to them. "Could you not have asked your boss to pick me up himself?"

"I'm sorry, Mom, but he was not available at the time." *She hated to lie, but she could hardly tell the truth...*

Lois sniffed. "Well, I heard some things down at the villa, including the fact that your boss comes from a *farming* background."

"Mom, *please*. He's my boss and his background does not concern me. Nor should it concern you." Neve felt her hackles rising. Five minutes hadn't gone by and her mother was already saying things that grated on her. "And at the moment, you are his guest."

"May I offer you some refreshment, Signora Wilder?" Neve and her mother both started at the voice behind them.

"I would like that, thank you." Lois nodded imperiously. "That dreadful cab had no air-conditioning and I thought I was going to pass out."

"Prego," Davide said, gesturing toward the castle. As her mother marched off ahead of them, Davide caught Neve's eye and winked. She exhaled slowly, shaking her head, and went inside.

Neve could tell that her mother was impressed, despite the nonchalant set of her shoulders. Lois's gaze was taking in every luxurious piece of furniture, the shiny marble floor and the curving sweep of the staircase. Davide directed her into the dining area and kitchen and asked if she would like tea, coffee or a cold drink.

"For now, a cold beverage, thank you, Signor Cortese." Lois glanced around as if she expected a butler or maid to suddenly show up. "I imagine you employ a large staff to maintain the place," she said casually.

Davide glanced at her, smiling thinly. "Not large, no." He handed her a glass of iced tea and poured another one for Neve. "Shall we proceed into the courtyard?" Davide took the tray with the two drinks and set it down on the bistro table. He pulled out a chair for her and Neve before going back to get the box of pastries.

Neve saw her mother's sculpted eyebrows lift when he returned. "I'm presuming that my daughter's reputation will remain intact while she's here?"

"Mother!"

"Now, Neve, I'm sure Signor Cortese can understand a mother's protectiveness…"

Neve shot her mother an icy look. "I'm going to check on Bianca," she said stiffly. Her stomach churning, she left, resisting the urge to slam the door behind her.

"Well, it seems my daughter doesn't appreciate my directness," Lois said before taking a sip of her iced tea. "A mother has to look out for her daughter's best interests," she sniffed, checking her manicured nails.

Davide leaned back in his chair and crossed his arms, his eyes pinning hers. "Have you ever thought, Signora Wilder, that your daughter can look out for her own best interests? She's not a child anymore…"

Lois blinked. "Have you ever raised a daughter? Because if you haven't, you couldn't possibly understand."

Davide felt a twinge in his chest. "I'm raising my niece, Bianca," he said curtly.

"Well, then, Signor Cortese, you can understand my point." Lois looked at him with a triumphant smile.

"And I can understand Neve's point," he said without smiling. "She can make decisions on her own."

"Apparently." Lois nodded. "Applying for this position and getting hired was quite a surprise to me."

"She was the most qualified of the applicants," Davide said crisply. "And she has not disappointed. In fact, *signora*, your daughter's personality and skills with my niece have exceeded my expectations."

"I'm glad to hear it. She's quite valued as a teacher back home. She had passed up the opportunity to work in the family computer business and chose teaching instead."

"She chose well. Neve is a natural around children and I'm glad she accepted the position of nanny for Bianca." He leaned forward and looked at her squarely. "So tell me, why have *you* come back to Valdoro?"

She looked taken aback that he would ask such a question. "I thought it would be nice to catch up with my friends at the Villa Morgana. And check in on Neve. Spend time with her on her days off."

Davide's eyebrows lifted. Neve had been right. Her mother couldn't untie the apron strings. Well, maybe it was time someone gave her a hand…and a firm one at that.

"Well, I'm afraid you're going to be disappointed, *signora*. I've already made arrangements to take your daughter sightseeing on her days off. It's the least I can do for her exceptional care of Bianca."

Lois blinked at him. "Really? Why would you—?"

"Because I've wanted to be with your daughter since I saw her eight years ago."

"You've what? Wh-what are you saying?" Lois sputtered. "What do you mean?"

Davide reached into his pocket and handed her the note. She read it, flipped it over, then looked up at him sharply, before reading the note again. "*Y-you* were the one who wanted to meet Neve?"

He nodded and took back the note. "And you were the one who kept it from happening." His words were stone cold.

Despite being in the shade, Lois reached for her napkin to wipe her forehead. "I—I won't apologize for that. Neve was young and—"

"She was eighteen," Davide replied curtly. "And I was—"

"You were out of line," Lois snapped. "And not suited—"

"Because I was working on a farm and therefore too lowly for your daughter?" Davide kept his voice steady, despite the agitation that he felt in his gut. "Tell me, *signora*, how did you manage to intercept the note? My friend, Agostino, slid it under Neve's door after going to the villa to give his mother a message…"

"I saw him do it and take off, and fortunately Neve hadn't come out of the shower." Lois fell silent for a moment, lost in her thoughts. "I replied and put it back in the envelope and then placed it under the flowerpot by the front door, as per the instructions on the envelope." She gazed at Davide defensively. "I did what I thought was right."

"I can't argue that," Davide replied coolly. "And we can't change the past. Or your feelings that I should remember my *place*. What's done is done." He leaned forward. "But things are different now. Neve is an adult and it would be nice if you treated her like one and stopped trying to control her life. She doesn't need your approval or your interference. *And neither do I.*"

Lois opened her mouth as if to protest, then promptly shut it. She stared at Davide for a few moments. "Well, *I've* been told."

Davide looked hard at the woman who had manipulated Neve's life since she was a child—and still seemed reluctant to relinquish total control. Eight years ago he might have had a difficult time confronting someone like her, but now he had no qualms about expressing his feelings, and no fears that he had to remember his *place*. "I think if you really gave it some thought you'd see that you deserved it, Signora Wilder. *You* were the one who was out of line."

Davide's piercing gaze didn't falter. He watched the play of emotions on her face: the furrowing of eyebrows, the arrogant tilt of her head at his effrontery and the wide-eyed blinking, probably from the shock of being brought down a few pegs.

Davide stood up. "Now, if you'll excuse me, I'll go and see if Neve is ready to come back down." He nodded and began to walk away. When he got to the door, he turned around. "Oh, by the way, Signora Wilder, your daughter is old enough to make adult decisions about her reputation. You would do well to let go of those apron strings…"

He met Neve as she was coming down the stairs. "I have some work to do," he said. "I'll listen for Bianca." He shook his head and gave an exaggerated sigh, aware that she was wondering how things had gone between him and her mother. "I think you and your mother might need some time alone…"

Davide took the remaining stairs two at a time, and after peeking into Bianca's room and seeing that she was napping soundly, he went to his study. He would give Neve and her mother ten minutes or so, and then go back down. After checking his email and replying to some of the messages regarding his planned renovations on another section of the castle, Davide checked his phone.

He'd give them a few more minutes…

Realizing it was rather dim in the room, he strode over to open the heavy shutters. The voices of Neve and her mother were suddenly audible, and although it hadn't even occurred to him that they'd be within hearing distance, and he had no intention of eavesdropping, the words Neve was saying immobilized him.

He had caught the last part of her sentence, the words

"peasant" and "unrefined" in a tone that clearly reflected her disgust. "Did you actually think I would give up my virginity to him? I had no intentions of sinking that low…"

Davide felt his heart crack as if someone had taken a hammer to the stone that it had instantly become. He missed Lois's reply. Neve went on, "He's not the same man he was back then, Mother. He's not in the same *place*. He's got money—lots of money—and more status than you could dream of—" Her voice sounded triumphant, as if she had just landed the biggest prize in the lottery.

Davide closed the shutters with a bang, not caring that they would hear him. He paced the room, disillusionment taking root in his gut and spreading tentacles of anger throughout him, constricting his heart to the point where he felt like collapsing.

Neve was a great actress, he thought bitterly, his hand gripping the back of his chair. And now he knew her true feelings. She may not have been the one who wrote that note, but clearly she was just like her mother, phony and obsessed about money and status. *And just as deceitful as the three nannies he had fired.*

Davide wanted to smash the chair against the wall. Neve wasn't interested in him as a person; no, she was obviously thrilled that she had hooked a guy who had an income and status even higher than hers. *Which is why she had allowed him to take her to his bed…* She had obviously thought it was a good trade…

He clenched his jaw so hard that the pain shot through to his temples. If Neve's note had devastated him eight years ago, her words moments ago had shattered every last ounce of trust and hope that had regenerated in his soul since she had arrived in Valdoro…

And now he'd have to go and face them both; mother and daughter, cut from the same rich cloth. His mouth twisted. He would keep his composure while Neve's mother was at the castle. *Put on the best act of his life.* And he would save his moment of reckoning with Neve till later…

He heard Bianca call out. His heart twisted, not only for himself, but for the way Bianca would feel when he eventually told her that Neve would no longer be staying as her nanny…

CHAPTER TWENTY-THREE

NEVE FELT A tightening in her jaw as she walked into the courtyard. What exactly had her mother bargained for, coming to the castle? And how was she supposed to do her job with her mother around? As her mother gazed at her expectantly, Neve felt her stomach twist with anxiety.

What *she* really wanted was to confront her mother about her manipulative and controlling actions to prevent her from meeting with Davide. Her need to manage Neve's life a decade ago, and even now. Would Lois ever change?

Well, it was time *she* did. Perhaps she had subconsciously allowed her mother to keep controlling her life. Perhaps *she* hadn't been ready to let go of the apron strings.

Not anymore.

There was no time for small talk. Lois had arrived against her wishes, made plans to come to the castle, had expected Davide to drop everything to accommodate her and pick her up, and had even had the effrontery to insinuate that he was making Neve do housekeeping along with her nanny duties.

It *was* time for her to stand up to her mother.

"I'm surprised you were civil to my boss, Mom," she said curtly. "But then again, he's not a *peasant* and *unrefined* as you thought him a decade ago. Did you actually think I would give up my virginity to him? I had no intentions of sinking that low…"

Her mother opened her mouth to reply, but Neve wasn't ready to let her have her say. "I wouldn't be sinking so low as to sleep with anyone unless I was in love with him. I can't believe you wrote that note, Mom. *Really?* What were you afraid was going to happen? That he would whisk me up into the hills and have his way with me? *Come on*, I hardly had the personality to allow *that* to happen!" She shook her head angrily. "It's so sad that you couldn't even trust me."

"It wasn't *you* I didn't trust, darling. It was *him*. I imagined it was the young fellow who had been making eyes with you. *I saw what was in them.*"

"Good God," Neve sputtered. "Admit it, Mom. You thought he was *below* me. *Us.* You didn't want me associating with *a farmer*." Her cheeks burned. *"You would do well to remember your place,"* she mimicked.

"A mother has to look out for her daughter's best interests," her mother said, dabbing her forehead with her napkin.

"No, you have always looked out for *your* best interests," Neve shot back. "He's not the same man he was back then, Mother. He's not in the same *place*. He's got money—lots of money—and more status than you could dream of. And when you found out about my boss, you had to come here to see how Davide's position and status could benefit *you* in some way."

"I came here because I care about you, Neve. It's hard to relinquish motherhood. You'll find that out for yourself one day."

Her mother sounded hurt, but Neve wasn't finished. "You don't have to relinquish motherhood. You just have to relinquish control." She took a deep breath. "And you don't care about me as much as you care about *you* and how you appear to your high society circles," Neve retorted. "I'm done with all of it." She glared at her mother. "If you really care about me, you'll leave and let me do my job here."

"Well... I've been told. *Again*," Lois huffed. "I can't undo what I did eight years ago, Neve. And I'm sorry you feel the way you do about me." She turned to grab her handbag. "I hope you will eventually find it in your heart to forgive me. And don't worry. I won't bother you anymore while I'm in Valdoro."

She started to walk toward the entrance to the kitchen, then stopped to pull a smaller bag out of her handbag. "This is a little something for Bianca. I'll leave it on the kitchen counter."

Neve stared at the retreating figure of her mother. Deflated, she took the box of pastries and followed her inside. Davide and Bianca were approaching. Bianca let go of Davide's hand and ran up to Neve. Davide introduced Bianca to Lois.

"Are you coming to live with us, too?" Bianca asked.

Lois gave an embarrassed laugh. "No, dear. I was just here for a visit."

"I'll drive your mother back to the Villa Morgana," Davide said coolly. "Bianca can stay and have a treat. I won't be long."

After they left, Lois walking stiffly past her, Neve tried to ignore the churning in her stomach. She gave Bianca a snack of almond cookies and milk, and after putting the pastry box in the fridge, Neve took the bag that was on the counter. "Come and open your gift, Bianca," she said brightly, not wanting to show Bianca how shaken the confrontation with her mother had left her.

Bianca ran over and pulled the tissue from the bag, letting it fall to the floor in her excitement. Neve picked it up and when her gaze shifted to the gift in Bianca's hand, she gulped.

It was a photo frame with a three-dimensional angel on one side. The top of the frame showed a sky with glittering stars, and the angel's arms were uplifted to hold one of them. The text at the bottom of the frame read: *Love never dies; it's true. Like the stars in the heavens, our love shines for you.*

And she had included a card.

To Bianca,
    For you to keep a special photo of your mommy and daddy.
God bless you.
Lois Wilder.

Neve didn't know how she had kept it together after seeing her mother's gift and note. She had set the picture frame on the counter, holding her tears back, and had ushered Bianca upstairs to get her overnight bag ready. Signora Lucia would be arriving to pick up Bianca later in the afternoon, Davide had said, which could be anytime now.

She arrived before Davide got back. Neve answered the door to greet her and Rosalia, and after Bianca had rushed to give them both a hug, Neve chatted with Lucia briefly and wished them all a good time. Neve almost lost her balance when Bianca unexpectedly turned around and hugged her around the waist. *"Arrivederci*, Bianca Neve," she giggled, before following Lucia out to her car.

Neve closed the door and promptly burst into tears.

CHAPTER TWENTY-FOUR

NEVE WAS STILL standing there moments later, staring out toward the dark strip of the Ionian Sea, when Davide returned. She felt the corners of her eyes prickling, and as he walked toward her, her tears prevented her from seeing him clearly. She wiped them hastily with her hands, and when her vision cleared, Davide was next to her, but instead of the look of concern that she was expecting, his face was expressionless, except for the hard line of his mouth.

She frowned. "What's the matter, Davide? Did my mother say something to upset you?"

He gave a harsh laugh. "No, it's not what your mother said that upset me." His eyes glinted. "It's what I heard *you* say..." He gestured toward the door. "Let's take this inside. I need a drink."

Neve followed him numbly. *What had she said to have caused Davide to speak to her so icily?* When they were in the kitchen, he poured himself a shot of brandy. She waited by the island, her stomach twisting apprehensively.

After he had downed it, he poured himself another one. Neve's heart thudded in her chest. *Why was he acting this way?*

"Davide, what is going on? Why—?"

"Why do I want to drink myself into oblivion tonight?" he rasped. "I'll tell you why, Signorina Neve." He spat out her name as if it was poison. "Because I hate myself for having trusted you. For believing that you…that you had *feelings* for me." His eyes narrowed. "What a fool I was, to think that you were any better than your mother." He swallowed his second drink. "You and your mother are a great team," he sneered. "You were both disgusted eight years ago when I was a *peasant* and *unrefined*, but how quickly you both changed your tune when you found out I had plenty of money and status…" He reached again for the bottle.

"No! Davide, don't! Please!" Neve grabbed his arm. "I don't know where you got these ideas…"

Davide's gaze swiveled to her hand and frowning, he pried her fingers off him. "You can cut the act now, Neve. I got those ideas from *you*, from what you said to your mother in the courtyard." He raked his hand through his hair. "Here, let me refresh your memory: *Did you actually think I would give up my virginity to him? I had no intentions of sinking that low…* But you had no problem sinking into my bed when you discovered I had more money and status than you could ever imagine. You and your mother can shake hands," he said icily. "And you can start packing. I'll have Lucia book the first possible flight back to Vancouver."

Neve froze as Davide brushed past her to stalk out of the room and into the courtyard.

"Oh. My. God."

She felt her eyes welling up. The glare he had fixed her with had pierced her to the core. *Such disgust in the depths of his eyes…* Neve blinked, but she could not stem the flow of tears. *How could Davide believe she had been so conniving?* With a sob, she ran up to her room and collapsed on the bed, letting herself cry until she was depleted.

When she got up and went to splash cold water on her face, she looked at the bathroom mirror and cringed at her red-rimmed eyes and mottled cheeks. With a heavy heart, she took her suitcase and started packing her clothes into it. Halfway through, she stopped.

What was she doing? She was not going to abandon Bianca, and she certainly wasn't going to accept Davide's damning judgment of her.

She *had* to find him and convince him that he had been wrong...

Davide's garden had always been a place of relaxation for him, but this time, his nerves were too jangled to allow him any hope of destressing. He had strode past the spot where he had kissed Neve and the pain that was already throbbing in his chest had intensified. He had to get out of there and away from the castle. Drive anywhere to distance himself from Neve.

He had just entered the kitchen when Neve appeared and planted herself in front of him, her eyes puffy and red.

"You said you were a fool, Davide. And you *were*, to believe those words you obviously heard without listening to the whole conversation. And I'm not leaving this castle, let alone this country, dammit, until I make you understand." Her eyes bored into his. "I'm not losing you again."

Davide's jaw tensed and he gripped the edge of the island chair. But as Neve kept talking, the muscles in his face and hand began to relax.

"I love *you*, not your money, Davide, and I would be happy living in a cave with you." Neve's eyes glittered. "And I've loved you from the day you stared at me across the road with your beautiful black eyes..."

When she was done, Davide groaned as he pulled her to him tightly. "I'm so sorry, *tesoro*. When I heard you say those words to your mother, my heart crumbled..." He brushed soft kisses on her cheeks. "Don't cry, *amore mio*."

As he reached for the box of tissues on the counter, his gaze fell on the photo frame. He picked it up and raised an eyebrow at Neve.

"My mother brought that for Bianca," Neve said, choking on her words.

Davide read the text on the frame. He set the frame down and closed his eyes. It felt like someone was squeezing his heart. *Hard.* He opened his eyes when he felt Neve wrap her arms around him. He swallowed.

"I miss her," he said, his voice cracking. "Why did this have to happen? To them, to Bianca... *She didn't deserve this.*"

"No child does."

Neve's soft voice and the compassion in her eyes pierced Davide's heart. He felt the pain and grief that he had been holding back for Bianca's sake begin to seep out. Letting out a moan, he broke away from Neve and went to sit down on the leather couch in the living room. He covered his face in his hands and tried to control the dam that was about to break within him. But when Neve came over to sit next to him and put her arm around him, the dam collapsed. He let the grief for the loss of his sister and brother-in-law burst out of him in deep sobs.

The feel of Neve's fingertips caressing his temples and face was calming. He inhaled and exhaled deeply. And then he turned to face her, looking deep into her eyes. He brought her fingers to his lips and brushed them with soft kisses. "Let's get out of here, *tesoro*," he murmured. "I want to take you somewhere special tonight."

CHAPTER TWENTY-FIVE

NEVE FELT RENEWED after her shower. She quickly dried off and chose a midnight-blue halter dress that fell just above her knees and a shimmering rose shawl. In case Davide was planning a walk along the coast, Neve decided on a pair of dressy navy sandals with laces that tied up at her calves. The anticipation of the evening and night ahead with Davide all to herself had her pulse spiking. Trying to keep her hand steady, she applied some dark brown eyeliner and a gentle brush of blue eyeshadow. And a rose lipstick to match her shawl.

She left her hair down but used her curling iron to give it extra body, and satisfied with the way she looked, she grabbed a navy clutch and made her way downstairs.

Davide was waiting in the foyer. He stood up when he saw her at the top of the stairs and strode over to the end of the stairway to wait for her. As she approached the final curve of the stairway, Neve could see the approving spark in his eyes as his gaze swept over her.

She reciprocated the gaze, her heart drumming at how incredibly handsome he was, with his well-fitting dark gray trousers and maroon shirt emphasizing his strong, muscled body. He was holding a single rose in his hands, and as she reached the bottom step, he held it out to her with a smile that sent her heart leaping.

Davide held out his other hand and led her outside toward his Lamborghini. Moments later, as he began the curving descent down the mountainside, Neve held her breath. She gasped at a few hairpin turns, and on one them, her hand impulsively shot out to grasp hold of Davide. He just smiled and when he reached the base of the mountain, he veered off in the direction of the interior, and not the coast, as he had originally mentioned.

"I'm heading to the *other* coast," he said, flashing Neve a grin. "And before too long, we'll be passing through the Aspromonte mountain range." He raised an eyebrow. "Brigand territory in the eighteen-sixties…"

The countryside took on a muted aspect as twilight set in. They passed through vast stretches of olive groves and craggy limestone hills, their shapes and shadows lending a haunting quality to the landscape. With the sensual thrum of the engine and the luxurious comfort of the vehicle, Neve couldn't help but relax, and she settled back in her seat and allowed her eyelids to close…

A soft pressure on her lips woke her up and her eyes blinked open. Davide's face was inches away from hers. She felt her pulse accelerate.

"We're here, Neve. And you must not have been under a deep spell, since it took only one kiss to wake you up…"

Neve quickly straightened in her seat. "Where are we?"

"In the Marina di Scilla, about twenty-two kilometers north of Reggio di Calabria on the Strait of Messina. *Andiamo*, the place where I want to take you is in walking distance."

Davide had parked on the side of the street flanking the beach. He climbed out of the car and opened the door for Neve. She stepped out and stood mesmerized by the yellow lights illuminating the clustered three-story houses across the beach and up the promontory to the castle that rose out of the hill, with its stark sides and square windows overlooking the hamlet and the strait. It looked like something out of a fairy tale.

"That's the Castello Ruffo," Davide said. "It was built by the priests in a time when they needed to protect themselves against Saracen invasions. Nowadays it's used for exhibitions and conferences."

Lampposts illuminated the stretch of beach where people were strolling, children were playing and others were dining. The aromas from the beachside restaurants were making Neve's mouth water.

As they walked along the road, with Davide's arm around her, Neve felt a contentedness she had never felt before. And despite the earlier confrontation with her mother, Neve resolved to make things right between them. Lois's thoughtfulness toward Bianca had touched her, and she hoped that they could work out their problems and come to a new understanding. And maybe in time, Davide could forgive her mother, as well.

Davide turned into a narrow alley that meandered past terraced steps and balconies festooned with geraniums and bougainvillea. These houses were steps from the strait, and the faint scent of salt and fish hung in the air.

A few moments later he was ushering Neve into an exclusive waterfront *trattoria* with a terrace that jutted out over the water. The waiter, who greeted Davide by name, led them to a table in a far corner of the terrace. The lights illuminating the terrace were reflected in the water around them, and with the movement of the waves, it gave Neve the impression that they were suspended above twinkling stars.

Davide pointed to the breakers in the distance. "That's the site of the sea witch, Scylla, the whirlpool personified in Greek mythology as a female monster devouring sailors and impeding the way of the hero Odysseus…" He turned to her, his gaze piercing. "You know, Neve, when I first saw you on my computer screen, I thought you might very well be a sea witch, with those mesmerizing eyes…"

Neve pretended to pout. "That wasn't the first time you thought me a witch."

At Davide's puzzled look, she added, "After you got that note and thought that I had written it…you must have thought me cruel and heartless."

Davide couldn't lie. "I was confused," he murmured. "What I had seen—or thought I had seen—in your eyes was so different from what I had seen written on that note."

"Did you hate me?" she whispered.

"I was crushed," he rasped, "but I never hated you. I admit, it was hard on my ego. But I think I despised myself, for not being your equal, for not being good enough for you."

"That was my mother's opinion, not mine. I wish I had seen the note…" Neve said wistfully.

"It wasn't meant to be…at least not then. If you had come, we might have stolen a kiss. But our destiny was not to meet that night, but eight years later. Our time is *now*."

The waiter approached and Davide ordered an aperitif for both of them and fried calamari as an appetizer followed by eggplant parmigiana and grilled swordfish.

After the waiter left, Davide rose and took Neve's hand. The way she looked in her blue dress and filmy shawl sent his pulse racing. He led her to the railing and for a few moments they looked up at the stars and the lights twinkling in the water. And then, with a muffled groan, he pulled her closer and inhaled the sweet floral scent at her temples.

"I suffered, Neve, losing you before I could even tell you how I felt… But maybe I would have suffered even more if I had spent treasured moments with you and then had had to let you go. Who would have ever believed that destiny would lead us to one another again?"

"I never really believed in destiny before…until now," Neve sighed, resting her head against his chest.

Out of the corner of his eye, Davide saw the waiter set down the drinks and appetizer on their table, but he didn't want to let Neve out of his arms. *Or out of his life.*

"I'm hungry," he whispered huskily against her ear. "For you." He drew back so she could see the love and passion in his eyes. "*Ti amo, tesoro mio.* You are my treasure, Neve, and I will love and honor you for the rest of my life, if you will have me. And Bianca."

Neve's eyes glistened. "*Yes.* I wouldn't have it any other way!" She gave him a lingering kiss. "*Ti amo*, Davide," she told him breathlessly. "And I'm just as hungry." She let out a tinkling laugh. "Let's eat, and we can have *dessert* back at the castle."

By the time they arrived at the castle, Neve was feeling drowsy from the effects of their fabulous dinner and wine. Before she knew it, Davide had scooped her up in his arms and was carrying her into the castle and up the stairs…

He deposited her gently on his bed and removed her shoes. "Don't move," he ordered gruffly and disappeared into his walk-in closet. When he returned, he was carrying a decorative box. He held it out to her somewhat sheepishly.

Neve glanced through the transparent cover and recognized the filmy coral nightgown she had liked at the market. She blinked in disbelief, and then gave Davide a teasing smile. "Either you were psychic or just confident."

"Impulsive and hopeful would be more accurate." He gave her a scorching kiss. "Would you like to wear it tonight, Bianca Neve, or on our honeymoon?"

EPILOGUE

Two weeks later

DAVIDE GOT DOWN on one knee in the same spot where Neve had collided into him when they had first played hide-and-seek. He reached into his vest pocket and pulled out a silver box. When he opened it, Neve gasped. The platinum ring was stunning, with an exquisite two-carat diamond and four small diamonds on either side of the band.

"The eight diamonds represent the years I waited," he said huskily, taking her left hand and slipping the ring on her third finger. "And the round diamond represents my infinite love for you—"

"Can I come in now, Zio Davide?" Bianca called out impatiently, a few steps away.

Davide let his head drop in feigned despair and Neve laughed.

Bianca rushed into the space, her orca in hand. "Can I be your flower girl?" she cried excitely, clasping Neve's arm.

Neve bent down and gathered Bianca in a hug. "I wouldn't dream of having anyone else, *tesoro.*"

"Oh, Bianca!" Lois Wilder joined them, throwing her hands up. "I told you I'd give you the signal when to go in, sweetheart," she said. "Oh, well!" She looked at Neve and Davide, who was still down on one knee, and smiled. "It's time for all of us to celebrate. Come on. I'm treating at the Pasticceria Michelina!" She gave Neve a hug. "I think I owe you two *that*, at the very least. Congratulations, darling!"

After Lois and Bianca had left, Davide held out his hand. Neve slipped her hand into his, and perched herself on his knee, her eyes glittering along with her ring. "*Sposami*, Neve," he said huskily.

Neve looked deep into Davide's eyes. "*Sì*, of course I will marry you, *amore*."

She leaned forward, but suddenly his knee shifted and she lost her balance, sending them both tumbling onto the grass, and the scent of the pink magnolia flowers was as sweet as their kiss.

* * * * *

THE BACHELOR'S BABY SURPRISE

TERI WILSON

For Cameron

Chapter One

"Come quickly… I am tasting stars."
—*Dom Pérignon, at his first sip of champagne*

Evangeline Holly was no stranger to guilty pleasures.

Like Audrey Hepburn, she had a fondness for a nice creamy chocolate cake. In fact, she was on a first-name basis with most everyone at Magnolia Bakery's Bleecker Street location in Greenwich Village.

She was also currently housing not just one, but *two* special-needs Cavalier King Charles spaniels in her very tiny, very *non*-pet-friendly apartment. So yeah. She had her vices.

But she also knew where and when to draw the line. Evangeline knew her limits. And for her, those limits included two noteworthy things she'd never once indulged in—bad wine and one-night stands.

Until now.

Her head throbbed. She dragged her eyelids open, and the first thing her gaze landed on was her pair of dogs snoring madly atop a man's Armani suit jacket that had been discarded on the bedroom floor. Beside it, a pair of trousers and a crisp white Oxford shirt rested in a heap.

Okay then.

She closed her eyes and reminded herself that there wasn't anything inherently wrong with cheap wine or casual sex. It was just that growing up on a vineyard in Upstate New York simply precluded her from experiencing the former. If she was a wine snob, she'd at least come by it honestly.

As for the latter…

Chalk that up to being involved in a devoted, monogamous relationship with the same man for most of her adult life. Also, no one actually had time for intimacy these days, did they? Evangeline had never quite believed everyone was spending as much time in bed as they cheekily hinted at.

She opened her eyes again. Early morning sunlight glinted off the pair of cuff links on her nightstand. There were *cuff links* on her nightstand. Cuff links from Tiffany & Co., but still.

She'd been wrong about everything. So. Very. Wrong.

Most notably the assumption that her relationship was in any way devoted. Or monogamous. On her end, yes. On Jeremy's, not so much. Apparently, he'd been spending plenty of time in bed...with his sous chef. Not Evangeline.

She'd been enlightened three days ago. It was startling how much could change in three measly days. She'd lost her boyfriend. She'd lost her job. Basic truths she'd believed about her life had gone right out the window.

As had Evangeline's previous avoidance of certain weaknesses.

The pounding in her head was a testament that she'd broken her *no bad wine* rule the night before. The evidence of her first-ever one-night stand was far more tangible—from the clothes and the cuff links to the startlingly attractive man lying beside her with his eyes closed, dressed in nothing but her nicest bedsheets.

"Good morning." He spoke without opening his eyes, as if he could sense her staring at him. His voice was delicious, low and unfamiliar. Not at all like Jeremy's.

"Um." She swallowed. What had she been thinking? She'd brought a complete stranger back to her apartment, and here he was. Naked in her bed.

She blamed Jeremy. This was 90 percent his fault. The other ten percent of the blame fell squarely on the shoulders of the pinot grigio she could still taste in the back of her throat. *Pinot grigio*, for God's sake.

"Good morning," she finally said, even though nothing about it seemed good.

She didn't know what to say or how to act. She wasn't even sure where to look, although she couldn't seem to force her gaze away from the owner of the cuff links. He stretched and rolled onto his back, giving her an eyeful of taut male skin and finely sculpted abdominal muscles.

Her throat grew dry. Where on earth had she found this beautiful person? And how had she summoned up the nerve to flirt with him? Flirting must have happened at some point for him to end up here, right?

Jeremy's voice rose up from the pinot-drenched fog in her mind. *Of course I've been sleeping around. What did you expect? You're not exactly a sexual person, Evangeline. I just need more.* Most *people need more.*

So that's how she'd found the courage. When your boyfriend insinuated you were terrible in bed, you either curled up into a ball or went about proving him wrong. Two days in the fetal position had been more than enough.

The sound of a deeply male throat clearing dragged her back to the present.

Evangeline's gaze flitted from the stranger's trim waist to his drowsy half grin. He'd caught her ogling him. Perfect.

Her face went hot. "Look, um…"

"Ryan," he said, tucking his arms behind his head, causing the sheet to dip even lower.

Don't look. Do. Not.

She looked, and a sultry warmth washed over her, settling in the very same areas that Jeremy had called dead just three days prior.

"Right." She bit her lip and met his gaze again. "Ryan. I knew that."

"I believe you." He winked. Clearly he didn't, even though Ryan had been the first name that came to her once she'd spotted the *RW* engraved on his cuff links. "Eve."

Eve?

No one had ever called her Eve. Always Evangeline.

She remembered hearing somewhere that *Eve* meant *living*. She tried not to think too hard about that while there was a naked man named Ryan with the body of a Greek god stretched out beside her. "Anyway, *Ryan*, what I'm trying to say is that I don't typically do this sort of thing."

"Yes, I know. You mentioned that last night. A couple of times, actually." He rested a warm hand on her upper thigh and gave her a smile that seemed a bit sad around the edges. Bittersweet.

She felt oddly transparent, as if the man in her bed knew more about her than was possible after only a handful of hours together. Her thigh was suddenly awash in goose bumps.

"Good. So long as we're clear—this was a one-night affair. A mistake, probably. I don't expect you to ask for my number or anything." She slid her leg out of reach, tucking it beneath the covers.

His smile faded. The dimples which had been barely visible beneath the layer of scruff on his chiseled jaw disappeared entirely. "A mistake?"

She nodded, because of course it had been a mistake.

A man was the very last thing she needed, even for one night. Particularly *this* man, whose hands she couldn't look at without imagining them on her skin. And whose mouth made her want to linger in bed and revisit the most wicked portions of the previous evening. "Good grief, how much wine did I have last night?"

She clamped her mouth closed. God, had she actually asked that question out loud?

"Quite a bit." Ryan's frown deepened. She couldn't stop saying his name in her head. *Ryan. Ryan. Ryan.* "Although you didn't seem drunk. Not even tipsy. Should I be apologizing right now? Something tells me I should."

Another perk of having a vineyard in your childhood backyard—an incredibly high tolerance. For wine, at least. Even on the rare occasion when she drank enough to *feel* like she'd overindulged, it never showed.

"You have nothing to apologize for. Truly." Memories flitted through her consciousness. The taste of him. The feel of him. The weight of him on top of her as he'd pushed himself inside.

It had been exactly what she'd wanted.

Exquisite.

A shiver coursed through her, and she leaped out of the bed to prevent herself from reaching for him again.

Ryan's gaze settled on her, and she felt it as keenly as if it were a caress. Her thoughts screamed. *Ryan. Ryan. Ryan.* She'd cried out his name last night, hadn't she?

Oh God.

She crossed her arms, and his gaze drifted lower, lingering on her bare breasts. She was every bit as naked as he was, which made perfect sense, given the situation. She'd just been so preoccupied with *his* nakedness that she hadn't noticed her own.

"What if I *wanted* to ask for your number?" he said, making no move whatsoever to evacuate her bed.

How long was he planning on staying? Did Ryan not realize how one-night stands worked?

Ryan. Ryan. Ryan.

Evangeline had repeated the name to herself so many times now that it no longer made sense. She wondered what the *W* on the cuff links stood for, but she didn't dare ask. If she knew his full name, she might be tempted to look him up later in another moment of weakness.

Not happening.

She grabbed the quilt off the end of the bed, wrapped it around herself and shook her head. "You don't want my number."

A muscle flicked in his jaw. "I'm certain I do."

"No." She shook her head even harder. "You don't."

If he knew the first thing about her situation, he'd run for the hills. She wouldn't blame him in the slightest.

"Then I must be an idiot," he said.

Did he have to be so charming? He probably couldn't help it. It was probably part of his genetic makeup, like the abs. And the voice. And the fathomless blue of his eyes.

Evangeline had never seen eyes quite so blue.

She averted her gaze from them.

"Honestly, you don't need to do this. Everything's fine. I'm fine. This was—" *Just what I needed.* She swallowed around the lump that had formed in her throat, seemingly out of nowhere "—fun."

"Fun," he echoed.

The word sounded oddly hollow, and Evangeline instantly wanted to take it back. She had to bite the inside of her cheek to stop herself from telling him the whole truth—that she was lost; she'd been lost for a very long time and that the real reason she never did this sort of thing was because it scared the life out of her.

Intimacy, in all its forms, involved a level of vulnerability that she couldn't quite handle. She thought Jeremy had understood that about her. Wrong again.

"Here you go, then." She bent to retrieve his abandoned shirt and trousers and handed them to him. When his fingertips brushed against hers, the lump in her throat doubled in size.

Leave. Please, leave.

He climbed out of the bed and started to get dressed. Thank goodness.

She glanced at the floor, where Olive and Bee were still sound asleep on top of Ryan's suit jacket. Olive's paws twitched. She was chasing rabbits in her sleep again.

Evangeline tugged gently on the wool Armani, trying her hardest to slip it out from beneath the sleeping dogs unnoticed. Like the old magician's tablecloth trick.

No such luck. Bee was completely deaf, therefore extremely sensitive to movement. She woke with a start, pawing at Evangeline's shins. Olive let out a squeaky dog yawn and hopped onto the bed, where she stood and stared at Ryan while he zipped up his pants.

He glanced up, spotted Olive watching him and then reached to scratch behind her ears.

"Pet her from the left side. She can't see out of her right eye, so you might startle her," Evangeline said.

He followed her advice. The little Cavalier's tail wagged furiously. Bee scrambled up onto the bed to join in the fun.

"Sweet dogs," Ryan said, and Evangeline's heart gave a little tug.

He somehow managed to look even more attractive, surrounded by adorable dogs. Because of course.

"Thank you. They technically belong to my grandfather, but he recently moved into an extended care facility, so they live here now." Why was she telling him this?

"I'm sorry to hear that." His voice went as soft as velvet, like he really meant it.

If he didn't leave soon, she'd probably offer to cook him breakfast.

"Here." She shoved his suit jacket at him. Every inch of it was covered in dog hair.

He pretended not to notice and slid it on, anyway. And that small act of kindness was almost more than she could bear. Maybe last night hadn't been a mistake after all. Maybe the mistake was happening right now.

Maybe she shouldn't be in such a hurry to let him go.

"Goodbye, then," she said in as firm a voice as she could manage.

He came around the bed, and when he was an arm's length away, he lifted his hand as if to cup her face. She took a tiny backward step.

His hand fell to his side. "Goodbye, Eve."

And then he was gone.

* * *

Ryan Wilde stood outside Eve's apartment and watched as the door shut in his face.

Well, he thought, *that was different.*

He'd never been so summarily tossed out of a woman's bed before. Then again, he typically didn't make a habit out of bedding women he didn't actually know.

Especially lately.

Ryan's love life had been rather complicated in recent weeks, thanks to the *New York Times*. He'd been doing his best to avoid romantic entanglements altogether.

He walked down the hall, making his way to the building's front steps and pulled his cell phone from the inside pocket of his suit jacket—which looked more like a fur coat at the moment—and rang the Bennington Hotel's driver.

The chauffeur answered on the first ring. "Mr. Wilde, how can I help you?"

Ryan didn't often take advantage of the more luxurious perks that came with being chief financial officer of the Bennington, but having a driver on standby was nice at a time like this. He glanced up and down the picturesque street. The sun was just coming up, bathing the neighborhood brownstones in soft winter hues of violet and blue. The snowy sidewalks were empty, save for an older man opening up the newsstand on the corner. "Are you free to come pick me up in the Village?"

He was, of course. Who needed a limo this time of day?

Ryan gave the driver his location, then pocketed his phone again. He rubbed his hands together. His breath was a visible puff of vapor in the crisp air. What the hell had he done with his coat?

He lifted his gaze to the row of windows on the third floor, trying to guess which one was Eve's. He wished he'd left his Burberry trench up there so he'd have a legitimate excuse to see her again, but he hadn't. He'd left it on the back of a chair at the wine bar the night before—forgotten, completely—right around the time he'd spotted Eve across the room, brandishing a butcher knife.

It had been one of the most bizarre things he'd ever seen. She'd grabbed a bottle of champagne and before he'd been able to process what he was seeing, she severed the neck of the bottle with the knife. Sliced it clean off, just below the cork. It made a loud popping sound, and she'd stood there with a quiet smile on her face while bubbles spilled down her arm. The group of people at her table cheered. All men, he'd noticed.

She wasn't on a date, though, from what he could tell. The table was piled with note cards, as if they were some kind of study group.

Note cards. In the middle of a wine bar on Friday night.

"That was quite the party trick," Ryan had said after he'd abandoned his coat, his drink and the trio of business associates he'd been meeting with.

He'd had to talk to her. *Had* to.

For the better part of a week, he'd been avoiding every marriage-minded single woman in Manhattan. But the knife-wielding goddess had gotten under his skin instantly. He wasn't even sure why.

Yes, she was pretty. More than pretty, actually.

Beautiful, with full red lips and long, spun-gold hair—the kind of hair that made him hard just thinking about what it would feel like sliding through his fingers.

But it had been more than her looks that had him spellbound from all the way across the crowded room. He'd felt an inexplicable pull deep in his chest when he looked at her. And as he came closer, there'd been something else. She'd had secrets in her eyes.

"It's not a party trick," she'd said, looking him up and down. A scarlet flush made its way up her porcelain face. "It's called sabering."

She'd gone on to explain that French cavalry officers had used their swords in a similar manner to open champagne during the Napoleonic Wars. Which didn't explain in the slightest why she was doing it in a wine bar on the Upper West Side, but Ryan hadn't cared.

It had fascinated him. *She'd* fascinated him…

Fascinated him enough that he very purposefully neglected to mention his last name.

A car rounded the corner. Ryan turned in the direction of the sound of tires crunching on packed snow, but it wasn't the Bennington limo. Where was the damned thing? He was freezing.

He bowed his head against the wind and walked toward the newsstand, hoping the old man could sell him some coffee.

He felt bad about the name thing, even now. Even after she'd shown him the door within minutes of waking up in her bed. It wasn't as if he'd lied to her. He'd just left off his surname.

Call me Ryan.

Thinking about that made him wince. It made him sound like a player, when in actuality, he was anything but.

That was the big irony of his current situation. Practically overnight, and through no fault of his own, he'd developed a *reputation*. A reputation that had no basis in reality.

It had been a relief when he realized Eve had no idea who he was.

Eve, with her butcher knife and lovely head full of history.

"Excuse me," he said.

The man behind the newsstand looked up. "Yeah?"

"Have you got any coffee back there?"

The man nodded. "Sure do. Extra hot."

"Perfect." Ryan opened his wallet and removed a few bills. As he handed the old man the money, his gaze snagged on a magazine.

Gotham. But the title didn't matter. It was the image on the magazine's cover that gave him pause.

A man's face.

His face.

If Evangeline Holly hadn't known who he was last night, she would now.

Chapter Two

Six weeks later

Ryan was late.

In the three years since he'd been named CFO of the Bennington, he'd been the first member of the executive staff to arrive for work every morning. He was notorious for it.

Sometimes the chief executive officer purposely tried to get there first, just to get under Ryan's skin. But Ryan had a sixth sense when it came to predicting moves like that, probably because Zander Wilde wasn't just the CEO. He was also Ryan's cousin. The two men had known each other a lifetime. Ryan knew Zander like a brother.

Consequently, he wasn't the least bit shocked to find Zander waiting for him when he strode into his office five minutes later than his usual arrival time. Annoyed, yes. Shocked, not so much.

"Well, well, well. Look what the cat dragged in." Zander was reclining in Ryan's chair with his feet resting on the smooth mahogany surface of his desk, ankles crossed. He folded the newspaper in his hands and shot Ryan a triumphant grin. "Looks like I got here first."

Ryan set his briefcase down and lowered himself into one of his office guest chairs. "Pleased with yourself?"

Zander's smile widened. "I am, actually."

"Enjoy your victory." Ryan lifted a brow. "Especially since it was three years in the making."

Zander shrugged. "I'll take it. A win is a win."

"If you say so, but would it kill you to get your feet off my desk?" He glared at his cousin's wing tips.

Zander rolled his eyes before planting his feet on the floor and sitting up straight. "I need to talk to you about something. But first, what's wrong? You're not dying or terminally ill, are you? You're never late."

"It's 7:35 a.m.," Ryan said flatly.

Zander's only response was a blank stare.

"I'm not dying. I was just…" He cleared his throat. "Delayed."

"Delayed?" Zander smirked. "I get it now. This is a bachelor-specific problem."

He cast a pointed glance at the framed magazine cover hanging above the desk. Gotham Names Ryan Wilde New York's Hottest Bachelor of the Year, the headline screamed.

Six weeks had passed since Ryan had learned about his "coronation," as Zander liked to put it. His feelings about the matter had remained unchanged since that snowy morning at the newsstand in the West Village. Namely, he loathed it.

He especially loathed seeing the magazine cover on the wall of his office every day, but it was preferable to having it on display in the Bennington lobby, where Zander had originally hung it. Ryan suspected it had been a joke and his cousin had never intended to leave it there, but he wasn't taking any chances. The terms of their compromise dictated that the framed piece made its home on the wall above Ryan's desk.

Oh joy.

"Let me guess." Zander narrowed his gaze. "You were out late last night fighting women off with a stick."

Hardly.

Ryan hadn't indulged in female company for weeks. *Six* weeks, in fact. Although his recent abstinence wasn't altogether related to the *Gotham* feature article.

He couldn't seem to get Evangeline Holly out of his head. A couple of times, he'd even gone so far as to visit her building in the Village. He'd lingered on the front steps for a few minutes, thinking about their night together.

It had been good.

Better than good.

It had been spectacular, damn it. The best sex of his life, which was reason enough to let it go and move on. That kind of magic only came along once. Any attempt to recreate it would have been in vain.

Maybe not, though. Maybe the night hadn't been magical at all. Maybe *she'd* been the magic.

He'd considered this both times he'd nearly knocked on her door. Then he'd remembered how eager she'd been to get rid of him on the morning after, and he'd come to his senses. The woman had refused to give him her phone number. That seemed like a pretty solid indication that she would've been less than thrilled to find him knocking on her door.

"I watched the Rangers game and then went to bed," he said. Then for added emphasis, "Alone."

"So what gives? Why are you late?" Zander frowned. "Wait. Don't tell me the groupies are back."

Ryan wanted to correct him. The groupies weren't technically back, because they'd never gone away. They'd been hanging around the Bennington for nearly two months—since the day the *New York Times* had decided to throw a wrench in his otherwise peaceful life.

He should have seen it coming. The Bennington had been the subject of a wildly popular series of columns in the *Times*' Weddings page. A reporter for the Vows column had speculated that the hotel was cursed after several weddings in the Bennington ballroom had ended like a scene from *Runaway Bride*.

But that was ancient history.

Should have been, anyway. Ryan had negotiated a cease-fire with the reporter. In exchange for exclusive coverage of Zander's recent nuptials, the reporter declared the curse over and done with. But Ryan hadn't anticipated that the last line of her column would imply he was on the lookout for a bride himself.

It had been brief—just a single sentence. But that handful of words had been enough. Women had been throwing themselves at him in a steady stream—

morning, noon and night. His photo on the cover of *Gotham* had only made things worse.

Ryan sighed. "There are half a dozen of them waiting for me in the lobby. I had to go around the block and come in through the service entrance in the back."

"You *had* to?" Zander let out a snort. "Here's an idea. Call me crazy, but why don't you go to the lobby right now, talk to the lovely ladies and ask one of them out on a date?"

He couldn't be serious. "Absolutely not."

Those women knew nothing about him, other than the fact that he was single. And rich. It didn't take a genius to know why they wanted to marry him, a total stranger.

No, thank you. He'd nearly been married once already, and once was enough. Never again.

Zander rolled his eyes. "You realize almost every man in New York would trade places with you in a heartbeat right now, don't you?"

"Is that so?" Ryan crossed his arms. "You wouldn't."

"Of course I wouldn't. I'm a happily married newlywed."

Precisely.

Ryan was thrilled for Zander. He really was. But that didn't mean he was going to pick a woman at random from the marriage-minded crowd in the lobby. This wasn't an episode of *The Bachelor*. This was his life.

"Good for you. I prefer my dalliances more temporary. Short-term and strings-free. Can we talk about something else now?" *Anything* else. "You said you needed to speak to me. I trust it's about something other than my personal life."

"It is." Zander picked up his discarded newspaper, spread it open and slid it across the desk toward Ryan. "Have you seen this?"

He glanced down. The *New York Times*. Not his favorite media outlet of late, for obvious reasons.

At least it wasn't open to the Weddings page.

"The food section?" Surely he hadn't merited a mention in one of the cuisine columns. "No, I haven't."

"The restaurant column contains an interesting tidbit. Right here." Zander indicated a paragraph halfway down the page.

Ryan scanned it.

Carlo Bocci was spotted checking into the Plaza last night, fueling rumors that he's in town for his annual month-long restaurant tour on behalf of the *Michelin Guide*. This time last year, Mr. Bocci visited a total of thirty-five New York eateries, ultimately bestowing the coveted Michelin star on fewer than ten. Only one of those restaurants, The White Swan, was awarded three Michelin stars, the highest possible ranking. The White Swan was recently named America's finest restaurant by *Food & Wine* magazine.

He looked up. "Let me guess. We're upset that he's staying at the Plaza instead of the Bennington."

"No. It doesn't matter where he stays. What matters is…"

Ryan finished for him. "The Michelin stars."

"Precisely." Zander's mouth hitched into a half grin. "Do you have any idea what a three-star Michelin ranking for Bennington 8 would mean?"

Bennington 8, the hotel's premiere fine dining restaurant, was located in the rooftop atrium. With its sweeping views of Manhattan, it already performed remarkably well as far as bookings went. But three Michelin stars would keep their reservations calendar full six months out.

It would mean money.

A lot of money.

An *obscene* amount of money.

The Bennington could use that kind of income since the runaway bride curse had put a serious dent in their cash flow. They were bouncing back, but not fast enough.

Ryan frowned and smoothed down his tie. "Three stars? Do you really think that's doable?"

They didn't even know if Bennington 8 was on Carlo Bocci's review list. The list was secret. Ryan suspected he booked his reservations under an assumed name and showed up when least expected, as most restaurant reviewers did.

Zander shook his head. "No, not the way we stand at the moment. Which is why you and I will be in interviews all afternoon today and tomorrow. As long as it takes."

"You want to hire a new chef? I'm not sure that's a wise idea." The chef they had was one of the best in the city. They'd never get anyone else of his caliber on such short notice, much less someone better.

"Agreed. Patrick is as good as we're going to get.

As far as food is concerned, we're golden. But that's only half the battle, isn't it?"

Ryan glanced back down at the newspaper and his gaze zeroed in on three italicized words—*Food & Wine* magazine.

"Wine," Ryan said, nodding slowly. "You want to hire a sommelier."

"A wine director—someone with impeccable credentials. Without a good somm, we haven't got a chance. Have we got room in the budget to hire someone?"

"I'll make room." He'd be staring at spreadsheets all day, trying to make it work. But that was fine. Numbers were Ryan's specialty. There were no gray areas with numerical figures, only black and white.

Just the way Ryan liked it.

Zander stood, folded the copy of the *Times* and tucked it under his arm. "Great. I've already put out some feelers. I'll start lining up interviews. Clear your calendar."

"Done." Ryan rounded the desk and reclaimed his seat.

Zander lingered in the doorway. "Let's hope we find someone immediately. This could be tough, but surely there's an out-of-work somm somewhere in the city who's also charismatic enough to impress Bocci."

Ryan's thoughts flitted back to six weeks ago. To a little wine bar in the Village. To Evangeline Holly, her butcher knife and the way her lips had tasted of warm grapes, fresh from the vine.

He pushed the memory away.

Zander was asking the impossible, but Ryan was

grateful for the challenge. He needed to get his focus back. He needed to forget about the numerous women who wanted to marry him. He especially needed to forget about the one who *didn't*.

He shot Zander a look of grim determination. "If the right person is out there, trust me, we'll find 'em."

Evangeline was getting desperate.

If she was being honest with herself—truly, *brutally* honest—she'd passed the point of desperation a few days ago.

Six weeks was a long time to go without a paycheck, especially when she was already contributing more than she could afford to her grandfather's care.

Maybe she'd been impulsive.

So she and Jeremy had broken up. So he'd been sleeping with his sous chef. Did that really mean Evangeline couldn't stay on at the restaurant?

Of course that's what it means. Are you insane? Don't even think about crawling back.

She lifted her chin and marched through the revolving doors of the Bennington Hotel.

She had to get this job. If she didn't, crawling back to Jeremy was exactly what she'd be forced to do by day's end.

"Can I help you?" The woman behind the reception desk gazed impassively at her.

"Yes, I'm here for an interview. I have an appointment at four o'clock." Evangeline forced a smile and tightened her grip on her Everlane tote bag—a leftover luxury from her previous life.

It was startling how much things could change in

a month and a half. She'd thought she'd had everything figured out. She'd been happy.

At least she'd thought she had been happy. Now she wasn't so sure.

You were *happy. You were perfectly content with Jeremy. Stop thinking about* that *night.*

She swallowed. The one-night stand was still messing with her head, six weeks after the fact. Which was all the proof she needed that one-night stands were *not* her thing. Lesson learned.

In the days since she'd woken up to the sight of those unfamiliar cuff links on her bedside table and the outrageously handsome man in her bed, she'd questioned nearly everything about her past relationship and life in general.

How was it possible to feel such an intense connection with someone she'd only just met? She'd gone to bed with the man, and she hadn't even known his last name.

She knew it now, though. Wilde. Ryan Wilde. It was kind of hard not to notice his name and face on every newsstand in Manhattan. *Gotham* magazine had named him New York's hottest bachelor or something ridiculous like that.

Of course. No wonder she'd been so charmed by him. There hadn't actually been anything special about their night together. He was just really, really good at sex. He probably couldn't even help it. It was an occupational hazard of being the city's biggest playboy.

Out of all the men in Manhattan, she'd fallen into bed with *him*. She was so mortified that she hadn't even bought the magazine with his face on the cover. She wanted to forget that night had ever happened.

Unfortunately, she couldn't. It was too damned memorable.

She blushed every time she thought about it, and she'd spent far too long trying to figure out why she'd never felt so passionate in bed with Jeremy.

So maybe she hadn't been as happy with him as she'd thought. Clearly she'd been wrong about things. *A lot* of things.

But she'd at least been on the verge of having her dream job handed to her on a silver platter. And now...

Now here she was, applying for a position she was in no way qualified for. Her only hope was that the Bennington Hotel was every bit as desperate as she was.

"Have a seat, Miss Holly. The general manager will be with you in just a moment." The woman behind the reception desk motioned toward one of the lobby's plush velvet sofas, situated beneath a glittering crystal chandelier.

"Thank you." Evangeline flashed another smile and headed across the marble floor.

She could do this. The hotel was, in fact, desperate. At least that's what Colin, one of the study partners in her wine group, had told her when he called to tell her about the job opening. They needed a sommelier, and they needed one fast.

Surely all the best somms in Manhattan were already employed. Evangeline hoped so. If she had to compete for this job against even one sommelier with actual credentials, she was toast.

"Hello," she said to the three other women sitting in the waiting area. Her competition, she assumed.

Odd.

Most sommeliers were men, particularly the ones who held wine director titles. At the highest certified level—master sommelier—men claimed 85 percent of the spots.

All three women swiveled their gazes in Evangeline's direction, but none of them returned the greeting. The one closest to her—a glossy brunette wearing a blouse that seemed far too low-cut to be considered professional—looked her up and down and finally spoke.

"Interesting, but I doubt you're his type." She sniffed and crossed one tawny leg over the other.

"I beg your pardon," Evangeline said.

His *type*?

Whose type?

And what kind of pervy work environment was this?

The brunette shrugged. "Just a hunch. There are a lot of us. It's going to take more than a tasteful pencil skirt and a red lip to stand out."

Evangeline blinked and fought the urge to flee.

Don't let her get to you. You know wine. She's probably trying to psych you out.

It was working. She was desperate, but not desperate enough to use her cleavage to make an impression.

What am I doing here?

She should have known this opportunity was too good to be true.

She stood, ready to bolt, but someone called her name before she could take a step.

"Miss Holly?" A man in a dark suit extended his hand. "I'm Elliot Ross, the general manager. We spoke on the phone earlier this morning."

She shook his hand, relief coursing through her when he kept his gaze firmly focused on her eyes. Not her pencil skirt. "Pleased to meet you."

The other women were no longer paying her any attention whatsoever. Things were getting weirder by the minute.

"The CEO and CFO are conducting the interviews upstairs in the restaurant. If you'll come with me, we'll get things underway." Elliot Ross waved her toward the shiny gold elevator doors.

Evangeline followed.

Once inside the elevator, he pushed the button marked Rooftop. "We appreciate your willingness to come on such short notice. The CEO is keen to fill this position as soon as possible."

Thank goodness. "I'm available to start right away."

"Excellent. You're the last of the candidates to be interviewed this afternoon, and I'm afraid I neglected to include your name on the list. Do you have a résumé?"

She'd hoped to avoid having to talk about her qualifications. A pipe dream, obviously. Couldn't she just talk about wine? She was good at that, regardless of what her résumé indicated.

"Here." She handed him a copy of her qualifications, minimal as they were.

Shake it off. This job is perfect for you.

Then the elevator doors swung open, and Evangeline realized she had something much more important to worry about than her lack of experience. Correction: some*one.*

Someone who'd been naked in her bed the last time she'd seen him, unless spotting his face on all those magazine covers counted.

Someone named Ryan Wilde.

Chapter Three

What was happening?

What was Ryan Wilde, her one-night stand, doing at her job interview—the most important job interview she'd ever had?

"Miss Holly, thank you for coming." Another man—the only man in the room she *hadn't* slept with—had spoken. She'd nearly forgotten he was there. Every bit of awareness in her body was focused squarely on Ryan. "I'm Zander Wilde, CEO of the Bennington."

"It's lovely to meet you," she said.

At least that's what she thought she said. She wasn't sure what words were actually coming out of her mouth.

Zander cleared his throat, and Evangeline realized she wasn't even looking at him. He was talking to her, and she was staring right past him, fixated on Ryan.

She couldn't seem to tear her gaze away from Ryan's chiseled face. He seemed even more handsome than she remembered. How was that possible? She swallowed—hard—and tried to figure out what was different about him.

He was a bit cleaner cut, for one thing. The dark scruff that had lined his jaw the last time she'd seen him was gone. Naturally. He'd probably woken up in his own bed, in his own apartment, where he'd shaved with his own razor.

He was also wearing glasses, which unfortunately failed to lessen the effect of his dreamy blue eyes. In fact, they looked even bluer behind the square cut black frames. Forget-me-not blue.

Zander cleared his throat again, louder this time. "Do you two know each other?"

"No," she blurted.

Ryan simultaneously said, "Yes, we do."

Zander glanced back and forth between them. "Which is it? Yes or no?"

She'd just told a bald-faced lie. The interview was off to a stellar start.

"Actually…" She took a deep breath and tried to figure out a way to change her answer that wouldn't make her sound like a crazy person.

"Actually, it seems I'm mistaken," Ryan said smoothly. "We don't know one another. Forgive me… Miss Holly, is it?"

He offered her his hand, and she had no choice but to take it.

"Yes, that's correct." Her voice sounded breathier

than it should have, and she couldn't make herself let go of his hand.

It was warm. Familiar. And when she looked down at the place where his fingertips brushed against her skin, all she could think about was the pad of his thumb dragging softly, slowly against the swell of her bottom lip.

Let go! Let go of his hand.

She dropped it like a hot potato and turned to face Zander. "I'm assuming the wine director reports to you since you're the CEO."

Ryan couldn't be her boss. No way.

Not that she'd gotten the job yet. Her chances were slim to none. Colin had mentioned they'd interviewed a master sommelier. Less than two hundred people in the world held that title. And presumably none of them had had sex with Ryan Wilde.

Zander's gaze narrowed. "Technically, the position reports to the CEO. But the wine director will work closely with the CFO, particularly with regard to the wine budget. So I suppose a certain amount of compatibility is important."

"Compatibility." Evangeline's gaze flitted toward Ryan, and he sent her a nearly imperceptible wink. She wanted to die. "Right."

"Shall we proceed?" Zander motioned toward a table in the center of the room.

"Absolutely." She did her best to ignore the way her knees went wobbly as she crossed the vast space and took a seat.

So it had come to this?

After a six-week-long job search, her only choices

were working for the man who'd dumped her or drawing up wine budgets with her one-night stand?

Lovely.

Also ironic, considering she'd so recently been accused of being an ice queen.

But she was getting ahead of herself, wasn't she? She hadn't been offered the job at Bennington 8 yet, and at the rate things were going, she wouldn't be.

She lifted her chin, met Zander's gaze across the table and decided to pretend Ryan wasn't even there. "The atmosphere here is stunning."

"Thank you," Zander said and glanced up at the glass dome ceiling overhead.

Snow fell softly against the atrium, and the twinkling lights of Manhattan glittered against the darkening sky. The interior of the restaurant was the epitome of cool winter elegance, with crisp white linens and pale blue velvet chairs. Evangeline felt like she was sitting inside a snow globe—trapped inside a perfect world, immune to the swirling chaos outside.

She took a deep breath and gave the snow globe a good, hard shake. "But your wine list is weak at best."

Ryan let out a quiet laugh, reminding her that he was still there, sitting beside her. She allowed herself a quick glance at him.

He arched a brow.

She kept her expression as neutral as possible and redirected her gaze at Zander.

A muscle flicked in his jaw. "Interesting. The other candidates didn't seem to think so."

"Are you sure? Or were they simply trying to flatter you?" She smiled sweetly at him. "I won't do that."

"Clearly," he muttered.

"But that means you can trust me to give you my honest opinion. And my opinion of your current list is that it's not good enough." She swallowed. If she didn't get the job, she'd at least make an impression.

Impressions were important. Being a sommelier was about more than choosing wine. It was about service. A good somm made drinking a glass of wine a memorable experience. There was an art to talking about wine and presenting a bottle—to opening it and pouring its contents.

People often overlooked that part of the job, and it was Evangeline's biggest strength.

"How would you change the list?" Zander said.

She was ready for this. Bennington 8's wine list was listed on its website, and she'd committed it to memory.

"For starters, I'd eliminate the pinot grigio. There are far better light-bodied whites." She studiously avoided Ryan's gaze, since it was apparently his wine of choice.

Then she told herself she was being ridiculous. He probably didn't even remember ordering multiple bottles of it all those weeks ago.

He laughed—with just a little too much force— and when she ventured a glance in his direction, the smirk on his face told her that his memory of their night together was just as intact as hers was.

Her face went hot, and she looked away.

"What else?" Zander asked, leaning forward in his chair. "Do enlighten us."

"I'd cut your California wines by two-thirds.

You've only got three old-world wines on your list. That's unacceptable."

"How so?" Ryan said.

"Wine is about history. The Roman army didn't march on water. Roman soldiers marched on wine. A good old-world wine lets you experience the past as you drink it. You can taste everything—the earth, the rivers, the sunshine of centuries. There's nothing quite so beautiful."

Ryan and Zander exchanged a look that Evangeline wasn't sure how to interpret. She was either nailing it, or she sounded delusional. There was no hiding the fact that she was a wine nerd of the highest order.

"I'm sure most of your customers walk in here asking for wines from Napa Valley and Sonoma, California, or the Finger Lakes region upstate because that's what they're familiar with." She shrugged. "They don't know what they're missing. That's why you need a wine expert."

Zander glanced down at the sheet of paper on the table in front of him. "But I'm looking at your résumé, and there's no mention of a sommelier certificate of any sort."

Here we go.

This was where each and every one of her other interviews had gone south. Way south.

"I'm self-taught. My family owns a vineyard upstate." *Not anymore, remember?* She blinked and corrected herself. "Owned."

Ryan's gaze narrowed ever so slightly, and she felt nearly as exposed as she'd been the last time they'd stood in the same room together.

She took a deep breath. "I'm studying for the certification exam, though. I should be prepared to take it when it's offered next April."

Zander frowned. "That's several months from now."

"Yes, I know." She smiled, but neither of the men met her gaze. Not even Ryan.

She needed to do something. Fast.

"Let me open a bottle for you," she blurted. "Please."

Zander glanced at his watch, which was pretty much the universal sign that time was up. The interview was over. "I don't think—"

Ryan cut him off. "Let her do it."

Evangeline felt like kissing him all of a sudden. Not that the thought hadn't already crossed her mind. This time, though, she had to physically stop herself from popping out of her chair and kissing him smack on the lips.

"Excellent. Why don't you point me in the direction of your wine cooler, and I'll select a bottle?" She stood before Zander could argue.

His gaze swiveled back and forth between her and Ryan again, just like when they'd given opposite answers to his question about whether they knew one another.

He knows. It was probably written all over her face. *News flash: I slept with your cousin.*

Was there a woman in Manhattan whom Ryan Wilde *hadn't* slept with? That was the real question.

"Very well." Zander waved a hand, and the hotel's general manager appeared out of nowhere. "Show Miss Holly to the wine cooler, please. And bring her a corkscrew."

She smiled. "Oh, I won't need a corkscrew."

* * *

Ryan watched as Evangeline studied the wines lined up on their sides in the cooler on the far side of the restaurant. He knew he shouldn't stare, but he couldn't quite help it.

After weeks of resisting the temptation to see her again, she'd fallen right into his lap. Metaphorically speaking, obviously. She clearly had no actual interest in his lap—or any of his other body parts. She didn't even want to admit they knew each other.

Maybe because they didn't. They'd shared one night together. What did he really know about her? Nothing. He'd learned more about her in the last half hour than he'd known when he took her to bed, a realization that didn't sit well for some reason. Especially the part about the pinot grigio.

"What's going on?" Zander muttered under his breath, dragging Ryan's attention away from the lush curve of Evangeline's hips as she bent to retrieve a bottle of red. "And don't evade the question, because something is most definitely going on here. It's written all over your face."

Ryan loved Zander like a brother, but he wasn't about to tell him the truth.

For starters, he didn't kiss and tell. What had happened between him and Evangeline was personal. She'd made it more than clear that she didn't want Zander to know they'd spent the night together, and Ryan wasn't about to out her as a liar in the middle of a job interview.

Because as uncomfortable as working together might be, she was perfect for the job.

"She's the one," he said. "Come on, can't you see it?"

Zander's eyes narrowed. "No, actually. I can't. We have at least half a dozen more qualified applicants. I'm not sure Carlo Bocci is going to be impressed by a self-proclaimed wine expert with romantic notions about tasting history in a glass of Burgundy."

"She knows her stuff. Admit it." She was smart. Ryan loved that about her. He could have sat there and listened to her talk about wine all night.

And then he would have gone home alone, obviously. Because he sure as hell couldn't go to bed with her again if she was going to work at the Bennington.

His chest grew tight at the thought. "She's a storyteller. Customers will eat that up, Bocci included."

Zander lifted a brow. "Again, why do I get the feeling there's more going on here than a simple job interview?"

Ryan didn't bother responding, but he couldn't manage to tear his gaze from Evangeline, even as Zander glared at him.

"I knew it," Zander muttered. "You're attracted to her."

"Enough," Ryan said through gritted teeth.

She was walking back toward them, cradling a bottle of Bordeaux in her hands as gently as if it were a baby.

"Just wait," he said. "Wait and see what she does with this bottle."

In actuality, Ryan wasn't sure what was about to happen. He just knew that if she didn't need a corkscrew, something interesting was sure to go down, possibly involving a butcher knife. Or maybe a hammer. He wouldn't have been surprised if she'd opened the bottle with a karate chop to its slender glass neck. Anything was possible.

"Gentlemen." She smiled and set the Bordeaux on the table. Then she swiveled her gaze back toward Elliot. "I'll need three glasses, a decanter and a small ice bucket filled with cold water."

"Of course." He gave her a little bow and disappeared to do her bidding.

She didn't even work there yet, and the staff was already treating her like she ran the place. Ryan couldn't help but smile. Even Zander was beginning to look intrigued.

Evangeline started removing items from her tote bag, one by one. First up was an old-fashioned shaving brush—the kind barbers used in the sort of establishments that had a striped pole as part of the decor. The next thing out of her bag was a small copper pot of red wax.

Just as Ryan was feeling a stab of disappointment that nothing resembling a weapon had made an appearance, she pulled out a long metal contraption with wooden handles and two arms that formed a ring where they touched.

He had no idea what he was looking at. The apparatus had sort of a medieval torture device vibe, which he supposed he shouldn't rule out as a possibility.

Beside him, Zander tilted his head. "Um…"

"Port tongs," Evangeline said. "They were invented in the eighteenth century, but these are a tad newer."

"Naturally." Ryan bit back a grin.

But it was the last item she plunked down on the table that was clearly her trump card.

It wasn't a butcher knife.

It was worse.

"Is that what I think it is?" Zander asked.

"An upright blowtorch?" She nodded. "Yes."

A look of intense alarm crossed Zander's face but before he could object, she fired it up. It made a whooshing sound, and a steady blue flame, tipped in orange, shot six or so inches into the air.

Here we go.

Elliot returned, carrying the requested items, and stopped a safe three feet away from the table. Evangeline thanked him, smiling brightly.

She's enjoying this, Ryan thought.

So was he—probably more than he should have been.

Once the items were arranged to her satisfaction, she presented the bottle of wine and described it, identifying the vintage, the vineyard and the specific area of France where it came from—the Médoc region on the Left Bank. She told them to expect a deep red liquid, with fruit scents and notes of cassis, black cherry and licorice.

Ryan had always been partial to white wine, but he had a feeling that was about to change.

Finished with her brief monologue, Evangeline set the bottle back down, picked up the port tongs and held them over the open flame until the ring burned bright red. Ryan was suddenly consciously aware of his own heartbeat and a heady combination of awe and dread pumping through his veins, as if he were on the verge of being branded.

What was happening to him? Did Zander feel it, too—this strange, sublime effect she had?

He couldn't tell, and he wasn't willing to take his eyes off her long enough to venture a glance in his cousin's direction. But he doubted it, because what he was experiencing felt an awful lot like desire.

He swallowed.

Maybe Zander was right. Maybe they'd be better off going with someone else, because having Evangeline around on a daily basis was sure to be complicated.

But that was absurd, wasn't it? He was a grown man. He could resist temptation.

Light glinted against the wine bottle in the center of the table, flashing a glimpse of the dark liquid it contained. Shimmering garnet red. Then Evangeline removed the tongs from the flame and slipped the ring over the bottle's narrow neck.

She pressed the ring in place and then loosened the tongs, rotating the ring slightly and pressing again. Satisfied, she removed the tongs altogether, placed them in a shallow pan of water and then dipped the shaving brush into the ice bucket. The bottle made a cracking sound, like ice under pressure, as Evangeline ran the brush over the spot where she'd heated the glass.

Instinct told Ryan what was coming next, but he was still thoroughly impressed when she wrapped a cloth napkin around her hand to take hold of the top of the bottle and it snapped off cleanly in her grasp.

"Voilà," she said quietly. Her bottom lip slipped between her teeth as her gaze collided with his.

Temptation.

Most definitely.

"Impressive." Zander arched a brow. "What exactly did we just witness?"

"It's called tonging," she explained as she held the little pot of red wax over the blowtorch's flame. "Traditionally, this method is reserved for opening vintage port. Aged properly, port sits for twenty, sometimes fifty years. The cork can disintegrate and crumble if you open it with a corkscrew."

She tipped the copper pot in a swirling motion until the wax ran smooth. "No one wants bits of cork in a wine they've waited half a century to drink. Tonging allows you to bypass the cork altogether."

Zander nodded. "Clever."

Evangeline dipped the severed top in the melted liquid and then did the same to the sharp edge of the bottle's remaining portion after she poured the wine into the decanter.

Crimson wax dripped down the bottle, and Ryan was struck by the fact that she'd managed to create a dramatic table decoration in addition to putting on a show.

She poured three glasses from the decanter and handed two of them to Zander and Ryan. "This is Bordeaux, not port, obviously. The method can be used to open any kind of bottle. It's rather fun, don't you think?"

Ryan sipped his wine. It was good, but try as he might, he couldn't taste cassis, black cherry and licorice. Instead, his senses swirled with the memory of their night together. He tasted Evangeline's lips, chilled from the winter air, rich with longing. He tasted her porcelain skin, sweet like vanilla.

He tasted trouble.

So very much trouble.

Zander stared into his glass. "I think—"

For the second time in the span of a half hour, Ryan cut him off. He was sure to hear about it later, but by then it would be too late. "Evangeline Holly, you're hired."

Chapter Four

She'd done it.

The job offer was conditional. After Ryan told her she was hired, Zander had added the caveat that she continue studying for her sommelier certification exam. If she didn't pass on the first try, she was out.

But that was okay, even though the test was notoriously difficult and people often had to repeat it several times. Evangeline didn't care. She'd make it work. She'd study until she knew every wine in existence.

She was a wine director! She'd gotten the job, and she'd done it all on her own.

Probably.

Maybe.

She liked to believe the tonging had secured her the position or that her knowledge and passion superseded the fact that she had no official qualifications. Or actual work experience as a sommelier, unless she counted pouring wine in the tasting room at her family's vineyard as a kid.

But that had been ages ago—nearly seventeen years. She'd been playing catch-up ever since, trying her best to put her world back together after her mother left, ripping the rug out from under her.

Ripping the rug out from under *all of them*.

Evangeline's heart gave a little tug, just like it always did when she thought about her mother, but she swallowed her feelings down. She shouldn't be dwelling on loss right now—not when she had every reason to celebrate.

"Almost every reason, anyway," she muttered.

Olive swiveled her head and gazed up at Evangeline. Bee stared straight ahead. They trotted at the ends of their leashes, tails wagging as they headed toward the dog park at the end of the block.

Their coats were dusted with snow, and tiny puffs of vapor hung in the air with every breath from the happy dogs' mouths. Despite their advanced ages, they loved going for walks. Unfortunately, the fact that they weren't supposed to be living in Evangeline's apartment meant they only got to go outside early in the morning and late at night. Thank goodness for puppy pads.

Now that she had a job—a *great* job—she needed to do something about the dog situation.

And she would.

She just wished she could shake the nagging feeling that the only reason she'd gotten the job in the first place had been because of Ryan Wilde.

He'd hired her, not Zander. And there'd been an unmistakable flash of surprise on the CEO's face when Ryan announced that the job was hers. She'd told herself to ignore it. She deserved the job. Wine was in her blood. She'd be great.

She'd simply have to avoid Ryan as much as possible. That shouldn't be too hard. He worked business hours, and Evangeline's day started at 4:00 p.m. That meant an hour or two overlap. She could survive that. Couldn't she?

Eventually, she'd be able to look at him without imagining his lips against her throat, his body rising and falling above hers. She'd be able to say his name without remembering the way she'd cried it out in the dark.

Ryan.

Ryan.

Ryan.

"It's going to be fine." She swallowed. Hard. "It's going to be fine, because it has to."

At the sound of her voice again, Olive's tail wagged even harder. Olive and Bee were the sweetest dogs in the world. She'd have kept them even if they'd been monsters, though. Even if it meant she was at risk of getting tossed out of her building.

Dogs weren't allowed at her grandfather's new extended care facility. But if Evangeline kept Olive and Bee, she could at least bring them to visit him every once in a while. She owed that much to her grandfather. Robert Holly was the one person who'd been there for her when the vineyard, and all that went with it, withered and died. The *only* one.

"You guys aren't the worst cuddle bugs to have

around," Evangeline said as they waited to cross the street. Taxis whizzed past in a dizzying blur of bright yellow against the early morning snowfall.

She glanced down at Olive, and a memory flashed instantly into Evangeline's consciousness—Ryan, shirtless, standing beside her bed, petting the little dog and looking like something out of a beefcake-bachelors-with-puppies calendar.

Oh God.

How was she supposed to work with the man every day when she couldn't stop thinking about what he looked like beneath his exquisitely tailored suit?

She'd slept with her boss. Granted, he hadn't been her boss at the time, but still. It couldn't happen again.

Obviously.

Not that Ryan had hinted at that possibility...other than a tiny wink, he'd acted purely professional during her interview. She probably should have been relieved.

Scratch that. She *was* relieved. The annoying pang in her chest wasn't disappointment. It couldn't be.

"I need to nip this situation in the bud. Right?" She clicked the double gate of the dog park closed and bent to unfasten Olive and Bee from their leashes. Olive let out an earsplitting bark—the sort of bark that would ensure their eviction if she dared to do it indoors.

Evangeline nodded. "I'll take that as a yes."

"Again?" Ryan paused in the doorway of his office and took in the sight of Zander sitting behind the desk, waiting. "Your new early hours are becoming a habit."

"Indeed they are. Get used to it." Zander shot Ryan a tight smile and waved him inside.

So this was it.

Zander had been called into a meeting immediately after their interview with Evangeline the day before, and then he'd gone home. He no longer worked late as often as he did before he married Allegra. A year ago, Ryan might have envied him.

He knew better now.

Ryan wasn't cut out for marriage…for family. He'd tried. He'd tried really hard, but it wasn't in his blood.

He'd suspected as much all along. Only a fool would grow up the way Ryan had and not wonder if a normal, healthy relationship was even in the realm of possibility. Still, when Natalie turned up pregnant, he'd allowed himself to believe.

What a mistake that had been.

A dull ache took root in Ryan's gut. He'd moved on from Natalie and her baby over a year ago. He shouldn't be thinking about that mess now—and he wouldn't be, if not for the damned *Gotham* cover hanging above Zander's head. Being heralded for his bachelor status was a pretty potent reminder that he was meant to go it alone.

"Any particular reason you're reading the morning paper in my office?" Ryan sank into one of the guest chairs. "Again?"

Zander lifted a brow. "You have to ask?"

So this *was* it.

Ryan was facing his moment of reckoning for making the unilateral decision to hire Evangeline

Holly. He should have known Zander wouldn't let it go.

"She was the right person for the job. End of story." He shrugged.

"That might be true, but as CEO I would have liked an opportunity to weigh in on the matter." Zander folded his newspaper closed and rested his elbows on the desk. "But what's done is done."

Ryan nodded. "I'm glad you see it that way."

"Are you still going to be glad when I tell you that you're going to be personally responsible for making sure Ms. Holly is a success?" Zander sat back in his chair, waiting.

Personally responsible.

What did that mean, exactly? Was Ryan supposed to hold her hand while she went table to table, recommending wines?

He'd heard worse ideas.

She's your employee now, remember?

Ryan cleared his throat. "Fine. She comes in around four. I'll plan on spending the last hour or so of each work day checking in on things upstairs."

He'd planned on keeping close tabs on Bennington 8, anyway. The chef and the rest of the staff were already aware that Carlo Bocci could turn up at any time, but Ryan wanted to ensure they were prepared. Overprepared, if possible. The Michelin ranking was too important not to oversee things personally.

"Think again," Zander said.

Something in his tone caused the ache in Ryan's gut to sharpen. "Explain, please."

Zander shrugged. Somewhere beneath his irritation, Ryan spied a hint of a smile, and he got the definite impression his cousin was enjoying playing the CEO card. "You're working nights now."

Ryan blinked.

"We'll split shifts. I'm taking days and you're handling nights. Four p.m. to midnight," Zander said.

"Whatever for?"

"So you can keep an eye on Bennington 8, obviously." Zander stood. "Someone needs to see Ms. Holly in action to make sure she's working out, and since she's your hire, that someone is you."

Ryan opened his mouth to object, then promptly closed it.

What Zander was proposing made sense on every level. Not to mention the fact that when Ryan made the decision to hire Evangeline on the spot, he'd known he'd eventually have to face the music.

And he'd done it, anyway.

Zander lingered in the doorway, arms crossed, leaning against the doorjamb. Now was the time for Ryan to fess up and tell his cousin everything.

Just say it. Do it now. Evangeline and I have a history, albeit a brief one.

He met Zander's gaze. "How long?"

"A month, probably?" Zander shrugged one shoulder. "Or until Carlo Bocci shows up. Whichever comes first."

A month, maybe even less.

Totally doable. "Sounds good."

This is about the Michelin star, he told himself. *Nothing else.*

It was work, and it had nothing whatsoever to do with Evangeline Holly. They were adults, perfectly capable of working together without falling into bed again.

Weren't they?

The closer Evangeline's footsteps got to the spinning gold door of the Bennington Hotel, the harder her heart seemed to pound in her chest. Her face was so hot she was surprised the snow flurries swirling in the air didn't sizzle and melt against her cheeks.

Was it going to be like this every day? If so, she wouldn't survive it. She'd have a heart attack right there on the rich red carpet lining the sidewalk in front of her workplace. Which might actually be convenient, because then she wouldn't have to face Ryan Wilde every day. She wouldn't have to smile politely when he held her paycheck in his hand, all the while knowing precisely where that manly hand of his had been.

One hour. She inhaled a lungful of frigid air. The immaculately dressed doorman smiled and tipped his top hat as she pushed her way through the revolving door. *Surely you can endure sixty minutes in the presence of your boss without imagining him pinning your hands over your head and kissing you against the wall.*

She swallowed.

No man had ever kissed her like that before. Like he *owned* her. She'd been shocked at how very much she'd liked it.

But she wasn't supposed to be thinking about that right now, was she? Besides, the notion that Ryan Wilde was running all over Manhattan in his Armani suit and Tiffany cuff links kissing women silly, *just like he'd kissed her*, was beyond mortifying. It actually made her sick to her stomach.

She glanced around the glittering lobby and reminded herself she was in survival mode. All she had to do was make it through the overlap in their schedules, and then she could focus. She could forget her recent lapse in judgment and concentrate on the sole area in which she excelled—wine.

It was an escape, of sorts. Tasting wine and evaluating it was almost like stopping to smell the roses. Everything around her seemed to melt away, and she lived fully in the present. It was a way of experiencing a moment in time, savoring it with every one of her senses. There was so much more to a wine than just the way it tasted. Sometimes when she swirled a particularly precious vintage in a glass, the beauty of the light shining through the liquid was so lovely, so luminous, that it almost made her weep. There were even words for that kind of clarity in a wine— brilliant, star bright.

One hour.

Then she'd be home free.

Except today it would technically be two hours, because she needed to set the record straight with her new boss, and she couldn't very well do that during her working hours. She wanted to keep her personal connection to Ryan completely separate from their working relationship—so separate that it ceased to exist.

She smiled at Elliot, the general manager who'd escorted her to the interview the day before. Her heartbeat kicked up another notch when she asked for directions to the CFO's office, but Elliot didn't bat an eye.

He motioned toward an expansive hallway and told her to turn left beneath the gleaming gold clock suspended from the lobby ceiling. "Mr. Wilde's office is second from the end, on the right-hand side. You're rather early. Can I get you anything before you head down there? Coffee or an espresso, perhaps?"

"No, thank you." She was jittery enough without adding caffeine to the mix.

Her hands were shaking, so she buried them in her pockets as she made her way across the cool marble floor. As she passed the velvet sofa where just twenty-four hours ago she'd sat waiting for her interview, she couldn't help noticing a cluster of glamorously attired women occupying the sitting area. A few of them looked familiar—so familiar that Evangeline was almost certain she recognized the brunette who'd maligned her pencil skirt.

What was going on? Were Zander and Ryan still interviewing applicants, even after offering her the job? God, she hoped not.

Relief washed over her when she reached Ryan's office and spotted him through the open door, sitting behind his desk. Alone. Not another sommelier in sight.

She took a deep breath and tapped her knuckles lightly on the open door. "Excuse me."

Ryan looked up, his crystal-blue gaze colliding with hers. Honestly, did he have to be so handsome? It was hardly fair. "Eve."

That name again. It stopped her in her tracks, and she wobbled in her stilettos.

"Evangeline," she corrected. "I don't go by Eve."

He looked at her for a beat, and she felt like she was standing in her apartment again, wrapped in bed sheets with him stretched out naked in her bed.

"Understood." He smiled, but it didn't quite reach his eyes. His gorgeous, gorgeous eyes. "Come on in."

She clicked the door closed behind her and took a seat in one of the chairs opposite his desk.

"You're early," he said before she could get a word out.

"Right." She lifted her chin. *This is it.* "I wanted to talk to you off the clock."

His gaze flitted to the windows of his corner office. Outside, the hotel's doorman stood in the center of the snowy street, waving down cabs for Bennington guests. "Shall we go elsewhere?"

"Oh." The suggestion was unexpected, but she liked the sound of it. Best to keep their personal business out of the office altogether. She nodded, but just as she was about to suggest a quick walk around Central Park, her gaze snagged on the framed picture hanging on the wall above his desk.

It was a magazine cover.

The magazine cover—the one proclaiming him bachelor of the universe or something ridiculous like that.

And he had it hanging *on the wall of his office.* "U-um," she sputtered, unable to tear her attention away from his picture on the *Gotham* cover.

Ryan followed her gaze and then stood. For once, his cool exterior seemed a little rattled. "Ah, don't pay any attention to that."

"Too late." She swallowed.

What had she been thinking? She couldn't go to
the park with him. Or anywhere else, for that matter.

"It's a joke." Ryan raked a hand through his hair.
"Zander thought it would be funny to hang it up in
here."

"Hilarious," she said flatly.

Then he started talking about the *New York
Times* and weddings and the whole thing being a
big mistake, and Evangeline couldn't quite follow
his rambling train of thought because something ex-
cruciatingly awful was beginning to dawn on her.

"Oh my God." Her voice echoed off the walls of
Ryan Wilde's luxurious office. "*Oh my God.* Those
women in the lobby—they're not here for job interviews, are they?"

"No, but…" Ryan sighed, came around his desk
and took a step toward her.

Evangeline flew to her feet and pinned him with
a glare. "But what? Is there or is there not a group of
women just sitting in the lobby waiting for a glimpse
of you, the bachelor king?"

"I'm not sure I'd put it quite that way." The corner of his mouth hitched into a self-deprecating grin.

Not that Evangeline was looking directly at his
lips on purpose. It's just that he was *right there*, and
his mouth was pretty much at eye level.

Still, she melted a little bit, which only magni-
fied her embarrassment. "They thought I was one
of them."

A muscle twitched in Ryan's chiseled jaw. "Pardon?"

Evangeline nodded. "Yesterday, when I was waiting for my interview, your fan club welcomed me

with open arms. They even gave me some advice—lose the pencil skirt. Also, I should give up because I'm not your type."

"I'm sorry. Truly," he said.

Something in his gaze told her he was being sincere, and the room felt smaller all of a sudden. Evangeline's head spun.

He arched a brow. "As you and I both know, they're wrong."

Why was he being charming? And why was she on the verge of falling for it?

Because he's New York's hottest bachelor, you idiot.

She took a backward step, and her calves bumped into the chair where she'd been sitting. "See, this is exactly why I came here to talk to you off the clock. This—" she motioned to the space between them "—can't happen again."

He crossed his arms, but inched closer. "I absolutely agree."

She could feel his heat. Sultry and warm, like a summer's day. "I mean, you're my boss now."

His gaze dropped to her mouth. "Indeed I am."

She licked her lips. "It would be inappropriate."

"Completely." His eyes locked with hers, and she realized they were suddenly standing just a whisper apart.

The chair was no longer touching the backs of her legs. In fact, it was a good three feet away. She'd been drifting closer and closer to him the entire time, drawn to him like a moth to a flame.

She'd inched so near that she could see the fine weave of his crisp white Oxford shirt and the dark threads of the buttonhole on the wide lapel of his suit jacket. She could smell the lingering notes of his aftershave—something rich and wholly masculine. Worn leather and mossy oak with top notes of pine, sandalwood and violet leaf.

If Evangeline had known men's fragrances as thoroughly as she knew wines, she'd have been able to identify it in an instant. Alas, she didn't. But she took a deep inhale anyway, breathing him in. She felt dizzy again. Dizzy and just a little bit drunk, even though she hadn't consumed a drop of alcohol.

Stop.

Stop this right now.

If she didn't dramatically alter her course, she was going to wind up kissing him. She could already feel herself rising up on her tiptoes and tipping her face upward, toward his.

Kiss him, and you'll have no one to blame but yourself.

This was *not* the way to begin her new career. She had to do or say something to kill the mood. Immediately.

She crossed her arms—a barrier—and told what might have been the biggest lie of her life. "We'd be fools to go down that road again anyway, since last time was such a disaster."

Ryan froze for a second, then frowned. "Disaster?"

"Sure." She shrugged and feigned nonchalance as best she could. Not an easy task when every nerve ending in her body wanted to lean into him. "I'm sure you agree. It was…"

He lifted an inquisitive brow.

"…awkward." Her face went hot.

Ryan's gaze narrowed, and a mesmerizing knot flexed in his jaw. Even enraged, he was one of the most beautiful men Evangeline had ever seen.

"Awkward," he repeated without a trace of emotion in his voice.

Evangeline couldn't bring herself to look him in the eye anymore, so her gaze flitted to a blank space over his shoulder. "At best. So it obviously shouldn't happen again."

"Don't worry," he said through clenched teeth. "It won't."

"Perfect." She nodded.

He gave her a long, hard stare—one that set tiny fires skittering over her skin. Her pulse roared in her ears… *Liar, liar, liar.*

There'd been nothing awkward about that night. Nothing at all. If that had been true, she'd be capable of standing in the same room with Ryan Wilde without wanting to kiss him, without wanting his hands on her. Everywhere.

Still, it hadn't been a complete and total lie. As much as the experience had meant to Evangeline, she knew it hadn't been the same for Ryan. It just wasn't possible. She wasn't good at that sort of thing. Jeremy had made that much clear. Besides, she was pretty sure Ryan dated supermodels. Apparently, he dated *everyone*.

If she was tempted to forget that notable fact, all she had to do was glance at the magazine cover hanging on his wall.

She looked at it again, and then squared her shoulders. "I'm glad we got that settled. I know we both want what's best for Bennington 8, so it's probably a good thing we won't be working together directly."

Ryan's mouth hitched into a half grin as he resumed his place behind the desk, and the tiniest trickle of dread snaked its way down Evangeline's spine. She wasn't sure why. She'd done what she needed to do. From now on, everything should be smooth sailing.

The amused look on Ryan's face said otherwise. "I guess I should have mentioned there's been a change in plans."

A change in plans.

Why did that sound so ominous?

Ryan clasped his hands together on the surface of his desk, and a flash of silver at his wrists caught Evangeline's eye.

Cuff links.

From Tiffany & Co.

The last time she'd seen them had been six weeks ago on her nightstand.

She swallowed, and when she met his gaze again, every last trace of amusement had vanished from his expression.

He gave her a tight smile. "I'm on the night shift now, and you're working directly for me."

Chapter Five

"Hello there, stranger. Aren't you a sight for sore eyes?" Emily Wilde wrapped Ryan into a warm embrace the moment he crossed the threshold of the Wilde family brownstone.

"Hi, Emily." Ryan hugged her back, inhaling the comforting scents of Sunday dinner—of *home*—and braced himself for the inevitable tongue-lashing that was coming his way.

Emily pulled back, holding him at arm's length, but keeping a firm grip on his biceps as she pinned him with a glare. "Do you have any idea how long it's been since you showed up for weekly family dinner?"

And there it was.

"Eight weeks," she said, giving his arms a squeeze. Ryan's aunt still had the slender frame of a dancer, but she was stronger than she looked. *"Eight."*

He winced and stepped out of her grasp. "Ouch."

"You deserve worse." She swatted at him with the dishtowel in her hand. "If Zander hadn't assured me you were alive and well and helping him run that hotel of his, I would have thought you'd dropped off the face of the earth."

"I'm sorry. I've been…"

Hiding?

Licking his wounds?

Avoiding participating in family gatherings where he wasn't technically immediate family?

All of the above.

"…busy." He smiled and handed Emily the bottle of wine tucked under his arm. A peace offering.

She turned the bottle over, inspecting the label. "What's this?"

"Douro—it's a red from Portugal." He nodded toward the kitchen. "It should pair well with the lamb."

"You're not a guest here. You're family. You know that. Since when do you bring gifts to family dinner?" Emily's gaze narrowed. "Who are you, and what have you done with my son?"

My son.

A bittersweet ache burned deep in Ryan's chest. He wasn't Emily's son. Not really. But she was the closest thing to a mother he'd had for almost as long as he could remember. His memories of his birth parents were few and far between, lost in a hazy watercolor blur. They only made sense from a distance. If he focused too intently on his early years, his recollections became nothing more than shapes and colors—moody grays and blues that left him feeling empty inside.

"I'm right here." He swallowed.

"Good." His aunt nodded.

Emily Wilde was no fool. Ryan suspected she knew precisely why his presence at Sunday dinner had been scarce over the past six months or so.

He hadn't meant to pull a disappearing act. He owed everything to the family that lived in this home. But sometimes it was difficult to witness how close they all were. It almost made Ryan believe he was capable of having a family of his own someday. Which was precisely why he'd fallen so easily for Natalie's lies.

But bless her soul, Emily didn't mention Natalie. Or her baby.

"What have you got there, Mom?" Zander's gaze shot immediately to the bottle in Emily's hands when they drifted into the crowded kitchen. "Let me guess. Ryan brought it."

Every head in the room swiveled in Ryan's direction. The entire Wilde clan was there—Emily's youngest daughter, Tessa, along with her husband, Julian. Zander and Allegra. Tessa's hearing assistance dog, Mr. B, was there, too. Even Chloe, whose attendance at Sunday dinner was even more sporadic than Ryan's, was standing at the stove with a wooden spoon in her hand.

Ryan was especially glad to see Chloe. Since all the other Wilde siblings had recently coupled up, he'd become increasingly aware of his loner status. Not that it would be changing anytime soon—or ever, for that matter. He simply preferred not to dwell on it every time he walked through the brownstone's front door.

He embraced them all, one by one, then scooped Mr. B into the crook of his elbow. The little dog licked the side of his face, and his thoughts flitted briefly to the last animal he'd petted.

Evangeline's wide-eyed marshmallow of a dog.

Ryan pushed the memory back into the recesses of his mind, where it belonged, and eyed Zander over the top of Mr. B's head.

"As a matter of fact, I did bring the wine." Ryan shrugged one shoulder. "It's polite."

"It's also a wine you probably never heard of until a week ago," Zander said.

Damn.

Ryan sighed. Why had he thought the Douro had been a good idea?

Probably because you heard Evangeline waxing poetic about it last night at Bennington 8.

She'd recommended it to a large party seated at the restaurant's most prominent table. They'd been leery, but after Evangeline worked her magic with a colorful story of the vintage's history involving wine counterfeiting and at least one shipwreck, she won them over. By the end of the night, they'd consumed eight bottles.

Ryan had been intrigued.

He'd been intrigued a lot lately. Intrigued and bewildered, most notably by Evangeline's dubious assertion that their night together had been a disaster.

"I'm broadening my horizons," Ryan said blithely. "Consider it a bonus of working the night shift."

"The night shift? What's that all about?" Allegra glanced back and forth between Ryan and her husband.

Zander reached into an overhead cabinet for a

corkscrew. "Ryan's heading up our efforts to secure a Michelin star rating for Bennington 8."

Allegra's brow furrowed and her gaze flitted back to Ryan. "But you're the CFO. That seems..."

Emily finished the thought. "Odd."

Julian's hands moved rapidly, slicing the air as he summarized the conversation for Tessa in sign language. Less than five minutes had passed since Ryan walked through the door, and already the entire household was entrenched in his personal life. Marvelous.

"It's fine. I'm happy to do it," Ryan said. He didn't particularly want to get into a family-wide discussion about how his change in schedule had come about.

So he ignored the curious stares and did his best to divert attention someplace else. *Any*place else.

"The wine should breathe for an hour before it's poured." He gestured toward the bottle.

When his family continued to stand there waiting for him to elaborate on his new work schedule and his sudden interest in fermented grapes, he took the bottle of red from Zander's hands and carried it to the dining room. Blessed escape.

Away from the crowded kitchen, he could relax a bit—breathe. Especially once he heard the conversation switch gears to ballet.

It was a common topic around the brownstone. Tessa and Chloe were both professional dancers. Emily had been running the Wilde School of Dance since before Ryan was born. Nowadays, Allegra worked alongside her, teaching a majority of the classes. Even Zander had hit the dance floor for a time, competing in ballroom contests as a teen.

Ryan could fake his way through a waltz. He didn't have two left feet—he wasn't quite *that* bad—but he was no Fred Astaire. He could remember hours spent after school shuffling around the mirrored studios at the Wilde School of Dance with his arms lifted into a dance hold and a broomstick balanced across his shoulders and elbows to better his posture. He could also remember Emily wincing the numerous times his broom clattered to the floor, bringing class to an abrupt standstill. Once, he'd tripped over it and crashed into his dance partner, a pretty girl who'd gone on to win several novice competitions with a more capable companion.

Eventually, he'd begged Emily to let him quit. She'd taken mercy on him, and spending afternoons on a baseball diamond instead of the dance floor had been a relief. But being the only member of the family who hadn't contributed to the shiny collection of trophies in the dance school's lobby was another reminder that he wasn't truly one of them.

He was different.

"Thought we might need these." Zander sauntered into the dining room carrying seven red wineglasses by the bases of their stems.

Ryan relieved him of half of them and wordlessly went about placing the glasses around the table.

Zander had more on his mind than simply being helpful. Ryan could feel it. He'd worked with his cousin long enough to know when he had something he wanted to talk about. But Zander was going to have to come out and say it. Ryan didn't want to play guessing games. Especially when he couldn't even utter Evangeline's name without arousing suspicion.

"Have you seen the paper today?" Zander asked finally.

"No." Ryan shook his head.

Zander sighed. "Bocci awarded a Michelin star to one of the restaurants he reviewed this week."

"Damn. Really?"

"Really." Zander crossed his arms. "It's a little French place near Lincoln Center."

"Just one star?"

"Just one." Zander nodded. "But at the moment, that's one more star than we've got at Bennington 8."

Point taken.

The voices of the other Wildes grew louder as they drifted from the kitchen toward the dining room. Zander glanced over his shoulder and then back at Ryan. "We can talk more later, but I'd like you to go check it out and see what all the fuss is about, if you don't mind. Tomorrow night?"

Ryan shrugged. "Sure. Bennington 8 is closed tomorrow night, so the timing is perfect. But do you think I can get a reservation?"

"I already made one in your name. They're booked for weeks, but when I mentioned New York's hottest bachelor was interested, a table magically became available." Zander smiled. "See? I told you all that tabloid stuff would come in handy eventually."

Ryan rolled his eyes. "Perfect. I look forward to reading about my solo dinner in Page Six on Tuesday. They'll probably rechristen me New York's loneliest bachelor."

Zander shook his head. "You're not dining alone. The reservation is for two at nine o'clock."

"I see. We're tag teaming them, then. You're coming with?" Ryan nodded. "Probably a good idea. Dining alone might make it obvious that I'm there as a culinary spy."

"I'm glad you agree." Zander crossed his arms. His expression morphed into what Allegra jokingly called his CEO face.

Which meant that Ryan might not like what was coming next.

"Evangeline will accompany you."

Bingo.

Ryan's jaw tensed. "That's hardly a good idea."

"Why not? You said yourself that dining alone could be a problem. You've been all over the papers. If I go with you, we'll probably both be recognized and it will be obvious why we're there. If you go with Evangeline, she can check out the wine." Zander shrugged. "It'll just look like you two are on a date."

"Exactly. I'm her boss. Don't you think dating her would be a tad inappropriate?" Ryan fixed his gaze on the table and straightened a wineglass that didn't need straightening.

Could he be a bigger hypocrite right now?

Granted, he hadn't slept with her while she'd been employed at the Bennington. In fact, they'd barely exchanged more than two words since their "off-the-record" discussion in his office on her first day. They'd been tiptoeing around one another every night, avoiding eye contact.

But there'd been one or two times he'd caught her staring when she thought he wasn't looking. And the way her cheeks went pink and her lips parted when she'd been caught told him she'd been lying through her teeth about their night together.

A disaster?

Hardly.

Zander snorted. "Of course I think dating her would be inappropriate. It would be worse than that, actually. It would be a disaster."

That word again—*disaster*.

Ryan's head snapped up. "I'm not sure I'd go that far."

"I would. We can't afford that kind of distraction while Bocci is in town. Besides, aren't you forgetting something? Tomorrow won't actually *be* a date," Zander said.

Right. Ryan had indeed forgotten that significant detail.

Zander frowned. "I'm not asking you to date her. In fact, I'm specifically asking you *not* to. I don't even want you pretending to date her. I'm just saying if people see you dining together and jump to the wrong conclusion, so be it. Why are you fighting me on this?"

Because date or not, he couldn't sit across from her without thinking about her blue eyes glittering in the darkness, her kittenish sighs and the way her breath caught in her throat when he pushed inside her.

Something in his chest tightened and closed like a fist. "It's fine. I'll do it."

Zander cut Ryan a glance as the rest of the family spilled into the room, piling plates onto the table. "Good. That was the answer I expected five minutes ago."

"Tell me about your new job." Robert Holly, Evangeline's grandfather, sat in his beige leather recliner with Olive and Bee piled in his lap.

If Evangeline tried really hard, she could almost pretend they were back in his old apartment on Forty-Second Street instead of a nursing home she could barely afford. But no amount of pretending could dislodge the lump from her throat. As grateful as she was that he'd been able to bring a few pieces of furniture from home and the staff allowed her to bring the dogs by to visit once a week, she still wished things could be different.

He was putting on a brave face, but the nurses had already told Evangeline he'd seemed depressed since he'd moved in. Somehow, the fact that he was protecting her feelings instead of the other way around only made her feel worse.

But that's how it had always been. Grandpa Bob was more than just a grandfather. He was her family—what was left of it, anyway. Old habits died hard.

"My job?" Where to start? *Let's see—with my famous bachelor boss who I accidentally slept with or the fact that the late-night hours are killing me?*

She'd fallen asleep standing straight up in the wine cooler the night before. When she'd woken up, she'd spied Ryan watching her from across the room, his dark gaze as penetrating as ever through the frosted glass. Or maybe she'd just been dreaming of him. She hadn't quite decided which prospect was more mortifying.

"The job is fine." She smiled, then blinked in an effort to eradicate the image of Ryan Wilde in one of his sleek designer suits from her mind. Hopeless.

"Fine?" Grandpa Bob's hand paused, midscratch, on the top of Bee's furry little head. "You thought you wouldn't be able to land a sommelier position until you passed your certification exam. I assumed the reason you've been glowing since you walked in here was because you'd snagged your dream job."

"It is. I have." Her face went hot. "I mean, I'm not glowing."

"You are," he countered.

"I'm not." Evangeline's gaze narrowed. "You're not wearing your glasses. I probably just look blurry around the edges."

That had to be it, because she was absolutely not *glowing* when she thought about Ryan Wilde. He had enough women glowing all over Manhattan.

Her grandfather laughed, and her face grew even warmer.

She cleared her throat. "It's definitely my dream job. It's just a tad more challenging than I thought it would be."

She would have liked to blame Ryan, just because. But while she might have been able to convince herself that his mere presence was distracting to the point of exhaustion, it didn't explain why she'd been unable to accurately identify any of the whites at her wine study group earlier this afternoon.

She was off her game.

That never happened.

Evangeline was the best taster in the group. Usually, anyway. When she'd confidently classified the second glass in the tasting as a sauvignon blanc from the southern Bordeaux region of France, the other members of the group had simply stared at her with their mouths agape.

Now wasn't the time to be making those kinds

of mistakes. Not when there was a Michelin star on the line.

"I'll be fine, though. I was born for that job." Again, she was distracted. That was all.

Had she been rattled by Ryan's announcement that he was changing to the night shift and she was to work directly under him? Sure. But she'd survived the first week, hadn't she?

Survived *might be a stretch. You've been hiding from him for five straight days.*

"Of course you were born for it." Grandpa Bob nodded. His smile quickly faded and was replaced with a pensive expression that made her heart feel like it was being squeezed in a vise. "I'm only sorry I couldn't save the vineyard. I didn't know…"

Evangeline shook her head in an effort to get him to stop.

She couldn't believe he'd brought up the vineyard. They'd spent almost two decades steadfastly avoiding the topic. It hurt too much to think about so much loss, and besides, he'd done nothing wrong. Not one thing.

Losing the vineyard had been her father's doing. And in a way, her mother's.

"It's okay. The job at the Bennington is the chance I've been waiting for. It's a fresh start." And boy, did she ever need one. For once she was glad that her grandfather never seemed to remember Jeremy's name. At least she wouldn't have to explain the breakup. And the subsequent job loss.

She wasn't exactly lying to Grandpa Bob. She was protecting him from the ugly truth. His whole life had recently been turned upside-down. All he needed to know was that she'd gotten a new job working as a sommelier at one of the most exclusive hotels in New York.

For now.

She pasted on a smile and ignored the churning in the pit of her stomach. She could be the best damn sommelier the Bennington could hope for. Better, even. She simply needed to get some rest, clear her head and most of all, rid her thoughts of Ryan Wilde.

That's what days off were for, right?

She nodded resolutely, and then, as if fate itself were mocking her, her cell phone chimed with an incoming text. She glanced at the display as Grandpa Bob switched gears and began talking about pizza night in the nursing home's dining room.

Zander Wilde: Sorry to bother you on your day off, but are you available to evaluate a restaurant tonight?

She stared at the words on the tiny screen. Before she could type a response, the phone chimed again.

Zander Wilde: Should have mentioned it's a Michelin-starred restaurant. Would like your input on the wine.

Here it was…her chance to get back on track and prove her worth without being distracted by Ryan's handsome face popping into her periphery every five minutes.

She really needed to stop thinking about how good-looking he was.

And she would.

Starting right now.

"Sorry, Grandpa. I just need to answer this text. It looks like I'll have to work tonight after all."

"Go right ahead. Do what you need to do, although we'll miss you around here this evening at pizza night." He smiled. Olive and Bee peered up at her, wagging their tails.

Pizza with a bunch of senior citizens and two snuggly dogs actually sounded lovely, but so did dinner at an upscale eatery that had been awarded a coveted Michelin star. Especially if she could enjoy said dinner with the very professional, very married Zander Wilde instead of his hot bachelor of a cousin.

She tapped out a response.

Evangeline Holly: Of course. Where and when should I meet you?

Zander Wilde: The Bennington limo will pick you up at 8.

Perfect.

Chapter Six

"We're here, sir." Tony, the Bennington chauffeur, met Ryan's gaze in the rearview mirror of the limousine. "Shall I go fetch Ms. Holly?"

Ryan glanced at the steps leading up to Evangeline's building and the intricately carved red door that, seven weeks ago, had been shut so resolutely in his face. "No, I'll do it."

He had no idea what Zander had told her about this impromptu field trip. When he'd mentioned calling Evangeline to discuss arrangements for transportation, Zander assured him it was already taken care of.

Surely he'd warned her that Ryan would be her companion for the four-course meal awaiting them at Mon Ami Jules on the Upper West Side. Then again, why would Zander consider Ryan's presence worth mentioning? As he'd reiterated more than once, this wasn't a date. It was business.

All the same, he doubted she'd be thrilled to find him waiting for her in the intimate confines of the limo's back seat unless she was expecting him. She might even consider it *disastrous*. If she was going to toss that word out again, Ryan preferred it to happen outside of Tony's earshot.

"Yes, sir," Tony said with a nod. "I'll wait at the curb."

Ryan climbed out of the sleek black car. Rock salt crunched beneath his feet as he made his way up the steps, and a sensation that felt too much like desire stirred deep in his gut as he approached Evangeline Holly's threshold.

It's not a date—pretend, real or otherwise.

His jaw clenched, and he rapped on the door.

The knock was met with an explosion of barks coming from within the apartment. The door swung open at once, revealing a panicked Evangeline stooping to shush the two little spaniels that Ryan had encountered on his previous visit.

"Olive and Bee," he said. The pendulum swing of their tails intensified at the sound of their names. "Nice to see you again."

Evangeline popped up, ramrod straight, with a dog tucked beneath each arm. They both squirmed gleefully as the color drained from Evangeline's exquisite face. Her perfect pink mouth fell open, and Ryan's gaze flitted briefly to her tongue.

A thousand inappropriate ideas came to mind. Possibly more.

Each and every one of them began with capturing her face in his hands and holding her still while he kissed her again. Slowly…deeply.

Thoroughly.

"You," she finally said, without any sort of preamble.

He'd been right. Zander clearly hadn't been forthcoming with the details. Score one for intuition.

"Expecting someone else?" Ryan arched a brow.

She shook her head. Too hard. Too fast. "No."

Ryan arched his brow a notch higher.

She sighed. "Okay, yes. I might have thought I was meeting Zander for dinner."

He shrugged one shoulder as he reached to give Olive a scratch behind one of her copper-colored ears, remembering to approach her from the left side since she was blind in her right eye. "Sorry to disappoint."

"I'm not disappointed," she said without meeting his gaze. "Just…"

"Rattled?"

The last time they'd been alone together, they'd nearly ended up in a lip-lock, despite vowing to one another it was a terrible idea. He knew she was rattled. Hell, so was he.

Her cheeks flared pink.

"No. Surprised, that's all," she countered.

"Good, because there's no reason to be nervous around me, Evangeline. None. I'm certainly not going to force myself on you." His attention drifted to her mouth again. Damn it. "Nor am I going to kiss you."

She swallowed hard, and he traced the movement up and down the slender column of her throat before forcing himself to look her in the eye. "You have my word. This is a business dinner."

For a long, loaded moment, neither of them said anything. Evangeline's eyes glittered like frosted blue diamonds, but somewhere in their luminous depths, Ryan could have sworn he saw a spark of disappointment. Or maybe that was just wishful thinking on his part.

"A business dinner." Evangeline nodded. "Of course. What else would it be?"

She shot him a bright smile. So bright that he knew it wasn't real.

What were they doing? This was absurd. They were obviously attracted to each other. Would it really be so bad to act on that attraction...again?

"Eve..." He knew he wasn't supposed to call her that, but it was a deliberate choice. It was easier to pretend at the Bennington, to deny the pull he felt toward her. The need.

But they weren't at the Bennington now. Here, they'd touched. Here, they'd kissed. They'd been different people here. It was impossible to pretend otherwise.

She took a deep breath, and he could see the struggle in her eyes. He could feel it in the way her body arched toward him, as if they were dance partners.

Then one of the dogs emitted a snuffling sound somewhere between a bark and sneeze, and the magic spell was broken. Ryan heard footsteps behind him. Evangeline's gaze shot over his shoulder, and faster than he could process, she shoved Olive at his chest, grabbed his wrist and hauled him inside her apartment.

The door slammed shut.

Ryan stumbled backward. "What the...?" Olive

licked his left eye before he could complete the thought.

He squeezed his eyes closed, and when he opened them, he found Evangeline peering through the peephole, clutching Bee. Her hand was clasped gently over the dog's mouth.

They were hiding, apparently. Ryan just wasn't sure why. Or from whom.

He watched, waiting, until she spun around.

"Good girl," she whispered, and set Bee down on the floor.

The little Cavalier immediately began pawing at Ryan's shins. He glanced at the dog, then back up at Evangeline. Her cheeks went crimson.

His eyes narrowed. "Care to let me in on your little secret?"

She crossed her arms, then promptly uncrossed them. In the light of her apartment, he got a better glimpse at what she was wearing beneath her blush-colored coat—a dress with a feathered skirt and a bit of sparkle on the bodice. She looked more elegant than he'd ever seen her before. Elegant, and fully embarrassed.

She bit her lip. Ryan had to force himself not to focus on her mouth again. "Olive and Bee might not technically be allowed to live here."

He glanced down at the dog nestled in the crook of his elbow and then at the other one—Bee—who flopped onto her back at his feet, begging for a belly rub. Sweet dogs. No doubt about it. High-maintenance, though. Not exactly the types of pets that could go unnoticed. They weren't goldfish, for crying out loud.

He set Olive down on the floor beside Bee and, as
if to confirm his thoughts on the matter, they immediately began chasing one another in a loop around
Evangeline's flowery, Shabby Chic sofa.

"I'm guessing that was one of your neighbors outside just now?" Ryan said.

She nodded.

He let out a laugh. "Good luck keeping them a
secret. You're going to need it."

She sighed. "It's not funny."

"Actually, it is. A little bit, anyway." One of the
dogs barked, and Ryan shrugged. "I rest my case."

"Bee is deaf. Her bark is loud because she's trying to hear herself."

Understandable, but somehow Ryan didn't think
her landlord would care about that sad little tidbit.
"You have one dog that can't see and another that
can't hear?"

"Yes," she said, as if it were completely normal.
"Bee is Olive's seeing eye dog. Olive is Bee's ears.
They help each other."

It was official. He was in a Hallmark movie.

Evangeline brushed past him, toward the kitchen.
He had a vague, wine-drenched memory of kissing
her there—Evangeline sitting on the counter, her lithe
arms draped around his neck. He blew out a steadying breath and averted his gaze. There was a slender
wine cabinet in the living room—empty, save for a
lone bottle of red.

She returned with two rawhide bones, one for each
dog. They immediately settled onto opposite ends of
the couch with their treasures.

Evangeline turned toward him, and a self-satisfied

smirk tipped her lips. "See? Easy-peasy. No one will know they're here."

"For the next five minutes maybe. Although I must say, I admire your ability to convince yourself otherwise. It takes a special kind of optimism to so willingly deny the truth." He shot her a pointed look.

They weren't talking about the dogs anymore, and they both knew it.

That ridiculous word—*disaster*—floated between them. Such a blatant lie.

Evangeline's gaze flitted around the room. She seemed to be focusing on anything and everything other than him. "Were you telling the truth earlier when you promised not to kiss me?"

"Yes." Somewhere in the back of his head, a voice told him not to make promises he couldn't keep. He paused and reconsidered. "With one exception."

She licked her lips, an unconscious gesture that would have no doubt rattled her if she'd been aware of it. "And what might that be?"

He waited for her to look at him before he answered. "If you ask me to. Nicely, of course."

It was the only way.

He was her boss, and he didn't want to take advantage of her. But if she wanted him badly enough to ask him to kiss her, to touch her, he'd never be able to deny her. Wild horses wouldn't be able to stop him.

Her blue eyes flashed. "Now who's delusional? You think I'm going to beg you to kiss me?"

"I never said beg. That was your choice of words." He couldn't suppress his smile any longer. He grinned at her, full wattage. "Although the prospect does have a certain appeal."

"If you want someone to beg, there are probably half a dozen women in the Bennington lobby right now who I'm sure would be more than willing to oblige," she said tartly.

Touché.

He took a step closer—close enough that he could see her pulse pounding in the hollow of her throat. "If you want me to kiss you, you're going to have to ask."

"Understood, but just so we're clear—that's never going to happen." Her voice was a ragged whisper, with a hint of vulnerability that crushed something tender and raw deep in his chest.

He had to pause for a moment before he responded.

"Fine. We should probably get going, anyway. There's a car waiting outside, and our reservations are in less than fifteen minutes." He steadied the un-characteristic tremble in his hands by busying him-self with buttoning his coat. "But you know what they say."

"What's that?" she asked warily.

"Never say *never.*"

The ride uptown through the snowy city streets was excruciating. Who knew it was possible to be so thoroughly miserable while sitting in the back seat of a luxury limousine?

Or quite so…restless.

Evangeline squirmed against the buttery soft leather at her back and did her best to ignore Ryan's presence beside her. But no matter how hard she fo-cused on the delicate snowflakes melting against the car's darkened windows, she could still feel the warmth of his body, so close to hers. She still shuddered when her thigh brushed against the smooth wool fabric of his bespoke suit pants.

If you want me to kiss you, you're going to have to ask.

She couldn't get those words out of her head. They twirled round and round—irresistibly sweet, like spun sugar.

Worst of all, he knew she couldn't stop thinking about them. She was certain of it. Every time she snuck a sideways glance at him, the corner of his mouth tugged into a sly grin. It was beyond embarrassing.

She wouldn't ask him to kiss her, obviously. His enticing little ultimatum might have planted the idea right at the forefront of her thoughts, but she'd never act on it. He'd lost his mind if he thought she would. Such reverse psychology might work on the hordes of bachelorettes who threw themselves in his path, but not Evangeline.

Then why are you still thinking about it?

She glared at Ryan.

He regarded her with those blue eyes that always seemed to see too much. "Something on your mind, Miss Holly?"

The man was impossible.

"Yes," she said primly. "Where are we going? Zander didn't mention the name of the restaurant."

Among other things.

The next time Zander requested her presence somewhere, she was going to make sure to get the details. She still couldn't believe she'd unknowingly walked right into this situation.

"It's a little French place near Lincoln Center. Mon

Ami something or other." Ryan's French accent was perfect, because of course it was.

But Evangeline didn't particularly care about his impressive language skills. A horrible sense of dread had washed over her, and she could barely force her next words out. *"Mon Ami Jules?"*

It couldn't be. *No.* Please, *no.*

"That sounds right." He angled his head toward her. "You know it?"

She knew it, all right. Mon Ami Jules was the restaurant where she was supposed to be employed— *Jeremy's* restaurant.

She couldn't have dinner there. Absolutely not. She'd rather cook dinner for Ryan herself.

Not that cooking him dinner would be in any way relevant to the Bennington or Carlo Bocci.

She was losing it. She was one hundred percent losing her mind. "I've heard of Mon Ami Jules. Honestly..."

Honestly? She had no intention of being truthful. She was planning on trying to diplomatically extricate herself from the situation by saying she already knew everything there was to know about Mon Ami Jules. But before she could say another word, the limo slowed to a stop in front of Jeremy's bistro.

Her mouth grew dry as she stared out the window at the fresh Michelin star insignia placed prominently on the building's glossy front door. She couldn't believe what she was seeing. The Michelin star hadn't even been on Jeremy's radar. Before their breakup, he'd simply been focused on getting his kitchen up and running—oh, and sleeping with his sous chef in his spare time. Who had the hours to pursue excellence when there was so much sex to be had?

And now the Michelin star had fallen into his lap. The unfairness of it churned in Evangeline's stomach, twisting into a sickening knot.

She'd been the focused one. She'd been the one who'd played by the rules. Always.

Almost always… She'd made one notable mistake, and he happened to be sitting beside her at the moment, clearly baffled as to why she couldn't seem to get out of the car.

Tony held the car door open for her, but she remained rooted to the spot, unable to move.

"Now's the part where we go inside and have dinner." Ryan straightened the already-perfect Windsor knot in his tie and nodded toward the dark green awning where *Mon Ami Jules* was spelled out in elegant script.

The tangle of dread in her stomach tightened, and bile rose to the back of her throat.

Oh God.

She was going to have to do it, wasn't she? She was going to have to walk in there and pretend she was having the time of her life while she shared a lengthy four-course dinner with Ryan Wilde in her ex's restaurant.

"Evangeline," Ryan prompted, his expression growing more serious. Wary even, as if he was afraid she might do something crazy like refuse to emerge from the back seat.

No way. She wouldn't give him the satisfaction of thinking he'd rattled her to such an extent that she couldn't do something as simple as sit across a table from him and eat a dish of beef bourguignonne. Nor would she jeopardize her job and hide from Jeremy when she'd done nothing wrong. *He* was the cheater. She had nothing to be ashamed of.

Still, her legs wobbled beneath her as she climbed out of the limousine. She was actually grateful for the gentle pressure of Ryan's palm on the small of her back, steadying her, as his touch seemed to smolder right through the beaded bodice of her dress.

"Wilde, party of two," he said to the hostess.

"Yes, of course." She fluttered her eyelashes at him without giving Evangeline so much as a cursory glance.

So this is what it must feel like to go on a date with the city's most eligible bachelor.

Oh joy.

They were quickly seated at a table for two in the far corner of the crowded dining room. At least six tables had been added since the last time Evangeline had stood in the cozy, wood-paneled space. Every one of them was full at the moment. She glanced around and didn't set eyes on a single unoccupied chair.

"I guess a Michelin star really does translate into a full reservation book," she muttered once she and Ryan were alone, menus in hand.

"Exactly." He reached for the wine list and slid it across the crisp, white tablecloth toward Evangeline. "Give it a look. See what you think."

She scanned the selection. Six reds, seven whites plus a generous offering of champagnes, ranging from extra brut to doux. All French. "It's a finely tuned list, but appropriate given the dinner menu."

Ryan frowned. "How can you know that? You haven't opened your menu yet."

Busted.

She blinked. "It's a French bistro, with a French name. I'm assuming all the cuisine is French, as well."

She really didn't want to get into the sad, sordid history of her love life. Not here. And definitely *not* with Ryan.

Was it too much to hope that Jeremy would stay in the kitchen all evening and she'd never be forced to look him in the face or, heaven forbid, introduce him to her bachelor boss?

God, she hoped not.

"Well, I hope you like foie gras because the cuisine here seems pretty one-note," Ryan said drily.

She pulled a face. "I don't, actually. Do you know how foie gras is made? It's inhumane and just plain mean."

"That makes sense coming from a woman presently risking eviction for the sake of two special-needs dogs." He closed his menu and pushed it aside. "What's the story there, anyway?"

Why did he care?

She swallowed. "I thought we established this is a business dinner."

"It is, but that doesn't mean we can't have a conversation about something other than the Bennington. It's going to be a long night if we sit here in silence, don't you think?"

He had a point.

She took a deep breath. *It's not a date.* "I think I told you that until recently Olive and Bee belonged to my grandfather. He can't have pets where he is now, so I took them in."

Ryan studied her in that way he had that always made her heart beat too hard. Too fast. "Even though you live in a building that doesn't allow animals?"

"I didn't have a choice," she said.

"Yes, you did. But not many people would choose what you did."

She rolled her eyes. "Why? Because I'm an idiot?"

"On the contrary. It means you're caring. Passionate." The still, silent way he held her gaze made her head spin a little.

It was a relief when the sommelier interrupted their conversation to take the wine order. Evangeline tore her gaze away from Ryan to consider the gentleman standing over them, holding a corkscrew. Her replacement, presumably. Her heart sank a little when she spotted the lapel pin on the man's suit jacket, indicating he'd already passed the advanced sommelier exam.

Without missing a beat, Ryan declined to choose a wine and instead asked the sommelier for a recommendation. A test. He suggested a Côtes du Rhône, an uninspired choice, as far as Evangeline was concerned. But what did she know?

She was beginning to get the definite feeling she was in over her head. Being back on Jeremy's turf was getting to her. He'd replaced her, in every way possible.

"Well?" Ryan asked after the sommelier had gone. "What do you think?"

"I think you're wrong. I'm far from passionate.

That seems to be the consensus, anyway." The words flew right out of her before she could stop them.

She didn't know what it was about Ryan that made her say things she ordinarily wouldn't dream of saying.

Ryan went still. "I was referring to the wine selection."

"Right. Of course you were. Um, the wine sounds fine." She clamped her mouth closed before she said something else even more humiliating. Although she was hard-pressed to think of anything more embarrassing than announcing she was deficient in the passion department.

"Fine? The wine is *fine*? I know that can't be right." He furrowed his brow, oh-so-handsomely.

She really didn't have the energy to argue with him. It was all she could do just to get through this horrible night. "It's a Côtes du Rhône. I'm sure it will be lovely."

"I've never heard you describe a wine in so few words before." Clearly he had no intention of letting it go. "The Evangeline Holly that I know tends to wax poetic about such matters."

She busied herself with meticulously unfolding and refolding the napkin in her lap so she wouldn't have to look him in the eye…

…until he said the words that made her heart stop. "Which is just one of the reasons that I know she's brimming with passion."

Her gaze collided with his, and the way he was looking at her left no doubt he was telling the truth.

"Shall I list the other reasons? Or would that be

inappropriate, given this is a business dinner? Your call." His deep voice rolled over her in a wave.

She sat stone still. She didn't trust herself to breathe, much less speak.

He was saying everything she'd once longed to hear from Jeremy. And for reasons she couldn't fathom, those words meant even more coming from Ryan. Somewhere along the way, his opinion had become the one that mattered. She wasn't sure when, or how, but it had.

"Seriously, Evangeline. Whoever told you that you lack passion is a fool." He leaned forward, looming above the candle in the center of the table, eyes blazing.

"It's there. I've seen it. I've felt it. I've *tasted* it. If you're wondering if I'm talking about the night we spent together, the answer is yes. But it's not just that. It's more. So much more. It's the way you sliced the top off that champagne bottle and the history lessons you give everyone before you'll let them taste a sip of wine. It's the way your eyes go all soft when you talk about your grandfather, and yes, it's the way your breath catches in your throat when you and I are in the same room together. It's the way you're looking at me right now. I go to bed every night—alone, contrary to what you might think—and I dream about that look. That's passion, Evangeline. And you're no stranger to it."

He stopped abruptly, sighing mightily as the sommelier returned.

Neither of them said a word while he presented the wine for Ryan's inspection, then uncorked the bottle. An agonizing lump swelled in Evangeline's throat. She felt like crying all of a sudden, and she wasn't sure why.

She did her best to focus on the swirl of dark liquid in her wineglass as the sommelier poured, but her gaze was drawn back to Ryan's like a magnet. And when their eyes met once again, she saw her own yearning written all over his face.

The sommelier lingered, waiting.

Evangeline had zero interest in the wine. None. She reached for her glass but stopped short of taking hold of it. There was a visible tremor in her fingertips as she rested her hand on the tablecloth.

Ryan sipped from his glass and nodded. "Very good, thank you."

At last the sommelier left.

Evangeline took a deep breath. Words were bubbling up her throat—words she'd been trying her best not to say since the moment she'd woken up beside Ryan Wilde. There was no stopping them now. Not anymore. Not after what he'd just told her.

"Ryan, I…"

From somewhere behind her, a voice interrupted. "Evangeline?"

And just like that, the warm glow rising up from deep inside her soul vanished.

She didn't turn around. She didn't have to.

Jeremy.

Chapter Seven

Another interruption.

Ryan's jaw tensed to the point of pain. He dragged his gaze away from Evangeline to get a look at the man who'd just said her name. It was the chef, if the toque on the man's head was any indication.

And yet not *just* the chef, Ryan realized as he watched the color drain from Evangeline's face.

"Hello, Jeremy," she said quietly.

The chef—Jeremy, apparently—shot a curious glance at Ryan, then turned back to Evangeline. "I didn't know you had a reservation. Did you come here to see me?"

Ryan had the sudden overwhelming urge to hit something. Or someone. At the moment, the chef seemed like a good target. Who exactly was this guy?

Jealous much?

He took a strained inhale. He had no claim on Evangeline and therefore, no right to feel this way. Somehow knowing that didn't help matters.

Ryan's own words from moments ago rang like a bell in his consciousness.

Seriously, Evangeline. Whoever told you that you lack passion is a fool.

"I'm here for dinner." Evangeline lifted her chin and leveled her gaze at Jeremy, undoubtedly the fool in question.

Her body language gave her away—the crossed arms, the fixed stare, the rebellious tilt of her head. But beyond the bravado, he saw the way her sapphire eyes seemed to go bluer than he'd ever seen before.

Jeremy had hurt her. The pain was real. Raw. Fresh.

"Excellent. I hope you enjoy yourselves." Jeremy glanced at Ryan again.

Evangeline's gaze flitted back and forth between the two men. "Ryan, this is Jeremy, the chef here at Mon Ami Jules. Jeremy, this is…"

An awkward pause followed, as if she wasn't sure how to introduce him. Ryan tried to imagine her possible options. Her boss? The one-night stand she probably regretted?

Neither of those was bearable.

"Ryan Wilde." He stood and offered his hand.

The chef took it and gave it a shake. "Jeremy Peters."

Ryan complimented the menu, and they exchanged a few words about French cuisine. Small talk. Ryan couldn't concentrate on any of it. He was too preoccupied with the dull ache that had formed at the base of his skull. He didn't want to be here in this man's restaurant, eating his food and shaking his hand while the tenuous connection he'd just made with Evangeline broke beneath the strain.

They'd had a moment, and it was fading away as surely as a pink-hued sky after a blazing sunset.

He sat back down, hoping Jeremy Peters would take the hint and go away. Instead, he droned on and on, oblivious to the way Evangeline blanched after her first sip of wine. She was so obviously disgusted by it that Ryan had to stifle a grin. Their eyes met, and her lips quivered with mirth when he reached for his glass. It tasted fine to him. Quite good, actually. But what did he know? After all, he still indulged in the occasional glass of pinot grigio.

He took another swallow, then a few more. Evangeline's eyes widened ever so slightly in amused horror. Again, Jeremy seemed clueless to what was transpiring at the table. He continued his monologue with a meticulously detailed description of his coq au vin.

They were sharing a secret right beneath his nose, and the connection between them—that glittering, gossamer thread—dazzled brightly once again, warming Ryan from the inside out.

He took another gulp of the Côtes du Rhône and then set his wineglass back down on the table, toying with the stem as memories he'd been doing his best to push away came rushing into his consciousness. Denying them was a hopeless effort. In recent weeks, he'd been semisuccessful in forcing his mind into submission whenever it strayed toward forbidden territory. But it was no use…there was no forgetting.

The memories weren't just in his head. They lived in his body—in his shuddering breath, in the featherlight nerve endings on his lips and the tips of his fingers. His flesh remembered her. It remembered every caress, every whispered sigh, every exquisite thing about that night.

He looked at her, sitting across from him in her glittering, feathered dress, and despite the suddenly awkward circumstances, she seemed to glow. God, she was gorgeous. Focusing so intently on her luminous eyes and lush, kissable lips was far too dangerous, so he dropped his gaze to her delicate hand resting on the table, just out of reach.

And yet so close...so very close...

Desire rippled through him, blossoming from somewhere deep inside, drawing him toward her. It was a fierce, fiery thing, visible in the uncontrollable tremor in his fingertips as his hands inched slowly toward hers.

He could have stopped himself. He could have simply withdrawn his hand and curled it into a fist under the table, but he didn't want to. Not after the way she'd looked at him as he'd confronted her with evidence of her passion. Not while a sly smile tipped her lips. Secret. Special. Only for him.

He slid his hand forward until the tips of his fingers made contact with hers. It was the barest of touches, little more than nothing. But somehow, some way, *everything*.

Evangeline let out a little gasp, and her gaze fluttered toward his. He waited a beat, and when she didn't pull away, he fully took her hand, weaving her slender fingers through his until he wasn't sure where his touch ended and hers began.

Ryan couldn't remember the last time he'd held hands with a woman.

College, maybe? As far back as high school?

PDA had never been his thing, but there was something different about Evangeline. If they'd been lovers—*real* lovers, not simply two people who'd once been intimate—he'd never be able to keep his hands off her.

But they weren't. Perhaps that was why there was a hint of melancholy in the warmth of their touch, and perhaps that was why the simple act of holding her hand felt more meaningful than he could ever have imagined. Perhaps that was why he couldn't seem to let go.

Jeremy looked down, spotted their interlaced fingers and at last grew quiet.

He cleared his throat. "Well, I've kept you long enough. Enjoy your dinner. Don't worry about ordering. I'll send over the chef's special tasting menu. It's on the house."

Ryan and Evangeline thanked him, and at long last, he was gone.

Their eyes met, and Evangeline's cheeks flared pink. She gave him a smile so soft, so vulnerable, that he forgot all the reasons he shouldn't be sitting across from her on a glittering Manhattan evening, holding her hand.

"Thank you," she said.

"For what, exactly?"

Her eyes flitted briefly in the direction where Jeremy had gone. The kitchen, presumably. "For making an awkward situation more bearable."

The sommelier returned to refill Ryan's glass, and Evangeline grew quiet. Ryan nodded his thanks, and was forced to release Evangeline's hand in order to accommodate the sommelier.

"Am I correct in assuming that Jeremy is an ex?" he asked once they were alone again.

"Yes. It ended badly." She nodded, and once again, a flash of pain glimmered in her eyes.

Ryan's gut tightened. Then he asked a question to which he somehow already knew the answer. "When?"

She stiffened ever so slightly, then shrugged an elegant, bare shoulder. "A while ago."

"A while." He took another, larger, taste of his wine. "As in six or seven weeks?"

"Thereabouts." She reached for her own glass, brought it to her lips, then frowned into it and placed it back on the table.

"Ah." He nodded.

Six or seven weeks ago, which meant the breakup occurred shortly before they'd met one another. The night he'd gone home with her.

Suddenly that evening made much more sense, as did Evangeline's skittishness the following morning. He'd wanted to see her again. *Needed* to. But there'd been no convincing her. Now he knew why.

He stared at the swirl of burgundy liquid in his glass, suddenly wishing it were something stronger. The timing shouldn't have mattered. He knew it shouldn't, but somehow it did. He wasn't even sure why.

Yes, you are.

The timing mattered because everything about that night mattered. It had mattered to him, anyway. And he was pretty damn sure it mattered to her, too.

"*Oeuf cocotte à la parisienne.* Parisian shirred egg, compliments of the chef." A server placed a small blue crock in the center of the table.

Ryan took an exploratory bite and was somewhat disappointed to discover the dish was delicious. "Not bad."

Evangeline didn't offer an opinion. Dishes kept coming, one after another. There was no more time for conversation, no opportunity to slip back into the quiet intimacy they'd fallen into before. Ryan was glad when the meal finally came to an end.

They sat side by side in the back of the limo as it crawled through the snowy streets, Manhattan nothing more than a silvery, sparkling blur through the frosted windows. The inside of the car was snug and warm, and once again, their fingertips came to rest a fraction of an inch apart on the smooth leather seat between them.

So close. And still so maddeningly far away.

The driver's voice crackled through the car's intercom system sooner than seemed possible. "We've arrived at Miss Holly's building."

Ryan pushed the button on his side of the partition. "Thank you, Tony. I'll escort Miss Holly to her door."

If it had been a day earlier, he'd have expected her to protest and insist that Tony walk her up the front steps of her building instead. Something had changed tonight, though. It felt as if he knew her now. *Really* knew her.

All that nonsense about their night together being a disaster?

She actually believed it, just not in the way he'd originally thought. Evangeline was convinced she'd been a disappointment, which couldn't have been further from the truth. It made him want to strangle that pompous foodie ex of hers...

Right after he took her to bed again and showed her exactly how much passion she kept hidden away in that beautifully guarded exterior of hers. But that wasn't going to happen. Not tonight, anyway. For a multitude of reasons, most of which had nothing whatsoever to do with Bennington 8.

He climbed out of the back seat and rounded the car, bowing his head against the winter wind, and then opened her door. "After you."

She stepped out and slipped past him, leaving a trace of airy floral scent behind her. Wholly feminine and just a little bit wild, like sun-kissed orchids.

Ryan took a deep breath and pressed his hand on to the small of her back as they navigated the icy sidewalk. Evangeline's neighborhood was dark. Quiet. Serenely so. The hum of the limo idling at the curb was the only sound piercing the silence. Ryan didn't have to glance at his watch to know that the time was closing in on midnight.

Twelve midnight—that notorious hour when fairy tales came to an end and Cinderella went home for the night, leaving her prince standing alone in the dark.

Except Evangeline wasn't looking at him with goodbye in her eyes. When she turned her gaze on him beneath the golden glow of the Village lamplights, he saw an unmistakable hint of something else. A new beginning.

"Ryan." For the first time since she'd walked through the revolving door of the Bennington, she didn't utter his name as if it were a curse word. On the contrary, it sounded more like a plea.

Something stirred deep inside him. Remembrance.

She whispered his name again, just as she had the last time she'd led him up these stairs.

"Eve," he said before he could stop himself, cupping her face in his hands.

Conviction churned in his gut. He knew good and well it was time to turn around and walk away. He shouldn't be letting her lift her arms and drape them languidly around his neck. His hands shouldn't be dropping to her waist, settling on the graceful dip just above her womanly hips. And he sure as hell had no business growing hard.

But he was. He was as hard as granite, and he'd barely touched her.

Step away. Do it now, while you still can.

He'd have given all he had—his shares in the Bennington, his penthouse overlooking Central Park and all the other pointless material possessions he'd accumulated—just to have her again. To hear her whisper his name on a broken sigh as he drove himself inside her.

What *things* matter, anyway? He'd spent a lifetime trying to make something of himself, trying to prove that he was better than his absentee parents... more than just the sum of their parts. Where had it gotten him?

Alone, that's where.

But he didn't just want Evangeline's body. He wanted...

More.

He wanted things he hadn't let himself want in a very long time. Since before the whole fiasco with Natalie. Things he wasn't prepared to want again. As ugly as the end had been between them, there'd been a certain sense of poetic justice in their parting. Only a fool wouldn't have seen it. Ryan didn't deserve the things he'd once wanted so desperately. He wouldn't have known what to do with them even if he'd had them.

Thanks for that, Mom and Dad.

Evangeline shifted, her breasts brushing softly against his chest. She gazed up at him through the lush fringe of her lashes, and her lips parted ever so slightly.

Don't. Don't ask me.

His thoughts were screaming even as his erection swelled, his mind and body in a full-on war with one another. To his great shame, he wasn't sure which would emerge victorious.

Please don't.

Evangeline rose up on tiptoe and every muscle in his frame tensed as her mouth hovered irresistibly close to his ear.

"Kiss me," she murmured, her breath dancing softly against his jaw.

How could he refuse?

He wanted her. There was no denying it. She knew it as well as he did, or she never would have dared to ask him for a kiss.

She's going to hate you after tonight. Rightfully so.

Her eyes were already closed, as her face tipped upward toward his. Then her mouth was just a whisper away, ready...wanting...

All he had to do was lean in and touch his lips to hers. One taste and he'd be a goner. No turning back.

He slid one hand along her jaw, pausing to brush the pad of his thumb gently along the swell of her lower lip before taking her chin in his grasp so that when her eyes fluttered open she was looking directly at him.

She blinked. Impatience creased her brow.

"We can't," he said as evenly as he could manage. "Not now. Not yet."

She blinked again, confused for a moment, as if he'd spoken to her in a foreign language. The moment was so bittersweet that Ryan wanted to swallow his words. Take them back and crush his mouth to hers.

He could practically feel her lips, cold from the biting wind, taste the forbidden warmth of her tongue sliding against his.

But it was too late.

"Oh my God." She shook her head, incredulous. *"Oh my God.* We can't? After everything you said to me tonight?"

He held up his hands. "Eve, let me explain."

"Don't call me that," she spit. "Ever again."

He nodded. "I deserve that."

It stung, nonetheless.

"You deserve worse. You told me to ask you when I wanted you to kiss me, so I did. And then you *refuse*?" She shook her head, blinking furiously as her eyes grew shiny with unshed tears. "Is this just some kind of game to you?"

"It's not what you think," he said, reaching for her.

She stepped backward, out of his grasp. "Is this something you do with all your other women? Are you playing hard to get, playboy-style?"

Ryan paused, and his jaw clenched with enough force to grind coal into diamonds. "First of all, there are no other women."

She rolled her eyes.

He sighed, not bothering to remind her she shouldn't believe everything she read in the papers, as she'd so clearly already made up her mind about him.

He narrowed his gaze. "Second of all, I don't play games. I'm a grown man, unlike..." *Him.*

He couldn't bring himself to utter Jeremy's name.

She lifted a brow. "Don't tell me Manhattan's hottest bachelor is jealous."

"I'm most certainly not." He most certainly *was.* Far more than he wanted to admit, even to himself. *Damn it.* "You and I both know that if I kiss you right now, it won't end there. Are you ready for that, Evangeline?"

He stepped closer, backing her up against the brick wall of her building, and planted his hands on either side of her head, hemming her in.

She stared daggers at him but couldn't seem to form a response. How on earth this woman could believe she wasn't passionate was a mystery he couldn't begin to fathom. She swallowed, drawing his attention to her neck, where her pulse boomed with such force he could see it flutter in the hollow of her throat. An excited little butterfly.

Lust shot through him, hard and fast. He needed to leave before he did something they'd both regret. But first she needed to know why he was willingly walking away from something they both wanted.

Needed. Craved.

He fixed his gaze on hers, staring into her eyes with such intention that she had no choice but to listen. "The last time I took you to bed, you were there because another man told you some things that were not only cruel, but also flat-out wrong. Maybe that wasn't the only reason, but it was certainly one of them. And that was fine. *Then.* I'm not judging your decision process in the slightest. We hardly knew each other. We were strangers."

She crossed her arms, but her hot gaze never strayed from his.

He continued, "Now I know you, Evangeline. I know you, and I want you now more than ever before. Hear what I'm saying—I want you so much that the next time I make love to you, there will be no one else in your head. Or your heart."

He swallowed. His throat felt raw all of a sudden, his words like razors scraping away at his deepest regret.

Maybe his refusal to kiss her wasn't as much about Jeremy as it was to do with Natalie. Either way, he was doing the right thing. Neither of them had a place here.

"The next time I kiss you…the next time I take

you to bed…it will be about us. And only us. Just you and me." His voice cracked on his parting words. "That's a promise."

Chapter Eight

In a perfect world, Evangeline would have called in sick the next day in order to avoid having to face her bachelor boss.

But she didn't live in a perfect world. She lived in a crazy, mixed-up place where Jeremy had become a culinary superstar without even trying, where she'd resorted to sneaking her dogs out in the middle of the night to do their business and worst of all, where she'd humiliated herself by asking Ryan to kiss her, only to have him adamantly refuse.

No.

He'd said *no.*

She couldn't believe it. *He'd* been the one who'd planted the idea in her head in the first place. *He'd* been the one who'd held her hand in the restaurant and given her that stirring speech about how passionate she was. And then he'd turned her down flat.

It was mortifying. Worse than mortifying. She'd never been so embarrassed in her life. Not even when Jeremy had confessed his affair.

She wouldn't have admitted as much to anyone, of course, least of all Ryan Wilde. She'd known the man for less than two months. She absolutely shouldn't be more emotional about his dismissal than she was about a breakup with someone she'd dated for two years.

And yet, she was.

Because he'd been right. She hadn't wanted just a kiss. She'd wanted more. She'd wanted all of him. Again. And he'd been fully aware of her intentions. He'd stood there and looked her right in the eyes as she'd yearned for him, burning with desire while snow fell around them, dusting his hair in a fine veil of frosty white.

Then he'd turned her down.

He'd framed his refusal in a promise, but Evangeline knew a rejection when she heard one.

Now, in the cold light of day, she was almost grateful. Sleeping with him again would have been a massive mistake. Nothing was going to change the fact that he was her boss. He also moonlighted as an expert playboy, apparently. And he was so skilled at it that he managed to trick women into throwing themselves at him, Evangeline included.

God, it was nauseating. She felt a sudden stab of sympathy for the Ryan Wilde fan club that gathered in the hotel lobby every morning. Bile rose to the back of her throat as she rounded the corner near Grand Central Station and the Bennington came into view.

The irony of her predicament wasn't lost on her. She legitimately felt physically ill, but calling in sick wasn't an option. She wouldn't have Ryan thinking she couldn't handle seeing him again. She preferred him to stop thinking about her at all, actually.

And vice versa.

Note taken, self.

"Good afternoon, Miss Holly." The general manager greeted her from behind the reservation desk as she clicked across the expansive lobby in her highest stilettos.

Power shoes.

"Good afternoon, Elliot." Her stomach churned, but she ignored it and shot him her brightest smile.

I might have begged my boss to kiss me last night, but I'm a professional, darn it.

Elliot's gaze flitted toward the hallway beyond the elevator bank. "Mr. Wilde would like to see you in the conference room adjacent to his office."

Her smile froze into place. *I'll bet he would.*

She shook her head. "I can't. I have a meeting with a vendor in half an hour. Would you let him know, please?"

Elliot frowned. "I'm afraid he's rearranged his schedule and stayed late specifically to meet with you and the other Mr. Wilde."

"Oh." He was talking about Zander, not Ryan. She really wished one of them would change his last name so she would stop getting them mixed up. "I see. Of course I'll make myself available."

Her tummy gave another sickening flip. Zander

had rearranged his day in order to meet with her and Ryan the minute she walked in the door?

He knows.

Her humiliation was multiplied one hundred times over. Was she about to get grilled about her personal life? Was Zander going to make her explain the awkward events of the night before?

Was she about to be *fired*?

She couldn't lose this job. She had an elderly grandfather and two dogs depending on her.

Relax. You've done nothing wrong.

True, thanks to Ryan's sudden virtuous streak.

Still, her faith in her power shoes was beginning to waver. She swallowed and pressed a hand to her stomach as she neared the conference room.

"Hello, Evangeline. Come on in." Zander waved at the empty chair beside Ryan when she poked her head inside the door.

She'd have preferred to sit someplace else. *Any-place* else, actually. But at least she wouldn't have to look at him.

She lowered herself into the designated seat. Ryan's gaze swept over her, but she kept her attention fixed firmly forward.

Zander sat back in his chair, a little too relaxed for a CEO who was about to fire someone. "Well?" he prompted. "How was last night? Give me the debrief."

Evangeline released a breath she hadn't realized she'd been holding. This was a simple discussion about Mon Ami Jules, not a termination. She could do this. Easy-peasy.

Where shall I start? With the fact that the chef was

*my ex or the part where a tiny brush of Ryan's thumb
against the palm of my hand gave me goose bumps?*

"The wine was substandard," she said flatly.

"I disagree," Ryan countered with a lazy shrug.

Of course he did. Would it kill him to cooperate
with her on one tiny thing? Especially when that
thing was her area of expertise?

Zander frowned and consulted the stack of papers
spread across the table in front of him. "I've got a
copy of Carlo Bocci's review for the *Times*, and he
specifically mentions the excellence of the sommelier's recommendation."

He glanced at the printed page on top of the stack
again. "It was a Côtes du Rhône."

Evangeline asked him to name the vintage, and
he rattled off the information that matched the wine
the sommelier had poured for her and Ryan the night
before.

"Interesting." She pulled a face. "I wasn't particularly impressed with it."

Zander's attention shifted toward Ryan. "But you
liked it?"

"I did," he said slowly. "But I'm not the expert."

That's right. You're not.

But Carlo Bocci sort of was, and he disagreed
with her, too.

Evangeline's smile grew tight. She wished they'd
move on to a critique of the meal. But now that she
thought about it, she'd barely eaten anything. She
hadn't had much of an appetite lately.

"Do we have this wine in-house?" Zander asked.

Evangeline nodded. "Yes, we do. Would you like
me to pour a glass for you?"

Zander held up three fingers. "Pour one for each of us. I think a tasting is in order."

"Very well. I'll be right back."

It was a relief to escape the room for a few minutes, even though she was beginning to feel like her job was indeed on the line. Her taste was being questioned. That's what was happening, wasn't it?

Fine. She had the utmost confidence in her ability to evaluate wines. She'd grown up surrounded by grapevines. She knew wine like the back of her hand. More so than Carlo Bocci, probably.

She returned to the conference room holding a decanter, a trio of balloon-style wineglasses and a bottle of the red in question. Once she'd placed the items on the conference table, she gave Zander and Ryan a brief lesson on Côtes du Rhône varieties. If she was going to present a wine for tasting, she insisted on doing it right. Like a proper sommelier, because that's what she was.

For the time being, anyway.

"A good Côtes du Rhône will never upstage a meal, but was instead created to enhance it," she said. "It's a fruit-driven, quiet wine. Medium-bodied with an earthy flavor."

She uncorked the bottle, and to her great dismay, realized that her hands were shaking. She blamed Ryan. His unwavering stare as she spoke was beginning to unnerve her. She felt exposed...vulnerable, as if she were standing naked at the head of the table.

"Are you feeling okay, Evangeline?" Zander asked. "You look rather pale."

She glanced up from the bottle in her hands, her

rebellious gaze veering straight toward Ryan. His brow was creased in concern.

"I'm fine, thank you." *I'm blowing this.*

Her original plan had been to stick to her guns and convince them she was right. The wine was bad, plain and simple, even though she ordinarily enjoyed a nice glass of CDR. And the vineyard that had produced this vintage had a sterling reputation.

She realized now that she was going to have to switch gears. Bocci was a Michelin star reviewer. *The* reviewer who'd hopefully be dining at Bennington 8 sometime in the coming weeks. Arguing against his opinion would be pointless.

She was going to have to fake it. She'd sip the wine and pretend it was the best Côtes du Rhône she'd ever tasted. It was her only option.

Easier said than done.

When she poured the wine into the decanter so it could breathe, she was hit with an aroma so strong that it nearly knocked her over. Fermented grapes, black plum, candied berries—she could smell it all. And everything seemed...*off.* The fruity notes were so pungent they almost smelled rotten. When she swallowed, she tasted vinegar at the back of her throat.

She covered her mouth with her free hand in an effort to stop herself from gagging. Something was wrong. Very, very wrong. Côtes du Rhône shouldn't have such a strong bouquet, even if it had somehow gone bad. It wasn't a heavy wine. Many experts called it cabernet light.

There was nothing light about the overwhelming smell of alcohol burning Evangeline's nostrils. She forced herself to breathe only through her mouth as she swirled the wine in the decanter so it could properly aerate.

"Evangeline." The silence in the conference room was broken by Ryan aggressively clearing his throat. "Can I see you in private for a moment?"

Seriously?

She stared at him and shook her head as subtly as she could manage.

No. Absolutely not.

Zander glanced back and forth between them. "What is it, Ryan?"

Ryan's gaze remained steadfastly fixed on Evangeline's face when he answered. "It's personal."

She was going to kill him. She was going to strangle him with his fancy Hermès tie right then and there.

"I'm sorry, Zander. I have no idea what he's talking about." A hysterical laugh bubbled up her throat. *Get it together.* She addressed Ryan without bothering to look at him. "I'm sure whatever you need to discuss with me can wait until after the tasting."

"It can't," he countered.

She pretended not to hear him as she poured three glasses, sliding two of them across the table toward the men.

Zander kept glancing around, appeared thoroughly confused, albeit handsomely so. The Wilde family had clearly lucked out in the genetic lottery.

"Evangeline," Ryan said tersely.

"Ryan." She pasted a smile on her face and fixed her gaze with his. *Would you kindly shut up?*

Zander held up his glass. "Cheers?" It sounded more like a question than a proper toast.

Evangeline reached for her drink, more than ready to get the tasting over with. She had no intention of speaking to Ryan one-on-one afterward. If he thought she was going to discuss anything remotely personal with him at work, he'd lost his arrogant mind.

She didn't *ever* want to speak to him alone again, and definitely wouldn't be asking him to kiss her again. No. Way. She just wanted to forget last night ever happened.

A glass of wine suddenly seemed like an excellent idea, even though the smell made her stomach turn. But just as her fingertips were about to make contact with the crystal stem of her wineglass, Ryan reached for it, too. It almost seemed as if he did it on purpose, she thought.

Red wine splashed all over her, from the cowl-necked top of her white angora sweater to the tips of her suddenly drenched power stilettos. As she stood there with Côtes du Rhône dripping from her hair, a wave of nausea hit her hard and fast, and she no longer cared whether or not the spill had been intentional. She needed to get to a bathroom.

Immediately.

She'd worry about pummeling Ryan Wilde later.

Well, that didn't turn out quite like I planned.

Ryan closed his eyes. Took a deep breath. When he opened them, red wine was dripping from the conference table onto the plush dove-gray carpet.

Zander was looking at him as if he'd just sprouted another head.

Evangeline was nowhere to be seen.

"Sorry," he said. "We reached for the same glass and…"

He didn't bother finishing. There was no way Zander would buy such a flimsy explanation. Not when every visible surface was drenched in Côtes du Rhône.

He'd panicked. He'd never intended to make such a mess. *Obviously.* He'd just wanted to stop Evangeline from taking a sip.

Mission accomplished, idiot.

"I should go check on Miss Holly." He turned and headed for the door.

He couldn't get into a discussion with Zander about this disaster. Not now. He could barely think straight, let alone come up with a reasonable excuse for his behavior.

He'd explain everything eventually. If what he suspected was true, he wouldn't have a choice.

"Send for housekeeping while you're at it, would you?" Zander said calmly.

Too calmly.

"Will do." Ryan strode out of the room.

He flagged down the closest hotel employee and requested help in the conference room, then headed for the nearby ladies' room. He didn't linger. Didn't think twice about what to do next. He ignored the feminine stick figure sign and pushed his way inside.

By some miracle, the restroom was empty, save for one stall with its door closed. He settled against the marble counter, crossed his arms and waited.

Sure enough, Evangeline emerged seconds later, looking as white as a sheet. Ryan's heart gave an undeniable tug. She was like a very lovely ghost of her very lovely self. Pale, fragile, delicate. All words he normally wouldn't associate with Evangeline.

Then she caught sight of him and managed to muster enough strength to narrow her eyes in fury.

"Get out," she croaked.

He shook his head. "We need to talk. Now."

"Do you have any idea how crazy you're behaving? You just tossed a glass of wine at me, and now you've ambushed me in the women's restroom." She waved her arms around the restroom's serene interior. "Is it even legal for you to be here?"

He didn't know. Nor did he care.

"I'm sorry about your clothes. I'll replace them with whatever you'd like. Take my Bloomingdale's card." He started to reach for the inside pocket of his suit jacket, then stopped.

What was he doing? He'd barged in here because he had something to say. Something important. Something that would change her life in a profound way. His, too, possibly.

If what he suspected was true.

How could this be happening again?

Sitting beside Zander while Evangeline poured the wine, struggling not to gag, Ryan had a deep sense of déjà vu. He was being revisited by his deepest desire and his worst nightmare, all rolled into one. Of course he'd panicked. It was a wonder he'd managed to hold on to anything remotely resembling sanity.

"Save it. I don't want your money. I just want you to let me do my job." Evangeline lifted her chin in defiance, but there was a telltale wobble in her bottom lip that told him that wasn't *all* she wanted. Like him, she wanted more. But for some reason, she couldn't bring herself to admit it.

The urge to close the distance between them and take her in his arms was overwhelming.

He didn't dare.

The door to the restroom flew open, and a woman holding a little girl by the hand stepped inside.

The young girl's eyes went as big as saucers. "Mommy, why is there a man in here?"

Ryan's throat clogged. *Mommy.*

He sighed mightily and tried his best not to look like a weirdo who cornered women in restrooms on a regular basis. "I'm sorry. Could you give us a minute? Please?"

After casting a questioning glance toward Evangeline, the girl's mother seemed satisfied nothing untoward was going on. She nodded. "Fine. One minute. But we'll be right outside."

"Thank you." He scrubbed a hand over his face. Super. Now he was being timed.

Once they were alone again, Evangeline strode to the sink, wet a paper towel and pressed it to her forehead. She closed her eyes and her voice dropped to a raw whisper. "I might need to go home for a while. I think I'm coming down with something."

Ryan watched as she tossed the paper towel in the trash and stared at her reflection in the mirror.

She wrapped her arms around herself, like she was trying as hard as she could to hold herself together. Her gaze dropped lower, and Ryan's heart lodged firmly in his throat as her hand slid to her stomach.

Surely she knew.

He couldn't be the only one. All the signs were there—the nausea, the fatigue. Hadn't he seen her nodding off in the wine cooler a few days ago?

But the clincher was her sudden aversion to alcohol. No one loved wine more than Evangeline. Ryan had never met anyone so knowledgeable or passionate about the stuff.

And yet she'd turned her nose up at every glass she'd come across in the past week. Somewhere on his desk he had a copy of an irate email from a vendor who'd written to him to complain that Evangeline had refused delivery on a case of Bordeaux shipped all the way from France because the wine had allegedly turned sour. It was a wonder he hadn't figured out what was going on days ago.

He hadn't suspected a thing until moments ago in the conference room when she'd opened the bottle of red and looked as though she might faint. The truth had hit him like a ton of bricks, and now it was so obvious that he couldn't believe he hadn't seen it sooner.

On some level, she had to know, too.

All that was left was for one of them to say it.

He took a deep breath and met her gaze in the mirror. "Evangeline, you're not sick. You're pregnant."

Chapter Nine

Pregnant.

Pregnant!

How could she have let this happen?

It was official. She was an abysmal failure at one-night stands. She would never, ever have one again. One little slip, and now her entire life had changed.

"No." She shook her head. "I can't be."

She'd missed her period last month, but not entirely. There'd been some spotting and even a little bit of cramping. Granted, she'd been tired a lot. And there'd been that strange night at wine group the other day when she hadn't been able to identify a single vintage. She hadn't had much of a taste for wine at all lately.

"Eve." Ryan's tone had suddenly gone so quiet, so serious, that she couldn't bring herself to chastise him again for calling her by the name she now associated with her adventurous, sexy alter ego…that passionate fool.

He was right, wasn't he? He hadn't needed to say it. The truth had slammed right into her right around the time she'd fallen to her knees in front of the toilet bowl—she was pregnant. She just hadn't wanted to believe it.

She had all the early symptoms. Every single one of them.

"It's going to be okay." Ryan's mouth curved into a tiny smile. "I promise."

He was *smiling*? At a time like this?

She tore her gaze from the mirror and turned to face him. Her knees wobbled, and she had to grip the counter behind her to steady herself, but something about the subtle lift of his lips took the edge off her panic.

Until some semblance of clarity descended on her and she fully grasped what his smile meant—the baby growing inside her wasn't just hers. It was his. She was pregnant with Ryan Wilde's child.

She shook her head. Hard. "We don't even know if it's true. It could be the flu. I need to see a doctor."

Maybe multiple doctors. A whole team of medical professionals. She needed to be sure before she could begin to wrap her head around this.

A baby.

Ryan's baby.

There was no doubt in her mind. She'd never been as amorous with Jeremy as she'd been that night with Ryan. She couldn't even remember the last time she and Jeremy had slept together, which should probably have been a warning sign that the relationship wasn't all she'd believed it to be.

Now here she was, possibly pregnant by a man with whom she had no relationship whatsoever.

She studied him, marveling at his composure. How was he so calm? Aside from drenching her in Côtes du Rhône, he seemed completely unruffled.

The wine.

She let her gaze travel to his hands, his fingertips, and she stared, remembering the way he knocked the glass out of her grasp...the unmistakable intention in his eyes. He'd deliberately stopped her from drinking because he'd suspected she was pregnant and he'd been worried about the baby.

It was sweet, in a controlling, maniacal sort of way. But it still didn't mean she was actually pregnant, and it definitely didn't mean she was chomping at the bit to start a family with him. Or anyone.

"I doubt it's the flu," he said evenly. "But seeing a doctor is a good idea. I'll ring the driver."

He gathered his cell phone from his pocket, but before he could dial, Evangeline grabbed his wrist. "Wait a minute. How are you so intimately acquainted with early-pregnancy symptoms?"

His expression went blank. Guarded.

Oh God.

"I see." She swallowed, and a fresh wave of nausea rolled over her. "You've been through this before."

Of course he had. How naive could she be? The man had a literal harem. There were probably tiny Ryan Wildes running around all over Manhattan.

She released her hold on his wrist and brushed a tear from the corner of her eye. She hadn't even realized she'd started to cry. And when had her hands begun to tremble so violently? Her body felt as though it was crumpling in on itself.

"Have I been through this before? Yes and no," he said after a long pause.

What did that even mean?

The bathroom door swung open again, revealing the young mother who'd tried to enter moments ago. She narrowed her gaze at Ryan and planted her free hand on her hip. Her tiny daughter maintained a firm grip on the other one. "It's been *three* minutes. Time's up. We're coming in."

Ryan held up his hands in a gesture of surrender. "My apologies. Do come in."

They had a brief conversation, wherein Ryan asked if she was a guest at the hotel and promised to have an extensive selection of complimentary desserts sent up to their room in return for her patience. Everything on the menu, from the Italian cream cake to the triple banana split. The little girl's eyes lit up, and her mother exchanged a few more words with Ryan.

Evangeline couldn't keep up with what was being said. All her attention was focused on the toddler— the bright red bow in her hair, her patent leather Mary Janes, the lace trim on her ankle socks. But above all else, Evangeline couldn't stop marveling at the way she never let go of her mother's hand.

She inhaled a shuddering breath. Fate had made some kind of terrible mistake. Evangeline didn't know the first thing about being a mother. The very word was almost foreign to her.

"Let's go." Ryan wrapped his hand around her waist

and ushered her out the door, toward the Bennington lobby.

She wanted to tell him not to touch her. Pregnancy aside, she still wasn't over the humiliating events of the night before. Plus they were at work. Zander was probably back in the conference room, mopping up wine and getting termination papers in order for both of them. The usual crowd of blushing bachelorettes was gathered beneath the massive gold clock that hung above the sitting area's sumptuous velvet sofas, beaming at Ryan as they walked past.

But Evangeline didn't protest. It had been a long time since she'd had anyone to lean on. A very long, very lonely time. And even though she knew she shouldn't—even though she was painfully aware that they weren't a real couple and never would be—she rested her head against his broad shoulder and let him bear the weight of her burdened heart.

Just this once.

Ryan had Tony take them to the closest urgent care center. A hospital seemed like overkill, but the likelihood of getting an appointment with a regular doctor in Manhattan on the spur of the moment was dubious at best. Evangeline sat beside him, growing paler by the minute as she stared out the limousine's window.

A baby.

Ryan's chest seized. He took a deep inhale, but the limo felt short on air all of a sudden.

Could he do this again? Could he hold Evangeline's hand through nine months of doctor's appointments, attend birthing classes and cater to her nutty pregnancy cravings?

Could he open his home and his heart to an infant? *This won't be like last time. It can't.*

He couldn't possibly be that unlucky twice in a lifetime. Then again, his present circumstances didn't have anything to do with luck. He'd chosen Evangeline that night. He'd known next to nothing about her, but he'd broken every rule he'd lived by since the Natalie fiasco and taken her to bed. He wasn't altogether certain he'd used a condom either. That was a definite first.

A shrink would probably tell him he'd chosen these circumstances, that a part of him still longed for the family he never had as a boy. A real family, a mom and dad instead of an aunt and uncle who'd been kind enough to take him in when he'd had nowhere else to go. Hell, Zander would probably say the same thing.

He'd be wrong.

Ryan knew better than to reach for things he'd never had. He'd wanted Evangeline. He still did, now more than ever. But wanting her…needing her… wasn't the same as believing they could have forever. He'd accepted his fate. Having a family, a life, ripped out from under you not once, but twice, did that to a person.

The car slowed to a stop in front of a small building just off Madison with a red cross in the window and a sign indicating no appointment necessary.

Tony met Ryan's gaze in the rearview mirror. "Shall I wait here, sir?"

Evangeline grasped the door handle closest to her, ready to bolt. "That's not necessary. I can take it from here."

"No," Ryan countered. Over his dead body. "I'll accompany Miss Holly, Tony. Stand by and I'll give you a call when we're finished."

"Yes, sir."

Evangeline sighed, but didn't put up more of a fight. Ryan suspected she was probably too preoccupied to argue, and for that he was grateful.

Once inside, Evangeline explained to the receptionist that she needed a pregnancy test. A *blood* test, she specified. The most reliable one available. The woman on the other side of the frosted glass partition nodded and handed her a clipboard full of forms, which Evangeline completed at warp speed despite her trembling hands.

A nurse in scrubs called her back almost immediately. At the sound of Evangeline's name, Ryan stood.

Evangeline squeezed his hand, but at the same time said, "No. Please. I'd like to do this on my own."

Then she was gone.

The door clicked closed behind her, and he found himself alone in the sterile waiting room, shut out and enveloped in antiseptic odors and the monotonous, even beeps of medical equipment. Sights, sounds and smells that were all too familiar.

He'd been in a waiting room eerily similar to this one when he'd learned the truth. When the grand charade had fallen apart. Natalie had given birth just five hours previously, and at first, everything seemed fine. Not just fine—wonderful. Better than Ryan ever imagined.

He and Natalie had only been seeing each other for four months when she'd told him she was expecting. To say it had been a shock would be a massive understatement. He'd been so careful. But there wasn't a birth control method on earth that was one hundred percent effective, and even though it would have been a stretch to say he and Natalie were in love, they were going to be parents. Together.

Letting her raise the baby alone was never an option. Ryan couldn't fathom the thought of not being a part of his child's day-to-day life. He moved in with Natalie right away, and he was there for every moment of the pregnancy—every bout of morning sickness, every sonogram.

Then came the contractions. The birth. And Ryan was there for that, too, squeezing Natalie's hand and urging her to push. The moment the baby boy's cries pierced the air, something had come loose inside Ryan—some part of him that had been bound up tight, cutting off his oxygen since the day his parents had abandoned him and left him to fend for himself at six years of age.

He could breathe again, and the future seemed so blindingly bright. A shimmering, soulful place where he had someone to call his own. He remembered with absolute clarity sitting in that hospital lounge—the one that so resembled the polished, sanitary space where he sat now—with his head in his hands, overcome with relief. As soon as he'd seen that baby, heard his plaintive cries, Ryan had loved that child. The doubts he'd had all along about Natalie didn't seem to matter anymore. They could raise the baby together. They could be a family, and love would come. Eventually.

Then came the hand, heavy on his shoulder, and the look of alarm on the doctor's face—the same doctor who'd just smiled at Ryan in the delivery room minutes before. *It's a boy.*

Ryan had known right away that something had gone terribly wrong. There was no misinterpreting that expression. He tried to ask for specifics, but the words stuck in his throat.

"The baby is in distress," the doctor bluntly stated.

After Ryan had stepped out of the room to call Zander and the rest of the Wildes, the baby had started bleeding internally. They'd stopped the hemorrhage right away but as a result he'd become severely anemic.

"Is there anything I can do?" Ryan had asked once he'd regained the ability to form words. "Donate blood, maybe?"

"That would be a huge help. In cases of neonatal transfusions, we try to use direct donations from family members as much as we can."

So Ryan had gone straight to the hospital's blood lab, and that's where he learned that Natalie's baby—the tiny little boy he'd fallen in love with on sight, the family he'd never had—wasn't his, after all.

His blood wasn't a match. Both Natalie and her son had O negative blood type, and Ryan's blood was AB positive. It was medically impossible for him to be the father.

Natalie had known the truth all along. Once the baby was out of the woods and she was presented with the irrefutable evidence, she'd confessed.

She never apologized, never shed a tear. "I wanted you to be the father. Shouldn't that count for something?"

With those words, the best day of Ryan's life had become the worst.

The crazy thing was, he might have still stuck around. He'd anticipated the birth of that baby for months. But Natalie didn't wait for him to decide. When he showed up at the hospital the following morning to talk things out with her, she'd packed up her son and gone.

"Can I get you anything, sir?"

Ryan looked up. The nurse who'd just escorted Evangeline to the back of the urgent care clinic stood a few feet away with a bottle of water in one hand and a steaming disposable cup in the other.

"You looked so worried, I thought you could use a distraction." She held both offerings toward him.

"Thank you." He chose the coffee. It was terrible, but he was grateful nonetheless.

"You're welcome. And don't worry. Your wife will be out in just a few minutes." She padded away, her white sneakers squishing softly on the polished tile floor.

Your wife.

The words echoed in Ryan's consciousness. He waited for the inevitable tightness in his chest that usually came when someone mentioned his name in the same breath as marriage. It happened on a surprisingly frequent basis, most notably on the pages of Vows, the *New York Times*' wedding section.

He usually laughed it off. Made a joke out of it, which was undoubtedly why Zander thought hanging the Hottest Bachelor magazine cover in his office was hilarious.

But he didn't feel much like laughing now. Nor

did his chest feel like it was being squeezed in a vise. For reasons he didn't want to examine too closely, he felt fine. Happy, almost.

Which defied all logic.

He was losing it, he thought bitterly as he sipped his coffee. Evangeline emerged moments later, just as he choked down the dregs. Their gazes locked, and he stood.

"You were right." She took a deep breath, and then her hand slid to her stomach and settled there in a protective gesture that rendered her following words unnecessary. "The test was positive. I'm pregnant."

Chapter Ten

She was going to have to quit her job.

Obviously.

It wasn't as if she could be an effective sommelier if she couldn't even drink wine. Although she knew her pregnancy wouldn't last forever. And she could always use a tasting spit cup. Sommeliers did it all the time, but something told her Zander Wilde would be less than thrilled to know his wine director was expelling every sip she took into an empty glass. Even if the empty glass was Baccarat cut crystal, which was what sat on every table at Bennington 8.

Besides, at the moment Evangeline couldn't tolerate even the smallest whiff of alcohol, much less the taste of it. So, the morning after the surreal visit to the urgent care clinic, she typed her letter of resignation and then strode into the Bennington with it tucked neatly into her handbag.

She glanced at the sitting area where Ryan's fan club usually assembled, but for once it was unoccupied. The little zing of relief that fluttered through her told her the resignation letter in her bag had less to do with her ability to do her job and everything to do with the father of her baby.

She couldn't work with Ryan day in and day out while his unborn child grew inside her. She just couldn't. It was hardly professional, but more than that, it was just plain dangerous.

She'd practically thrown herself at him before she knew she was pregnant. How was she supposed to maintain her distance from him now? When he'd turned her down before, she'd been embarrassed. But there was more at stake now than her pride. So much more. Now she had everything to lose.

A future.

A family.

Her heart.

The ride home from the urgent care clinic had been excruciating. No one had said a word, which Evangeline took to understand that Ryan wouldn't argue when she handed him the letter and told him she thought they should go their separate ways. He'd probably be relieved.

Neither of them had planned this pregnancy. Neither of them wanted it. Except now that it was happening, Evangeline *did* want it. She wanted the baby—her baby, *Ryan's* baby—very much. More than she'd wanted anything in as long as she could remember.

She didn't know a thing about being a mother. Her own mom hadn't exactly been a stellar example. But if her own childhood had taught her anything, it was that her baby came first. From here on out, all of her focus had to be on her pregnancy. Potentially getting her heart crushed by the bachelor of the year didn't belong anywhere in the equation.

She took a deep breath as she rounded the corner and walked the remaining steps toward Ryan's office. She hadn't set foot inside the luxe space since her first day of work when she'd vowed to keep everything between them strictly business.

Epic fail.

"Ryan, I…" Her voice faltered when she stepped inside, looked around and found the office empty.

Great. He wasn't there. It had taken her an entire day's worth of pep talks to bring herself to face the playboy father of her baby, to say the things she needed to say, and he wasn't even there.

Maybe it was for the best. Maybe fate had finally cut her a break. She wasn't sure if she could go through with it if she had to look him in the eye while she pretended she wanted to have the baby all on her own.

She didn't.

But she also didn't want to end up like her father had after her mother left.

Losing her had broken him. Evangeline didn't want to be broken like that. She'd spent her entire adult life protecting herself from that kind of pain. It was why she'd stayed with Jeremy as long as she had, even though deep down she'd always known she deserved something different. Something better. Something real.

It was also why she'd been in such a hurry to kick

Ryan out of her apartment when she'd woken up with his cuff links on her nightstand and her head on his chest. She couldn't be broken by the loss of something she'd never really had.

The letter inside her bag seemed like a terrible, living, breathing thing. Evangeline was eager to be rid of it, before she changed her mind. She reached for the crisp white envelope, crossed the spacious office and placed it on Ryan's chair. Right where he couldn't miss it.

She paused for a beat, and Ryan's words from the night outside her apartment danced in her mind, like a magical, mystical snowfall.

I want you so much that the next time I make love to you, there will be no one else in your head. Or your heart.

Just you and me.

But it would never be just the two of them. There were three of them now. Everything had changed.

I can't do this.

She couldn't walk away with her typed resignation letter as her only goodbye. That would make her no better than her mother.

She turned back for the envelope, but a voice stopped her in her tracks.

A woman's voice, calling out, "Knock knock!"

The singsong quality of the greeting turned Evangeline's stomach. This was obviously someone who was close enough to Ryan to feel comfortable strolling into his office in the middle of the day. And to top it off, she was beautiful—willowy thin and graceful, with a neck like a swan and masses of thick dark hair piled on her head in the kind of casually elegant updo that Evangeline had never managed to master.

"Oh, sorry." The woman glanced around the office, registering the absence of its occupant. "Ryan's not in?"

So this stunning person and Ryan were on a first-name basis. Evangeline wasn't the least bit surprised.

"No, he's not." A lump lodged in her throat. She couldn't have felt more like a third wheel if she'd plopped right down in the lobby with all the other members of the Ryan Wilde fan club.

"Can I give him a message for you?" She hated the way her voice wavered, betraying her emotion. Resigning was the right thing to do. She couldn't stay here and linger on the fringe like an extra on an episode of *The Bachelor*.

"Oh my God. You think I'm one of them, don't you?" The balletic stranger laughed. "You think I'm one of Ryan's women."

Evangeline felt sick. *Ryan's women.* "You're not?"

"No." She rolled her eyes. "God, no. Those women are delusional. Although you have to admire their persistence. And their optimism. As far as I know, Ryan hasn't even gone out on a date in close to a year."

Wait…*what*?

"But he's New York's hottest bachelor." Evangeline's face went hot. "At least that's what the magazine cover says."

She gestured toward the framed issue of *Gotham* hanging above his desk, but it wasn't there anymore. The wall was bare.

The dancer followed her gaze. "He took it down a

while ago. My husband gave it to him as a joke, but Ryan never found it quite as amusing as Zander did. Men, am I right?" She rolled her eyes.

The pieces were falling into place. Evangeline remembered hearing something about Zander's wife being a ballet teacher. "You're Allegra?"

She nodded and extended a lithe arm. "Allegra Wilde."

Evangeline shook her hand. "Nice to meet you. I'm Evangeline."

Allegra smiled. "Ah, so you're the wine director I've heard so much about."

She nodded. She was still the hotel wine director... for now, at least. "I'm not sure where Ryan is at the moment. I need to speak to him myself, actually."

Allegra's gaze ventured over her shoulder and landed on the envelope in Ryan's chair. "I stopped by to have lunch with Zander. I thought I'd poke my head in to tell Ryan hello and see if he's coming to Sunday dinner this weekend. It was nice to see him last week. He's kept to himself for way too long. Such a hermit."

Hermit? Was she serious?

Evangeline probably shouldn't be having this conversation. Scratch that—she definitely shouldn't. It felt like prying. And the fact that she was seriously tempted to interrogate one of Ryan's family members to get more information on his supposedly notorious love life was pathetic.

"That whole bachelor business is just something a reporter for the Vows column at the *Times* made up because she was looking for another big story after the Bennington Curse was proven to be bogus." Allegra's voice softened, and something in her gaze made Evangeline's heart skip a beat. "Ryan Wilde is no playboy. You know that, don't you?"

The Bennington Curse. It had been all over the internet a few months ago. Evangeline wasn't sure about the specifics, other than it had something to do with runaway brides. It had always sounded more like a Julia Roberts romcom than real life.

The story about Ryan, however, she'd bought. Hook, line and sinker.

It was just so believable. He was handsome, charming and kind. Beyond swoon worthy. Weeks after they'd met, he still remembered which eye Olive could see out of. He'd gone out of his way to make her feel special at Mon Ami Jules. If he hadn't been there, she never would have made it through the first course. And he'd been so desperate to stop her from drinking the Côtes du Rhone in the conference room—desperate to protect her baby. Their baby.

Even his hands were nice. Strong. Manly…as if they'd be perfectly capable of assembling complicated furniture. A crib, perhaps.

Who wouldn't want to marry him?

She swallowed around the lump that was rapidly forming in her throat.

No.

No, no, no.

She would *not* start thinking she had actual feelings for him. Because she didn't. She *couldn't*.

"Why are you telling me this?" she asked Allegra in a near whisper.

Allegra smiled. "Because it's the truth. And because it seems like something you needed to hear."

Allegra's attention flitted to the envelope again and then back to Evangeline. She looked her right in the eye for a long, silent moment—a moment in which Evangeline's heart fluttered wildly in her chest.

Then before Allegra turned to go, her gaze drifted lower...to Evangeline's hand resting lightly, unconsciously, on her stomach, where Ryan's child grew inside her.

Ryan returned to his office after his monthly accounting meeting to find Evangeline standing beside his desk. Her arms were crossed, and she had the same determined expression that she'd worn the last time she'd sashayed into his inner sanctum.

Back then, she'd come to tell him she wanted to keep things between them purely professional. Back then, she'd also been pregnant. They'd just been oblivious to that significant detail.

"Evangeline." A trickle of worry snaked its way down his spine. He knew that look. "To what do I owe the pleasure?"

He sat down on the corner of his desk and did his best to ignore the clench in his gut that told him she'd come to deliver another unpleasant ultimatum.

She'd been alarmingly quiet on the way home from the clinic the night before. Shell-shocked. He'd thought it best to give her some space—time to absorb the fact that she was going to be a mother. Of course they needed to talk about how they were going to proceed, but he hadn't wanted to push. After all, they had nearly nine months to figure things out.

Looking at her now, he realized his silence had been a mistake. A big one.

"Why didn't you tell me?" She looked him up and down, her gaze lingering briefly on his hands. Then she lifted her glittering eyes to his.

She was breathtaking, even in her anger. So beautiful that it took him a moment to respond.

"You're going to have to give me a hint here, love." Her cheeks flared deliciously pink at the endearment. "What didn't I tell you?"

She took a step closer to him, so close that he could feel the heat of her indignation...of the passion that she still didn't quite believe she possessed. A wave of desire crashed over Ryan. If he hadn't already been seated, he might have fallen to his knees.

"All this time you let me think you were some kind of womanizer. A swinging bachelor." She swallowed, drawing his attention to her slender neck, where her pulse boomed furiously at the base of her throat. "And you're not."

Swinging bachelor?

Other than Hugh Hefner, had anyone ever used that term nonironically? What kind of cad had she thought he was, exactly?

"You're upset," he said evenly.

"Of course I'm upset," she spit.

"Because I'm a decent guy." Ryan lifted a brow.

She was so adorably furious, full of fire and light, and she wasn't making a lick of sense. But it was killing him not to touch her, to take her in his arms and kiss the righteous smirk right off her face.

"Precisely. Yes." She blinked, then frowned and

shook her head. "I mean, no. Not because you're decent, exactly. It's just…"

It's just that she was pregnant. They were having a baby together, and her reaction to the news had progressed from shock to panic.

She's scared.

She's scared out of her mind, and she's pushing you away.

He swallowed, suddenly far more troubled than amused.

Don't let her.

He stood, closed the distance between them and took her face in his hands. She glanced over his shoulder, toward the opened office door. Anyone in the building could have walked in on them right then, but Ryan couldn't have cared less. Their days of hiding were numbered. The truth was bound to come out eventually.

Not that he had a full grasp himself on what exactly was happening between them. What *was* the truth? They were going to be parents, but was that the extent of it?

Not if he could help it.

"What is it that you're trying to tell me? Talk to me, Evangeline," he said.

She looked at him for a long, loaded moment, as if he were some kind of complicated puzzle she was trying to understand. Then her voice dropped to a fragile whisper. So fragile that something broke inside Ryan when she finally spoke. "I hardly know a thing about you, and I'm having your baby."

His baby…

His.

Warmth radiated through Ryan's body, starting at the center and spreading outward to the tips of his fingers and toes. *Mine.*

He let his forehead fall against Evangeline's and ran his thumb in gentle, soothing circles over her cheek. He could have stayed that way all day, breathing her in. The mother of his child. "That's easily fixable, Eve. If there's something you want to know, just ask me. I'm right here."

Her eyes went wide. Glowing. "I can ask you anything. Really?"

"Really." He pulled back and waited, wondering just how deep she wanted to go.

Evangeline bit her lip as her gaze flitted to the wall above his desk. "When did you take the *Gotham* cover down?"

"On your first day of work, right after you came in here reading me the riot act."

She bit her lip. "Why?"

"Because I could tell it upset you, and because I always despised it myself."

The corner of her mouth tipped into a quiet grin.

"At last, a smile. Right answer?" He raised a brow.

She nodded. "Right answer."

"What else? I know there are more questions swirling in that gorgeous head of yours." He reached to tuck a stray curl behind her ear, enjoying the new-found intimacy between them, hoping it would last.

She took a deep breath. "Yesterday on the way to the clinic, when I asked if you'd been through this before, you gave a cryptic answer—yes and no. What did that mean?"

Ryan grew still.

He never discussed Natalie and her baby. With anyone. The Wildes knew what had happened of course, but Ryan resisted Emily's many efforts to get him to "talk it out." He wanted to forget. He didn't want to talk about it, hence his prolonged absence from Sunday dinner.

But Evangeline needed to know, before she jumped to more conclusions.

"Last year, a woman I was seeing became pregnant. She told me the child was mine, but on the day the baby was born, I found out she'd lied. I wasn't the father. We parted ways afterward." He tried to keep his gaze locked with hers, but in the end he couldn't. He didn't need to look her in the eye to know what he'd see there—pity. And he didn't want pity from Evangeline.

He wanted more.

Her breath hitched audibly in her throat, and then her hands reached for his. "Oh my God, Ryan. That's terrible."

"It's in the past." He looked up, and to his infinite surprise and relief, there wasn't a trace of pity in her expression. Only a promise.

She took his hands and placed them low on her stomach where their unborn child was growing inside her, its heart beating beneath his fingertips. "This baby is yours, Ryan. I want you to know that, without a doubt."

He was holding life in his hands—a life they'd

made together. It may have been unintentional, but it was no mistake. It was fate. Destiny. And he couldn't shake the feeling that it was another chance, somehow. For both of them.

If only they could find their way back to each other again. "I know. I trust you."

He did.

Maybe that made him a fool. He preferred to think it made him an optimist, but he believed her. There wasn't a chance that the baby was Jeremy's. If it were, she wouldn't be here, desperately trying to know him better. She wouldn't have reached for his hand and gripped it like a lifeline during the strange, silent ride back to her apartment last night.

She wouldn't be looking at him right now with that wild combination of terror and desire in her eyes.

The yearning between them was palpable. He could feel it in the way she shivered beneath his touch as his hands moved from her tummy to her hips. Pulling her closer...and closer still...until she was nestled neatly between his thighs. Her fingertips brushed against his leg, and that's all it took. He went hard in an instant. He wanted their baby, but he also wanted *her*. He'd wanted her for weeks. No amount of doors slammed in his face could change that.

Kiss me.

The words floated between them, as tender and lovely as snow caressing the treetops in Central Park.

"Eve," he said, clutching the fabric of her pencil skirt in his grip. Desperate. Devoted. "Is there something else you'd like to ask me?"

He'd promised his lips wouldn't touch hers until

she asked for it, and he was keeping his word. The pregnancy didn't change the fact that he wanted her to be ready. He wanted her to want him as badly as he wanted her. He wanted her to be *his*.

"Ryan." Her gaze dropped to his mouth, and his erection swelled.

He took a deep breath and forced himself to focus. To wait for her to ask. Then, in an effort to stop himself from crushing his mouth to hers prematurely, his gaze strayed over her shoulder.

That's when he finally saw it—a plain white envelope sitting in his chair.

His name had been printed on the front of it in feminine hand. Not just his first name, but his surname as well—Ryan Wilde—as if it had been left there by a stranger.

But it hadn't. He knew exactly where it had come from, and he was fairly sure he knew what was inside.

His hands stilled on her hips just as her lips parted, poised to say the words he'd been waiting for.

"Evangeline." His voice was hushed and flat, yet it sliced through the office like a knife. "What is that?"

She froze for a moment, her brow crumpling in confusion…and just a little bit of hurt.

Despite the spike of irritation that had hit him hard in the chest when he spotted the envelope, he registered the distress in her gaze. And a very real part of him hated himself for putting it there.

But the other part of him—the tender part, the damaged part, the part that needed to know she was *all in* before they went down this road again—was livid.

Her head spun slowly around, following his gaze. A second passed, maybe two. But they were among the longest seconds of Ryan's life. When she faced him again, the desire in her eyes had melted into something else. Regret, laced with a hint of fear.

"Tell me you didn't come in here while I was out and leave a resignation letter on my chair," Ryan said through gritted teeth.

"I didn't." Evangeline shook her head. "Well, I did. But it wasn't like that. I…"

Ryan knew he should give her a chance to explain. He knew she was scared. But damn it, so was he. Couldn't she see that? From the moment he'd woken up in her bed, she'd been pulling away from him, and she was still doing it. Only now, things were different. Now if she fled, she'd be taking their baby with her.

"Do you have any idea how finding a letter like that would have felt?" he said.

She shook her head. "But I wasn't going to leave it there. That's why I stayed. I…"

"Excuse me," someone said from the direction of the office door. It was followed by a pointed clearing of a throat.

Evangeline, still standing between Ryan's legs, flew backward, as far away as she could get.

"I apologize for interrupting your…ah…meeting, Mr. Wilde." Elliot's face had gone beet red. He stared so intently at the floor that Ryan half expected it to open up and swallow him whole. "But there's an urgent phone call for Ms. Holly."

Evangeline grew deadly still. "Do you know who it is? It's not about my grandfather, is it?"

Ryan shot to his feet. *No, damn it. Please no.*

Elliot shook his head. "It's your landlord."

Chapter Eleven

As if Evangeline's life hadn't already become enough of a train wreck, she was now officially homeless. At least that's what the scary-looking eviction notice posted on her door implied.

Her landlord hadn't minced words when she'd picked up the phone at the Bennington. *No dogs.* That was it. That's all he'd said, then he'd slammed the phone down. Hard.

She hadn't known what to do, and at first she'd been more concerned about Olive's and Bee's safety than the pesky detail of where she'd sleep at night. What if her landlord had called animal control and reported them? What if they were sitting in a cement cell at the pound? What if they'd been separated?

In her panic, she hadn't objected when Ryan insisted on accompanying her to her building to see just how bad the situation was. She'd been grateful for Tony and the limo, otherwise she never would have made it home so quickly. She'd been grateful for Ryan's presence, too. For some reason she felt like things couldn't come completely apart while he was there, even though she had a sneaky suspicion he simply didn't want to let her out of his sight in case she fled.

Her fault, obviously.

She should have done something with that letter of resignation when she realized what a mistake it had been. She should have buried it in the depths of her handbag. Or shredded it. Better yet, she should never have written it in the first place.

But she couldn't think about that right now. Because even though Olive and Bee were completely fine, snug in their dog bed, right where she'd left them, there was a horrible red sign on the door of her apartment. It said Notice to Vacate in a font large enough to be read from space, because Evangeline hadn't already experienced enough humiliation in recent months.

Once satisfied that the dogs were indeed safe and sound, she went back outside to square off with her landlord, who was busy pacing back and forth on the narrow sidewalk in front of the building. It would have been nice if he'd shoveled it while he was out there, but she refrained from making that suggestion.

"Please, Mr. Burton," she said, just shy of begging. "I just need a few days to figure something out, to find a new apartment. A week, maybe?"

What was she saying? She'd never be able to find an affordable, pet-friendly building with a move-in date in less than seven days. She'd been combing the real estate ads since the day she'd brought Olive and Bee home and hadn't found a thing she could afford. If she had, she wouldn't be standing on the snowy sidewalk arguing with her landlord while her boss/erstwhile lover and his chauffeur looked on.

She'd asked Ryan to leave, but so far, he'd stayed put. She didn't bother getting angry. He'd had a front-row seat to all of her recent humiliations. Why should this one be any different?

"This is a no-pets building. You knew that when you signed the lease." Mr. Burton, who'd never had a particularly friendly demeanor to begin with, frowned beneath his supersized mustache.

"I did. But the dogs are my grandfather's, and they had nowhere else to go. They're very well behaved. Just one more week? Two?"

"You can stay, but those dogs can't. No way." He shook his head. "I want those filthy animals out of here. If I let you keep the dogs, everyone will want to have dogs. This is an apartment building, not an animal shelter."

Ryan shot the man a murderous look and came to stand at her side. "There's no reason to be so harsh. Surely we can all work something out."

Her landlord looked Ryan up and down, and then he glanced briefly at the limo and rolled his eyes. "You can't buy her way out of this. She broke the rules."

Evangeline cut her gaze toward Ryan. "It's fine. I'm handling it."

She took a deep breath and faced Mr. Burton again. "Five days. Surely you can give me that long."

He shook his head. "Zero days, unless you get rid of the mutts."

Mutts? She gasped. "You did *not* just call them that."

Ryan reached for her hand and gave it a squeeze. "Come on, love. Let's take Olive and Bee and go. You don't want to stay here anymore."

He was right. She didn't. But where was she supposed to go with two elderly, special-needs dogs?

She shook her head. "I just can't believe you're throwing me out with no notice whatsoever. Is this even legal?"

Mr. Burton shrugged. "I'm not throwing you out. I'm throwing those dogs out. Get rid of them, and you can stay. They're not yours, anyway. You just said so. If that's true, send them to stay with your mom and dad. Your sister. Anyone. They just can't stay here."

She flinched as if she'd been slapped. "For your information, I don't have a mom and dad. *Or* a sister."

"We're finished here." Ryan's arm came down between her and Mr. Burton, then before she could object, he pulled her close to his side and began steering her toward the car.

She couldn't believe this was happening, but she should have seen it coming. She had, after all, broken the rules.

Still, it would have been nice if she'd been evicted before she found out she was pregnant. She already had serious doubts about her mothering instincts, and this wasn't exactly inspiring confidence in her ability to properly care for a helpless baby.

"Sit." Ryan pointed at the buttery leather seat in

the back of the limousine. The look on his face told her arguing wasn't an option.

Besides, she didn't have much fight left in her after squaring off with her landlord. His suggestion to send Olive and Bee to live with her parents had caught her off guard, stripping her of every last shred of confidence.

The truth was, sometimes she forgot just how alone she really was. Sometimes she was too busy trying to forge ahead, preparing for the sommelier exam or thinking about what wine she'd suggest to Carlo Bocci if she ever actually had the chance to serve him, live and in the flesh. Sometimes she very purposefully didn't allow herself to think about what the future would look like once her grandfather died and once Olive and Bee were gone, and she had no one left.

Sometimes she was simply distracted from her loneliness by the devastatingly gorgeous man who'd fallen into her lap and didn't seem to have any plans to go anywhere, no matter how convinced she was that he'd eventually break her heart.

And here he was. Again.

Somehow, some way, even though she was homeless, and even though she didn't have the first clue how to be a mother and she was probably going to get fired for fleeing her workplace two days in a row, she didn't feel so alone anymore.

Maybe this was what hope felt like.

"Give me your keys," Ryan said.

She dropped them into his outstretched hand.

"Wait here. I'm getting the dogs." A vein throbbed in his left temple. His gaze shot toward Tony, giving

Evangeline a perfect view of the fascinating, angry knot that had formed in his jaw. "Make sure that jerk leaves her alone while I'm gone. Got it?"

Adrenaline trickled through her veins.

Tony nodded. "Yes, Mr. Wilde."

It wasn't adrenaline. It was something more... pleasant. She squirmed in her seat. Was she seriously feeling aroused at a time like this?

Impossible.

She called after him. "Ryan?"

He turned. The resolve in his gaze sent a shiver coursing through her.

Not so impossible, after all.

She swallowed. "Can you get the bottle of wine, too? The one in the wine cabinet in the living room?"

She couldn't leave it there. That wine was special. One of a kind. It would have been easier to go get it herself, but she didn't dare move. Not when Ryan had suddenly gone into alpha male–protector mode.

He gave her a curt nod and stalked back toward her building.

While he was gone, she concentrated on getting her skittering heartbeat under control. And reminding herself that she was an independent woman who didn't need rescuing. Except it felt good to let someone take control, for once. She'd been on her own for so long, she'd forgotten what it felt like to be cared for. Protected. Jeremy had never stood up for her as Ryan just had. In all fairness, she'd never given him the chance. She hadn't wanted to.

Moments later, Ryan emerged, holding the bottle of red in one hand and two dog leashes in the other. Olive and Bee trotted merrily out in front of him.

They were obviously on doggy autopilot because they tried to drag him in the direction of the dog park, but he made a few adorable cooing sounds and they immediately turned around, ready to follow him off into the sunset.

Evangeline's heart gave a wistful little tug. She averted her gaze, but not before her eyes went misty.

She blamed pregnancy hormones. And the frosty winter air. Because she absolutely couldn't be getting emotional at the sight of Ryan Wilde walking her dogs.

A tear slid down her cheek.

Too late.

He exchanged a few words with Tony, who helped the dogs into the limo, and then slid in beside her with the bottle of wine tucked neatly under his arm. Bee immediately scurried into Evangeline's lap. Olive settled on the back seat between them.

"Thank you," she said as the car pulled away from the curb.

"You're welcome," he said quietly.

He was saying and doing all the right things, but now that they were alone again, he couldn't seem to look her in the eye anymore. It hurt. More than she wanted to admit.

His words from earlier kept echoing in her mind, on constant repeat.

Do you have any idea how finding a letter like that would have felt?

She'd messed up. He was probably counting the seconds until they got back to the Bennington and he could put her and her troublesome dogs into a hotel room and walk away from this mess.

"Once we get back to the hotel, I'll figure something out," she said. There had to be somewhere she could go. New York City had more Realtors than the rest of the country combined. She'd find something. She had to.

But then the limo turned right when it should have turned left. Evangeline could see the snow-tipped trees of Central Park on the horizon when Grand Central Station should have been coming into view instead.

She swiveled toward Ryan. "Wait a minute. This isn't the direction of the Bennington."

"No, it's not," he said evenly.

He smoothed down his tie, which now had a large puddle of dog drool in the center of its woven silk pattern. Ryan didn't seem to notice. Either that, or he didn't care.

Evangeline blinked furiously again. *Do not cry. He's probably got an entire walk-in closet full of Hermès. The fact that he's letting your half-blind dog drool all over one necktie doesn't mean anything.*

She cleared her throat. "Are we taking some secret alternate route back to the hotel?"

It was possible. Tony was a miracle worker. He clearly knew Manhattan like the back of his hand.

But somehow she doubted it. Ryan was too quiet. His eyes were too steely, the set of his jaw too tense.

"No, Evangeline." Olive crawled into Ryan's lap. He rested a hand on her back, but his gaze remained glued on the scenery out the window, whizzing past them in a crystalline blur of white. "I'm taking you home."

* * *

"This really isn't necessary." Evangeline stood in the center of Ryan's living room, looking far too much like she belonged there, and crossed her arms. "I mean, thank you. I appreciate it more than I can say. But it's a huge imposition."

Bee shuffled into view from the direction of Ryan's bedroom with Olive hot on her heels. Each dog had one of his shoes dangling from their destructive little mouths. The shoes weren't a matching set, either, ensuring maximum damage.

"It's not an imposition at all," he lied. Somehow he managed to keep a straight face.

What was he supposed to do? Watch and do nothing while the mother of his child got tossed onto the street? Over his dead body.

"I'm sure if I called Elliot and explained the situation he'd find a room at the Bennington we could use for a day or two." She bit her lip, not looking entirely sure.

Ryan knew calling Elliot would be her absolute last resort. Evangeline didn't believe in mixing business with her personal life, a fact Ryan knew all too well. "Think again. Elliot is severely allergic to pet dander. I don't think you'll get much sympathy from him."

She blinked. "How do you even know that?"

"A certain former US president spent two nights in the Bennington penthouse with a certain pair of Portuguese water dogs last year, and Elliot sneezed for three straight weeks afterward."

She let out a snort of laughter. "Are you making that up?"

Some of the tension in Ryan's muscles loosened slightly. For the first time since their near kiss in his office earlier he fully met her gaze. "No, it's true."

She smiled at him, and it seemed to blossom from somewhere deep inside. That thing about pregnant women glowing? He'd never believed it before. Until now.

"I thought Portuguese water dogs were supposed to be hypoallergenic," she said.

"Not for extreme allergy sufferers, apparently."

"Like Elliot?"

Ryan nodded.

Were they really going to stand there and discuss their coworker's dog allergy instead of talking about what was—or *wasn't*—going on between them? He sighed. "I haven't kidnapped you, Evangeline. You're free to go."

Olive or Bee—Ryan wasn't sure which—made a snuffling noise. Then, as if to prove a point, the furry nonhostages abandoned their stolen shoes and curled into a contented pile by the fireplace.

Evangeline's glow dimmed, ever so slightly. "I never said you'd kidnapped me."

No, but you're already planning your escape.

"It's only temporary, though. Until I find something else." She nodded resolutely. "Obviously."

"Obviously," he echoed.

What were they doing?

They were having a baby together, and they couldn't even manage to have an honest conversation about their feelings.

She looked up at him, and he could see his own

doubts swirling in her sapphire eyes. They were both in over their heads, drowning in all the words they couldn't say…desires they couldn't quite contain. And like most drowning victims, they were flailing, lashing out, when in reality, they just might be destined to save one another.

"I was never going to just leave that letter in your chair, Ryan. I want you to know that." Her lips curved into a sad smile.

In another time, another place, he'd kissed those lips. He'd tasted them, worshipped them. When the time was right, he would again. "Do you really want to resign?"

He wanted to be supportive. He wanted to tell her it was okay if she still wanted to quit. But it wasn't okay, damn it. The Bennington needed her.

He needed her.

"What is it that you want, Evangeline?"

Tell me.

Say it.

Her gaze flicked toward his bedroom and then back to him. She exhaled a shaky breath. "I don't want to resign."

It wasn't everything he wanted to hear, but it was enough. For now. "Promise me you'll stay until Bocci shows up."

She nodded, then frowned. "What if he never comes?"

"He will." He'd better. "He's in New York until the end of the month. Just give it until then."

And then what?

He didn't know. He was just trying to buy some time—time to convince her to stay.

"Okay, I promise." Her lips parted, as though she wanted to say something more.

He waited, but then she grew quiet again.

He narrowed his gaze. "Tell me something?"

She nodded. "Anything."

He'd let her ask the questions before. It was only fair that the tables were turned.

"What happened to your mom and dad?" He'd seen the pain in her eyes when her jerk landlord suggested she pawn Olive and Bee off on her parents. There was a story there.

She grew very still for a moment, then took a deep breath. "I don't know, actually. I haven't seen either one of them in years. My mom left when I was nine years old. Afterward, everything just fell apart. My father couldn't cope. He stopped hosting tours at the family winery, stopped harvesting the grapes. The vineyard crumbled around us."

And what about her? Had her father stopped taking care of Evangeline, too?

Ryan didn't have to ask. The answer was in her eyes. It was in the door she'd slammed in his face, not just once, but twice. It was in her stubborn reluctance to let him help her, even when she needed it most.

"My grandfather didn't realize how bad things were until my dad lost the winery. He saved me, but he was too late to save the vineyard. I went to live with him. It was supposed to be temporary, but my dad just kind of drifted away and never came back for me." She squared her shoulders and drew herself more upright, defiant in the face of rejection.

"That's why you and your grandfather are so close." Ryan nodded. "I understand. I went through something similar."

She blinked. "You did?"

"Yes, my parents were both addicts. They weren't ready for the responsibility of a kid, so my aunt and uncle took me in."

"Zander's family?" A lock of Evangeline's hair fell from her messy bun, a casualty of her tumultuous day. It was the only outward sign that anything was amiss.

He reached and tucked it behind her ear, somehow resisting the urge to let his fingertips linger on the elegant curve of her shoulder. "Yes. My uncle died a few years back, but he was like a father to me. Emily Wilde still treats me as one of her own."

She nodded, and a shiver coursed through her at his touch. "Then I guess you really do understand."

She had walls. They both did. But every so often, when they lifted their gazes skyward at the same time, they caught a glimpse of pure blue heaven. In each other.

What would it be like once those walls finally came tumbling down?

Ryan shoved his hands in his trouser pockets to stop himself from touching her again. Cleared his throat. "Tell me about the wine you asked me to bring with Olive and Bee."

"It's from the family vineyard. The last remaining bottle. As far as I know, anyway." She lit up like she always did when she talked about wine. "It's a cabernet franc. Bold, richly bodied, with notes of tart red cherries and brambly raspberries mixed with warm toast and cedar."

She made it sound so nostalgic. So cozy.

Like home.

"It's the perfect wine to pair with food. I defy you to show me a meal that it wouldn't complement." This was the woman he'd fallen for that night, the one who'd drawn him out of his self-imposed exile. Smart, bold...so full of life.

Utterly captivating.

This side of her couldn't be hidden away, no matter how hard Evangeline tried. Because she was real...as authentic as the little girl who'd been forgotten by her father. She just didn't know it. If anyone understood that warped sense of self, Ryan did.

"I wouldn't dare." He smiled.

She reached for the bottle, turned it over in her hands and ran the pad of her thumb reverently over the label. "It's also star bright, which is rare for a deep red wine. Almost impossible, actually."

"What does *star bright* mean, exactly?" He was still languishing in the ranks of the pinot grigio drinkers, clueless.

"It's a measure of the wine's clarity, its ability to absorb and reflect light. A wine that's star bright is vivid and luminous, but not quite clear. It has light running through its darkness, like a sparkling ribbon. It glows." She paused, searching his face. "Does that make sense?"

He let his gaze travel from her sparkling blue eyes

to her cheeks—soft and pink, like rose petals. Her mouth beckoned to him. Ruby red.

She was beautiful. She'd always been beautiful, but now she was more. Now she was radiant. Star bright.

"It makes perfect sense," he said.

Then he bade her good-night while he still could, and went to bed.

Alone.

Chapter Twelve

Hours later, Evangeline lay awake in Ryan's spacious spare bedroom with Olive and Bee nestled at her feet.

His apartment was nothing like she'd imagined it would be. Granted, he lived in a penthouse. Because of course he did. But it was hardly the sleek bachelor pad she'd envisioned. Ryan occupied the top floor of a prewar limestone building in the nine hundredth block of Fifth Avenue. Instead of chrome and black leather, the rooms were filled with rich velvets and elegantly weathered pieces that gave the space a comforting feel.

The French doors in the living room overlooked a terrace with a view of the boathouse in Central Park. Before Evangeline had gone to bed, she'd stood with her hand pressed to the glass, watching skaters twirl across the frozen pond. Come springtime, the ice would thaw and people would race tiny wind-driven sailboats on the water. It was one of the best spots in the city for children. For families.

Under the covers, Evangeline's hands slid over her nightgown and splayed on her stomach. She was only in her first trimester, but already she could feel her body changing—growing rounder, softer. It was a potent reminder that the life she and Ryan had created was real. They would be a family someday. Someday soon.

Whatever did or didn't happen between them, they'd be bonded together forever.

She'd been so wrong about Ryan. And yet, deep down she'd known he was a good man. She'd sensed it on that morning so many weeks ago when he'd stood there with dog hair clinging to his Armani jacket while he tried to convince her to see him again. Otherwise, he wouldn't have frightened her so.

She'd had reason to be afraid. Ryan was everything she wanted, everything she needed. Just the kind of man who could break her heart.

But something about lying there in the dark with her head on his pillows and his child growing inside her made her bold. Fearless. Ryan was right next door, and they weren't at the Bennington anymore. There were alone—in his home. And he'd brought her here. He could have taken her anywhere, but he'd brought her home.

What would happen if she went to him now? What would happen if she tiptoed into his room and slid into bed beside him?

The thought was intoxicating. It sent liquid warmth

skittering through her body, like she'd just sipped from a glass of rich Spanish sherry.

What is it that you want, Evangeline?

He'd given her a chance, and she'd blown it.

You. I want you.

The words had been right there, on the tip of her tongue. They tasted as wild and sweet as sun-ripened grapes plucked straight from the vine. But she hadn't been able to say them, hadn't been brave enough to give voice to her desire. Because this time was different. This time, it would be more than just physical. She could lie to herself all she wanted, but no amount of denial would change the fact that she had feelings for Ryan. She just wasn't altogether sure what those feelings were.

He's the father of your baby.

Maybe this need to touch him—this need to feel his hard flesh beneath her fingertips and his mouth, hot and needy, against hers—was biological. Maybe it was primal, her body crying out for more of him.

Or maybe it was just fate.

Either way, she was tired of trying to fight it. So very tired. She slipped out of bed as quietly as possible so as not to disturb Olive and Bee. Then she closed the door behind her and made her way to Ryan's room. The door was closed. She considered knocking, then thought better of it. She didn't want him to turn her away. Not again. Not this time.

Her hand was steady as she turned the doorknob, and that's when she knew she was sure. No hesitation. No doubt. No regrets.

Moonlight streamed through the bedroom windows, casting shadows of gently falling snow over the massive bed in the center of the room. The bed sheets took on a lavender hue in the darkness, and Evangeline felt as if she were entering some strangely beautiful winter wonderland, a frosted fairy tale.

But this was no fairy tale, and the man whose lean body was stretched out before her, all hard planes and sculpted flesh, was very much real. He gazed up at her, his eyes glittering in the shadows. If he was surprised to find her sneaking into his bedroom in the middle of the night, he hid it well. He looked more as if he'd been lying there, waiting for her. As if he'd summoned her with the pure intensity of his desire.

"Evangeline." His voice scraped her insides, making her heart beat hard and fast.

She leaned down, letting her hair fall against his cheek and whispered, "Call me Eve." She swallowed. "Please."

He nodded, cupped her face in his hands then slid his fingertips into her hair. His hands curled into gentle fists, and she could feel the tension in his body, flowing from him to her. Days…weeks…of wanting one another, of desire, of denial.

No more.

No more denial. No more waiting.

"Let me see you, Eve," he growled.

She rested a hand on his chest and straightened, savoring his gaze on her as she gathered the hem of her nightgown in her hands and lifted it slowly over her head. His gaze raked over her bare body, and she felt it as keenly as a caress, traveling down her neck, over her collarbone and then lingering on her breasts. A delicious warmth pooled low in her center, and even though she'd undressed for him before, she had the unmistakable feeling that she was being seen for the very first time. Truly seen, body and soul.

When his gaze moved to her newly rounded belly, a smile tipped his lips and his eyes grew shiny in the darkness. "Mine."

His.

He was talking about the baby, not her. But for a minute, she let herself pretend he wasn't. She closed her eyes and let the word wash over her, bathing her in love and light.

Ryan's hands found hers, and he pulled her toward him until she straddled his body on the bed. When she opened her eyes, he looked at her with such adoration, such reverence that she thought maybe, just maybe, he'd been talking about her, after all.

Mine.

His.

He rested his fingertips gently on her stomach. "Ours."

She smiled down at him. "Kiss me, Ryan."

He rose up, captured her chin in his grasp and in the torturous moment before his lips touched hers, he murmured. "Oh, baby, I thought you'd never ask."

Evangeline's breath caught in her throat. The kiss was slow and gentle. Achingly tender. She fought back tears as she opened for him and his tongue slid languidly against hers. Every movement, every taste was delicately drawn out. The sweetness of it caught her off guard.

She'd been prepared for heat—for a shuddering, frenzied end to the attraction that had been swirling between them for so long. But this was no frantic coupling. They weren't just looking for a release.

They were seeking something else, and as much as Evangeline wanted it, *needed* it, she was terrified of what it meant.

This isn't sex, she thought as she let her hands roam his chest and abdomen, exploring every tantalizing dip, every ridge of muscle. *This…this…is making love.*

Still, beneath the tenderness—beneath the feather-soft kisses and the broken sighs—an excruciating need burned deep inside. Evangeline's nerve endings felt like they were on fire. His erection pressed against her center, thick and hard. She ground against him, whimpering.

"I'm here," he whispered against her lips. "Right here."

Then his mouth dropped to her nipple and the whimper turned into a low, sultry moan. It was a sound she'd never heard herself make before, and in a strange, sublime way it made sense because this body was new to her. It was changing every day, blossoming into something wonderfully different. Her breasts had grown fuller, sensitive to the barest touch. When he moved to the other nipple and drew it into his mouth, sucking gently, she nearly came apart.

"Please," she breathed, and she wasn't sure what all she was begging for.

She wanted him inside her. Now. She wanted to feel his hardness pushing into her until they became one, but she wanted more than that. She wanted all of him—all of this beautiful, broken man who made her believe she could have a life she'd never dared to imagine.

A future.

A family.

So she reached for him, reveling in the way his breath caught when her fingers wrapped around his erection. Then she guided him to her entrance and lowered herself over him, taking him in. He rose up to kiss her as their bodies came together, and at first there was nothing but an overwhelming, exquisite sense of relief. Like she could finally breathe again after a long, lonely season underwater.

But all at once the heat began to build. He curled his strong hands around her hips and thrust into her. Harder. And harder, until she felt like a shimmering, heavenly thing—a brilliant, beautiful fire. More light than dark. A flame in the night.

Star bright.

It felt like a fever dream. Too colorful, too vibrant to be real.

But Ryan knew it couldn't be a figment of his imagination, because as long as he'd waited for this night, as much as he'd wanted it, the reality of making love to Evangeline was infinitely sweeter than any fantasy he could have conjured.

She looked so beautiful rising and falling above him with her hair tumbling over her shoulders and spilling over her bare breasts. He remembered everything about their previous night together, every supple curve of her body. But she'd changed in the weeks since they'd been together. There was a new softness to her—and it was more than the pregnancy, more than merely physical.

She was more open to him now, more vulnerable. When he rolled her over so that she was beneath him and then gathered her wrists in one hand, pinning them over her head, she purred like a kitten. The sound was nearly enough to bring him to climax right then and there, but he clenched his jaw and fought the release. This night had been months in the making. He wanted, *needed*, to make it last.

For her.

For *them*.

He slid from her body, murmuring wicked promises at her whimper of protest. Poised over her, he moved down the lovely, writhing length of her, pausing to take a nipple into his mouth again. She arched toward him, crying his name as his hands found the tender insides of her thighs and guided them apart.

His mouth moved lower, and she opened her eyes, questions glittering in her gaze.

"Trust me," he whispered, smiling at the knowledge that this was new for her, that even after making a baby together he could show her a new kind of intimacy. A gift for them both.

He pressed an openmouthed kiss to her belly, then dipped his head even lower, giving her the most intimate kiss of all. She gasped at the first touch of his tongue. Then he circled her slowly, gently with the pad of his thumb as he licked his way inside. She shivered against his mouth, and her hips rose up off the bed. He slid his hand beneath her perfect bottom, holding her still.

She was close. So close.

Her hands were tangled in his hair, and her breath was coming hard and fast. He could taste the honeyed prelude to her release, so decadently sweet. He stopped, moved over her once again and braced his hands on either side of her head.

Her face was deliciously flushed, her eyes were closed and her lips bee-stung, swollen from his kisses. Ryan had never seen anyone so radiant. Lost in pleasure, lost in love.

His erection throbbed at her opening.

Love.

Is that what this was?

How would he know? He knew nothing of love, nothing of commitment or what it took to build a home—a real home where the walls rang with laughter and where people took care of each other. Where they *stayed*.

But when Evangeline's lashes fluttered open and she looked at him through heavy-lidded eyes, he almost believed he could.

"Just you and me." He pushed inside her again.

He'd made her a promise, and he'd honored it. There were no ghosts in this bed. This was about them, and only them. Except they weren't a couple anymore. They were a family…almost. "Just *us*."

Then she shattered around him for a second time, and he couldn't hold back any longer. He thrust into her and came with a deep, shuddering groan that felt like it had been ripped straight from his soul.

For a prolonged moment, neither of them moved.

He squeezed his eyes closed tight, savoring the sound of their intermingled breath and the snow falling lightly against the windows. New York… Bennington 8…the Michelin star…all of it felt so far away. So long as he was inside her, nothing else could touch them. Nothing could tear them apart.

"Ryan."

He opened his eyes. Evangeline gazed up at him, her sapphire irises shining bright with unshed tears.

"What if I'm just like her?" she whispered. "What if I'm just like my mother?"

"Oh, baby, you're not." He shifted, and pulled her close, tucking her head beneath his chin. Her panicked heartbeat crashed against his, and he wrapped his arms around her as tightly as he could.

She'd undressed for him. Not just in body, but also in soul. He knew without having to ask that she was sharing her deepest fear—the thing standing between them, threatening to pull them apart. Even here, even now.

"How do you know?" she said into his chest.

He wondered if she could hear his heart breaking in that moment—breaking for her. Evangeline Holly, the woman who cared more about a pair of blind and deaf dogs than where she slept at night, was afraid she'd follow in her mother's footsteps and abandon her own child.

"Because I do." He swallowed. *I do.* Wedding words. "Look at me, Eve."

He captured her chin and tipped her face upward, so she met his gaze. "I never knew your mother, but I know you. You have more love and devotion in your heart than anyone I've ever known. I see it. I see *you*. Even when you're trying to push me away, I see you. Our baby couldn't ask for a better mother."

She gave him a wobbly smile. "Our baby."

"Yes, ours. Yours and mine."

She closed her eyes and burrowed into him, and while his chest was still wet with her tears, she fell into a deep sleep. And still he held her, whispering reassurances into her silky hair, hoping they would somehow take root. She didn't have to do this alone. He'd be there, too. Neither of them had had a perfect childhood, but that didn't matter. They were two broken people, but together they were whole. So long as they helped each other, just like Olive and Bee, everything would be all right.

More than all right. It would be perfect...

If only she believed.

He wasn't sure how long they stayed that way, wrapped around one another, before he finally drifted off. But sometime before dawn, after the heavy snow had lightened to delicate flurries that coated the city in a fine layer of sugar, a shot of arousal dragged him back to consciousness. When he opened his eyes, Evangeline was moving over him, taking him in again. He groaned, reaching to cup her full breasts, running his thumbs over their soft pink peaks.

She leaned forward to kiss him, and her hair fell around them in a shimmering gold curtain, sheltering them from the outside world. It was slow this time, gentle and easy.

Easier than it should have been in a room swollen with doubts.

Chapter Thirteen

Ryan didn't know if Evangeline would come to him again the following night, or if she'd considered their most recent coupling another one-time thing. A moment of weakness.

The relief that coursed through him when she entered his bedroom, undressed, with her hair gathered in loose waves over one shoulder, was frightening in its intensity. It wasn't until she'd slipped into his bed for five nights in a row that he let himself come to expect it. On the sixth night, they didn't even go through the pretense of retiring to separate bedrooms. Olive and Bee claimed the guest bed as their own, and Ryan led Evangeline to his bed by the hand. Her lips tipped into a bashful smile as he undressed her and as always, he marveled at the sight of her ever-changing body. So beautiful in its purpose.

But their trysts were always ushered in by the violet hour and ended when the sun came up. They never spoke of the change in their relationship. At work, everything remained the same.

Which was fine.

For now.

Evangeline had promised to stay until Carlo Bocci made an appearance at Bennington 8, but the month would eventually come to a close. Until then, Ryan was certain of only two things—he wasn't ready to give Evangeline up, and he couldn't keep lying to Zander. It was time to confess.

The events of the past few days couldn't have gone unnoticed. Ryan and Evangeline had bolted out of the building without providing any sort of explanation. Twice. And then there'd been the near kiss in his office, witnessed by dog-averse Elliot. Ryan had some explaining to do, and it seemed like a good idea to do it before Zander grew impatient and decided to fire them both.

Not that Zander could actually fire Ryan. He owned shares in the Bennington. Ryan served on the board of directors. They were family, and they'd always operated as a team. As CEO, Zander had never pulled rank on Ryan before.

Then again, Ryan had never even considered dating a hotel employee, much less moving in with one of them. And having a baby.

Damn.

It sounded bad. Really bad. How had he let things get so out of hand without talking to Zander? His cousin had every right to be pissed. The triple espresso Ryan had waiting on his desk as a peace offering first thing Thursday morning seemed wholly inadequate.

Zander's gaze snagged on it the moment he crossed the threshold. He stared at the coffee, then slowly switched his attention to Ryan, sitting in one of the wingback chairs opposite his desk.

"A triple." He arched a brow. "Things must be dire."

"Not dire," Ryan said. *Just...big.* "But I did give some thought to adding a shot of whiskey."

"At seven in the morning? I'll pass." Zander set down his briefcase and downed half the espresso in a swift gulp.

He sat and leaned back in his chair. His posture may have been casual, but his stare was pure intensity. Pure Zander. "I suppose you're here to tell me you're sleeping with our wine director."

If only it were that simple.

Ryan released a breath. "How long have you known?"

"I suspected as much the day she turned up for her interview. There's no mistaking the way you look at her. I've known you my entire life, remember? I haven't seen you look at a woman like that since—" Zander paused to reconsider "—ever, actually."

"Evangeline and I met before the interview," Ryan admitted.

Zander's eyebrows rose. "When?"

"A couple of months ago. I didn't expect to see her again, and then she showed up here. It was a nice surprise." An understatement, obviously. He was going to have to be more forthcoming, but he also wanted to respect Evangeline's privacy. Zander didn't need a play-by-play of their entire relationship.

So now it's an actual relationship?

He cleared his throat. "There's more."

Zander nodded. "I suspected as much."

"She's pregnant."

Zander grinned, but didn't seem the least bit surprised. "I wondered when you were going to get around to telling me."

Ryan shifted in his chair. "You knew that, too?"

Clearly he and Evangeline hadn't been as successful as they'd hoped at keeping things under wraps.

Zander let out a wry laugh. "I figured it out around the time you doused her in Côtes du Rhône. It wasn't the subtlest of moves."

Touché.

"Plus Allegra had an interesting conversation with your Miss Holly a few days ago. She had a feeling you two had some news to share."

Ryan nodded.

My Miss Holly.

She wasn't his. Not yet, anyway.

He cleared his throat. "Things between Evangeline and me are...complicated. Neither of us were expecting this."

"But is it what you want? That's the real question, isn't it?" Zander leaned forward. "I never expected Allegra to come back into my life. I wasn't ready, and neither was she. She was probably *less* ready. But deep down, it's what we wanted. Ready or not."

Zander made it sound so simple, but Ryan had been there. He'd seen the way Zander fought for

Allegra. And now here they were, months later… married and happy.

A wistful ache churned in Ryan's gut. He didn't realize he'd grown quiet until Zander broke the loaded silence by opening and closing one of his desk drawers.

When Ryan looked up, he found Zander watching him with an expression he hadn't seen on his cousin's face since they were kids growing up together in the Wilde family brownstone. He'd dropped his CEO aura and was giving off a distinct big brother vibe.

"Look, cousin. There's no easy way for me to do this, so I'm just going to come out and say it." Zander took a deep breath. "Evangeline is great and if you two end up together, no one will be happier for you than I will. I promise you that. But I've been worried about you for a long time now. The whole family has."

The ache in Ryan's gut sharpened. Zander was going to bring up Natalie. He probably should have seen it coming. Maybe on some level, he had. Maybe that's why he'd waited so long to tell him what was going on.

"You don't need to worry about me. I'm fine," he said through gritted teeth.

"I know." Zander's gaze dropped to his desk. "But after what happened with Natalie, I also know you want to be sure."

A trickle of alarm snaked down Ryan's spine as Zander bent to retrieve something from the opened drawer and set it on the surface of the desk between them. It was a flat white box with some sort of laboratory symbol on the side. Zander pushed it toward him, and he got a better look at the block lettering in the upper right-hand corner of the cardboard.

Noninvasive Prenatal Paternity Test.

Ryan glared at Zander. "What the hell is that?"

"A paternity test. You just said yourself that your relationship with Evangeline is complicated. You barely know one another."

"I know enough," Ryan said quietly.

Did believing Evangeline make him a fool? Perhaps. Zander apparently thought so.

"I care about you, man. You were a mess after Natalie's baby was born. I just don't want to see you go through that again."

"I won't," he snapped. His mood was suddenly black enough for a fight. He and Zander hadn't come to blows since they were twelve years old, but something about seeing that box on the table made his hands curl into fists.

Zander held up his hands. "I'll drop it. It's your call. Just do me a favor and take the kit in case you change your mind."

Ryan took the box and slipped it into his pocket, out of sight. Looking at it made him feel sick. "Fine. But for the record, Evangeline is nothing like Natalie. She's..." He was at a sudden loss for words as a series of images flashed through his consciousness— Evangeline sabering the top off a champagne bottle; grabbing him by the lapels and hauling him into her apartment so her neighbor wouldn't spot Olive and Bee; smiling at him as she reached for him in the night.

Zander, waiting, lifted a brow.

"She's special," he finally said.

Zander nodded. "She's also important to Bennington 8."

"Yes, I'm aware. She can still do her job, if that's what you're worried about. Quite effectively, I might add." She'd been pouring wine like a pro for six nights running. She knew enough about the various vintages to make recommendations without having to sample bottles. She was ready for Bocci. They all were.

"Exactly. I need to know she's all in," Zander said. *All in.*

"She is. There's nothing to worry about. We've talked about it, and she's assured me she's staying on until Bocci's visit. She knows how important it is. She gave me her word. She's all in."

All in as far as Bennington 8, anyway. As for the rest of it, he wasn't so sure.

Evangeline felt a little faint as she walked into the nursing home with Olive and Bee bobbing gleefully at the ends of their leashes. Pregnancy hormones. Or more likely, nerves. Tonight was her weekly pizza date with Grandpa Bob, and she'd also decided it was the night she was going to tell him about the baby.

She couldn't keep it from him. He meant too much to her. She couldn't lie to him if she tried. Not about something like this.

Being the supportive person he was, she knew he'd be happy for her. But she still wasn't looking forward to the conversation, probably because it wasn't as if she could just drop a bomb like a pregnancy on her elderly grandfather and not expect him to ask about the father.

Oh, didn't I tell you? I broke up with the guy you hated, and now I'm having an affair with my boss.

Her face went hot.

An affair? Is that what it was?

She had no idea. She was still trying to wrap her mind around the fact that she was having a baby. It was hard enough to start thinking of herself as a mother. She couldn't begin to think of herself as someone's wife.

Getting ahead of ourselves, aren't we? Who said anything about marriage?

No one had. Certainly not Evangeline.

Olive and Bee twitched their noses as they trotted past the dining room. The air was already heavy with the scent of pepperoni, and Evangeline held her breath. Just in case. Her body couldn't seem to decide if it was prone to morning sickness or not. One day, she'd feel fine and then two days later the smells coming from the kitchen at Bennington 8 would make her want to hurl. This biological ambivalence certainly didn't improve her confidence in her mothering abilities. Even her body didn't know what it was doing.

When she reached Grandpa Bob's room, he was sitting in front of his television with his back to the door. His hearing wasn't what it used to be, even with his hearing aids, so he didn't turn around. She paused for a moment, swallowing around the lump in her throat.

He looked so frail. She couldn't get used to the sight of the walker sitting beside his recliner or the guardrails that had been installed on either side of the bed that he'd brought with him from his apartment.

Everything in the room was so familiar, but somehow managed to look different. Smaller somehow. Evangeline's grandpa had loomed so large over her life. He'd always been the one reliable presence in a sea of confusion. The dependable one. The strong one. Now they'd switched places, and she was still struggling to live up to the task.

She bent to unclip Olive and Bee from their leashes, and they scurried over to him at once, vying for space in his lap.

He laughed. "Hello there, little ones."

Evangeline settled onto the matching recliner—the same one where she'd curled up and done her homework as a little girl—and waited for the dogs to calm down. After five full minutes of tail wagging and excited yips, they planted themselves on either side of Granda Bob. Within seconds, they were both snoring.

"They miss you," Evangeline said, as her heart gave a little twist. She had zero regrets about the whole eviction thing. None whatsoever.

"I miss them, too, but they certainly seem to be happy." Grandpa Bob let out a laugh. "Not to mention well-fed."

Evangeline cleared her throat. Ryan liked to bring home doggie bags for Olive and Bee from Bennington 8. Last night they'd dined on leg of lamb. "We should probably keep them away from the pizza."

"Easier said than done. I speak from experience," he said.

"I'll guard my slice with my life."

"That might be what it takes." He glanced at the

digital clock on top of the television. "Shall we head on down to the dining room?"

"Can we chat for a minute first? There's something I want to talk to you about." Her tummy gave another nervous flip.

"Sure. Is everything okay?" His brow furrowed.

Spit it out.

"Everything's fine. It's good news, actually. At least I hope you'll think so." She took a deep breath. "I'm pregnant."

For a sliver of a moment, her heart seemed to stall while she waited for his reaction. But then his face split into a wide grin. "Pregnant? Really?"

She nodded. "Yes, really."

"Of course that's good news. It's the best news possible." He beamed. She hadn't seen that kind of light in his eyes in months. Years, maybe. "I'm going to be a great-grandfather."

"And I'm going to be a mom," she said.

"You'll be a wonderful mother, sweetheart. Your baby couldn't ask for a better mom."

"You sound just like Ryan." The words flew out of her mouth before she could stop them. She didn't even realize her mistake until Grandpa Bob's smile faded.

"Who's Ryan?"

"Ryan Wilde." She swallowed. "He's the baby's father."

"So no more what's-his-name, then." Grandpa Bob's eyebrows lifted.

She didn't bother scolding him about pretending to forget Jeremy's name. It was probably time she forgot it herself. "Nope."

"Good. I never liked that guy."

"Yes, I know. You mentioned that a time or two." Why had she never listened? Why had she never believed her grandfather when he'd insisted she deserved better?

Because you never believed it yourself. But you do deserve better.

The words in her head sounded as if they'd been spoken by Ryan, as so many of the thoughts spinning in her consciousness had lately.

Bee stirred, and Grandpa Bob gave the dog a reassuring pat. "Tell me about Ryan. Will I like him?"

"He's wonderful. Olive and Bee are certainly fond of him." *And so am I.* She was afraid to say it out loud, though. Afraid to admit that she might be letting herself fall, when that was the last thing in the world she'd wanted. The risk to her heart was greater now than ever before.

"I trust them. You should, too. They're excellent judges of character." Grandpa Bob winked. "So when's the wedding?"

And there it was.

"There isn't going to be a wedding," she said with a little too much force.

Her adamancy didn't go unnoticed. The light in Grandpa Bob's eyes dimmed, ever so slightly. His expression grew serious. "Ever?"

"Ever." She nodded. Over her grandfather's shoulder, she could see a few of the other residents making their way down the hall toward the dining room. They should probably get down there. Pizza night was really popular around here.

Besides, she was suddenly ready to put an end to this conversation.

"If this Ryan Wilde is so wonderful, why would you say something like that?"

"Because." There was that darned lump in her throat again. *Do* not *cry.* The last thing she wanted was for Grandpa Bob to worry about her, because she was perfectly fine. "It's the twenty-first century. I don't have to get married just because I'm pregnant."

"True." He nodded, but something about the way he looked at her caused the lump in her throat to quadruple in size. "But why do I get the feeling that whatever century we're in has nothing to do with your reluctance to tie the knot?"

"I don't know." She stood, picked up the walker and positioned it closer to his chair. "We're late for dinner. We can talk about this another time."

He glanced at the walker, but didn't budge. "Don't let the choices your parents made rob you of a lifetime of happiness, Evangeline. Your mom and dad both made terrible mistakes. Mistakes that caused you deep pain. No one knows that more than I do."

She shook her head. *No. Please no.* She didn't want to go there. Painful childhood memories had no place at a pizza party.

But Grandpa Bob kept on talking. To make matters worse, Olive and Bee were gazing up at her as though she'd just crushed their dreams of being flower girls. Or in their case, flower dogs. "But it's time to let the past die. You're having a child. That means a new life. A new future. Not just for the baby, but for you, too."

"I know," she whispered.

"Do you? Because I'm not so sure you do. Trust yourself, sweetheart. You'll know love when you see it. It won't look anything like what your parents had. It will look more like sacrifice than selfishness." At last he stood, meeting her gaze head-on. "It'll be like nothing you've ever experienced before. And when it's real, it has a way of repairing old wounds. Believe it."

She smiled a bittersweet smile. "I'll try."

Believe it.

Believe.

Again, the echo in her head sounded so much like Ryan's voice that it was almost as if he was right there.

Whispering in her ear.

Chapter Fourteen

Evangeline stood at the head of one of the larger dining tables in Bennington 8 with six bottles of wine lined up in front of her. Three reds and three whites, arranged from light to dark.

"So to recap, the wines we're featuring this evening are all from France." She glanced at the eight people seated at the table—all of them servers scheduled to work when the restaurant opened in fifteen minutes. Then she pointed at one of them. "Gia, can you name the regions represented by this selection?"

Gia nodded. "The chenin blanc and muscadet are both from the Loire region. We've got a sauvignon blanc and a red blend from Bordeaux, plus two reds from Burgundy—one light and the other bold."

"Excellent. I think we're ready. Any questions before the doors open?" Evangeline gave the group a final once-over, but no one raised a hand. "Very well. I'll be here all night if you need anything. As always, I'll drop by each table personally, but it's important for everyone to have a good understanding of all the wines on offer."

The servers thanked her, and the few that still had wine remaining in their tasting glasses finished it off before leaving to prepare their tables for the evening. Evangeline's glass was still full, of course. But she'd placed it discreetly behind the row of bottles, and no one appeared to notice that she wasn't actually drinking anything.

So far, so good. Her evening wine briefing with the staff had gone exceptionally well, and according to the maître d', Bennington 8 would have a full house tonight. They were booked solid from opening until close.

She'd be on her feet for hours. With any luck, she could escape to Ryan's office for a few minutes of rest before the doors opened. It wasn't until she gathered the bottles and returned them to the wine cooler that she realized he hadn't stopped by her evening tasting like he usually did.

She situated the muscadet back in place, only to realize she'd put the chenin blanc where the Bordeaux was supposed to be. An atypical mistake. But she was feeling a bit...unsettled.

She and Ryan had barely seen one another in the past twenty-four hours. He'd left her a voice mail message while she was at the pizza party letting her know that he'd been called away overnight on business. Something about a hotel property that was about to go on the market in Chicago. He and Zander were thinking about buying it.

She'd been relieved at first. At least that's what she'd told herself. She needed time to shake off the things that Grandpa Bob had said to her. Time to get the ridiculous idea of marriage out of her head. And she couldn't very well do that while she was sleeping in Ryan's bed, with her head on his chest and his hands buried in her hair.

Time to herself would be good.

But then she'd let herself into his apartment, and it had felt so cavernous without him there. So empty. Even Olive and Bee missed him. They'd kept hopping off the sofa during her *Say Yes to the Dress* marathon to scour the penthouse in search of him.

Something's wrong, she thought as she switched the chenin blanc and the Bordeaux. She'd thought he would be back by now. She should have at least heard from him, shouldn't she?

Then again, why should he keep her apprised of his every move? As Grandpa Bob had so bluntly pointed out, she wasn't his wife. She wasn't even his girlfriend. She just happened to be pregnant with his baby.

There's more to it than that, and you know it.

She squared her shoulders, shut the door to the wine cooler and made her way to the maître d' stand. Now wasn't the time to analyze her relationship. Or obsess over why Ryan hadn't contacted her. Or, more disturbingly, why she'd watched six straight episodes of a show that centered around women choosing their wedding dresses. She had less than ten minutes to herself before she began recommending wine for Manhattan's elite.

"If anyone needs me, I'll be in Mr. Wilde's office until we open," she said.

The maitre d' nodded. "Yes, Miss Holly."

His office was empty, which she supposed should be a relief. She wasn't sure how she would have felt if he'd been here all evening and hadn't popped in on her tasting like he usually did. But he'd assured her he'd be back before Bennington 8 opened for dinner. Everyone was on high alert in case Carlo Bocci showed up.

Evangeline doubted he'd come on a Friday night, though. So far all of the restaurant reviews he'd conducted in New York City had been done on weeknights, and Mon Ami Jules was still the only one that had been awarded a Michelin star.

Still, she was starting to worry.

She kicked off her shoes and stretched out on the brandy-colored distressed leather sofa that was situated in the corner of the office, and a chill coursed through her. The snow hadn't let up for days, and it was beginning to look like the city was sleeping beneath a fluffy white down comforter.

She sat up and spied one of Ryan's impeccable suit jackets draped over a hanger on the back of the door. A blanket would have been sublime, but also Armani wool would do nicely.

After sliding the jacket from its hanger, she returned to the sofa and snuggled beneath it in a semi-fetal position. The cool silk lining was soft against her cheek. She closed her eyes and took a deep inhale, filling her senses with his scent—that unique bouquet that was pure romance. Pure Ryan. Oak and pine, with just a hint of sandalwood and crushed wild violets. If he'd been a wine, he'd be a rich, bold red. Her favorite kind.

A second passed, maybe two. If she wasn't careful, she'd fall asleep.

Thank you, first trimester.

She wasn't sure when exactly she gave up the fight or how long she'd been unconscious when a low, familiar voice dragged her from her slumber.

"Hey there, sleeping beauty."

Her eyelashes fluttered open, and she found Ryan bent over her. There were snow flurries in his hair, and laugh lines around his eyes and it was such a surprise, such a *relief*, to see him that the hot sting of tears pressed against the backs of her eyes.

This was bad.

So very bad.

Don't fall in love with him. You can't.

"You're back." She blinked furiously.

"I am." He leaned down and pressed a slow, soft kiss to her lips. His mouth was cold against hers. He tasted of icicles and roasted chestnuts. "Happy to see me?"

More than she wanted to admit, even to herself. "Very."

They'd never kissed in the office before. Never even held hands. This was a first, and it should have scared her, but it didn't. It felt right. "How was your trip?"

"Quite productive." His smile dimmed. "But now I'm worried about you. Are you okay, love?"

"I'm fine. I had a few minutes after the staff tasting, so I thought I'd rest for a bit before we open."

He went quiet for a beat too long, and that's when she noticed the glittering lights of the theater district shining through the office's corner window. The sky was inky black.

"Oh my God." Panic gathered in a tight knot in her chest. She sat up so fast that her head spun a little. "What time is it? How long have I been asleep?"

"It's about eight thirty. Don't worry. I'm sure everything is fine." He brushed the hair back from her face. "Just tell me again that you're feeling all right."

"I am. I promise, but I need to get upstairs. We're booked solid tonight." She'd promised to visit every table personally. Why hadn't anyone come to find her? What was going on up there?

She flew to her feet, and Ryan's jacket—her makeshift blanket—fell to the floor. She'd forgotten all about it. "Oh, sorry."

She bent to pick it up, but he beat her to the punch. "It's okay. I've got it."

He gathered the Armani in his hands, but as he stood back up, something fell from one of its pockets. Evangeline was already hurrying toward the door, and she tripped over it. She stumbled into Ryan, and he caught her by the shoulders so she wouldn't fall.

"Oops, that was a close one." She laughed, but when she pulled back and caught a glimpse of Ryan's face, she knew something was wrong. He'd gone ashen.

"Ryan, what is it?"

"Nothing. It's nothing. Zander…"

She wasn't sure what he said next, because when she followed his gaze to the white box at her feet all she could hear was the sound of her own heartbeat. Impossibly loud, impossibly fast, as if her heart was trying to burst out of her chest.

"Eve, don't," Ryan's voice managed to cut through the fog in her head. "Please."

But it was too late. She'd already bent to pick up the box. She had to. She needed to be sure the letters on the cardboard really spelled out the words she thought she'd read.

They couldn't.

But they did.

Noninvasive Prenatal Paternity Test.

This can't be happening.

Ryan had spent just about every minute he was away thinking about the things he wanted to say to Evangeline upon his return—the promises he wanted to make, the question he wanted to ask her. He'd run through a dozen different scenarios in his head, but not one of them had involved the box that she was currently clutching in her trembling hands.

That godforsaken paternity test.

Damn you, Zander.

A knot of regret wound itself tightly around his throat. He couldn't blame Zander for this disaster. His cousin's motives had been pure. The blame for the wounded look in Evangeline's sapphire eyes rested squarely on his own shoulders. The minute he'd laid eyes on that box, he'd known it was trouble. He should have disposed of it instead of shoving it inside his coat pocket.

But he hadn't. He'd dropped it in the pocket of his Armani as if it was something as inconsequential as a paper clip instead of a hand grenade. And now that grenade had just detonated in the face of the woman he loved.

"Here." She shoved the box at his chest. "You dropped something."

"This isn't what it looks like. I promise it's not." God, he hated himself.

"It looks like a paternity test," she said flatly.

He chucked it in the trash can beside his desk with such force that the wastebasket fell over, rolled across the floor and bumped into the wall. "It's garbage."

She held up a hand. "You don't have to explain, Ryan. I understand. I really do."

But the pain in her gaze told him she didn't. She thought he felt no different about her than he'd felt about Natalie. She thought he didn't trust her. Hell, she probably thought he'd toss her and her sweet little dogs out on the street if the baby she was carrying wasn't his. Why else would he be toting around a paternity test in his pocket?

That wasn't how he felt at all. Not even close. "Understand this, Eve. I'm in love with you."

"No." She shook her head. "You're not."

They were right back to square one. Right back to the morning he'd woken up in her non-pet-friendly apartment in the Village and she'd insisted that he didn't actually want to see her again.

Once more, he was losing her.

"This is all a terrible misunderstanding, and I can explain." She had to believe him. He'd drag Zander into this if he had to. It couldn't be too late.

"I need to go," she said quietly.

She walked past him, and he turned to stop her,

struggling to find the words that would convince her to stay and hear him out. But then she opened the door, and Elliot stood on the other side with his hand poised to knock.

His gaze shot back and forth between them, and he let out an audible sigh of relief. "Thank God you're both here."

"No. Not now." Ryan held up a hand. "Whatever it is, it's going to have to…"

"Carlo Bocci is here," Elliot blurted, cutting him off.

Evangeline froze. *"What?"*

Elliot nodded frantically and tried to elaborate, but his head bobbed up and down faster than he could get the words out. "Yes…he's…"

"Let's calm down," Ryan said, stunned at how calm he managed to sound. "We're ready for this. We've been preparing for weeks."

"You're right. Of course. We're ready." Beads of sweat were breaking out across Elliot's forehead. He looked anything but ready.

Ryan's temples throbbed. Why the hell did this have to happen now? He could barely think straight. All his focus was concentrated on Evangeline and repairing the mess he'd just created. At least Bocci's appearance had kept her there. For the time being, anyway.

Focus. "How long has he been here? Where *exactly* is he?"

Elliot took a deep breath and managed to get himself together long enough to spit out the facts. "He just checked in with the maître d'. He's early. He's got a nine o'clock reservation under a fake name—Mark

Spencer. The maître d' recognized him right away and is planning on seating him at table twenty-five."

"Good." Ryan nodded. Situated in a semiprivate alcove at the right of the entrance, table twenty-five was the best seat in the house. It was spacious and had a sweeping view of the city. They'd been limiting reservations at this particular spot for weeks in anticipation of this exact scenario. "Why hasn't he been seated yet?"

"He asked to visit the bar for a cocktail first." The last remaining splash of color drained from Elliot's face. They hadn't planned on such a request.

Evangeline frowned. "Is that normal?"

"I have no idea," Ryan muttered. "But at least it buys us some time."

"Right." Evangeline took a deep breath. "I've got to go. I need to select his wine."

She was correct, of course—they couldn't keep standing there.

But Ryan was reluctant to let her out of his sight. Actually, that was an understatement. The thought of her walking out the door was killing him.

All in, remember?

He had to trust her. They could finish their discussion later, after Bocci had gone. Everything would be fine. It had to.

"Go." A dull, cavernous pain bloomed in place of his heart.

He implored her with his gaze. *We're not finished here.*

But she turned around and left without casting even a cursory glance in his direction.

"Mr. Wilde." Elliot cleared his throat.

Ryan tore his attention from the empty spot that Evangeline had just vacated and tried to act as if he was on top of things. Totally in control. "Yes?"

"Should I call the other Mr. Wilde and let him know Bocci is here?"

"I'll do it." Zander would want to know what was going on, and Ryan should be the one to fill him in.

Plus, making the call and dealing with Zander would give him something to do. He couldn't pace around Bennington 8 for the duration of Bocci's meal, analyzing every bite the reviewer ate. Nor could he pace the length of his office, waiting to talk to Evangeline. He'd lose his mind.

"Very well," Elliot said. "I'll get back to work."

"Perfect." Someone needed to keep an eye on the rest of the hotel. The night was spinning out of control. Ryan didn't want to contemplate what else could go wrong. "Thank you, Elliot."

The manager gave him a final nod and then left.

Ryan raked a hand through his hair, suddenly exhausted beyond measure. He looked around the office. The overturned trash can and his suit jacket, forgotten in a heap on the floor, were the only outward signs of the chaos that had just taken place. He'd expected worse. It felt like a tornado had just ripped through his life. Shouldn't the paint be peeling off the walls or the building be crumbling down around him?

He righted the trash can, and bile rose to the back of his throat when he caught a glimpse of the paternity test lying at the bottom of the bin. He swallowed it down, picked his jacket up off the floor and hung it back on the hanger where it belonged. Small things, but it helped him feel like he had some semblance of control over his world.

But his life no longer revolved around the Bennington. Not the way it used to. Evangeline was his world now. He wasn't sure when exactly it happened. But it had. At some point during the past two months, everything had shifted. Everything had slipped so perfectly into place—his mind, his heart, his very existence.

For the first time in his life, he was happy.

He was head over heels in love, and he was going to be a father. He didn't need a paternity test to tell him what he already knew. The irony of the whole thing was that he would have loved Evangeline and her baby, regardless of genetics. They belonged together.

Now he could only hope that once this surreal night was over, Evangeline would listen.

He took a ragged inhale, pulled his cell phone from his pocket and dialed Zander. His cousin answered on the third ring.

Ryan didn't mince words. "Carlo Bocci is here. He's got a nine o'clock reservation."

"I'm on my way. I'll meet you upstairs at Bennington 8." Zander hung up without saying goodbye.

It was showtime.

Ryan checked the inside pocket of his jacket, adjusted his cuff links and smoothed his tie before he headed out. He strode down the hall on his way to the elevator and cast a quick glance at the sitting area in the lobby. It was empty, just as it had been for nearly a week. Once Evangeline had moved into his apartment, he'd issued a new mandate—the hotel lobby was for guests only.

No more bachelorettes.

They were free to hang out in the jazz bar if they wanted, but after a few days without a Ryan Wilde sighting, they'd given up. At least he'd gotten something right.

He seized on to this thought as he stepped onto the elevator, clung to it as he climbed closer to the restaurant. With each passing second, the night was coming closer to an end. But when the elevator doors swished open and he made his way to the snow-swept atrium that was Bennington 8, a chill came over him. He didn't need anyone to tell him what had happened, because he sensed her absence. He already knew.

Evangeline had left the building.

Chapter Fifteen

"**I** thought you said she was all in." Zander's panicked gaze shot back and forth across the elegant restaurant, searching for Evangeline.

He could look all he wanted. She wasn't there. Ryan had checked. "I did say that."

All in.

She'd promised to stay and make the night with Carlo Bocci a success. She'd given him her word.

He'd hurt her. He knew that. God, how he knew it. But he couldn't believe she'd gone. Minutes ago, she'd been in his office, talking about selecting wine for Bocci's meal. What had happened?

No one at Bennington 8 had seen her. Not the maître d'. Not the bartender. None of the servers. Which meant she hadn't ever gone to the restaurant floor at all. She'd simply walked out of his office and left.

"Then where is she?" Zander said through gritted teeth.

Ryan cut his cousin a sideways glance. "Not now."

Zander did a double take. "Not now? Seriously? Carlo Bocci has about an inch left of his gin and tonic. In less than ten minutes, he'll be seated at the best table we've got, waiting for a sommelier who just went AWOL. If not now, then when?"

At first, Ryan didn't respond. He didn't trust himself to speak without saying something he'd later regret. Zander wasn't just his cousin. He was his oldest friend, the brother he never had. In some ways, he'd even become a father figure. The paternity test had been his way of protecting Ryan.

"She found it," he finally said in a voice as calm as he could manage.

"What are you talking about?" Zander was still standing with his arms crossed, looking out over the restaurant floor, shooting surreptitious glances toward the bar whenever possible. But a few seconds later, his face fell.

He turned his back to the restaurant and faced Ryan. "Wait a minute. Do you mean the test I gave you a few days ago?"

Ryan nodded wordlessly.

"When?"

"About a minute before Carlo Bocci checked in for his reservation. It fell out of one of my jacket pockets. She has no idea where it came from."

Zander sighed. "I'm sorry. I'll talk to her. I'll explain everything."

"That's going to be difficult, considering we have no idea where she is." He didn't allow himself to consider the possibility that she'd gone back to his apartment to collect her things and take Olive and Bee elsewhere. He was almost afraid to go home, in case he walked into an empty penthouse.

Damn it.

This was what he'd been worried about all along. She was so scared of ending up like her parents that she'd been looking for a reason to run. And he'd given her one.

"I was going to ask her to marry me tonight."

He hadn't planned on saying those words out loud, but there they were, hanging between him and Zander like a breath of cold winter air.

Zander cleared his throat, but Ryan couldn't look at him. He'd bared enough of his soul already.

"Maybe you still can." There was an unmistakable smile in Zander's voice, which told Ryan that he had no idea how upset Evangeline had been. But then he added, "Your bride just walked through the door."

Ryan spun around, and there she was—striding across the room with a bottle of wine in her hands. At first he thought he must have made a mistake. She'd been there all along, and somehow he hadn't seen her. But that couldn't be right, because no one else had seen her either.

Then he took a closer look at the bottle in her hands, and everything suddenly made sense.

Whatever you do, don't drop it.

Evangeline tightened her grasp on the vintage bottle of red and willed her hands to stop shaking. If she dropped the bottle now, the madness of the past twenty minutes would have all been for nothing.

Tony had really pulled through. If everything turned out well tonight—if her extreme long shot managed to pay off—she was going to tell Ryan to give his driver a raise. A big one. He'd gotten her to Ryan's penthouse even faster than she'd hoped. After she'd dashed upstairs to get the bottle of wine, she'd come back down to find the car idling at the curb, pointed in the direction of the Bennington. The return trip had taken less than half the time of their initial dash across Manhattan.

Tony was a miracle worker. The unicorn of chauffeurs.

Evangeline would miss him after tonight. She'd miss a lot of things.

But she couldn't think about that now. If she did, she'd never get through the next few hours without breaking down. She was having enough difficulty keeping the tears at bay already.

Ryan's presence certainly wasn't helping. He and Zander were standing in the far corner of the dining room, just outside the door to the restaurant's kitchen. Did they honestly think they were being discreet?

Actually, they were. Carlo Bocci probably wouldn't even notice them. Evangeline, however, was consciously aware of their presence. Ryan's, especially. He'd honed in on her with his gaze mere seconds after she'd crossed the threshold. The look on his face was so bewildered, so full of raw hope that she'd had to look away.

If he thought she was doing this for him, he was only partially right. She was also doing it for herself. And for her unborn baby. It was time to say goodbye to the past, once and for all.

"Mr. Bocci has been seated at table twenty-five. He's using the alias Mark Spencer," the maître d' said as he met her halfway across the room.

"Perfect. I have his selection ready."

The maître d' cast a wary glance at the bottle. "You're not going to ask him what kind of wine he'd prefer? Or give him a chance to go over the list you've been working on for weeks?"

"No." She shook her head. "It's this one."

It was one of a kind—the only vintage like it in existence. What more could he possibly want?

"All right, then. You're the expert. I think he's ready."

Evangeline took a deep breath. "Here we go."

Bocci sat with his back to her as she approached. Unfortunately, Ryan and Zander were situated on the exact opposite side of the room, making them impossible to ignore. She dropped her gaze to the floor and tried her best to focus on the elegant pattern of the black-and-white marble tile beneath her feet, but it was no use. She couldn't help but look at Ryan. After this evening, she wouldn't get to see him like this again.

She'd never keep his baby from him. If he had any interest in seeing the child or being involved in the baby's life, they'd work something out. She'd see him on alternating weekends when they traded diaper bags and strollers and she pretended that she'd never once believed that the three of them could live happily-ever-after.

But she'd never see him look at her the way he was regarding her now—as if she were the most beautiful woman he'd ever set eyes on.

She bit down on the inside of her cheek to keep from crying. It didn't matter if he thought she was beautiful. Nor did it matter if he thought he loved her. She knew the truth now. He didn't trust her. Grandpa Bob insisted she'd know love when she saw it, and while she still wasn't altogether convinced that she would, she knew that love and trust were intertwined. You couldn't have one without the other.

As she slowed to a stop beside Bocci's table, Ryan mouthed something to her.

You don't have to do this.

But she did. She wanted to.

"Mr. Spencer, welcome to Bennington 8." She gave herself a mental pat on the back for remembering to use Bocci's fake name. After all, they weren't supposed to know it was him.

"Thank you." He glanced up from the menu in his hands, and his gaze snagged on the wine bottle. A frown tugged at the corner of his mouth.

Maybe this was a crazy idea, after all.

Too late.

"My name is Evangeline Holly, and I'm the hotel's sommelier." She presented the bottle on his right side, as proper wine etiquette dictated. "I'd like to recommend a very special vintage tonight, a rare and unique opportunity to experience a one-of-a-kind wine."

He lifted a dubious brow. "One of a kind? How so?"

"This wine is a cabernet franc from Chateau Holly in New York's Finger Lakes region. The vineyard ceased operations more than twenty years ago, and this is its last remaining bottle. It's a rich wine, aged to perfection, with notes of tart berries, cedar and warm toast." She smiled, and from some forgotten place deep inside, a tiny spark of pride flickered to life.

The bottle in her hands represented her heritage. Her parents had given her more than brokenness. They'd gifted her with a passion for wine and its history—her life's work. Someday she'd pass it along to her own child. Her baby wouldn't know what it was like to grow up and eat grapes fresh from the vine, but she'd teach her child other things—how to identify a fine Bordeaux, how sipping a good wine was the best way to slow down and experience a moment, how loving wine was an exercise in appreciation.

"I see." Bocci scanned the label. His face was a blank slate, but at least his frown had disappeared. "This is highly unusual."

"As I said..." Her smile widened. "This is a rare and special opportunity. If you'd prefer something else, I'd be happy to show you our house wine list."

She held her breath while he took another look at the label.

"I usually prefer old-world wines." He looked up, and she thought she spied a trace of a smile in his eyes. "But you've won me over with your confidence. I'll give it a try."

"Excellent." She pulled her sommelier knife from the pocket of her fitted blazer and used it to score the foil around the top of the bottle, being careful not to let the bottle come in contact with the table.

During a proper wine presentation, nothing in the sommelier's hands should touch the tabletop. Not even the wine itself. It could be something of a juggling act. Evangeline preferred to think of it as a dance.

She removed the loosened foil top and slipped it into her pocket, along with the knife. Then she pulled out her corkscrew and inserted it into the center of the cork.

Please don't be rotten.

This wine was old. She'd done her best to store it properly, but it wasn't as if the bottle had been sitting in a climate-controlled cellar for two decades. Recommending a wine she'd never actually sampled as an adult was risky enough without the added chance of a crumbly, dried-out cork. If the cork fell apart into the bottle of wine before she could remove it, Bennington 8 could kiss its Michelin star goodbye.

For once in Evangeline's life, fate was on her side. The cork slid out as smooth as butter.

She handed it to Bocci for his inspection. The underside of the cork was wet, just as it should be. He nodded his approval.

By some miracle, her hands didn't shake as she poured a small amount into a wineglass. Nor did she recoil at the wine's bouquet. She could smell the berries—plump red cherries and crushed raspberries, the kind just ripe enough for making jam. She could smell the cedar, too, balsamic and smoky.

She didn't even need to taste the wine to know it would be good.

No, not good.

It would be perfect.

Bocci tasted the sample sip she poured for him, and she could tell the moment that the wine touched his tongue. His eyes widened in surprise and he lifted his gaze to hers.

"Miss Holly, I'm stunned to tell you that this is the best wine I've ever tasted."

Three stars.

At the end of his meal, Carlo Bocci had walked right up to Ryan and Zander, revealed himself to be the Michelin reviewer and announced that he'd be awarding Bennington 8 the highest ranking possible—three coveted Michelin stars. There were only a dozen other three-starred restaurants in America. Bennington 8 would now go down in history as one of the best of the best.

It was more than they'd dared to hope for.

And all because of Evangeline.

Ryan wanted to sweep her off of her feet and twirl her around until she tossed her head back and laughed. He wanted to kiss her full on the lips right there in front of everyone who'd stayed for the impromptu victory party at the Bennington bar. Then he wanted to take her home and make love to her until the sun came up.

But he couldn't do any of those things, because she was in the middle of packing up her things—her champagne saber, the port tongs she'd used during her interview, the now-empty wine bottle from Chateau Holly. They were all neatly tucked away in her bag. The message was clear.

She wasn't coming back.

She'd kept her promise. She'd stayed until Bocci paid them a visit. She'd knocked it out of the park, and now she was done.

They were done.

Ryan took a deep breath. *Not if I can help it.*

"You're not just going to stand here and let her leave without telling her how you feel, are you?" Zander said under his breath as he sipped his champagne. Dom Pérignon. They were in the big leagues now.

"Absolutely not." He was going to do more than just tell her. He was also going to show her...in the best way he knew how.

"I didn't think so." Zander gave him a firm pat on the back. "Go get her."

He set his champagne glass down on the bar and walked to the table by the wine cooler where she was slipping one last thing into her bag. A cork.

"Is that from tonight's bottle?" he asked.

She looked up and smiled, but the glimmer in her eyes was bittersweet. "Yes."

She toyed with the cork, rolling it back and forth with her fingertips. It took great effort on Ryan's part not to stare. The thought of never kissing those hands, never seeing them cradle their newborn baby, was killing him.

His voice dropped an octave. "Why did you do it? That bottle of wine meant the world to you."

"It was time to let it go. Not just the wine, but all of it. I don't want to bring a baby into the world who I'm afraid to love. I want to be the best mother I can possibly be." Her bottom lip began to quiver. "The other night, my grandpa told me that love looked a lot like sacrifice. I wanted to make that sacrifice— for you, and for our baby."

She loved him.

She hadn't said it, but she did. That knowledge

should have made him happy, but the light in her eyes had dimmed on those last two words.

Our baby.

"The baby is yours, Ryan. I wish you believed me, but I understand why you don't. If you want me to take the paternity test, I will." Her eyes grew shiny with tears. Two bottomless pools of blue. "Either way, it's over between us. I know you think you love me, but this isn't love."

"Yes, it is. Eve, I've loved you since the night I met you. You pulled me straight out of my past and into the present. You saved me. Can't you see that? I hadn't so much as looked at a woman in over a year until I saw you in that wine bar, wielding that butcher knife like some kind of ninja wine goddess. I wanted you then, but I want you more now. I want forever with you." He blew out a breath. "And as for that test… I didn't have anything to do with it. Zander gave it to me, because he thought I needed proof. I don't. I'm ready to leave the past behind and start a new life with you and our baby. *Our* child. I told Zander I didn't need proof almost a week ago. He's standing right over there if you'd like to confirm it."

She blinked, and a tear slipped down her cheek. The cork in her hands fell to the floor. Neither one of them bothered to pick it up. "Is that true?"

"Yes but, I'm not finished. I didn't go to Chicago last night. I went somewhere else." He wished he could have avoided lying, but he'd wanted to surprise her. It seemed insignificant at the time, back when the trust between them wasn't so fragile.

But maybe it was better this way. Maybe this was the only way to move forward. As one.

"I don't understand. Where did you go?"

He reached into the inside pocket of his jacket and pulled out an envelope. "I went to the Finger Lakes region. To a little place near Cayuga Lake, where the soil is supposed to be perfect for growing grapes. The land hasn't been tilled in years, but it seems like just the place for a new beginning...just the place to start a family."

He reached for her wrist, turned her hand over and set the envelope gently in her palm. "Open it."

She took a deep breath and slid a finger beneath the envelope's flap, breaking the seal. A slow smile came to her lips as she unfolded the contents, and then all at once, her face broke into a beatific grin. "This is a deed. You *bought* a vineyard?"

"Love, it's not just a vineyard. It's your vineyard. It's the exact parcel of land where Chateau Holly was located. I got the information from your bottle's label and tracked down the owner." Purchasing the land had been the easy part. If they were going to turn it into a working vineyard, they had a lot of work to do. If Evangeline just wanted to hold on to it and let it stay as it was, that was fine, too. He just wanted to give her back a piece of her childhood. The piece she loved most.

"I can't believe you did this." She couldn't stop staring at the deed.

When she finally looked up, he was no longer standing beside her. He'd dropped down to one knee. The paper in Evangeline's hand fluttered to the floor, alongside the confetti that had been tossed around while the champagne was being poured—tiny gold stars.

And there, with stars scattered at her feet and their baby growing inside her, Ryan Wilde asked Evangeline Holly to be his wife.

Her answer was an unequivocal yes.

Epilogue

One year later

Evangeline sat near the head of a rustic farm table
that had been placed between two rows of grapevines
located in the most scenic portion of the vineyard.
The farm table had been her husband's idea, and it
had been a good one. It was made of repurposed
wood, perfect for a harvest party. Even more perfect
for celebrating a place where they'd made something
beautiful out of the discarded remains of the past.

The table was set for ten. All the family was
present—Tessa and Julian, Allegra and Zander,
Chloe, Emily, Grandpa Bob. Even Olive and Bee
were there, snoozing in a dog bed that Julian had
made out of a sawed-off wine barrel stuffed with a
generous amount of cushions. And of course Ryan

was there, too. He stood beside Evangeline, holding their daughter in the crook of his arm and raising a glass in a toast.

"Eve and I want to thank you all for coming out here today to celebrate the first vintage from Wilde Hearts Winery." He grinned down at her.

In the beginning, once plans for the wedding had been made and after Evangeline's morning sickness had passed, they'd been stumped as to what to name the vineyard. Ryan insisted he'd be fine with calling it Chateau Holly. But Evangeline wasn't. The winery represented a new beginning, so it needed a new name.

Choosing a name for their daughter had been far easier. Holly Wilde was the obvious choice, and they both loved it. Boom. Done.

Naming the vineyard was a far more difficult task, until their wedding night when Ryan finished unbuttoning Evangeline from her wedding dress and groaned as it fell to the floor in a puff of white tulle.

Be still my Wilde heart.

The second he'd uttered those words, she knew they'd found a name.

No one knew the story of how they'd come up with it. It was their little secret.

"We couldn't have pulled off the challenging feat of getting this vineyard off the ground without each and every one of you," Ryan continued.

"I'll drink to that," Zander said wryly.

Allegra gave him a playful swat. "Let the man finish his toast. I'm ready to sample this wine."

It was their first bottle from their very first barrel—a cabernet franc, just like the vintage Evangeline had poured for Carlo Bocci a year ago. Ryan kept suggesting they create a pinot grigio instead. He was joking, obviously.

Evangeline hoped he was, anyway.

"I also want to congratulate my beautiful wife for recently passing her Certified Sommelier exam." Ryan lifted his glass a little higher and shot her a wink.

"Hear, hear!" Grandpa Bob said. He'd been spending weekends at the vineyard, away from his assisted living facility, and seemed to be getting some of his old spunk back.

"This doesn't mean you're going to give us a long description of what this wine is supposed to taste like before we're allowed to take a sip, does it?" Julian stared into his glass.

"No." Evangeline shook her head. "It means Zander is going to let me keep working at Bennington 8."

"Nonsense. The three Michelin stars negated that whole condition. Surely I told you that." He frowned.

"You didn't, actually. But I would have gone through the certification anyway, if it makes you feel any better."

"It does." Zander arched a brow and cut his gaze toward Ryan. "Although what would really make me feel better is if your husband would finish his lengthy toast and let us drink."

Holly let out a happy squeal.

Evangeline stood to hand her little girl her favorite stuffed toy and wrap her arms around Ryan's waist. "I hate to tell you this, but it sounds like even your daughter wants you to wrap this up."

"Her wish is my command." Ryan brushed a ten-

COMING SOON!

We really hope you enjoyed reading this book. If you're looking for more romance, be sure to head to the shops when new books are available on

Thursday
23rd August

der kiss to the top of Holly's head. "Cheers, everyone! To the harvest!"

"To the harvest," they all echoed.

Glasses clinked all around, and a breeze blew
through the valley, rustling the grapevines. The air
grew heavy with the lush perfume of good wine,
good grapes and good people. Family.

Drunk on happiness, Evangeline rose to her tiptoes and pressed her lips to Ryan's ear, to the sensitive, secret spot she knew so well.

"And to you, my handsome husband," she whispered. "Be still my Wilde heart."

* * * * *